FLASH POINT

STEELE RIDGE: THE BLACKWELLS

TRACEY DEVLYN

STEELE RIDGE
www.SteeleRidgeSeries.com

TEAM STEELE RIDGE
Edited by Kristen Weber
Copyedited by Martha Trachtenberg
Cover Design by Stuart Bache, Books Covered
Beta Reads by Liz Semkiu, Sandy Modesitt and Isabel Hofmann
Author Photo by Lisa Kaman Kenning, Mezzaluna Photography

Print Edition, May 2022, ISBN: 978-1-948075-82-4
Digital Edition, May 2022, ISBN: 978-1-948075-81-7
For more information contact: tracey@steeleridgepublishing.com

STEELE RIDGE CHRISTMAS CAPERS

DISCOVER MORE STEELE RIDGE

STEELE RIDGE: THE BLACKWELLS

Flash Point, Book 1

Smoke Screen, Book 2

STEELE RIDGE: THE STEELES

The BEGINNING, A Novella

Going HARD, Book 1

Living FAST, Book 2

Loving DEEP, Book 3

Breaking FREE, Book 4

Roaming WILD, Book 5

Stripping BARE, Book 6

Enduring LOVE, A Novella, Book 7

Vowing LOVE, A Novella, Book 8

STEELE RIDGE: THE KINGSTONS

Craving HEAT, Book 1

Tasting FIRE, Book 2

Searing NEED, Book 3

Striking EDGE, Book 4

Burning ACHE, Book 5

ALSO BY TRACEY DEVLYN

NEXUS SPYMASTER SERIES

Historical romantic suspense

A Lady's Revenge

A Lady's Temptation

A Lady's Secret

A Lord's Redemption

A Lord's Bargain

BONES & GEMSTONES SERIES

Historical romantic mystery

Night Storm

TEA TIME SHORTS & NOVELLAS

Sweet historical romance

His Secret Desire

FLASH POINT

STEELE RIDGE: THE BLACKWELLS

TRACEY DEVLYN

STEELE RIDGE
www.SteeleRidgeSeries.com

To Sarah,
the daughter of my heart

1

ZEKE BLACKWELL SHIFTED HIS ATTENTION FROM THE antiquities dealer's hopeful face to the incredible array of weapons splayed out before him—an Italian stiletto dagger, an English mortuary sword, a Polish rapier, and a longsword of indeterminate origin.

It's not here.

The stab of disappointment cut deeper this time, and the hope he'd been holding on to for the past year took a severe nosedive. He couldn't keep this up. Couldn't continue staving off the inevitable collapse of all he held dear while searching for an artifact he would never find.

Even so, he went through the motions of examining the sword on the off-chance that someone over the past one hundred years had replaced the longsword's distinctive wooden grip and twisted quillons.

He indicated the sword. "Do you mind?"

"Not at all. Please." The antiquities dealer made an encouraging motion.

With gloved hands, Zeke lifted the longsword from its black velvet bed. No four-headed wolf on the pommel or ancient Latin etched on the cross guard.

An extraordinary piece, but not the one he was searching for. A familiar, yet efficient numbness slid through his mind and loosened his taut muscles. He returned the artifact and picked up the other pieces, appreciating their craftsmanship and excellent condition. He saw no telltale signs of modern construction or technology, but, as much as he'd like to think otherwise, he was no expert.

But Lan Sardoff could identify a reproduction in a single glance, so Zeke didn't question their authenticity.

"The pieces are not to your liking?" his friend asked, a note of concern in his voice.

"You've outdone yourself, Lan."

"But none are the one you seek."

He shook his head. "You have provenance for each?"

"Do not say after all of these years you doubt me now?"

"I would be a fool to overlook the fact that yours is a for-profit business."

A slow smile etched tiny lines in Sardoff's perfectly tanned face as if he intended to deliver one of his oily salesman quips. Then the curve of his lips straightened and an uncharacteristic seriousness took hold of his features. "Anyone else would need to be concerned about my profit margin. If not for you," he waved a ringed hand around his expansive shop, "my business empire would have crumbled before it ever had a chance to rise."

Zeke's friendship with the dealer stretched back to their days at UNC, when Sardoff had helped him join the fencing team. Sardoff, two years older, had been fencing since grade school. He was a master. The best on UNC's team, and he'd taken the raw promise in Zeke's technique and molded it over the course of many private lessons.

A few years later, Zeke had been presented with an opportunity to pay his friend back when Sardoff told him about suspecting a potential buyer of stealing a vintage comic book, worth more than a quarter of a million dollars, from the shop after Sardoff refused to negotiate the price.

Zeke had broken into the thief's home and taken back the stolen comic book, and Sardoff had thanked him by recommending his "services" to trusted clients.

His occasional recoveries—or what his brothers referred to as shadow operations—became the precursor to what would eventually become a lucrative family business. But Zeke's first recovery hadn't been smooth. In fact, Zeke's ass hadn't even cleared the thief's office window sill before the guy entered and caught him in the act.

Even now, reliving how his surprised expression had turned into a furious, you'll-pay outburst, as Zeke slipped, er, fell out of the window, still made him smile.

Zeke waved off his friend's words. "Sardoff's Antiques and Uncommon Treasures would have survived the loss of the comic book. Its owner is too stubborn, and too smart, to fail."

The dealer bowed his head in amused acknowledgment, then studied him with a salesman's intensity. "I've heard whispers about an early sixteenth-century British longsword with a four-headed wolf carved on the pommel and *familia primum* inscribed on the guard," Lan said. "Is this something you would be interested in?"

Familia primum. Family first.

Shock turned Zeke's muscles to glass. One wrong move, and his world could shatter into a million fragments. Had

Sardoff found Lupos, the sword that had defended the Blackwell family for generations until it was stolen from his great-great-grandfather a century ago?

"An antique longsword," Zeke said, infusing amused disbelief into his voice. "Do you really have to ask?"

"No, I suppose not. But *I* cannot obtain something the possessor has no desire to sell."

Disappointment coiled in his gut. "Can you get me a name?"

Sardoff lifted a brow. "Do you really have to ask?"

Zeke grinned, despite the tension still gripping his insides. "I suppose not."

Always the businessman, his friend swept his hand over the antique arsenal displayed on the table. "Which one should I wrap up for you?"

Zeke snapped off his Nitrile gloves and stuffed them into the front pocket of his jeans. "All of them."

"All?"

Lifting a duffel bag from the floor, Zeke dumped out two stacks of Ben Franklins onto the table. "All."

2

AFTER RETURNING TO HIS HOTEL, ZEKE CARRIED HIS DUFFEL bag of artifacts to his room, showered, and changed into a gray button-down shirt and black slacks for his prearranged dinner with his older brother Ash.

Now, he followed the hostess of the Grand Marquis Hotel restaurant to a booth across from the bar, feeling like a stink bug amidst a kaleidoscope of butterflies.

His idea of a nice evening involved him wearing a T-shirt and jeans, on his deck, with a beer in hand, steak on a plate, and a sunset beautiful enough to bring tears to his eyes.

But his brother had more refined tastes, and he'd insisted on this hotel and warned Zeke to wear something besides said deck-wear. Normally, he ignored fashion advice from his brother, but he didn't want to set their rare get-together off on the wrong foot. Plus, today was his birthday. Why not celebrate in style?

The hostess handed him a menu and laid another in the empty place opposite him. "Your server will be with you shortly, Mr. Blackwell. I'll show your wife to your table once she arrives." She smiled at him with generous red lips and blue eyes. Long black hair draped over a bare shoulder, the perfect complement to the strapless white dress that outlined her curves in all the places he liked.

The slight emphasis she put on "your wife" sounded like a question to his ears, one he found himself not interested in answering, despite the obvious temptation.

"Thank you," he said, picking up the menu.

She had barely turned away before his mind shifted to Lupos and Sardoff's promise to text him the name of the longsword's owner. Zeke had allowed his hopes to rise many times over the past year, only to be disappointed. But this was the first time the description matched his family's heirloom so perfectly.

"Hello, I'm Keith. I'll be your server tonight," a tall young man with curly brown hair and a sunburned nose said. "Can I get you anything to drink while we're waiting for your guest?"

Zeke glanced down at his watch and noted the time.

8:27 p.m.

Way to cut it close, bro.

"Two glasses of your best bourbon." He scanned the menu. "I'll have the beef tenderloin."

"Would you like for me to put your order in now or wait for your guest?"

"Put it in now." One thing the last decade had taught him—never hold up food for his brothers. Out of the five of them, he seemed to be the only one who didn't lose track of time. It's why he'd made such a great operations manager.

He pushed the thought away. Later. He would get into that later.

The restaurant buzzed with guests. A few were men like him in town for business. Most of them dined on a tumbler of amber liquid. A large group of people in business casual, with matching blue lanyards around their necks, sat at the bar, releasing a continual series of ear-grating laughter.

Several couples dotted the dining room, each sharing different levels of longing looks and intimate touches. Except for a twenty-something couple near the fireplace, who seemed more captivated by their electronic devices than each other.

Everyone in the restaurant had a story. Stories that had led them here, to this place and time.

Zeke allowed his curiosity free rein, picking out the loners, the seekers, and the drinkers.

His surveillance snagged on a guy at one of the high tables in the bar. He didn't know why, exactly. There wasn't anything particularly interesting about the man's stocky build, tousled hair, or stubble-cured face, nor did his plain loafers, dark jeans, and pressed polo shirt inspire the imagination.

Then he keyed in on the intensity of the guy's face. He followed the man's line of sight until it stopped on one of the bar sitters. A woman.

He stopped short of snorting. It didn't take a detective to unravel that bit of domestic drama. Unrequited love. The worst, most devastating kind.

What sort of scenario would elicit such visual fervor? Did he fall in love with his childhood friend? Coworker? Boss? Best friend's wife?

Or maybe the guy just had a hard-on for redheads.

"Here you go," server Keith said, placing twin glasses on the table. "Two Old Fitzgeralds."

Zeke looked at his watch. His jaw clenched.

8:42 p.m.

Would it be so hard for Ash to take a few seconds and

send him an update on his status? Or couldn't G-man be bothered with common courtesy anymore?

"Would you like me to put in an appetizer?" Keith asked.

"No appetizer. Bring out my meal when it's ready." An image of his Gram's narrowed eyes flashed through his mind, and he added, "Please."

Once the server left, he fired off a text to his brother.

We still on for dinner?

He lifted the glass to his lips and took a healthy swallow. Old Fitz's headwind smoothed a path down his throat for the crackle of fire that soon followed.

No longer interested in Intense Dude, he focused on the woman. With her back to him, all he could make out was the curve of her slender neck, her long, red ponytail, black pantsuit, narrow waist, long legs—and sensible shoes. Nothing jaw-dropping extraordinary like the hostess, but nice.

He didn't take her for a seeker. Not with those shoes. Even if she thought leather slip-ons were sexy, she seemed more interested in the booklet spread out on the bar before her than anyone around her.

Too bad for Intense Dude.

A fruity cocktail sat sweating by her left elbow, so not a drinker.

Loner then.

By choice? Or circumstance?

Did she know Intense Dude? Or was she oblivious to her wannabe-lover's existence?

Broad shoulders wedged into a tailored charcoal-gray business suit snuffed out his view of the woman. Zeke looked into the familiar blue eyes of his brother Ash.

Zeke rose and extended his hand. "About damn time, asshole."

Energy poured off his brother, despite the late hour. Unlike Zeke's constant five o'clock shadow, the G-man's jaw was clean shaven and his silver-striped red tie was still cinched tight at the neck.

Ash gripped his hand. "Sorry, something's come up."

A tall, fifty-something black woman, wearing a purple silk blouse and knee-length skirt, materialized next to Ash, along with a blond-haired man carrying a thick, canvas briefcase.

All three wore the same blue conference lanyard as the group of loudmouths.

Now Zeke understood why Ash had picked this swanky hotel restaurant over a billion others in the city. He was attending an FBI conference.

Which meant Zeke sat in the epicenter of his enemy.

INTELLECTUALLY, ZEKE UNDERSTOOD HIS DISLIKE OF THE FBI was irrational. After all, they didn't seek out Ash and rip him from the family business, leaving Zeke reeling at the loss and scrambling to take his brother's place at the helm.

No, Asher Cameron Blackwell had done that mindfuck all on his own. To follow his passion, his dream. Something he had failed to share with Zeke, until three years ago, when he'd called it quits and left Steele Ridge.

He'd even left his fucking name behind. Wanted the family to call him Cameron now. A clean split.

To hell with that shit.

Tonight was going to be the first step in fixing things with his brother.

Or so he'd thought.

Instead, the FBI crammed the knife deeper into his heart.

"Let me guess," he took in the other two agents, "duty calls."

Ash's jaw worked, as if he wanted to say something, but not in front of an audience. Instead, he stuck with the tried-and-true. "I'm sorry, Zeke. I'll make it up to you."

He felt the woman's eyes on him, but he refused to look at her. Had no wish to stare empathy in the eye.

Zeke sank back in his chair and lifted his drink to the trio. "Have fun at the office."

Ash slipped five twenties from his wallet and placed them on the table. "Happy birthday, bro."

He stared at the money. The sight of the fanned-out bills caused the whiskey in his gut to heave.

"Here you are," server Keith said, sliding a plate in front of him. "Can I get y'all anything else?"

"No, thanks." Zeke placed the pristine white napkin in his lap and used his fork and knife to cut a thick slice of tenderloin. By the time he lifted his head, he was alone.

The beef all but disintegrated in his mouth. Any other time, he would sigh in carnivorous satisfaction. Not tonight. Tonight, he swallowed the meat with all the excitement of changing a newborn's hundredth shitty diaper.

But he kept cutting and chewing and swallowing with mechanical efficiency.

He took a sip from his third bourbon.

He drummed his fingers against the table.

His gaze strayed to the woman at the bar, then to Intense Dude. The guy's seat was empty and a server was clearing away his empty drink.

Back to the woman. He couldn't figure out why a red ponytail and an uninspired pantsuit would compel his attention, but here he was staring. Again.

This time, he searched the back of her neck and around

her jacket collar. No blue lanyard. Normally, once people put those things on, they didn't remove them until they were rolling their suitcase out of the hotel. Which meant she wasn't part of the G-con. Relief tumbled through him.

Sensible Shoes took a drink of her fruity cocktail before dropping her reading material into an oversized purse at her feet. After paying her bill, she slid off the stool and turned toward the dining area.

Thick, perfectly arched eyebrows accented wide, catlike eyes. Her full lips were without lipstick and, somehow, the absence captured his interest even more. When his gaze roamed lower, he cursed, unable to assess the rest of her assets in that damn formless business suit.

She scanned the room, as if looking for someone. Her eyes met his, and something shifted inside his chest. Something warm and familiar, though he'd never met her before. He didn't understand the sensation, but he liked it. A lot.

He nodded, and she smiled in return.

"Happy birthday to you, happy birthday to you."

Oh, no. *Oh, hell no.*

Server Keith, followed by several other similarly uniformed staff, snaked through the dining room, holding aloft a small plate of *tiramisu* skewered by a single, flaming candle.

Fucking Ash.

"Happy birthday to Zee-eeke. Happy birthday to you!"

Keith set the plate in front of him and waited expectantly.

Sensible Shoes smiled and mouthed, "Happy birthday," as she breezed past his table.

Disappointment burned his chest. He sat there in indecision. Should he call out to her? Invite her to share his dessert? A drink? Hot stranger sex?

The pressure of four politely impatient pairs of eyes kept his mouth shut and his butt in the chair. He blew out the candle and Keith and friends disappeared.

A harsh breath pushed out of his lungs. Ignoring the *tiramisu,* he knocked back the last of his bourbon, not even bothering to savor it. He wanted the fire. Needed the lick of alcohol to wake the hell up.

His traitorous gaze kept going to the barstool where Sensible Shoes had sat. The longer he stared, the more he regretted not going after her. Not to hook up, though he wouldn't have said no, but to simply talk to someone who knew nothing about him or his family or his business.

Uncomplicated, no-expectation conversation.

By the time he finished his meal, the mild regret had turned into a full-blown, alcohol-induced flagellation. He signed off on his bill, grabbed what was left of Ash's whiskey, and began the long journey to his room on the ninth floor.

Alone.

He chinked the air with his glass. "Happy fucking birth-day, to me."

ONCE ZEKE WAS BACK IN HIS HOTEL ROOM AND CLOSED THE door, he stood in a slightly buzzed state, staring at his surroundings.

A thick file folder on the small desk near the window caught his eye. Before he even formed the thought, his legs were moving in that direction. He flipped it open and thumbed through the mounds of research he'd collected over the past year, pausing on an illustration of a medieval knight brandishing Lupos while standing on a mound of bodies, complete with severed limbs and heads.

He slid the illustration aside to reveal a 1909 newspaper article with a picture of the sword hanging above an enormous stone fireplace. A young, serious-looking man holding a pipe stood below it.

Theodore Blackwell. His great-great-grandfather.

Not long after the newspaper published the article, Lupos had disappeared and was never recovered.

The tip of his finger smoothed over the sword above his grandfather's head. "I will find you, Lupos, and you will rest in a place of honor in the Friary's Great Hall." A place where he could draw on its strength, every day. Where his family could unite around it, every night.

Turning away from the file, he weighed his options. Stay and go to bed? Leave and go for a swim?

He wasn't the least bit tired and had no interest in flipping channels for hours. Decision made, he replaced his evening wear with a pair of swim trunks he'd decided to bring at the last minute, along with some old flip-flops. Yanking a bath towel off the rack, he grabbed his keycard and stalked out of his room.

Rather than take the elevator to the pool, he hoofed it up the four flights of stairs. Relief hit him when he pushed open the door leading to the roof and found the pool unoccupied. An odd reaction given he'd just escaped his empty room.

The rooftop wasn't completely devoid of people. A few couples reclined in lounge chairs, quietly talking or gazing at the stars, and a small group of men sat around at the back-lit bar, watching a previously recorded NASCAR race on the big screen above. He ignored them all.

Dropping his towel and keycard at the edge of the deep end, he dove in. The cool water slicked by his face for three, four, five, six seconds before he angled his body upward, his head breaking the surface. Night wrapped around him, lulling him into rhythmic, exhausting laps.

By his fifth rotation, his muscles screamed for him to stop. He pushed himself through one more lap before pivoting onto his back. Snatches of his conversation with Ash tried to push aside his serenity, but he shook them off and, instead, searched his memory for an image of the redhead.

Who was she? With that outfit and those shoes, her presence had to be business-related. Would he see her tomorrow at breakfast? Before he checked out? If he did, what then?

Zeke cursed beneath his breath. He'd screwed up his opportunity to learn more about her when he'd sat there like an idiot and watched her walk out of his life.

A large splash interrupted his whirling thoughts and a ripple of water rocked his world. A yell preceded another splash, and a spray of chlorinated water coated his chest and skipped up his nose.

Uninterested in dodging drunken human cannonballs, he swam to the edge of the pool, his muscles heavy from their exertion. He climbed out, dreading going back to his room. Already thoughts of the stolen sword and shithead Ash and his brothers' growing frustration were returning. A sense of helplessness thundered against his temples.

Steam and flickering light at the opposite end of the roof caught his eye. A few minutes in the Jacuzzi might be what he needed to calm his frenzied mind enough to fall asleep.

A pergola of sorts, replete with wooden lattice and viny green plants, surrounded the pool of steaming water, giving the space a more intimate feel. It wasn't until he cleared the greenery that he noticed the Jacuzzi wasn't empty. Annoyance made his steps slow. Until he realized the occupant was a woman.

She sat with her head tilted back, obscuring her features. Steam glistened on her cheeks, her throat, her chest. Water rippled around her, concealing everything below the surface. If not for the thin black shoulder straps, he would question whether she wore anything at all.

Why was she out here, alone? Was her seclusion by choice? Or would she mind company?

He took a step toward the hot tub, then checked himself as his mother's voice rose in his mind, cautioning him.

You're a stranger. A virile man approaching a lone woman at night wearing little more than your underwear.

Glancing around, he noticed several of the lounge chairs had emptied during his swim. He couldn't help but appreciate the irony of the situation. If there had been more people around, he wouldn't have thought twice about joining the woman—or at least asking if he could share the jets.

Doing so now would only result in her making a hasty retreat off the roof or both of them enduring an indeterminate amount of awkwardness before one of them bolted. Neither option appealed to him tonight. Clutching his keycard in a death grip, he turned to leave, already feeling the pang of loss.

"I won't bite," the woman said in a soft, languid voice.

He peered over his shoulder and found her eyes on him, a teasing smile curving her lips.

Catlike eyes. Full, kissable lips. Red hair coiled atop her head.

Sensible Shoes.

His heart punched against his ribcage, as if a temperamental goat had rammed its bony head into his solar plexus.

"Sorry." His throat felt as if he'd swallowed a cobweb. "I didn't want to disturb you."

She shifted in her seat. "There's more than enough room for both of us."

"You're sure?"

"I won't hesitate to scream if you misbehave."

He grinned at her teasing tone. Dropping his belongings, he lowered himself into the hot water and groaned.

"You'll let me know if you're on the verge of an orgasm?" she asked. "I'd prefer not to be in the water when it happens."

He opened one eye, not sure what to make of her, but played along. "I'll give you plenty of time to run."

With their heads resting on the edge of the tub and their eyes closed, they sat in comfortable silence for several minutes, listening to the hypnotizing rumble of the water jets. Although his body remained keenly aware of his hot tub companion, his mind relaxed and his frenzied, tangled thoughts unraveled, one by one, until they finally floated away.

All except one. His curiosity about the loner went into overdrive.

"What brings you into the city?" she asked, beating him to the Q&A period.

"What makes you think I don't live here?"

"I have an eye for detail."

He lifted his head. "What detail gave me away?"

Her eyes caressed his face before trailing down his chest and into the depths of the water. "Your hands, for one."

"What about them?" He raised them out of the water, turning them one way, then the other.

"Not a single paper cut."

He smiled. "What else?"

"Your necklace. It lacks the requisite bling for the city."

A thin, brown leather rope encircled his neck with a black onyx stone resting in the center. He'd picked it up at a farmer's market in Black Mountain last year. The woman who made it said the stone would help him make wise decisions and feel more centered and calm. He never took it off.

"Anything else?"

"The most telling bit of evidence is your mud-splashed truck."

That she'd seen him in the parking lot without him noticing her gave him pause. "Are you stalking me?"

"Nothing so dramatic. My shuttle bus pulled into the parking lot at the same time you were exiting your monster truck."

"That was a few hours ago, yet you still remembered me."

"Well, you are hard to forget."

Did she remember him from the dining room? Remember wishing the loser sitting alone a happy birthday?

His fingers tingled with the sudden urge to release the mass of red hair coiled on top of her head. With deliberate movements, he braced his arms on the rim of the Jacuzzi. "Good detective work..."

"Olivia—or Liv, if you prefer."

"I'm Zeke."

"Zeke," she repeated. "I've heard that name only once before. Is it short for something?"

"Yes, but my birth name was buried in a vault at the bottom of the sea."

She laughed, and the sound went straight to his groin. "Business or sightseeing?"

A droplet of water slid down her cheek, over her jaw, and along her neck. "The sights."

"By yourself?"

Her fishing expedition made him smile. "I'm selfish that way."

"Avoiding someone or something?"

"A little of both." He rotated his neck, working out the kinks. "An entire day without a single responsibility."

She studied him. "No one else's schedule. No one else's likes or dislikes to consider."

"And no one waiting on a decision."

They both grinned. He couldn't remember that last time he'd enjoyed a conversation so much.

"Actually, I was supposed to have dinner and hang out with my brother, but the shit—but he got caught up in work."

"Work? This late?"

"It happens."

Her expression turned to one of empathy. "You're disappointed."

He shrugged. "Not the first time. Besides, had he stuck around, I wouldn't be here now." Which was infinitely better than attempting a reconciliation with his big brother. He lowered his voice. "And I like where I am now."

"So do I."

Silence stretched between them. She might like being in his company, but that didn't mean she was interested in anything beyond a bit of playful conversation.

"What kind of business brings you to the Grand Marquis?" he asked.

Her smile dimmed a second before turning appreciative. "It seems you have your own powers of observation."

"You're hard to forget too, Liv."

"Yet so many do."

He chewed on her cryptic remark for all of three seconds before a bead of moisture trailing down her chest diverted his attention. The drive to go to her, to set his mouth on that smooth expanse of skin, vibrated through his veins. He shifted his attention up her neck, over her slightly parted lips, to her eyes.

The moment stretched.

But rather than act on the charged tension pulsing between them, they both stayed rooted in their corners.

A silent, sensual duel.

"Are you staying in town through the weekend?" she asked.

"I leave tomorrow." He hesitated a moment before deciding to throw out another lure. If this one didn't hook some serious interest from her, he'd do his best to settle his raging hard-on and simply enjoy her company. He hoped to God she bit. "Unless I have a reason to remain for a few more days."

"I leave tomorrow, too."

He waited a heartbeat, then another, to see if she'd offer to linger another day. When she didn't, he felt the loss in the deepest part of his gut. He drew in a long breath to quell the ache.

Friendly conversation, it was. He took in her glistening cheeks and the damp tendril of hair against her shoulder. At least his torture came with a view.

"You never said what you do for a living," he asked.

"Are you truly interested in talking about work?" Her gaze lowered to his mouth. "Or do you have another topic you'd like to explore?"

Later, he would not recall who made the first move. All he would remember was that they met in the middle. Tendrils of steam rising in the small space between them.

"Shall we end the battle?" she whispered, trailing a damp finger along his whiskered jaw. "Or continue wasting precious hours before dawn?"

For the past three years, he'd been embroiled in his own personal war. He'd put down skirmish after skirmish. But the war still raged, and he was tired. So fucking tired.

Tonight, he would lie in her arms and allow unsuspecting Liv to tend his wounds.

"Truce, my lady."

4

LIV WAS GOING TO DO THIS. SHE WAS GOING TO SET ASIDE every rational thought she possessed and have sex on a hotel rooftop with a perfect stranger.

Emphasis on perfect.

Zeke epitomized every erotic fantasy she'd ever had. From his dark lashes to his scruff-covered jaw to his superhero abs to his sun-kissed skin.

When he rose from the pool and stalked toward her, she figured fate had to be at work. Their paths had crossed three times in one night. That had to be some kind of metaphysical sign. Not that she followed such things, but there must be some pixie if-you-don't-get-laid-tonight-there's-no-hope-for-you dust in the air.

She had first noticed him in the hotel parking lot. Coming back from a workshop excursion, she had rested her head against the shuttle bus's seat and stared out the window as their vehicle wound its way through the lot toward the drop-off location.

Zeke had exited his giant pickup truck at that precise moment, and her breath had literally caught in the back of her throat. The intense expression he wore as he dragged a bulging duffel bag from the cab had her twisting in her seat to keep him in sight.

By the time she shuffled her way off the bus, he'd disappeared inside the hotel. The keenness of her disappointment had been surprising. In that short stretch of time, she'd envisioned them sitting at a table for two, the soft glow of candlelight illuminating their faces, while they enjoyed an evening of flirtatious banter.

Reality had knocked her daydream into the proverbial trash can, so she soothed the sting with a drink. Many had accused her of having eyes in the back of her head, but not tonight. Tonight, she'd sat in inexplicable misery at the bar while her dream guy dined alone. Right. Behind. Her.

She'd been so unprepared for the discovery that, when she stood to leave and found his gaze on her, all her years of training for the unexpected had blinked out under the intensity of his bottomless brown eyes. Instead of making her fantasy come true, she'd chickened out and buzzed right by him with nothing more than a whispered happy birthday.

But the third time he entered her orbit, she'd sensed him the moment he stepped foot on this rooftop oasis. Had even pressed her face close to the pergola's lattice to watch him stride toward the pool.

While he swam laps, her mind fired on fifty cylinders, working through scenarios and witty responses and logistics. She'd even crossed her fingers and silently chanted, *Please join me. Please be single. Please be into women. Please like what you see.*

When he'd left the pool and started her way, she'd experienced a moment of vulnerability. Initiating a one-night stand with a stranger came with so many risks. She knew them all. Yet, she could no more ignore his testosterone pull than a monarch could ignore the call of its winter home in the Sierra Madre Mountains of Mexico.

The monarch followed its instincts, and so had she.

When his big hands clasped her waist and she hooked her legs around his hips, she decided to always follow her instincts.

She took a moment to simply feel his nearness. Soak up the press of his hands on her hips, the waft of his breath over her damp shoulder, the soft skin protecting hard, delicious muscles.

She missed this connection, this anticipation, this . . . this loss of self.

Liv skimmed her fingers up Zeke's biceps and over his shoulders until they reached his corded neck. If Callie could see her serious, responsible, lonely sister now, she'd be dancing a celebratory jig.

"So," she said, her thumbs drawing idle circles in the water droplets beading on his skin.

He nuzzled her nose. "So."

Her bold talk had brought them this far, but she had never been the aggressor in her relationships. She left that mindset at the day job. When in her lover's arms, the only decision she wanted to make was slow and thorough, or hard and fast.

At the moment, she needed the latter. Needed to get past the upcoming anniversary of her husband's death. Needed to put an end to four years of celibacy.

But she would make an exception to her no-decision rule, if that's the price she had to pay for mind obliteration. A price she would happily pay with this man.

"I'm not interested in a weekend," she said. "Only tonight."

"Sounds good to me." His mouth brushed hers. "Though, don't be surprised if I try to change your mind."

"Don't be surprised when I say no."

A slow smile curled his lips and softened his already unbearably sexy eyes. "Blackwells always love a challenge."

Zeke Blackwell.

Any misgivings she had about hooking up with a stranger vanished at the confirmation of his identity. With his unusual first name, she had suspected this was Cameron's brother. Now she knew. Knew she could put an end to her dry spell without worrying about getting killed in the middle of the night.

But it was Cameron's brother. A complication. Another secret in her long list of secrets to keep.

Zeke leaned in and kissed her. All thoughts of complications and secrets disappeared behind a haze of want and need. He took his time exploring her mouth with a patience and a thoroughness that made her toes curl and her nipples ache.

From one stolen inhalation to the next, he deepened the kiss, sliding his tongue into her mouth and pressing his hardness against her stomach.

Tonight, she would live for pleasure. Seek it with a man who'd been pulled out of her most vivid dreams and deepest longings. Her legs tightened around his hips, and she ground her starving center against his thick length.

A hiss escaped his lips. "As much as I would like to have a *Tequila Sunrise* moment with you in this Jacuzzi," he murmured between hot, drugging kisses. "I don't have any protection with me."

She traced the ridge of his strong jawline with her fingertip, loving the rasp of his stubble against her water-softened skin. "In your room?"

"Yes." His head turned into her touch. "Will you join me?" He drew her finger into his warm mouth, never taking his eyes off hers while he waited for her answer.

Every muscle in her lower body contracted around his erotic invitation. Wanting, seeking, needing the wicked things he would do to her.

She nodded. "One night."

5

Two weeks later
FBI Resident Agency Office
Asheville, North Carolina

THE MUSCLES IN OLIVIA WESTCOTT'S NECK AND SHOULDERS were so taut that if someone had hailed her from behind, she would have had to turn her whole body to acknowledge them.

Thanks to an accident on I-240, her annoying ten minutes late had turned into *WTF Westcott?* late.

Maybe she'd get lucky and Mitch would be in a meeting and have no idea what time she had arrived. She tried to tiptoe past her SRA's office and would have succeeded if Peppy Patsy hadn't zipped by her at that precise moment.

"Morning, Olivia." Patsy tapped her own earlobe. "Love your earrings. They go great with that top." She kept walking at the speed of a Maserati. "I put the information you were looking for yesterday on your desk."

"Thanks, Patsy," Liv said through clenched teeth.

"Westcott," Senior Resident Agent Mitch Lawson called from inside his office.

Closing her eyes briefly, she drew in a bracing breath before pivoting toward his open door. "Sorry, sir. I—"

"Save it. Get your pretty earrings in here."

Rather than pounding away at his keyboard, Mitch was standing. His blond head angled down, searching for something amongst the mounds of case files on his desk. Already, he'd rolled up the sleeves of his white dress shirt and loosened his blue, white, and black striped tie. In the two years she'd worked under his supervision, she had never beaten him to work. Callie teased her about never leaving work. Liv wondered if Mitch ever actually went home.

Setting her heavy handbag just inside his door, she paused by the pair of chairs facing his desk, clasped her hands together, and waited.

"I had hoped to brief you on this yesterday, but you'd left by the time my meeting ended."

He made it sound like she'd slinked out of the building early, when in fact she hadn't packed up her things until after six-thirty. Given he was already irritated with her, she kept this bit of clarification behind her teeth.

Lifting his attention from his desk, he looked at her in that familiar, unnerving way of his. Part indifferent, part exasperated, part something that shouldn't arise in a supervisor's gaze. She hoped for both their sakes that he never let go of the tight hold he kept on whatever was brewing behind those green eyes.

"Anything you need to tell me, Olivia?"

"A transportation issue at home, sir. It won't happen again."

"Since when did your son start driving?"

Her clasped fingers strangled each other. "My sister

Callie is living with me at the moment. Her car is at the shop."

"I suggest she get a rental or Uber tomorrow."

"Yes, sir."

He handed her a thick file folder. "Go drop off your belongings and meet us in the conference room."

Her heart skipped a beat. "Us?"

"That's all."

As punishments went, it was effective. She turned to leave with her proverbial tail between her legs. When she bent down to grab her bag, he said, "Special Agent Westcott."

Shit. He really was pissed to use her title like that. She met his gaze.

"Not a word in the meeting. You're there to observe."

A ball of dread dropped into her stomach. Unlike other times when she'd been asked to sit in on meetings for informational purposes, this one felt different. Something in his eyes told her she wouldn't like what she was about to hear. "Yes, sir."

As she wove her way through the squad room, Liv pushed back her misgivings and brushed off her SRA's ass-whooping. She'd gotten pretty good at compartmentalizing conflict over the years. In her line of work, it was a good day if she only had to put out three fires instead of ten.

After stuffing her handbag into a cabinet drawer, she flipped open the file folder to see if she could glean something, anything, about the upcoming meeting. She hated, absolutely hated, the feeling of unpreparedness, of being ignorant of something she—or other people believed she—should know.

Mitch had said "meet us." Who else would be there?

Would she have to present something? Give her opinion on a case?

No, he'd all but told her to keep her trap shut. Why?

She released one long, slow breath, read the top page of the case file in front of her, and frowned.

Drugs? She, like her fellow special agents, assisted with other cases when the need warranted, but she'd never worked drugs before. Had no desire to do so now, either. Most of her time was spent on art theft and cultural property crimes, and that's the way she liked it.

"Hey Olivia," a deep voice said.

Still mired in the mystery meeting, she didn't at first recognize the blue-eyed, black-haired man, wearing a charcoal gray business suit by . . . *classic lines mixed with a slim, tailored fit . . .* Ralph Lauren, she decided.

She had little in common with her socialite mother, but an appreciation for fashion ran in both their bloods. Liv wondered why Cameron Blackwell was sporting Lauren today, rather than his normal Men's Wearhouse garb. Granted, the man looked stunning in any brand.

But not as gorgeous as his brother Zeke.

"Cameron, what are you doing here?"

"Good morning to you, too."

A flush of embarrassment heated her chest. Whether it was the result of her rudeness or remembrance of what she'd done with his brother, she didn't know. She held out her hand. "Sorry, but I didn't expect you."

She watched for indicators that he knew about her night with Zeke, which was ridiculous. During their rooftop introduction, she'd been careful not to share her last name or the reason for her stay at the hotel. And she'd slipped from his bed before dawn to avoid any awkward after-sex chitchat.

Disentangling herself from Zeke's warm body had been a great deal more difficult than she'd expected.

Cameron smiled and shook her hand. "No offense taken."

When the two of them happened to be at the same work function last year, he'd all but pounced on her after learning she was the region's go-to agent for working art crime. New special agents were notorious for volunteering to help more senior agents in order to build their experience, but few showed much interest in recovering art or cultural heritage pieces.

It was for that reason alone that Liv had called Cameron when several pieces had gone missing from the Asheville Art Museum, a few weeks later. Unlike most history geeks, Cameron's expertise wasn't limited to one area of interest. He had an extensive knowledge base about many genres. A base she'd tapped into several times in the past year.

He looked toward the conference room. "I'm not looking forward to this."

"This, what?"

"Our meeting."

Evidently, Cameron was part of the "us" club.

Recognizing her I-don't-know-what-the-hell-you're-talk-ing-about expression, he said, "You have no idea what this meeting's about, do you?"

"I only got the file five minutes ago."

"Now I know why I got the call from Mitch yesterday instead of you. Thought you might have been enjoying a spa day or something."

She smacked the back of her hand against his steel-encased bicep.

"Careful. You could break a finger that way."

Shaking her head, she peered down at the case file

again, ignoring the fact that Mitch bothered to call Cameron, but not her.

"Why did Mitch bring you in?" Cameron worked out of the Charlotte office and specialized in cybersecurity when he wasn't assisting her with art crime.

"I have a unique connection upper management decided to exploit."

"Connection . . . ? " Her voice trailed off as her gaze settled on a familiar name.

Ezekiel Blackwell.

Blackwell Asset Recovery Services.

Ezekiel Blackwell.

Ezekiel.

Zeke.

Although she already knew the answer, she still had to hear the confirmation. "Your brother?"

He gave her a pained smile and nodded.

She closed her eyes and wondered if this day could get any worse.

6

For a brief period in ancient Persia, they deemed it legal to commit fratricide for the greater good of the Ottoman Empire.

Zeke Blackwell reflected on this fact as he paced the FBI's conference room, waiting for his brother, Ash, to show his pretty face.

He glanced at his watch.

8:59 a.m.

The moment felt too reminiscent of two weeks ago, when he'd sat alone in a fancy restaurant, waiting for Ash to arrive so they could finally clear the rotten air between them —and catching his first glimpse of a redheaded woman who would gift him with the best birthday ever.

He shook his head, refusing to go *there* while standing in enemy territory. He didn't know why the hell Ash had summoned him to Asheville or why he'd fucking complied, but if his big brother didn't appear in the next thirty seconds, his reasons would remain a mystery.

Once again, he took in the eighty-plus-inch display

attached to the far wall with the Federal Bureau of Investigation's logo emblazoned on the screen.

Fidelity-Bravery-Integrity

"Fidelity, my ass." Even after three years, Ash's defection to the FBI still rankled.

Ash had led the family business for several years after their father had passed away—until he hadn't. One day, everything slogged along like normal and the next day, his brother announced he was deserting the family business to become a G-man. The only person who hadn't appeared surprised by the news was Grams.

Whether from her keen, almost eerie intuition, or because Ash had confided in her, he didn't know, but something inside Zeke had shattered that day. Something he had yet to reclaim in the years since Ash left.

How could he have not known that the brother he damn near worshiped wanted to work for the feds? Wanted out of the family business?

He'd known his brother wasn't passionate about repo work—who the hell was? But hating it enough to leave? He hadn't seen that coming.

In hindsight, Ash's refusal to implement any of Zeke's ideas to enhance the company made sense. Ash hadn't wanted to get in any deeper. Or maybe he'd gone into lame duck mode and didn't care enough to try.

Why hadn't Ash confided in him? Prepared him for the inevitable disappointment, rather than dumping a ton load of shit on him at the last minute?

Every childhood memory he possessed included Ash. Zeke recalled the time when a neighbor boy had come up behind him and swiped his chocolate fudge brownie ice cream cone. While he'd wailed his frustration, Ash had taken off after the thief and retrieved his cone.

Without the ice cream.

Like any ungrateful little brother, he'd stamped his feet and blamed Ash for the loss.

In retaliation, his brother had eaten the waffle cone while laughing at Zeke's new tantrum. Which made him want to *end* his big brother.

The meeting room door opened, and Ash stepped inside, carrying a thick file folder. He eyed Zeke's jeans and T-shirt with a frown.

"Glad to see you dressed for the occasion," Ash said with a shake of his head. "As usual."

"I hit my dress-up quota for the year a couple of weeks ago. Too bad you didn't stick around to enjoy—"

A woman with her hair pulled back in a flawless pony-tail, wearing business attire similar to Ash's, entered behind his brother. Zeke blinked in rapid succession before his gaze banked down to her shoes. This pair of black shoes had a shinier finish and a tiny silver buckle on top, but still sensible.

Liv.

Where irritation sat heavy in his chest seconds ago, something more powerful, lighter, took its place. Of its own volition, his face pulled into a grin. He hadn't thought he'd ever see her again. But here she was, standing in front of him.

Staring at him with neither surprise nor joy nor recognition.

Something clunked in his torso. He thought it might have been his heart falling, but he was too preoccupied *willing* Liv to acknowledge him.

He got nothing from her. Absolutely nothing. His smile faded. Vaporized as if it had never been.

Irritation returned. And maybe a keg of hurt.

"You'll have to save the verbal guilt trip for later," Ash said into what felt like a century of silence.

If she wanted to play the stranger card, he'd follow along. For a while. "What am I doing here, Ash?"

Liv's eyes narrowed on his brother. "Ash?"

"Asher Cameron Blackwell," his brother explained. "Only my family calls me by that name."

Zeke folded his arms. "He needed a clean break when he became a G-man. Isn't that right, brother?"

Ignoring him, Ash answered his previous question. "I can't say anything until the SRA arrives." He indicated Liv. "This is Special Agent Olivia Westcott. Olivia, my smart-mouthed brother, *Ezekiel,* and CEO of Blackwell Asset Recovery Services or BARS, for short."

She was a fucking FBI agent. Why hadn't that realization come to him yet? Because he was too focused on seeing a trace of recognition in those devastating blue eyes.

Zeke thought back to their encounter two weeks ago, to the large group of men and women wearing matching lanyards, to Liv sitting at the bar perusing a booklet—no doubt a program schedule, to her sensible conference shoes.

He shook his head at his own stupidity, his own subconscious desire that she not be one of *them.*

Why in the hell had she been sitting alone?

"Zeke," he corrected through clenched teeth as he lifted a hand in Liv's direction.

She stepped around Ash and grasped Zeke's hand in a firm grip. No hesitancy. No bolt of electricity when skin met skin. No recognition of the hours they'd explored each other's bodies.

Her features softened in greeting, an expression she'd probably delivered a thousand times. Nothing special. No hint of her sexy hot tub smile.

Did she not remember him?

The thought made his stomach turn.

Ash waved a hand toward the oval conference table surrounded by six leather chairs. "Have a seat."

Liv and Ash took seats next to each other. Zeke sat across from them.

"Sorry, I'm late," a blond forty-something man with narrow-set eyes said. "I'm Senior Resident Agent Mitch Lawson." He held out his hand. "Good to meet you, Mr. Blackwell."

"Zeke." He threw Ash a disgusted look before turning back to Lawson. "We've already met."

Lawson paused in the act of sitting. "Have we?"

"Two weeks ago, in Charlotte. You and some woman hijacked my dinner date."

"The woman was Special Agent in Charge Shanice Williams from the Charlotte field office," Ash said, sending Zeke a warning look.

Lawson studied Zeke a moment. "That's right. Now I remember."

Something about the entire exchange felt off to Zeke. If he had to guess, he'd say that Lawson recalled their first meeting before Zeke's reminder. Why would he act otherwise?

Secrets already. Great.

Lawson reached across the table and drew a remote from a basket at its center. "What I'm about to share with you cannot leave this room."

"I'm not surprised, given the mysterious nature of my brother's call."

"Special Agent Blackwell was under strict orders to get you here. That was it."

"Then he was a good little special agent."

His brother cut him a sharp look.

Zeke focused on the SRA. Who was he to fault his brother for following the rules? One phone call from Ash, commanding him to his side with no details, and here he was. Even after years of leading BARS, he'd slid right into the familiar—and more comfortable—role of second-in-command without a thought.

"We're working a high-profile case and my UCA's confidential informant has made a demand," Lawson said.

"I don't speak G-geek. What's a UCA?"

The skin around Lawson's eyes tightened the slightest bit. Good. Now they both had each other's measure.

"Undercover agent," Lawson explained.

Zeke stared hard at his brother. "Are you this UCA?"

"We can't get into the specifics of the operation, at this time," Lawson interjected.

Ash gave nothing away, not by word or expression. A good soldier, following orders.

Unable to tune out Liv any longer, he flashed her a glance, only to find that she wore the same impassive expression as his brother. Zeke set his jaw and gave the SRA his full attention, ignoring the way his guts were curling into a cold knot. "What does any of this have to do with BARS?"

"The CI—confidential informant—claims someone stole an item from him several months ago."

"What kind of item?"

"A valuable antiquity."

Comprehension dawned. "You want BARS to retrieve it."

Surprise shot across Liv's face. "Why are you contracting a recovery for an antiquity? I'll take care of it."

Lawson stared at Liv for a long moment. His anger ricocheted around the room, though his expression, nor his body altered. "You're nose deep in the O'Fallon case." He paused a palpable second. "Even if you weren't, you don't have the skillset this recovery requires."

Liv leaned forward. "My success rate is a hundred percent." Her tone hardened. "Exactly what *skillset* do I lack?"

Bright red rimmed Lawson's ears. Either he wasn't used to someone challenging him—or something else was at play here. "Do you recall the warning I gave you in my office, Special Agent Westcott?"

Liv's entire upper body moved on a deep inhalation, then she slowly sat back.

"The ability to cross the line," Zeke supplied, answering Liv's question, though he directed the comment to his brother.

Ash's gaze slammed toward the table a brief second before he looked at Zeke. His brother's sign of discomfort was all the confirmation he needed. And yet, something else lurked in the depths of his brother's eyes.

A challenge, Zeke thought. Nothing new. Ash was a Blackwell. Challenging each other was a rite of passage.

No, what bothered Zeke far more was the thing Ash was concealing behind his challenging stare.

"What line?" Liv asked, missing, or ignoring, the tense exchange.

Lawson and Ash said nothing. Not within these hallowed walls. Where justice and law ruled every decision, guided every action.

Not so with BARS.

After he'd reorganized the family's repo company, the newly branded Blackwell Asset Recovery Services had slowly grown into a multimillion-dollar business. BARS specialized in recovering property that was deemed unrecoverable. If, at times, they employed methods that would in some circles be considered illegal, so be it.

They had played by the rules for years, and the family barely scraped by. He had no problem righting wrongs by whatever means necessary. Not all of his brothers agreed with his fluid ethics. But for now, he was the one calling the shots, and everyone but Phin seemed to have no problem adjusting their mindsets.

"The fine line that separates recovery from theft." Zeke's gaze landed on his big brother, the man he'd idolized his whole life. The man who'd handled every difficult situation with ease and grace. The man who'd walked away from the family business to find *legitimate* work.

The man who was now asking him to break the law.

"You can't be serious."

Zeke turned toward Liv's incredulous voice and found her staring, thunderstruck, at her supervisor.

Whatever warning Lawson had given her in his office, she was clearly ignoring.

The SRA's lips firmed into a thin line of annoyance before he said, "The Bureau can't be linked to this recovery."

"Why not?" Liv said in a low, dangerous voice. "If someone has stolen a piece of art, it's my—our—job to recover it."

Was she goading Lawson to speak the unspoken? Or was she truly that naïve? He suspected the former. Because it was more than obvious to him that Lawson doubted their CI's ownership claim on the artifact. That the agent knew from the onset that this *recovery* was nothing more than a smokescreen for theft.

Zeke turned to Ash. "Did you tell them about us?"

"We learned about BARS through other means," Lawson answered for Ash, drawing Zeke's attention. "Though we did question him about your business's integrity."

"And?" Zeke's gaze shifted back to Ash, remembering how Lawson and the female agent from Charlotte had snatched his brother away during their dinner. "Did BARS come highly recommended?"

His brother clasped his hands together on top of the table. The tips of his fingers turned white.

"As a matter-of-fact, you did," Lawson said.

Something wasn't adding up. Ash wouldn't want his career with the FBI and the family business within ten feet of each other. He'd started using his damn middle name for that reason. Distance.

Zeke turned back to Lawson. "What happens if the recovery goes wrong?"

"The Bureau will disavow any knowledge."

Of course they would.

Ash sat there, stone-faced, while his boss, or whoever the hell Lawson was to him, laid out a plan that would abandon his brothers to an uncertain fate the moment the Bureau smelled trouble.

"If you don't trust me to handle this," Liv said to her supervisor, "why am I here, Mitch?"

Zeke's gaze sharpened on the SRA. Was Lawson hiring BARS to protect her?

"This isn't about trust or distrust." Lawson's voice was hard. "You will be Mr. Blackwell's handler."

"His . . . *handler*?"

Zeke's hackles rose at the level of disgust she'd infused in that one word. What right did she have to be upset?

After an amazing night of sex, she was the one who'd disappeared the following morning without a damned goodbye. And now, she didn't appear to even recognize him. On top of that fucking humiliation, his straitlaced brother seemed to have no problem using BARS to steal a priceless object to further his "legitimate" career.

"What do you say, Mr. Blackwell," Lawson said. "Will you assist the Bureau?"

He should tell the bastard—all of them—to go fuck themselves. It was right there on the tip of his tongue.

"What does BARS get out of this arrangement?"

"Twenty percent over your normal fee and, if all goes well, the Bureau will keep you on its Rolodex, so to speak."

Although BARS was doing just fine without being on the FBI's speed dial, Zeke couldn't allow his personal feelings to get in the way of business. Nor could he keep his attention from straying to Liv. He didn't like unfinished business, and she was definitely unfinished.

"I'll discuss your offer with my team and get back to you in a few days."

"The Bureau's offer is with you, not your team," Lawson said. "More people knowing about this raises the likelihood of the case getting compromised. I can't chance it."

Zeke rose, wanting no part of this job if he couldn't involve the rest of his team. "Then you picked the wrong guy." He glared at his brother. "You know BARS's success is due to the team and not me." As he strode to the door, he could almost feel his brother's building anger. Pissed off—he could handle. Disappointment—he couldn't take on anymore. He was already drowning in a boiling vat of it.

He yanked on the handle, but not before his gaze touched on Liv's. Regret pinged inside his chest.

"Wait, Zeke."

Two decades of habit brought him to an immediate halt.

Clenching his jaw, he let the door swing closed and turned to face his brother.

"I get it," Ash said. "I get your conflict. I get your suspicion." *Even your resentment,* his eyes said. "But the Bureau needs you. Your community needs you." He paused, looking down at his clenched hands, visibly struggling for the right words. "If we don't hand over the antiquity to this asshole CI, he won't give us valuable information that we need to save lives."

Zeke caught the note of urgency in his brother's voice, but also a hint of fear. Nothing ever riled Ash. He was the ultimate cool cucumber. Which meant there would be major fallout if the case failed.

Sonofabitch.

Zeke looked at Lawson. "It's the team or nothing."

A muscle twitched in the SRA's jaw before his gaze flicked to Ash, who nodded. "Okay, but everyone must sign a confidentiality agreement."

"No problem."

Ash released an audible breath.

"I'll e-mail the agreements to you," Lawson said, rising.

"I have two more conditions."

Lawson dropped back in his seat. "Name them."

"If things go wrong, I, and I alone, will take the fall. The rest of my team gets immunity."

"I'll do my best to insure they're protected against any criminal fallout."

"Not good enough. I want a guarantee or no deal."

"You have it," Ash said in a quiet, firm voice.

Zeke looked to the SRA for confirmation.

Lawson nodded, muscle twitching again. "And two?"

"Special Agent Westcott will assist us with the recovery, rather than be my handler."

Liv's eyes widened, then narrowed into blowtorches. Aimed at him.

"Out of the question. I told you the Bureau can't be linked to the recovery. Having her be the case agent is risky enough."

"My conditions are nonnegotiable." He grasped the door handle. "I don't need the Bureau's gidgets and gadgets. Just Westcott. I'll be in touch with our answer."

"When?"

"When I have it."

"By the end of the week, Blackwell."

As Zeke shut the conference room door behind him, he heard Lawson demand, "What the hell is going on—?"

Zeke didn't know if Lawson spoke to Ash or Liv—and didn't really care. He had a lot of his own shit to sort out.

Like how the hell he was going to get his brothers on board with this recovery and how he was going to keep his hands off his new FBI partner.

7

"Hurry up," Liv said to her sister, three days later.

"You need to get laid."

"Callie!" She cut a look at the door across the hall. "Keep your voice down."

"If you're worried about Brodie overhearing us, don't be." The twenty-two-year-old, recent college graduate blocked the bathroom doorway, wearing nothing but a towel and a scowl. "He's in the Zone."

Liv closed her eyes for a moment and pushed out a slow, slow breath. "You should be dressed by now. My boss warned me not to be late again." She shouldered her way into the only full bathroom in her small, single-story bungalow and popped open the medicine cabinet.

Adding a master bathroom and walk-in closet was one of a dozen things she and Tyler had planned for this house when they had purchased it. Then life threw their budding family a curveball and all of their dreams were now buried in York Memorial.

Not for the first time, she considered selling this house

and buying something that didn't need renovation, especially now that Callie was living with her.

"Your boss is being a jerk," Callie said. "Does he know how late you're there, every night?"

Liv sent her sister a don't-go-there glare. Last week, she finally had a breakthrough on a case she'd been working on for months, but that didn't mean her late nights were ending. There was a great deal of aftermath work to do. Way too much for one person, but she couldn't think about that right now. Especially now that Mitch had added handling Zeke Blackwell to her load.

She tossed back two ibuprofens and took a gulp of water to prepare for her next battle. Her boss.

"Which brings us back to you getting laid. You used to be fun when you were getting it on a regular basis."

As it had a hundred times since the conference, an image of her body tangled with Zeke Blackwell's surfaced. The intensity of his brown eyes as they trailed a hot path down her torso, the slight smile on his gorgeous face as she writhed beneath his touch, the shocking fullness as he thrust into her, again and again.

The transformation of his surprised expression to confused hurt to something else she couldn't identify.

The boiling anger when he included working with her as one of his nonnegotiable conditions.

Liv rolled her fingers and dug her nails into her palms to tamp the torrent of emotions surging through her body. If he'd been so keen on working with her, why hadn't he called to accept the job? His silence had everyone in the office on edge, especially after SAC Shanice Williams paid Mitch an unexpected and rare visit the day before.

Shoving away the Zeke problem, she glared at her sister. "Could you be any more crude?"

"As a matter of fact—"

"Don't." Liv left the bathroom and crossed the hall. "We're leaving in ten minutes."

"Arggh!" Callie slammed the bathroom door. "I can't wait until my car is fixed," came her muffled reply.

"That makes two of us!"

Liv knocked on Brodie's door, but didn't bother waiting for his permission. When her nine-year-old-soon-to-be-ten-year-old son was in the Zone, the world beyond his noise-canceling headphones ceased to exist.

Sure enough, he sat at his desk, headphones on, destroying ancient alien worlds. Or L.A. It was hard to tell with his screen moving so fast.

She tapped a fingernail against his left earmuff, causing him to jump. He yanked off his retreat-from-the-real-world device. "Mom!"

"You know the rules. No video games in the morning. They're too distracting."

"I'm dressed, my bed is made, and my pack is ready."

"Teeth?"

He groaned, and mummy-walked toward the bathroom.

"Brush them all, young man."

"Yes, ma'am." He banged on the door. "Hurry up, Cal!"

Liv grabbed his dirty clothes off the floor and threw them into a hamper inside his closet. When she turned, her gaze landed on the four-by-six picture frame lying facedown on his bedside table. The sight no longer sent an ache deep in her chest or made her eyes blur with tears.

Now she looked at it with a numb sort of sadness and the hope that tomorrow would be the day the frame would be upright once again, and she would see her smiling son standing in between his father and Charlotte Knights's first baseman Jimar Baker.

Drawing in a breath, she left her son's room and rushed into the kitchen to make their lunches. Eight minutes later, Callie strode in as if she had all the time in the world. She plucked an apple out of a bowl sitting on the island and bit into it.

"Sandwich or salad?" Liv asked.

"Neither. Jessica wants to try the new sushi place that opened up close to the bookstore."

Having finished her last day of college a week ago, Callie had three months before her architect position with Boone and Kaye Architecture and Design begins. She could have easily spent those ninety days lolling around Liv's house.

Not her sister. When Callie wasn't shelving books at the bookstore, she was volunteering her time at the women's center, where Liv also volunteered. Her little sis might be a pain in Liv's ass sometimes, but Callie had the work ethic of a Baby Boomer and a heart bigger than the sun.

"Need any money?"

"I'm good." Callie took another bite. "Want me to cull through the candidates for you?"

Right before she left for the conference in Charlotte, she had allowed her sister to talk her into creating an account on one of the dating apps. It was time, she reasoned. Time to find love again. Find someone to share her and Brodie's lives.

After Charlotte, she still wanted those things—more than ever—but now she couldn't bring herself to view any of the matches piling up. Nor could she stop thinking about Zeke Blackwell. Unfortunately, if he agreed to work with the FBI, he would become taboo, romantically.

"I don't have time to deal with men right now."

"Two hours. Three hours tops. That's all you need to

meet and greet and do the vertical nasty. That should be enough to take the crank out of your style."

"What are you talking about?"

"Drinks, wall sex, smile."

"I'm not cranky because I need sex. I'm cranky because I live with two people whose sole purpose is to make me late for—" She glanced at the clock on the stove "—shit. Brodie!"

"Ow!" Callie reeled back. "Watch the ears."

Liv shoved Brodie's lunch into her sister's arms. "Get into the vehicle, *please*." She ran toward the bathroom, knowing even before she opened the door that there was no way he was still brushing his teeth. "Brodie, it's go time." Empty.

Inhaling a long, calming breath, she prayed for extreme patience. Somehow, some way, she would figure out how to get her boy back outside if it was the last thing she did.

She smacked her hand against his open bedroom door. "Brodie, if you're not buckled up in one minute, I'm taking away your game for an entire month."

Standing and playing, he dropped the controller and snatched his backpack off his bed. "Sorry, Mom!" He tore out of the house.

Liv fast-walked to a computer nook off the family room, where her suit jacket, handbag, and keys were waiting. She knifed her arms through her jacket, one at a time, covering her service weapon. Most of her neighbors had no idea what she did for a living, and she was happy to keep them in the dark.

She checked the front and back door locks again before exiting the house through the mudroom, hitting the garage door button on her way out. She climbed into the driver's seat.

Halfway down the driveway, Brodie yelled, "Wait! I forgot my calculator."

"You're going to have to borrow someone's."

"But I have a test. The teacher won't let us share during tests."

Liv slammed on the brake and hit a button to stop the garage door's descent. "Same warning. You have one minute."

Brodie took off, and Liv's head fell against the headrest. "I'm so going to get fired."

"Sex is a great stress reliever."

Damned if Callie's words didn't conjure the feeling of Zeke's phantom lips working their way down her thigh. Filling her lungs with air, she gave her sister a sidelong look. She had no doubt Callie was sexually active, but she didn't need the reminder.

"So I've heard." Callie flung her apple core out the window. "Don't worry, I'll pick it up later."

A heavy sigh escaped Liv's lips as she raised her head and watched Brodie scrambling back to their vehicle. Maybe her little sister was right. Maybe she should set up another one-nighter. Be with someone who could excise the tension from her body and Zeke Blackwell from her mind.

Sensing victory, Callie smiled and tapped several buttons on her phone. "I'll find someone who'll take good care of you, Sis."

8

ZEKE LOOKED AT HIS WATCH AND MARKED THE SECONDS AS they sifted away. It was all he could do not to boot their new recruit, Clay Neuman, out of the way and pick the damn lock himself. His brother, Cruz's, assurance that the young man had what it took to be a recovery artist was the only thing keeping Zeke's foot anchored to the floor.

His mind took the opportunity to wander into more tempting, but no less dangerous territory, also known as Liv. *Special Agent* Olivia Westcott. What were the chances that the same woman he'd had mind-blowing sex with two weeks ago would walk into a meeting he was present at a hundred and thirty miles from their penetration point?

Had she known who he was when she slept with him? Had she been the tenderizer to the FBI's plan to soften him up? Make him more amenable to their offer?

Another more disturbing, more bile-inducing thought hit him. Had she felt sorry for him? She couldn't have missed that he'd been flying solo during the humiliating birthday serenade.

For the hundredth time, Zeke analyzed their conference

room reunion. Something about the extreme neutrality of her expression didn't ring true. It was as if she'd been fore-warned of his presence, but had no idea of how to navigate the situation.

She certainly hadn't known Lawson's intention of assigning her as Zeke's handler. No one could fake that level of shock and repulsion.

Zeke leaned closer to Neuman's kneeling form when a cloud of noxious fumes sailed up his nose. Jumping back, he hooked an elbow over the lower part of his face and sent a savage look at Cruz, who guarded their backs at a safe distance away.

His brother's shoulders shook with laughter, and Zeke could almost hear the humiliating words being carved on his headstone.

Here lies Zeke Blackwell, a noble thief, who died from compli-cations of an ass bomb.

His brothers would do it. Without a second's thought. Then they'd go have a drink in his honor.

"Neuman, what the hell did you eat for lunch?" Zeke wheezed.

The rookie glanced up before quickly turning back to the lock. Even in the dim light, Zeke could see red blotching his fair, freckled cheeks.

"Didn't I tell you no more spicy foods before a recovery?"

"Red pepper flakes clear my mind. They help me focus."

"What the hell kind of voodoo you-do logic is that?"

When he opened his mouth to explain, Zeke held up a hand. "I don't want to hear it. Not now. Finish what you're doing."

Impatience gnawed at Zeke's nerves. He could almost smell the anxiety wafting off the rookie as he unrolled the soft leather housing his picklock set. Zeke understood he was, in large part, the reason for Neuman's nervousness, but he didn't much care. Every step of a recovery was timed to the minute. If one RA blew his mark, he put the whole recovery at risk.

While monitoring Neuman's slow progress, he followed the team's chatter in his ear.

Rohan: "Chickadee is at the dessert table."

Phin: "On my way."

Rohan: "Last month, she purchased the collector's edition of *i-Werewolf*."

Phin: "You're shittin' me."

Cruz: "Good luck with that one, bro."

Phin: "Hit me with the short version."

Rohan rattled off a description of the novel and two talking points.

It was all their little brother needed to strike up a conversation. The guy was a master at small talk and drawing out even the most reluctant target's secrets. Especially if the target was female. For reasons Zeke didn't understand, women found Phin's tailored clothing, bling watches, and product-tamed hair appealing.

Zeke said into his throat mic, "We're about ready to breach the antechamber door. I need that code in three minutes, Phin."

"You'll have it in two."

If the boast had come from any of his other brothers, he would have busted their balls. But Phin's track record justified his cocksure attitude.

"Shit," Neuman said.

"What's the matter?" Zeke asked.

"It's not here."

"What's not here?"

"My rake."

Zeke checked his watch again. Fuck. "You have your tension wrench?"

"Yeah." Neuman held up a three-inch stainless steel pick that had both ends flared at a ninety-degree angle.

Thank goodness for small miracles. "Get out your backup rake and let's get this door unlocked."

"My . . . what?"

Zeke grit his teeth. "You don't have backup equipment?"

Neuman squeezed his eyes shut. "Sorry, Zeke."

Zeke gave his second-in-command a hard sidelong look, while fishing his own picklock set out of his pocket.

Cruz shrugged as if the rookie's mistake couldn't have killed the recovery, right then and there.

After enduring months of his brother's harping, Zeke had finally agreed to bring on Neuman and train him to take Zeke's place on the team so he could focus on the administrative side of BARS. The twenty-three-year-old showed promise, but his broad learning curve might be the death of his budding career.

Patience at an end, Zeke said, "Move aside, Neuman."

The recruit scuttled out of the way, and Zeke knelt before the lock. He didn't have time to train someone to do a job he could accomplish himself in a tenth of the time. As team leader, he had a hundred things jostling in his mind at any given moment. Like the FBI's job offer and how the hell he'd get his brothers to agree to recovering—scratch that, stealing—an unknown item for the federal government. A government ready to cut the safety rope if they got in a jam.

Discontent was already brewing on the team, and Zeke knew he was at the core of his brothers' frustration. He was *trying* to let go of some of his responsibilities, but Neuman's colossal mistake was a perfect example of why letting go wasn't always a good thing.

And why hadn't he heard from Sardoff yet? How many layers of whispers and rumors did the antiquities dealer have to sift through before uncovering the sword's location? Evidently a lot, because his friend was a man of action. Once he had a scent, he didn't stop until he had the thing cornered.

Zeke inserted his tension wrench in the bottom of the keyhole plug and his rake in the top. Two seconds later, the bolt slid free. The second lock took even less time.

Shaking his head at the primitiveness of the target's security, he moved to enter, his finger resting on the trigger guard of his pistol.

"Stay put," he ordered Neuman, when the rookie made to follow.

"But—"

"No buts. You're here to perfect your breaching craft. The rest will come later."

"Stay by the door," Cruz said, sending Zeke a you're-an-ass look. "You can follow what's going on inside while keeping an eye on the hallway."

Zeke pushed his way into the vault's antechamber. Cruz on his six.

Two eighteenth-century chairs huddled around a small round table against the wall. A decanter of amber liquid and two squat glasses sat on a mirrored tray in the center of the table. The out-of-place ensemble faced a six-by-six gold-plated door.

Cruz released a long, slow whistle. "Wealth protecting wealth."

"Phin," Zeke said into his mic. "We're at the vault."

"Let me know when you're ready for the code."

Zeke checked his watch.

Two minutes.

He shook his head. One day, his little brother would come up against a woman immune to his charms. He hoped he was there to witness the moment.

Cruz stood before a digital panel to the right of the massive door. "Hit me, bro."

Phin rattled off an eight-digit combination.

Once Cruz entered the last number, a loud click echoed through the room.

Grabbing one of the gold handles, Cruz used his body weight to pry open the door. Automatic lights flickered on inside the vault, illuminating enough precious gems and priceless artwork to fund a small country.

Zeke ducked inside and began searching for a centuries-old, bedazzled sphere while Cruz kept watch at the door. He spotted the piece inside a glass enclosure in the far corner. Triumph pulsed through his veins. This was what he lived for. That moment when all of their planning came together, and they took home the prize.

He would miss this once his role became largely administrative. Though considering how much training Neuman needed, he wouldn't be stuck in the office for a while.

When he reached the display case, he found three more spheres arranged behind the first one in a diamond shape.

Dammit.

He racked his brain for Rohan's description, but quickly realized that he'd only been listening with half an ear. Who had more than one bedazzled sphere?

"There are four of them," he said to Cruz.

"Who cares? Grab the target and let's get out of here."

"Can you confirm the description?"

"No, man. Guard dogs don't get into the weeds."

Rohan spoke into Zeke's ear. "You have company headed your way."

Setting his teeth, Zeke said, "Rohan, give me the description again."

"I gave it to you twice already."

A man with near-perfect recall of everything he sees and reads, would never understand the limitations of a mere mortal's brain. Especially a mortal who was more interested in getting things done rather than in miring himself in finite details.

Only sometimes those details really mattered.

Ash would never have made this mistake.

"I don't have time to discuss the obvious," Zeke said. "There are four spheres. Which one am I recovering?"

Silence filled his ear. When Rohan finally spoke, static butchered his words. Man-made static, no doubt.

Realizing he was on his own, he scooped up the sphere on the left side of the diamond quartet and set it in a specially designed padded box before placing it in his backpack.

"Asset secure," he announced, and turned to leave.

Blinding strobe lights stopped him in his tracks.

Cruz cursed, Rohan sighed, and Phin laughed.

Zeke lifted his gaze to the elevated observation catwalk that spanned the entire length of the shoot house. There, he found three faces staring down at him, observing that he, the team leader, not the recruit, was the one who'd killed their practice run of the Warner recovery.

Behind a makeshift workstation attached to the catwalk's metal railing, Rohan's fingers paused over his laptop's keyboard. He wore the same contemplative look he always did, but with a slight bit of tension around his jawline.

Zeke's shoulders tightened when he took in his mother's ever-present erect posture and splayed feet, both evidence of the twenty years she'd spent in the armed forces. As always, and especially with him, Lynette Blackwell's expression wavered between concern and narrow-eyed scrutiny.

The face on the far right, the one that neither approved nor disapproved, was the one that captured and held Zeke's attention.

Out of everyone in his life, including Ash, his grandmother, Johona Blackwell, was the one person he wanted to make most proud. He didn't know why exactly, but it had always been so. She could dole out tough love like a dominant wolf or extend comfort like a matriarchal elephant. Her mind was as sharp at ninety as it was in her heyday as a nurse during the Korean War.

"Ezekiel," Grams said, "please join me in the chapel." All four foot nine inches of his grandmother strode down the catwalk, her shoes clanking against the metal grate flooring. Lynette followed in her mother-in-law's wake.

No one said a word until the sound of an exterior door opening and closing reached them.

Then the shitheads let loose.

"Taken down by a ball," Cruz said as Zeke began his walk of shame.

"Bling does matter," Rohan said from the catwalk.

"I'll meet you assholes at the Annex for the debriefing." He had intended to bring up the FBI's offer after the practice run, but Zeke wasn't in the right mindset to field his brothers' questions or navigate their reactions. Especially Phin's.

Later. He would discuss it with them later.

Zeke approached Neuman, visually daring the new guy to add more salt to the wound. If Zeke's screwup hadn't eclipsed the recruit's, Neuman would be enduring their jabs instead of Zeke.

Any time one of them screwed up a test mission, the

others did their best to leave a deep mental scar, so that they never made the same mistake again. It was a custom their father started years ago.

Many would find the practice cruel. Blackwells called it a life raft.

With BARS taking on riskier recoveries, they couldn't afford to get it wrong. Their lives, and livelihoods, depended upon every team member's success.

Especially the team leader's.

But Neuman didn't add salt. He did something far worse.

"You'll get it next time, Z."

Zeke's step hitched. Anger tried to boil to the surface, but he wrestled it back to a simmer. Empathy ranked right up there with disappointment on his Suck-o-Meter.

He didn't need a dirt-behind-the-ear rookie telling him what he already knew. Of course he'd get the damn thing right next time. There was no other option.

A large hand clamped on his shoulder. "Relax," Cruz said as he squeezed by.

His brother's warning had the opposite effect of what he had intended. Zeke wasn't a damn keg about to bust under pressure. He could control his roiling emotions.

Most of the time.

When he really, really wanted to.

Neuman shifted on his feet and swallowed hard enough for Zeke to hear. It was the rookie's telltale sign of nerves that allowed him to shake the dirty pond water off his back.

He handed Neuman the backpack containing the sphere reproduction with a little more force than was necessary before he stalked through the shoot house, passing a handful of rooms decorated to replicate the home of multi-millionaire Dane Warner's palatial Asheville home.

As he passed the makeshift ballroom, he glimpsed his

brother, Phin, in a tux, dancing in circles with a delighted ten-year-old Sadie, wearing her finest pale yellow dress.

Sadie was the daughter of one of their long-time, trusted employees, Alejandro Rios, and his wife Clara. She was also Neuman's stepsister.

Everywhere he turned, he could find traces of the girl. She flitted around the estate, playing bit parts, as she did with their recovery scenario, helping Lynette and Clara set up the rooms, assisting his mom in the office, and shooting targets with him and his brothers.

She was a never-ending whirl of energy and a constant source of joy to everyone she touched.

Jumping in his vehicle, Zeke drove past the Annex, a term they'd used for their office building while it had been under construction. They hadn't come up with a better name, so the word stuck. His truck rolled by the former Friary, a large stone structure the family had recently renovated and now called home.

It had taken a little over a year, a boatload of money, and a bazillion decisions to update the seventies monstrosity. Oddly, no Blackwells had died during the process.

Each family member had their own suite of rooms where they could disappear when family got to be too much. The original Great Hall dominated the center of the main level, where a wall of twelve-foot windows overlooked the backyard and forest beyond. At opposite ends of the Hall, two enormous fireplaces flared to life, during the cooler months, warming the family as they indulged in spirits and gossip.

As he neared the chapel, he waved to his mom, who was hiking up the drive and likely headed to her office in the Annex. He parked beside Grams's UTV, scanning the off-road vehicle for fresh scratches or grass clumps clinging to the roof. His grandmother could literally do anything she set her mind to, except drive.

Lynette did her best to reduce the time Grams spent behind the wheel, but the wily old girl liked to burn rubber and found ways to evade her daughter-in-law's keen eye.

He climbed the three stone steps leading to the chapel's entrance, turned both handles, and swung open the double doors with ease. The long, open room still retained its austere origins—white walls, high ceiling, stained glass windows, organ pipes, altar, and godlike pulpit overlooking the masses.

Beyond the altar, two hidden doors were carved into the paneled wall. One led to a small kitchenette and restroom, the other to a secret bunker below ground level. The former youth camp leadership, or the Franciscan monks before them, must have been expecting one hell of an apocalypse, given the number of canned goods they'd found on the shelves. The bunker even had an emergency exit out the back that poured its occupants into the forest about fifty yards away.

Since his family had purchased the property, this building was no longer a place of worship, but of reflection. At the far end of the chapel, wooden steps led up to a dais where the altar languished in all its wooden glory.

Grams sat with a mug of coffee on the top step, waiting.

Time for reflection.

Much reflection.

9

GRAMS STUDIED ZEKE, WITHOUT EXPRESSION ON HER BROWN, lined face. Today, she had gathered her silver-white hair into a long braid down her back and she wore a multicolored T-shirt with beige pants that stopped at her calves, showing off her thick-soled white gym shoes and purple-and-yellow-striped socks.

To keep BARS running efficiently and profitably required the Blackwell trifecta—Zeke led the business and oversaw the operations, Lynette managed the money and office, and Grams was their heart, their foundation.

The one he answered to when he screwed up.

He stopped a few feet away. "Sorry, Grams."

She indicated the spot beside her. "Have a seat, *she'ashkii yázhi.*" My little boy.

Once he lowered himself onto the hardwood step next to her, a long, stomach-clenching silence stretched between. A master strategist, his Grams knew how to leverage quiet time to great effect.

A trait she shared with Special Agent Olivia Westcott. He could still remember how his body ached to see one hint of recognition in her eyes during their meeting in Asheville. How his breath suspended and his eyes locked on her face for the slightest quirk of her mouth to indicate she would keep their secret from the rest of the room's occupants. How, when neither happened, his heart plummeted like a rock down a dry well.

Whether her lack of recognition was real or some sort of self-protection measure, he couldn't be sure. All he knew was that she'd given him an out. One he'd be an idiot not to accept, because he didn't need one more complication in his life.

So why had he all but forced Liv to work side by side with him?

He dug his fingertips into his forehead in an attempt to forestall the oncoming headache.

"Something occupies your mind," Grams said.

He closed his eyes briefly, wishing he hadn't promised himself to never lie to this woman.

"Yes."

"Business or personal."

A shaft of light stole over a large stained glass window above the chapel's entrance door. The sun pierced through the window, projecting a kaleidoscope of colors onto the floor a few feet from where they sat. He never tired of watching the noonday ritual. But today, it did nothing to lift his spirits.

"Unfortunately, both," he said.

"You have a decision to make."

Her ability to discern trouble was downright frightening. "Yes."

"Have you shared it with your brothers?"

He rested his forearms on his knees and stared at his clasped hands. "Not yet."

"Are you concerned they won't approve?"

"Phin won't." Cruz was iffy. Rohan would say his piece, then follow Zeke's lead. "BARS has been offered a recovery job, one that's riskier than anything we've done to date and straight-up illegal, but will somehow save lives and potentially establish a lucrative long-term relationship."

"Illegal in what way?"

"The FBI wants us to recover"—he lifted his hands to do air quotes—"a *stolen* piece of art to appease an informant who can give them information that will stop something big. They won't give me all the details until we sign a confidentiality agreement." He lowered his voice. "Ash was there."

He didn't need to explain to Grams how that fact tore at his insides.

She grew silent for a long time, then in a voice that usually reignited his flailing confidence, she said, "You must trust your instincts."

But not today. No fire, no spark. Only a cloud of darkness where his instincts used to be.

"What if I end up tearing this business apart?"

"Tearing the family apart, you mean?"

An invisible fist sucker-punched him in the chest. "They are one and the same."

"No, *she'ashkii yázhi*." A hand that had weathered nearly a century of triumphs and disappointments settled on his arm. "Businesses rise and crumble and disappear from the landscape as if they never existed. Family endures." She wrapped both hands around her coffee cup and sipped. "But you must listen to its heartbeat as you would any living being, especially when it has sustained an injury, unintended or not."

His throat grew thick. He *was* listening. He just couldn't understand the words.

"Coordinating so many recovery missions must feel overwhelming, at times."

Unlike his brothers, Zeke's role in BARS required him to not only execute his part of their missions, but he also had to plan them, organize logistics, order supplies, meet with new and potential clients, write up proposals . . . His duties were endless and so fucking fatiguing.

"It's nothing I can't handle," he said.

Most days.

Other days, he felt the weight of a thousand sleepless nights pressing on his skull.

"A leader's most valuable trait is respect," Grams said. "Respect you earn and respect you give."

"I thought vision was the most valuable."

"A leader can lead a team to war, but he can't win it without their respect."

"Are you saying I've lost my brothers' respect?" The possibility, one he'd considered a thousand times, made him sick to his stomach.

She shook her head. "But respect is a fragile thing. Easily shattered. Difficult to repair."

He sent her a sidelong glance. "I sense a suggestion coming."

The creases around her mouth deepened in humor. "One you've already worked out for yourself."

"My brothers have a lot on their plates already. I depend on them to figure out how best to execute their part in each recovery."

The double doors opened, and Cruz appeared, leading the pack of Blackwells.

Nosy bastards.

"Don't worry, Grams. Once Neuman is operational, I'll

get back some much-needed time." He leaned over and kissed her wrinkled cheek. "I won't let the team down."

Her hand rose to cup his jaw and her dark eyes, cloudy around the edges, conveyed a message for him and him alone. But the sight of his brothers had pushed his barriers back up, blocking whatever wisdom she tried to convey.

"Come on." Zeke rose and held out a hand to his grandmother. "Let's get you to higher ground before these apes run you over." Even though she was sharp as a whip and healthier than many fifty-year-olds, her body didn't fire on all cylinders that low to the ground.

She gave him a knowing smile before accepting his assistance.

He escorted Grams down the aisle. "What are you all doing here? I told you we'd debrief at the Annex."

Light fanned over the group when the chapel doors opened again, and another figure crowded in behind Phin.

The newcomer's eyes met Zeke's.

Ash.

10

A BATTERY OF EMOTIONS HIT ZEKE AT ONCE. DESPITE THEIR less than cordial parting in Asheville three days ago, Zeke's mood lightened at the sight of his brother. Until he remembered he hadn't discussed the FBI's offer with his team yet. Had Ash come to force a decision?

Of course he did. When they'd met in Charlotte, Ash had no plans to return home until Grams's birthday, months from now.

Zeke steeled himself for his brother's next move. He could visit Ash in Charlotte without blinking an eye, but the moment his big brother set foot on Blackwell soil, Zeke experienced a series of turbulent emotions—longing for old times, wavering self-confidence, suspicion.

No matter how much BARS had flourished under Zeke's leadership, he couldn't shake the feeling of being an interloper when his brother visited home. BARS had always been meant for Ash. Their father had trained Ash on different aspects of the business, mentoring him for the day his eldest would take over.

A memory, old and muddy, surfaced.

"*Zeke can handle it,*" Ash said to their dad, Ashkii Duke Blackwell.

"*No, he can't. Your brother is a great number two, but he doesn't have the right mindset or temperament for the top position.*"

"*You underestimate him.*"

"*I* know *him.*"

Zeke's jaw clenched so hard, he was certain he'd cracked a molar. At seventeen, he hadn't realized that Ash and Duke had been talking about Zeke's ability to lead the family business. His father had no faith in him, and Ash hadn't wanted the business—them—as far back as high school.

The weight of this revelation slowed his steps to a crawl until he finally stopped a few feet away from the circle of men.

Phin hooked a thumb over his shoulder. "Look what we found loitering outside the house."

"Hello, Grams." Ash strode forward and bussed her cheek. "How are you doing, old girl?"

Even his brother's quick-to-tan skin couldn't hide the dark circles under his eyes. His near-black hair appeared finger-combed and his normally clean-shaven face sported several days' growth. He still wore a navy sports coat over a pristine white button-down shirt, though his ever-present tie was missing.

In short, he looked like shit.

Grams cupped Ash's face. "Better than you, I think."

Ash grasped her much smaller hand and kissed the backs of her knuckles. "Nothing a shower and eight hours of sleep won't cure." When he lifted his gaze to Zeke, flint sparked in their depths. "I need to speak with you. Alone."

Rohan said to Grams, "How about we wait out the storm in a more comfortable setting?"

Grams squeezed Zeke's arm in warning before accepting Rohan's assistance. Phin followed the two from the chapel, and after a long, considering moment Cruz strode out on silent feet.

As soon as they were alone, Ash accused, "You haven't spoken to them yet."

"Observant as always, Ash."

"Why?"

"The timing hasn't been right." And he wanted the FBI to sweat, just a little.

"Well, your *timing* issue has created a critical situation. Something spooked the CI, and he's demanding his property back by the end of the week."

"Five days?" Zeke shook his head. "Guess you have your answer now. There's no way we can plan and execute a recovery in that amount of time."

"Bullshit. You recovered the Salvatores' painting in three."

"How the hell—" Zeke took a deep breath. Ash always seemed to have an insider's understanding of the business. He didn't know who was giving him updates, but a tiny, resentful part of him wondered how often his leadership came up in the conversations.

"You could have called for an update. Why travel all of this way when you had no interest in doing so?"

"Look," Ash ran his fingers through his thick hair, "it's not that I don't want to visit—"

Suddenly tired of his brother's cat and mouse games, he asked in a harsh voice, "Why are you here?"

Ash shrugged, avoiding his eyes. "My supervisor thought I needed to burn some vacation."

Zeke's attention sharpened. His beef with his brother faded into the background at the scent of a common enemy.

"Is that true?"

"Considering that I haven't taken any time off in two years, true enough."

"What about the case? How does it move forward without its UCA?"

"I'm not the UCA."

"What's your role with the case?"

"Co-case agent."

"Co-what?"

"Over the past year, I've teamed up with Liv on some of her art or cultural property crime cases."

A red cloud filled his vision at the thought of Ash and Liv working together. "Anything going on between the two of you?" The question ripped from his throat.

"Me and who, exactly?"

"Liv—Olivia—Agent Westcott, dammit."

Ash studied him for a long, too-knowing moment. "Did she say something was going on between us?"

"Forget it." Zeke made a slashing motion with his hand. "You still working cybersecurity?"

Ash smirked. "That's what I do full-time. Art crime is my collateral job."

"You're Westcott's backup on this case?"

"That was the plan, until you took your sweet damn time." His brother's mask slipped into hard, uncompromising lines. "They expected your answer before now."

"What are you saying? Your sups didn't get what they wanted, so they're punishing you instead? What kind of fucked-up organization do you work for?"

"The kind that doesn't wait around for perfect timing."

"Did they also place Agent Westcott on leave?"

"Doubtful. She's your *partner,* after all."

Zeke gritted his teeth. "Tell Cruz to keep everyone on

target for the Warner recovery. I'll be back tomorrow, at the latest."

"Tell him yourself, *when you discuss the Bureau's offer with the team.*"

"I need to clear up something before I can have that conversation."

"Clear up what?"

An image of Zeke standing on Mitch Lawson's neck was quickly replaced with one of Liv's beautiful body spread out beneath him. "Some unfinished business."

11

"You did what?" Liv stared at her SRA, sitting at his desk as if he hadn't just thrown a bomb in her lap, and wondered how she would ever look at Mitch Lawson with respect again.

Since their discussion with Zeke, Cameron Blackwell had temporarily occupied a desk two cubicles down from hers. When he'd disappeared yesterday afternoon and failed to show up today, she decided to discuss her concern with Mitch.

But her SRA not only knew why Zeke's brother was gone, he had conspired with Cameron's supervisor at the Charlotte field office to make it happen.

"I have no desire to repeat myself, Olivia."

"You've gone too far."

Mitch's eyes turned harder, colder. "We don't have time to dillydally. This was the most expedient way to light a fire under Zeke's ass."

"By punishing his big brother? Why didn't you call him before taking such drastic measures?"

"I did."

"And?"

"Voice mail, every time."

"Then you should have sent me or Cameron to talk to him." She shook her head. "All you accomplished was to piss him off. Zeke will never assist us now."

"He will."

"How can you be so sure?"

"Protecting one's family is a powerful motivator."

Something Liv knew a great deal about. What had happened to this man? He'd always been tough and willing to take things right up to the edge, but he'd never turned on one of their own.

"Does Shanice know?" Something this big couldn't have gotten far without the region's Special Agent in Charge's seal of approval.

"You could say the SAC was almost enthusiastic about the arrangement."

Everything she understood about her coworkers had been upended in the space of a five-minute conversation while listening to the whir of the microwave.

"If Zeke Blackwell is as smart as I think he is," Mitch said, "he'll be in contact soon. Prepare yourself."

"Me? I had nothing to do with this."

Mitch stared at her with his usual desire-laced exasperation, but this time she sensed something more volatile bubbling at the edges. Something his iron grip of control might not be able to contain "It's your case, and he seemed quite keen on working with you." His voice lowered. "Is there something you need to tell me?"

She'd rather walk around the NASCAR Hall of Fame naked than share the details of her one-night stand with her supervisor. Especially one whose interest in her personally seemed to be growing by the day. Not good.

"He's not going to do it," Liv said, "and I'm not going to be his verbal punching bag."

Mitch shrugged. "Since when do you care about what others think?"

That stung.

To be successful as an FBI special agent, Liv had trained herself to be sparing with her emotional responses at work. She wasn't an ice queen and she didn't try to blend in with the guys.

Sometimes she cared too much, but she didn't let it get in the way of doing her job. She kept her momentum moving forward. Always. But she was loyal to the Bureau and to her fellow agents. In many ways, the Bureau had saved her after losing her husband to a freak accident. The work gave her purpose during a time when she struggled to understand life's myriad of cruelties.

"We're done here," Mitch said. "Let me know when Zeke Blackwell makes contact."

"There's something else."

He sighed and leaned back in his chair. "What?

"The case file mentions Nicola St. Martin."

"That's right. She's in possession of the artifact BARS needs to recover."

"She and my mother are good friends."

"Will that fact prevent you from doing your job?"

"No, but—"

"That's all I need to know." Mitch leaned forward and began shuffling papers on his desk. "Your insider's knowledge might prove useful to the case." When she stood there, speechless, he raised his head. "That's all, Agent Westcott."

Liv turned to leave, but this thing with Cameron continued to gnaw at her thoughts. Words crammed in her throat, fighting for release. Nothing she could say would change the situation. Like it or not, events were already in motion. Yet...

She peered over her shoulder. "In your quest to get Zeke's cooperation, did you stop to think about what all of this will do to Cameron? How he'll view the Bureau from this point forward? How will he ever trust leadership again after this?"

"How little you understand Special Agent Blackwell."

"What do you mean?"

Mitch smiled. It wasn't pleasant. "Ambition makes the most unendurable endurable."

She strode away.

It would take a special person, especially in law enforcement, to forgive his supervisors for something like this. Leadership should be an agent's buffer, their protector, their trusted mentor. Not someone who viewed them as collateral damage.

She had to get out of here. Breathing the same air as her SRA was like sucking in exhaust fumes. Toxic. She'd go to the warehouse and see how the UNC professor and her interns were coming along with cataloging the O'Fallon treasure trove.

Glancing at her phone, she spotted a text message alert. Her heart took off like a rocket when she saw it was from Zeke.

We need to talk. Be there in thirty.

"Shit." She checked the message's time stamp. "Shit, shit, shit." He would be here any second. No way would she give Mitch the satisfaction of witnessing this showdown.

Grabbing her purse and laptop from her cubical, she practically sprinted to the elevator. A few minutes later, she pushed through the front entrance of the federal courthouse, but saw no signs of Zeke. She descended the stone steps and looked up and down Otis Street. Nothing.

She checked the clock on her phone and decided she had enough time to get her vehicle out of the secure parking area. After sending a quick text to Zeke, she turned to the left and marched the short distance to the security gate.

As she paused beside the small black box outside the guardhouse, Paul waved to her from inside before returning to his animated conversation on the phone. Impatience hummed through her veins as she waited for the wrought-iron fence to yawn open. Once there was enough room for her to squeeze through, she checked her phone again to see if Zeke had responded.

Nothing. She hoped he was making his way through the parking garage across the street and not already headed upstairs.

Maybe Zeke's visit wasn't about his brother's forced leave. Maybe Cameron had gone to Maui instead of Steele Ridge. Zeke could be on his way to give them his decision, unaware of the lengths to which the Bureau had gone to secure his cooperation.

Or...what if he'd been stewing for the past three days about her perceived lack of recognition? What if he was coming to remind her of what she'd forgotten?

What if she let him?

An image of his I-know-you smile, followed by its slow death, still haunted her.

She'd been torn between kissing him senseless and pleading with him to run. From the moment she'd seen his name on the same page as fentanyl, heroin, and methamphetamines, she had wanted to protect him from whatever Mitch had planned.

Instead, she had followed orders and kept her mouth shut.

Liv unlocked her SUV and reached in to set her purse and laptop into the passenger seat. When she straightened, something hard slammed into the back of her head. Her vision grayed and her knees buckled. She slumped forward into the driver's seat, disoriented and confused.

But not for long. Her training kicked in and her mind identified the threat before her vision cleared. She pushed against the seat at the same time her foot struck out, connecting with her assailant's body. A whoosh of alcohol-infused air rushed over the side of her face.

Before she could twist around, he shoved her into the driver's compartment again. Her right cheek struck the center console and her dominant arm got wedged between her body and the seat.

A blade pressed into the hollow below her jawline. He dug the knife into her flesh enough to cause a warm trickle of blood to coil its way around her throat.

"Be still," he growled, pressing his forearm harder against her shoulders.

"Who are you?"

"Someone you shouldn't have messed with."

Liv took stock of her body, searching for a way to disarm him. But with his arm pinning her down and his foot anchored against the back of her left knee, she was trapped. There was no escape, no way to shape this to her advantage. "What do you want?"

"To gut you right now for all the trouble you've caused us."

"Hey!" a man's distant voice called. "What's going on?"

Her assailant stilled, then spoke rapidly in her ear. "Keep your nose out of our business, or I'll have to pay a visit to 217

Western Avenue." He gave her a shove for emphasis, making her wince. "Don't you forget it."

The pressure-pain disappeared, as did her attacker.

"Stop!" Running feet tore past her, across the asphalt parking lot.

Hanging half in and half out of the vehicle, she pushed up until she was standing on unsteady legs.

"Ma'am, are you okay?"

She latched onto the man's voice. A rich, soothing, familiar voice.

Zeke.

"Liv?" He was at her side, steadying her with one hand beneath her elbow. "What the hell's going on?"

"I don't know."

217 Western Avenue.

There was something familiar about the address. Something right. . . there. . .

217

21— Terror ripped through her. "I have to go." She pushed out of his hold and bent to pick up her purse and laptop bag from where they had fallen at her feet.

Pain knifed through her head, and a wave of dizziness made her stumble into her door.

"Whoa." He gently probed the back of her head. "You're not going anywhere. I'm calling for an ambulance."

"No, you're not."

When she made to bend down again, he snatched up her belongings. "Hospital. I'll drive."

Panic fractured the small amount of self-control she held on to. "Give me my fucking keys, Zeke."

12

Zeke wavered.

Liv was not in any condition to be driving. But fear gripped her features, and he didn't think it had anything to do with the aftereffects of her assault.

"I'm not letting you behind the wheel," he said. "I'll drive you anywhere you need to go."

She opened her mouth to argue, but he'd spent thirty-four years battling his brothers for the upper hand. She couldn't win. "Either I drive you, or I'll call nine-one-one. You choose."

Whatever ticking clock was chiming in her head won out over stubborn pride.

"My keys are in the side pocket of my purse."

He retrieved the keys, and she nearly ripped his arm off, reclaiming her purse and laptop. With one hand braced against her vehicle, she circled around and climbed into the passenger seat. Any other day, he would have opened the door for her, but he liked having his head attached to his neck.

He took his place behind the wheel and started the vehicle. "Where to?"

"Western Avenue." She spewed out the directions while hitting the speed dial on her phone. "Come on, come on," she said in a broken whisper, "pick up." When no one did, she left a voice mail message. "Pierce, it's Liv. Call me as soon as you get this."

Who the hell was Pierce? Husband? Boyfriend?

She jabbed her thumb against the phone's screen to disconnect. "You're driving like an old man. Faster, Zeke."

"If I drive any faster, we're going to have liftoff."

She propped an elbow on the window seal and clenched her fingers around her nose, closing her eyes.

"Headache?"

Silence.

"The cut on your neck needs attention."

Silence.

His irritation spiked. If either of them should get the silent treatment, it should be her. "Dammit, Liv. Are you hurt?"

She cringed. "Keep it down, or it will be on your head if my brain explodes."

"You may have a concussion."

"Wouldn't be the first time."

"Do you have a first aid kit?"

"Why?"

"Your neck is bleeding."

"It's just a scratch." She reached up to inspect the damage and her fingers came away covered in blood. "Shit."

She fumbled to open the console between their two seats. From inside, she retrieved a plastic package filled with tissue paper, removed half, and slapped the wad against her cut.

"That works, too," Zeke said. "Who was he?"

"I don't know."

He gave her a sidelong glance, trying to determine if she was telling him the truth. It was difficult to decipher any emotion beyond the intensity riding her features. He tried to think of something that would take her mind off whatever was bothering her, but the only thing that surfaced was what brought him to Asheville in the first place.

The bullshit the FBI pulled on his brother in order to get his cooperation. He wanted to ask about her role, but couldn't bring himself to add to her stress.

"Did your attacker say anything?"

Ignoring his question, she shot back, "Why are you here?"

"You know. But we'll save that conversation for later."

She pointed. "Make a right at the next light."

"Where are we going?"

"I told you—"

"What's at the address?"

She said nothing.

"Liv—"

"Pull over."

He did as instructed, parking her vehicle in front of a large brick building. Above the entrance, carved in stone, was a sign that read *Hawthorne Elementary School.*

Liv yanked on the door handle, and he grasped her arm. "Wait."

"Let go of me. Now." He released her, and she made to bolt again.

"You've got blood all over your neck and top. It'll be a shock to whoever is inside."

"Dammit." She reached behind the driver's seat and lifted what looked like a go-bag from the floorboard. Plopping the black duffel in her lap, she unzipped it and drew out a navy button down top with a collar. She shook it out and laid it across her bag.

Grabbing the ends of her soiled shirt, she ripped it over her head in a quick, jerky motion. Zeke glimpsed a no-nonsense beige bra that molded around full breasts and the outline of strong muscles gliding beneath smooth skin before remembering to avert his gaze.

Through his peripheral vision, he watched her scan their surroundings, as if searching for someone or something, while donning her clean shirt.

"Why are we here, Liv?" He glanced at the building again.

Rather than answer, she pulled a wet wipe from her bag and cleaned her neck with efficient strokes. She appeared paler than normal and on the verge of losing her stomach's contents.

Zeke's hand strangled the steering wheel. He called on his limited cache of patience while his brain frantically tried to process the sequence of events.

"Did that guy threaten someone who works here?"

She flipped down the visor and checked her reflection in the mirror.

"Liv?"

Removing her service weapon from her hip, she placed the pistol, holster and all, into her bag, along with her soiled shirt. She dropped the bag between her feet. "Don't leave this vehicle."

In less than a minute, she'd transformed from victim to businesswoman. All evidence of her ordeal was gone. Except for the pebbling of blood at the cut site.

He held out a square of gauze and pointed toward her injury.

She accepted the offering and exited, jabbing her arms into a business jacket while walk-running up to the school's entrance, completing the illusion.

Nearing her destination, she slowed her pace. A dark-haired man, carrying a young girl in a flower-covered dress, exited the building. Liv paused to exchange a few words before pushing through the entrance door.

Zeke knew next to nothing about kids. What ages attended elementary school? The little girl in her father's arms looked young. Six? Seven? He had no idea.

What about Sadie? Two months ago, she'd celebrated her tenth birthday. Then he remembered the girl was home-schooled. No help there.

He gave the area another scan before his attention strayed back to the spot where Liv had disappeared. The longer she was gone, the tighter the knot in his stomach grew.

What was she doing here? His mind refused to settle on the obvious. But the look of terror on her face and her sense of urgency all but hammered it home.

Ten minutes later, Liv emerged with a brown-haired boy at her side. He wore jeans and a lightweight blue and white hoodie over a graphic T-shirt. His thumbs were hooked in the arm straps of a bulging red backpack.

Zeke checked the rearview mirror and noted the absence of a car seat or booster. North Carolina required kids to be in one or the other until they were eight years old. He didn't think the boy was older than Sadie, but who the hell knew?

Heart hammering, he opened his door, slid out, and made his way over to the passenger side.

Liv stopped a few feet away. "Brodie, this is my friend Zeke. Say hello."

The boy cast him an uncertain look. "Hi."

"Howdy." Zeke shoved his hands into his front pockets. "How was, um, school?"

"I beat Imar at spelling today."

"Oh, yeah? First time?"

The boy nodded, shrugging off his backpack. "He's really smart."

Liv took his bag and opened the back door. Brodie climbed inside and grabbed for the seat belt, while she placed his pack next to him.

The whole exchange was all so. . . ordinary, but it set Zeke's nerves on fire.

When Liv shut the door, her gaze touched his before she strode around to the driver's side back door and slid in beside what he could only assume was her son.

They shared the same blue eyes, and Zeke hadn't missed how the sunlight picked up the red streaks in the boy's brown hair.

Staring at the tinted back windows, he thumped the side of his thumb against his thigh, a sign his patience had been poked one too many times today. He splayed his hand wide before balling it into a fist.

Once he was behind the wheel again, he caught Liv's eye in the rearview mirror. "Where to?"

"Back to your vehicle."

"Then what?"

"We go our separate ways."

"Are you going to call someone to drive the two of you home?"

"You don't need to worry about us."

He set the vehicle in motion. "Driving in your condition," he looked from her to Brodie, "isn't smart."

She brushed a hand over the boy's head, but said nothing.

"Why is Zeke driving your car, Mama?"

Mystery solved.

"So I can listen to the rest of your story."

"I can drive you home." The thought of her losing consciousness while driving did weird things to his chest. "And call for a ride back to the field office."

She gave the boy one last loving look before meeting his eyes in the rearview mirror. Her expression was no longer loving. It was resigned. "Okay."

Rather than give him directions to her home, she punched a few buttons on her phone and engaged her vehicle's GPS. He spent the next fifteen minutes listening to Brodie's excited chatter and Liv's encouraging comments.

When they finally pulled to a stop outside a modest gray and white bungalow, he knew everything about the boy's day. Right down to the clump of disgustingness that his friend Liam pulled from his right ear during lunch. The interplay between mother and son was both charming and exhausting.

He had only one burning question left unanswered. Opening her door, he asked, "Married?"

She swallowed before answering. "Widow."

The tension in Zeke's gut eased. He'd figure out who Pierce was later.

He held out her keys. "Are you going to be okay?"

"After a few ibuprofen, I'll be fine."

"And the... incident?"

"I'll deal with it."

Any other woman might have sobbed in his arms after getting bashed in the head. But not Special Agent Olivia Westcott. The only thing that streamed from her eyes was the promise of retribution, now that she knew her son was safe.

Had her assailant threatened the boy? It was the only thing that explained her single-minded flight to the school.

Brodie jumped down from the backseat, his eyes fixed on the action streaking across the tablet in his hands. Zeke squeezed his narrow shoulder. Something he'd done a thousand times with his brothers. "It was nice meeting you, Brodie."

The boy said nothing, absorbed in his death and dismemberment fest.

"Is that Fortnite?"

Brodie shot him a wary glance, though he nodded.

"Have you made it to Champion Division yet?"

The boy's eyebrows rose as he shook his head. "Have you?"

"Not yet, but I'm close."

"Thank Zeke for driving us home," Liv said.

"Thanks."

Liv nudged him toward the house. "Let's get you inside, sweetheart." She started to walk away, but paused and looked back at Zeke. "Thank you for driving. It was—" she grimaced as though a bug had flown into her mouth "—the right decision."

He suppressed a grin. "We have some unfinished business. Tomorrow?"

The bug must have latched onto her tongue, because her grimace deepened. "There's a restaurant, Plate It, on the corner of Baldwin and Granite. I'll meet you there at nine a.m."

Every step Liv took away from him made his gut contract tighter and tighter until he realized his lungs hadn't expanded for a while. He pushed out a breath and turned away.

Pull it together, Blackwell.

Fishing his phone out of his pocket, he tapped the ride share app, punched in his information, and moved to the foot of the driveway to wait.

It would be the longest ten minutes of his life.

13

LIV STOOD IN FRONT OF THE LARGE PICTURE WINDOW IN HER family room, watching Zeke pace back and forth at the end of her driveway. The familiar, delicious aroma of the slow-cooker's contents—tomatoes, oregano, basil, garlic, and parsley—filled the house and calmed her jangling nerves, even as guilt thrummed in her ears with each heartbeat.

If he hadn't shown up when he did, she would have made the disastrous choice to drive to Brodie's school. Twice on the way there, she'd experienced an overwhelming urge to close her eyes. The only thing that had kept her conscious was Zeke's incessant questions.

"Such a waste," her sister Callie said with a sigh. She stood beside Liv, watching Zeke prowl with a look of female appreciation.

"I'm not biting."

"You're cruel to keep him from me."

"Won't you be around guys all day today?"

Callie made a face. "The guys at the bookstore are all so . . . sooo—"

"Serious? Smart?"

"Young."

Liv thought about the men working at the bookshop. Besides the manager, who was in his mid-fifties, most of the men were in their early twenties. "When is college-aged old?"

"They're infants compared to that one." She nodded at Zeke.

"*That one* is trouble."

"Even better."

"Did you go to the women's center today?"

Callie gave her a knowing look, but nodded. "I wanted to check in on Debbie and see how the twins are doing. She had a doctor's appointment this morning."

Liv's blood boiled at the mere mention of the pregnant sixteen-year-old. For two years, the girl had been sexually abused by her stepbrother. No one, including her mom and stepdad, believed the good-looking, blond-haired, blue-eyed football star could be a predator.

Several weeks ago, she'd found the girl in Pritchard's Park, huddled against the low stone wall that partially surrounded the tiny urban greenway, during a craving-induced walk for biscuits and blueberry jam. After coaxing Debbie's story from her, Liv's thirty-minute lunch break turned into several hours while she helped the pregnant teen get settled in at A New Beginning Center for Women. Liv volunteered for the center whenever she had a spare moment and her sister had followed suit soon after moving in.

"Thank you for checking in on them," Liv said. "Did you happen to see Claudia Rogers?" Liv had first met Claudia about three months ago. She'd been covering the center's reception desk when the older woman's call had come in. It had taken some time, but she'd managed to talk Claudia into meeting her for lunch the next day.

Wary, she had refused to go to the center, but walked away with Liv's business card, promising she would call if things got worse. They had a couple weeks ago, and Liv had managed to talk her into sheltering at the center, but for only one night.

Yesterday, Claudia had shown up at the center, bruised and battered, because her husband didn't like the way she had ironed his work uniform.

"From a distance. I'm sorry, Liv, but I'm not sure she's going to stay. She paced the whole time I was there."

"I'm free tomorrow. I'll stop in and check on her."

A small body wedged between them. "Can Zeke stay for dinner?" Brodie asked, casting hopeful blue eyes her way.

Callie grinned.

So much for her attempt to redirect the conversation. Liv frowned at her son's empty hands. Glancing over her shoulder, she located his tablet, sliding off a throw pillow and flopping onto the sofa.

When she turned back, Callie met her gaze, one dark eyebrow raised in surprise. "You gotta say yes now."

"I'm sure Zeke has better things to do this evening."

"Lame."

"What's better than spaghetti and meatballs?" Brodie asked.

"With homemade sauce," Callie added with a sly smile.

"And garlic bread!"

Tension snapped along Liv's spine. "He's already called for a—"

"Please, Mama?" Brodie bounced on his feet.

"How can you deny this face?" Callie pushed her nephew's cheeks forward to make him look like a chipmunk.

Brodie blinked his eyelids rapidly, ripping a chuckle from Liv's throat.

She loved seeing the two of them so playful. Despite losing his dad at such a young age, Brodie was a happy kid, though one area of his life remained irrevocably changed. His refusal to play sports of any kind, especially baseball. Grief wrapped around her chest.

"Zeke and I—" She paused to pick her words carefully, digging her fingers into her left temple. Had she even thanked him properly? She couldn't remember. Her entire focus had been on getting to Brodie, then separating him from Zeke as quickly as possible. "Our association has had a rocky start. He will probably say no."

What if her icy behavior made him decide not to help them with the case? Mitch would freaking kill her. Or fire her. Neither option boded well for her career.

"Leave him to us," Callie said, grabbing Brodie's hand.

Liv set her jaw. "No, I'll go."

"But he might say no to you."

"Exactly." She moved toward the door. "If he stays, it'll be because he wants to, not because he can't say no to a siren and a cherub."

"Don't go out there with your cop face on," Callie warned, "Ask him as Liv. The woman who helps those in need and takes walks in the park to pet other people's dogs."

She sent her sister an annoyed look. "Yes, Mom."

Zeke stood staring down the street, his hands in his pockets. When she stopped beside him, he said, "I'm not loitering to annoy you. My ride will be here in a few minutes."

"My family," she sent a pointed look toward the house where two faces pressed against the picture window, "would like you to join us for dinner."

He followed her gaze, then returned to watching for his ride. "Are you here to encourage me to decline?"

"No."

"But you're not encouraging me to stay, either."

She scanned her surroundings. "No."

"I can't read you, Liv. Am I welcome or not?"

"Of course. My family has invited you to be their guest."

"But not yours."

She met his gaze straight on. "This has turned messy, Zeke. You being here muddies the line between my personal and professional life, which I try like hell to keep separated."

"What do you call two weeks ago?"

A ticker tape of images flashed through her mind—Zeke eating dinner alone, Zeke rising from a midnight swim, Zeke moving over her with firm, hard strokes.

"Two consenting adults passing time."

"You do remember me. I wasn't sure."

"I told you once, you're hard to forget."

"Why did you pretend otherwise at your office?"

"Mitch handed me the file on the meeting minutes before it started. I barely had time to absorb the situation before you were standing in front of me. I'm sorry, I just—"

"I get it."

Of course he did. He would've been as shocked to see her as she had been to see him.

A white sedan slowed to a stop in front of them. His rideshare had arrived.

"Tell your family thank you for the invitation, but I have other plans for dinner." He moved toward the sedan's back door just as a fast-moving silver BMW swung into her driveway.

A tall man in a gray Armani business suit pushed out of the beamer. "What's wrong?"

Liv frowned at her brother's tone and his unexpected appearance. "What are you doing here, Pierce?"

"You sounded upset on your voice mail message."

"Why didn't you just call me back?"

"I tried, but you didn't answer."

She flinched, forgetting she'd called him on their mad dash to the school. "Sorry, I had a small freak-out moment, but everything is fine."

Pierce eyed Zeke, who stood next to the sedan, his hand gripping the top of the door. "Who's this?"

"This is Zeke, a . . . work associate. Zeke, this is my brother Pierce."

The two men shook hands, neither smiled.

Finally, her brother turned back to her. "You never freak out. What happened?"

"It was nothing."

"She was attacked," Zeke said.

"Attacked?" Pierce echoed.

"Keep your voice down." She pointed toward the house. "They'll hear you."

"Are you hurt?"

She glared at Zeke, daring him to contradict her. "I'm fine."

"Looks like everything is under control here." Zeke climbed into the waiting car. "I'll see you tomorrow morning."

"I'll text you the address."

Nodding, he shut the door, and the vehicle drove away.

"Date?"

"I don't date people I work with. We're going to meet at Plate It to sort out a business issue."

Behind her, an angry hand *whopped* against the picture window.

Pierce smirked. "I take it Callie wanted him to stay."

"Ya think?" She blew out a tense breath. "Do you want to take Zeke's place at the dinner table?"

"Somehow, I think I'll fall short of my sister's expectations."

"We're having spaghetti and meatballs," she coaxed in a singsong voice.

"Homemade noodles?"

"And sauce."

"In that case, I'll brace myself for my little sister's disappointment."

Liv bumped her brother's shoulder with hers. "Come on. I'll let you grate the parmesan."

As they strode up the driveway, they both glanced toward the departing white sedan.

14

ZEKE FOLLOWED THE HOSTESS THROUGH THE FRONT DINING room of the upscale restaurant, Plate It. The farther back they traveled, the sparser the people and the dimmer the lighting. A perfect place to have a private conversation.

"Here's Liv," the hostess said, indicating a high-backed booth where the agent already occupied one side. "Your server, Hailey, will be with you in a moment. Will you need a menu?"

Liv dropped her phone into her handbag. "Not this time, Andrea. Thank you."

Zeke slid into the seat opposite Liv. "Nice place."

"Yes, it is."

"You must come here often, if you're on a first-name basis with the staff."

"What makes you think we didn't introduce ourselves?"

"Tone. Your voices held a friendliness that's absent in strangers."

A grudging smile appeared, but she didn't offer an explanation.

"How's your head?"

"Sore, but okay."

"No lasting headache or dizziness?"

"I have a very hard head. No need to worry about me."

"Did you send Brodie to school today?"

She nodded. "School is the most secure place for him while I'm at work. Mitch contacted the APD. The police chief agreed to have an officer drive by the school once or twice a day until school's out in a few weeks."

"Any ideas on your attacker's identity?"

"None. Based on the parking area's security tape, he'd been lying in wait for me for a while. He kept his face hidden from the surveillance cameras, but we could see enough to determine that he's Caucasian, close to six feet." She cleared her throat. "I failed to thank you for your intervention yesterday."

"All I did was yell at him."

"It was enough to spook him and get him off my back."

"Good timing. I came out of the public parking garage just as you turned down the sidewalk." He drummed his fingers on the table. "What did he say to make you believe your son was in danger?"

"Zeke, there's no reason for you to get involved in this any further."

"The hell there isn't. What did he say?"

"I can see why you were selected for the job. You don't give up."

"We all have our talents."

When he stared at her expectantly, she sighed. "He complained about me causing him a lot of trouble, then warned that he'd keep an eye on my son's school."

"Besides mine, who else's life have you screwed with lately?"

Her eyes flashed. "I didn't screw with your life."

"What do you call sneaking out of my hotel room before dawn?"

A flush shot up her throat and into her cheeks, though she didn't break eye contact. "Believe it or not, I don't have a great deal of experience with—" she paused, waiting for a server to walk by "—one-night stands."

He leaned forward on his elbows, clasping his hands together. "Do you have experience with common courtesy?"

She stared at him, a slight frown gathered between her eyes.

"Let me give you an example. 'Goodbye, Zeke.' Followed by a soft kiss on the lips."

For a brief, tantalizing moment, her gaze dipped to his mouth, and an answering warmth stirred between his legs. When her eyes lifted, he noted genuine remorse in their depths.

"I'm sorry, Zeke. I—I'm sorry."

The cold knot he'd been carrying in his stomach for days—*weeks*—disappeared. But not the want. Not the need. Those continued to claw deeper into his gut.

He sat back. "Who else might want to hurt you?"

She blinked, covering the quick flare of surprise in her eyes. "Every case I successfully close has a negative impact on someone."

"This has the feel of a fresh wound, one not yet scabbed over. What was your most recent case?"

"O'Fallon. I—" She flinched. "I shouldn't say anything. The case hasn't gone to trial yet."

"Give me the three-thousand-foot overview, so I know what we're up against."

"We're?"

"We are partners, of a sort." He cocked his head to the side. "Right?"

She sighed. "Don't make me regret this. Please."

"Spill it, Westcott."

"I uncovered a collection of priceless antiquities in the basement of a home in rural Marion. The former politician had been stealing pieces for decades, intending to sell them on the black market in order to provide his five kids with an inheritance."

"You got to be shittin' me."

"I'm not creative enough to make up a story like that."

"Did the kids know about his scheme?"

"I suspect so, though Ted O'Fallon denies it. The basement looked like a distribution warehouse, complete with computers and shipping materials. There's no way that was a one-man show."

"What about his wife?"

"Deceased."

"Worse-case scenario, the kids knew and were eagerly awaiting their inheritance. That's not one pissed-off person, that's six."

"Eleven, if the children's spouses were also in on the scheme." Her eyes took on a faraway look as if she were rewinding through a mental surveillance video, then she murmured, "He said, 'us.'" Her focus sharpened. "My attacker. He said, 'the trouble you caused *us.*'"

"Sounds like there are a lot of *us* in this O'Fallon case."

Deep in thought, she didn't respond.

"What did he smell like?"

"Who? O'Fallon?"

"Your attacker." He lifted the perspiring glass of water at his elbow and took a drink. "Everyone has a scent. Could be natural, could be sprayed on, or it could be absorbed from their environment like smoke or paint or manure. It might be a clue to his identity."

"Alcohol. He'd definitely been drinking."

"Anything else?"

"Oil or grease or maybe something metallic."

"That's good. It's more than we had five minutes ago and something you can keep in mind as you complete your background checks on O'Fallon's clan."

Amusement softened her eyes. "Perhaps you would be better suited for the FBI."

"Hell, no. I'll leave the bureaucratic bullshit to my big brother."

Her features slid back into neutral.

Way to destroy progress, Blackwell.

"Hi, Liv." A twenty-something brunette leaned down to air-kiss the agent's cheek. "Thanks again for helping my sister deal with her"—she stabbed a glance in Zeke's direction —"situation."

"It was my pleasure, Hailey. But any success belongs to Ivy—and her determination."

Tears glistened in the server's eyes before she cleared her throat. "Can I get you something to drink?"

Liv deferred to Zeke.

"Coffee. Black," he said.

"I'll have the cappuccino."

"A slice of banana nut bread?" Hailey asked Liv.

"I shouldn't."

"It just came out of the oven."

She looked at Zeke. "You allergic to nuts?"

"Just my brothers."

A smile flashed. "Bring us a nice, thick slice, please, Hailey."

"Will do. I'll be back in a sec."

Once the server left, Zeke said, "A weakness. Good to know."

"Enjoy the moment. It's the last one you'll learn."

He remembered her reaction when he'd licked the delicate hollow between her leg and mound. If he'd had more time with her, he was certain he could have found a few more places that would make her moan his name. "I doubt that."

She shifted in her seat as if recalling the same memory.

"What was this thing you helped Ivy out with?"

Her hands smoothed out the nonexistent wrinkles on the linen napkin draped over her lap. "Nothing much. A guy issue."

"Considering a guy bashed you in the back of the head, I'd say nothing related to guys is too small right now."

He could tell she didn't want to discuss the incident with him, but finally said, "Ivy is a social media influencer who makes a living off sponsorships for fashion, beauty products, and even luxury vehicles."

Sadie could spend hours watching videos of dancers and dogs and other dipshits trying to make their mark on a platform that was nothing but roiling pots of poor grammar, high drama, and unnecessary risk.

Jeez-Almighty, he sounded old.

"A guy started leaving comments on Ivy's posts. A lot do, so she thought little of it. Just hearted his comment, like she does everyone's, and moved on."

"Let me guess, the tone of his comments changed. Became more suggestive and salacious."

"Actually, no. What turned him into freakin' Frankenstein was when Ivy missed hearting his comment one day."

"He took it as a slight?"

She nodded. "He sent her an angry message, and Ivy apologized. For a few weeks, everything was calm. Until she did it again."

"As an influencer, she must receive hundreds, maybe thousands, of comments."

"She does. Acknowledging each of her fans was another level of engagement. Needless to say, I've discouraged her from further hearting."

"What did he do after the second perceived slight?"

"He sent her more messages filled with a weird mixture of hate and love. She blocked him, but somehow, he got her phone number and started leaving her voice mails with similar love-hate messages."

"How'd you get involved?"

"I happened to be at the restaurant when Hailey received a phone call from her sister. Ivy was hysterical, certain someone was stalking her."

"Did you see him?"

More napkin smoothing. "I not only saw him, I spoke to him."

Zeke bit down on the scolding comment before it left his lips. In a strained voice, he asked, "What happened?"

"When I arrived at Ivy's, I spotted an SUV matching the description she gave me, idling two doors down from her house. I knocked on his window and asked if he needed assistance. He told me to fuck off, so I pulled out my badge and asked again."

"What kind of bullshit story did he give you?"

"He apologized and explained that he didn't want attention drawn to him."

"No shit."

"He told me his girlfriend lived down the road and he was keeping an eye on things because she thought someone was stalking her."

"The guy is either certified or was ballsing his way out of trouble."

"Probably a little of both." Her rubbing switched to her temple as if warding off a headache. "I referred to him by his social media handle, which, in hindsight, might not have been my most strategic move." She gave him a small self-deprecating smile. "I told him I was seeking an Order of Protection against him on Ivy's behalf and, if he ever called, texted, or came near her again, I would—"

She broke off, and frost coated his heart. "You would, what?"

She grimaced. "I would make sure he never posted, commented, or hearted again."

"Did he go apeshit?"

"Oddly no. The mutinous expression on his face cleared and, before he drove away, he nodded as if I had given him directions to the nearest gas station."

"She hasn't heard from him since?"

"Not as far as I know."

"Suspects are piling up."

"Welcome to Complications 'R' Us."

"I have stock in that store."

They shared a smile, and he considered asking her about Intense Dude while they were on the subject of strange guy incidents, but couldn't bring himself to shatter the moment.

"I wish you would've stayed." The words he'd been harboring for over two weeks tumbled out of his mouth like boulders down the face of a mountain. Their thunderous clatter rocked to a halt, leaving an unbearable silence in the wake.

Her smile faded, replaced by a familiar neutral expression. "Do you have an answer regarding the Bureau's offer?"

15

ALL WISHFUL THOUGHTS OF WAKING UP, WRAPPED AROUND Liv's beautiful body, and coaxing her into spending the day making love with him blinked out as Zeke recalled the reason why he had hightailed it to Asheville. To Liv.

"I wasn't aware the Bureau's offer came with a caveat."

"What do you mean?"

"If I don't agree to the recovery, Ash pays the price."

She broke eye contact.

"You knew." All the way here, he'd hoped that when this moment came that he'd see confusion on her beautiful face. Not guilt. Something sharp pricked the back of his throat. He swallowed.

Could he get into bed with an agency who would treat their own in such a way? What would keep them from reneging on their promise to protect his family from any legal fallout? He tilted his head back and stared at the ceiling as if the answer to The Great Question could be found in the track lighting.

Hailey returned with their order, then bustled off again.

"I only found out this morning," Liv said quietly. When

he lowered his gaze to hers, she continued, "You don't have to give in to their bullying tactics. Despite what Mitch said in the meeting, I'm more than capable of retrieving the art piece."

The thought of her taking on the recovery alone sent a slice of fear through his middle. "What else can you tell me about the case?"

"I can't get into—"

He held up a hand, not wanting to hear the company line. "At least tell me what I'm getting my team into. What am I recovering?"

"The situation is highly sensitive. We can't take the chance of revealing details to someone outside the Bureau."

"Other people trust me with the secrets all the time."

She sipped her cappuccino. "I'm well aware."

He raised a brow. "From Ash?"

"No. I dug deeper into your background after our meeting."

"We've come full circle again. I need information, and you won't give it."

"Your answer is no, then?"

"Depends."

"On what?"

He broke off a piece of the banana nut bread. "On how my answer affects my brother's career."

The furrow in her brow deepened with something like indecision a moment before her features hardened into a you're-a-big-boy-figure-it-out stare.

He weighed his options. If he walked away, could someone at the Bureau be asshole enough to fire Ash in retribution? It happened in the private sector all the time, but government? He knew little about his brother's job and nothing about his relationship with his colleagues. Discounting the possibility would be a mistake.

If Ash returned home to lead the family business, Zeke wouldn't have to pretend like he knew what the hell he was doing anymore. But Ash would hate it. He'd already spent eight miserable years at the helm.

Even so, Zeke heard himself pushing back. "You're bluffing."

"Agents, especially undercover agents, are master manipulators. They're used to blending in with some of the worst, most evil elements of humankind while keeping one finger gripped on reality." She paused, as if chewing on something rotten. "Finding someone's vulnerability and putting out a few comments to rip it open and make it bleed is an afterthought. The true test on their grip is—will they let the person bleed out or sew him up?"

In other words, a carefully placed word in the right ear could not only affect Ash's future opportunities at the FBI, but kill his career entirely.

He lifted his coffee cup to his lips. "I'll do it."

To his surprise, she didn't smile her triumph. She simply nodded and popped a piece of bread in her mouth.

"On two conditions. Scratch that—three conditions."

She stiffened. "More conditions?"

"I put the job to a vote. If I get a unanimous 'yes' from my brothers, we're in."

"If you don't?"

"We're out."

"Number two?"

"I know what you know about this recovery. I won't send my team in blind."

"You'll keep me informed on anything you discover?"

"Yes."

"Three?"

"The Bureau brings Ash back from his *vacation* immediately."

"I'll see to it."

"We agree on all three counts?"

She nodded.

"Should we kiss on it?"

Her eyes narrowed. "I have a condition of my own?"

"Why am I not surprised? Let's hear it."

"There will be no repeat of what happened in Charlotte."

"Ever?"

She hesitated a moment, toying with the edge of her napkin. "I can't afford any distractions while we're working this case."

"Agreed." If any of his brothers had been sitting at the table, they could have warned her that his easy capitulation did not bode well. "Two agreements in five minutes. Surely that calls for a seal of a kiss."

She shook her head and smiled, one reminiscent of their rooftop banter, appeared. A quiet moment followed, the only sound the distant clink of silverware.

Clearing her throat, she said, "We would both do well to forget that night."

"Not possible." A cold hand gripped his chest as a thought occurred to him. "Was our hookup part of this op?"

"No," she said in a sharp tone. Her attention drifted to the small wall sconce illuminating their booth. "That was. . . "

"A mistake?"

"Not at the time."

"Then what?"

She shook her head. "It doesn't matter. Not now. We

both got what we needed." She dug into her wallet and tossed a ten onto the table. "Don't worry about the check. Everything's comped."

Comped? Zeke shook his head. A mystery for another day.

Instead of leaving like he expected, she studied him for a long moment, then muttered, *"Fuck it,"* beneath her breath. "What I'm about to tell you can't go beyond this booth."

"Understood."

"The CI knows the time and location of a major drug shipment. If we don't intercept the shipment, a high volume of fentanyl, heroin, and methamphetamines will hit, not just city streets, but small towns across Western North Carolina, including ones like your hometown. You know what that means, right?"

People he knew would die. People Ash knew. Adults, kids, anyone stupid, or naïve, enough to put that shit in their systems.

Zeke understood then. Understood why Ash would intermingle his family's business with his career, something he'd gone so far as to change his name to avoid. Understood why he now toed the line between right and wrong, legal and illegal.

To protect his community and the people he loved.

"Thank you."

Nodding, she gathered her things and stood. "Time's ticking, Zeke."

"I'll speak to the guys tonight." When she turned to leave, he said, "Fair warning, Liv."

She looked back.

"I don't like unfinished business."

Confusion crinkled at the corner of her eyes.

"You and me."

She strode away, then stopped abruptly, and marched back. Leaning forward, she whispered near his ear, "You finished your business just fine, Zeke." She plucked the last of the banana nut bread from the plate and left without another word.

He watched her weave her way between the tables before she disappeared from sight.

Zeke smiled.

Game on.

16

After leaving Zeke at her parents' restaurant, Liv had gone straight to A New Beginning Center for Women to check in on Claudia Rogers.

The battered wife had been on her mind ever since her conversation with Callie yesterday. Like most women who showed up at the center, Claudia feared her husband would find her and, with equal fervor, feared leaving her home.

Liv hadn't missed the old scar on the woman's right cheek or the permanent hook to her left pinkie, likely from a break that had never been properly set.

Rather than make her customary circuit around the common room to say hello to those present, Liv made a beeline for the woman rolling her small travel-size suitcase her way.

"Claudia, where are you going?"

The older woman glanced around the safe house, taking in the gray vinyl flooring, gold-plated light fixtures, clean but well-worn furnishings, and its occupants—women of every race, color, age, and socioeconomic background. "I don't belong here."

"Please," Liv motioned toward a small table with two chairs near a window, "sit with me for a moment."

Claudia stared at her, one bloodshot eye at half-mast, swollen and severely bruised. Her split lip trembled and her fingers tightened around the telescopic handle of her suitcase.

"Please," Liv urged, wrapping an arm around the woman's stooped shoulders and urging her toward one of the chairs.

Claudia didn't resist, and a few seconds later Liv sat across from her, holding the battered woman's cold hands in hers.

"I know it feels unfamiliar, but this is a safe place. He won't find you here."

"I'm not unsafe at home."

Liv studied the woman's injuries, which included a scraped jaw and bruised neck. "He hurt you, Claudia. And this wasn't the first time."

"Sam's been under a lot of pressure at work. He's short-staffed and there's a backlog of repair work. Once he's caught up, everything will go back to normal."

"Until things get busy again?" Liv lowered her voice. "Until his work shirt hasn't been pressed to his specifications again? Or his dinner isn't ready at whatever time he decides to come home? Or he finds an empty soda can on the coffee table?"

Claudia's shoulders rounded even more and tears filled the narrow space of her swollen eye.

"Stay, Claudia. Stay the full five days you're allotted while I continue to work on finding you longer-term housing."

"My cousin lives in Raleigh. I might could stay with her for a few days."

As if on cue, Claudia's phone vibrated. She picked it up and peered at the screen. The gathering tears tipped over the rim and slid down her flushed cheek. "He must be sick with worry. I've never been away from home before."

More like he's lost without his live-in maid these past two days.

Liv kept her opinion to herself as she watched Claudia turn away to answer her phone. Across the common room, Liv met the Center's director's questioning gaze and shook her head.

The moment Claudia answered her husband's call, Liv knew she had failed. The bastard would talk his wife into returning home, and there wasn't a damn thing she could do to stop her.

Claudia hung up and faced Liv, though she continued to stare at her phone. "He apologized and swore he would never lay a finger on me again."

"He will, Claudia," Liv said, unable to let the woman leave without trying one more time. "You know he will."

The battered woman grabbed the handle of her overnight bag and rose. "You didn't hear him, Olivia. He sounded so m-miserable." Her voice broke. "He was crying."

"There's no life for you there. Only his wants, his needs." Liv's heart pounded with her desire to make Claudia see reason. "His anger will explode again when you fall short of his expectations."

"I've made up my mind," Claudia snapped, wrenching her hand from Liv's.

"My apologies. I didn't mean to upset you. I want only the best for you."

A pained expression replaced Claudia's anger. "I'm sorry." She squeezed Liv's forearm. "I know my husband. He's not an evil man. He loves me." She smiled. Or tried to.

It was a broken effort. "Thank you for your kindness, but it was a mistake to come here."

Liv rose and hugged her, then pressed her business card in the other woman's hand. "Promise me you'll call if—if anything changes."

Claudia's gaze slid away. "I will."

The fifty-three-year-old woman left the safe house and got into her white pearl sedan. Liv waited until Claudia turned down the next block before rushing to her vehicle and following. She didn't think twice about tailing the other woman. Although she had the Rogers's home address, Liv wanted to witness the couple's reunion.

Maybe then she would believe Sam's apology.

Maybe.

Twenty minutes later, Claudia drove into a middle-class neighborhood and slowed when she approached a navy-blue ranch with stacked stone trim. She pulled into the driveway and parked behind a black pickup with an *SAR Performance* logo on the passenger side door.

Liv's vehicle crept forward for a few more feet before stopping next to the curb.

The moment Claudia exited her car, a salt-and-pepper–haired man rushed out of the house, a severe expression on his face. Claudia froze near the trunk of her car, and Liv's fingers tensed on the steering wheel.

Another man with dark-blond hair emerged from the house. This one was in his late twenties, early thirties. He had the same stocky build as the older guy. Must be Claudia's son, Alan.

Sam wrapped his arms around Claudia and buried his face in the crook of her neck. She stood still for several seconds before she hugged her husband back with equal ferocity.

The younger man held back, watching the couple until finally Sam and Claudia, arm-in-arm, disappeared into the house. Liv waited for the relief to hit her.

It didn't.

A sick, coiling dread continued to slither inside her stomach.

Alan shoved his hands into the pockets of his dark blue uniform pants and trailed after his parents.

17

————

LATER THAT NIGHT, AFTER ANOTHER SUCCESSFUL RECOVERY, Zeke and his brothers poured into the Annex and headed downstairs. As usual, they didn't stop to kick up their heels on the plush leather sofas or go to war with each other at the foosball table.

Weapons first.

Always.

It was a cardinal rule their dad had established years ago, and one they continued to this day.

Take care of your weapons, boys, and they'll take care of you.

Once he hit the lower level, Zeke hung a left toward the Vault and strode to the electronic panel on the far wall. A dark screen lit up at his approach, and he laid his palm on the smooth surface. A blue light scanned his hand, and a red light above his middle finger blinked to green.

The wall rolled back in a *whoosh,* revealing rows of various handguns, long guns, and knives. Metal cabinets below the arsenal display contained ammo and technolog-ical devices that only Rohan seemed to know how to operate. On the opposite wall was an assortment of wigs, beards, costumes, and special effects makeup.

He wondered what Liv would make of the Vault. Did the FBI have anything like it? Would she be impressed? Or horrified?

Time's ticking, Zeke.

Her reminder from breakfast had him snapping open his chest holder with a little more force than necessary. He removed his nine-millimeter and, after clearing the bullet from the chamber, he placed his weapon in its designated spot, then he unfastened the knife and sheath secured to his thigh and stowed them away, too.

In the three years they'd been doing this work, he'd never drawn his gun and hoped he never would.

Moving deeper into the Vault, Zeke paused in front of a six-foot-by-three-foot door. He pulled a key fob from around his neck and clicked it into the top insertion point. Cruz shouldered past him to insert his fob in the lower hole. After he tapped in an eight-digit code, metal clanked against metal and Cruz dragged the heavy door open.

A light flickered on inside the steel-reinforced concrete safe, illuminating rows of empty, black-velvet-lined shelves. Zeke unzipped his backpack and retrieved the bejeweled sphere they'd recovered from the Warner mansion and settled it on its plush, temporary home. Backing out of the safe, he and Cruz reversed their actions and secured the sphere within.

Ten minutes later, they all lounged in their usual spots, except for Rohan, who busied himself behind the bar, making everyone's drinks.

"Family first." Zeke said the words as he did at the conclusion of every mission. A moment of complete solidarity with his brothers.

"Through blood," Phin said, continuing the tradition.

"Through hate," Rohan said.

"Through fear," Cruz said.

"No exceptions," they all said in unison.

Whiskey glasses chinked together, and everyone downed their shots. They had started the tradition after the first recovery, when his team walked in as he tipped back a thank-God-we-didn't-get-caught shot.

He'd been so bound up with nerves that he'd turned to alcohol to take the edge off. Running, archery, and, Lord help him, Grams's meditation had done nothing to stop his insides from twisting in on themselves.

The moment Rohan saw him, he stepped behind the bar and poured them all a shot. With his calm, steady gaze on Zeke, Rohan made their first toast and, one by one, his brothers chimed in, making up the chant as they went along.

In that moment, he knew that, with their help, he could build BARS into something amazing, something that would change their lives.

He hadn't been wrong.

BARS had changed everything. At times, like this thing with the FBI, he wasn't sure it was all for the better. Tomorrow, he would introduce Liv to the team and finally get the full details of the recovery.

Which meant he had to convince his brothers to take on the job.

Tonight.

His attention strayed to Phin. His youngest brother would take the news the worst. More and more of late, he'd voiced his displeasure about their cash-only side of the business. The side some folks might perceive as illegal.

Stolen property was stolen property. In Phin's way of

thinking, that fact didn't change just because law enforcement didn't have a perfectly laid yellow brick road leading up to the thief's house.

Unfortunately, his little brother's moral compass pointed due north, whereas the rest of the Blackwell clan sat somewhere southwest. The irony of Phin's bruised morals was that the money they made off the books was the money that paid for his thousand-dollar suits and designer watches. But his little brother's struggle was real. Zeke might not fully understand Phin's inner workings, but he respected him and tried to keep him out of that part of the business as much as possible.

Cruz, leaning his butt against the foosball table, studied him. "You look like someone whose rubber ducky drowned."

He ignored his smart-mouthed brother and belted back the last of his whiskey. "There's something I need to tell you all."

"Oh, shit," Phin said, striding to the bar for another drink. "You're going to piss on my high, aren't you?"

Rohan raised a brow.

Cruz crossed one ankle over the other. "Don't keep us in suspense, brother."

He wished Grams were here. She would be a welcome voice of reason—either for or against taking the job. But she had gone to bed early in order to get enough sleep in before Lynette drove her to an early appointment in Asheville tomorrow morning.

"I've lined up another recovery."

Phin's jaw hardened. "What sort of recovery?"

"One that if successful might solidify a lucrative, ongoing partnership for BARS."

"With whom?" Rohan asked.

Heat flushed up the back of his neck as he looked at each of them. Cruz and Rohan's expressions held only curiosity, but Phin's grew more mutinous by the second.

It was an expression he knew well. Ash had worn the same one in the months leading up to his defection. Would his announcement cost him—the company—another brother? He was about to find out.

"The Federal Bureau of Investigation."

Phin's face cleared. "Dammit, Zeke. Don't pull that shit again. I thought from your tone that this was going to be another one of your shadow ops."

"What are we recovering?" Rohan asked.

"An antiquity."

"Doesn't the FBI have an Art Crime Team?"

Damn Rohan and his bottomless hat of useless information. "Right, as always."

Phin's head nearly snapped off. "What's going on, Zeke? Why do they need us?"

He met his little brother's gaze. "Because we can do something they can't."

"Which is?"

He let the silence set between them, let it stretch while Phin's brilliant mind worked it out.

Phin's confusion cleared and was replaced by a look of disappointment.

Regret clutched Zeke's chest for a long moment before he hardened his heart. Phin might not agree with the black ops side of their business, but that didn't make it wrong.

Justice didn't always favor law-abiding citizens. BARS retrieved stolen property and gave it back to the rightful owner. Sometimes—most of the time—the retrieval required methods not wholly supported by local, state, or federal laws.

Not wanting to hold anything back, he said, "There's a level of danger to this one that we haven't come up against before."

"What are we stealing back?" Phin asked.

"I don't know."

Phin's eyes flared wide.

"Who's the target?" Cruz asked.

"I don't know."

This time, he caught disbelieving glares from all three of his brothers.

"What do you know?" Rohan asked.

"Not much. They won't divulge the full details until they get our commitment."

"Wait," Phin said, "You haven't agreed to do the job yet?"

"Not until I have everyone's buy-in." He let that sink in a moment. "One thing I know for sure is that this recovery won't succeed without the entire team."

"Why is the FBI so keen on recovering this item that they would engage an outside company?" Rohan asked.

He hesitated. Not because he worried his brothers wouldn't protect the intelligence, but sharing the details that would get their agreement would betray Liv's trust.

"If you want our buy-in," Cruz said, "you're gonna need to share what you have. No matter how little."

His responsibility was to this team, to his family. Not the FBI. Or agent Westcott.

"The FBI is involved in a high-profile drug case. Their confidential informant has logistical details for a large shipment coming into North Carolina. In exchange for the information, the CI wants the undercover agent to retrieve an antique that was allegedly stolen from him—or her. That's where we come in."

"I don't like it," Phin said. "Their informant could be

putting the screws to a competitor, for all we know. We steal the item and get caught in the middle of a gang war."

"He's got a valid point," Cruz said.

"If the FBI can't stop the shipment, the drugs will pour into our small towns. And we're not talking pot. It's nasty shit."

"Does Ash know about this?" Rohan asked.

He nodded. "In addition to offering twenty percent over our normal fee, they brought him in as incentive."

"Incentive how?"

"I was left with the impression that if we turned the job down, Ash would suffer professional consequences."

"Sonofabitch," Phin snarled.

"What's Ash's take on this?" Rohan asked.

"Ash is Ash. He won't pressure us one way or another, but the FBI is his life. If they dick with his career, he'll—"

"What?" Phin said. "Resent us? Blame us?"

He shrugged. "We're in an impossible situation."

"The way I see it," Rohan said, "there's only one way forward."

"Which is?" Phin asked.

"We steal the item, take the FBI's generous payment for our services, and watch our backs."

"Everything about that is wrong. You know that, right?"

"I disagree. We get paid, Ash keeps his job, and the drugs stay off the streets. Triple win."

Phin looked at Cruz. "Would you talk some common sense into our brother's too logical techno-geek mind?"

Cruz studied Rohan as if he were working through a complex puzzle.

"Not you, too." Phin said in disgust.

"The only real negative is that we don't know who or what our targets will be," Cruz said. "Once we agree to do the job, the FBI will disclose more details. Once we have those, we'll know what we're up against and can take all necessary precautions."

"So that's it," Phin said. "We're doing this."

"Only if you're on board, too," Zeke said. "It's all or nothing."

"If I say no, you'll decline the FBI's offer, and they'll do God-knows-what to Ash's career."

"That about sums it up."

"Ash will blame me and not the fuckers who screwed him over."

"Technically, you could say we all screwed him," Rohan said.

"But you're right," Cruz put in. "Ash would blame us —you."

Phin pointed to the group at large. "If this thing goes south, it's your fucking fault, not mine." He ran his fingers through his perfectly styled hair. "We're going to wind up on America's Most Wanted. Mark my damn words."

Zeke shook his head. "One of the conditions I demanded before agreeing to the job was that if things go to hell the team has immunity." Everyone on the team except him, but he'd keep that detail to himself.

"Somehow that doesn't make me feel any better," Phin muttered.

"It's settled then," Zeke said. "I'll invite our liaison to the Friary, so we can work out the details."

Three pairs of eyes stared at him in surprise.

He'd surprised himself.

"You want to bring the FBI onto our property?" Cruz asked.

They had purchased the property to protect their activities from prying eyes. No one but family and trusted caretakers of the estate was allowed beyond the entrance gate. Even deliveries were left at the gate.

None of this had crossed his mind when he'd decided to allow Liv inside the secure zone. He trusted her, he realized. An oddity in and of itself, given their short acquaintance. Doubly odd given the fact that she worked for the government.

"I'd rather have her on our turf than us be on theirs."

"Her?" Phin asked, his eyes lighting up.

"Back off, Romeo," Zeke warned. "This is business."

Phin smiled. "It's always business."

"Liv's off-limits. Understood?"

Phin's humor faded, and he studied Zeke with a keenness his brother normally reserved for targets. "Yes, I think I do, brother."

"Cheers," Rohan said, holding up his glass.

Everyone air-clinked their glasses.

"Now that we have that out of the way," Cruz said, "let's review our performance on the Warner recovery."

Zeke sat back, allowing the conversation to flow over him. The tension in his muscles loosened now that he had the team's agreement. He didn't feel triumph, nor excitement. Just a low buzz of anticipation.

Problem was, he couldn't decide if he was looking forward to the challenge of the job or seeing Special Agent Wescott again.

An image of Liv rising from the Jacuzzi, water sluicing off her gorgeous body, flashed through his mind. Something stirred low in his gut.

His phone dinged with an incoming text. Unlocking the screen, he read the message. It was from Sardoff.

I have the location of the sword.

18

LIV'S VEHICLE ROLLED TO A STOP OUTSIDE THE MASSIVE STEEL gate demarcating the entrance to the mysterious Blackwell compound. Several warning signs covered the barrier— *Private Property—No Trespassing—DO NOT ENTER—Guard Dog on Duty*—giving it a creepy survivalist camp vibe.

Rolling down her window, she took a moment to inhale the fresh morning air before pushing the intercom button.

"State your business," an authoritarian female voice said through the speaker.

"Olivia Westcott to see Zeke Blackwell."

"Hold your I.D. up to the camera."

She did as instructed.

"Leave your electronic devices in the lockbox below the intercom."

She looked down at the three-by-five metal box with a key sticking out of the lock. It reminded her of the mailbox system at her old apartment building.

"I'm sorry, but I can't leave my phone." How would the school get ahold of her if something happened to her son?

"Give the number printed on the box to your office. That number is monitored 24/7."

Liv gritted her teeth. If she didn't do as required, she would no doubt be denied access. Zeke had made it clear in his text that he had no intention of returning to the Asheville office.

She texted the number to her emergency group, which included an assistant at her office, Callie, and Pierce. If Brodie's school couldn't get a hold of Liv, they would work their way down the list.

After she sent the message, she opened the metal box and placed her phone inside.

"Your watch too," said the disembodied voice.

Liv gave the camera a blistering stink eye before unfastening her Apple Watch. She placed the device in with her phone.

"Remove the nondisclosure agreement, sign, and bring it with you."

"You're kidding, right?"

"Do I sound like I'm kidding?"

Liv wrenched the one-page agreement out of the box and read it to make sure she wasn't agreeing to anything that would impair her case. After scribbling her signature at the bottom, she tossed it on the passenger seat before retrieving the lockbox key.

"Follow the signs to the Annex." The gate swung open, and Liv accelerated through, dropping the key in her cupholder.

Large stands of oak, maple, and pine trees lined the winding asphalt road. A blue jay screeched a warning from deep in the woods and an enormous redheaded woodpecker soared from one side of the road to the other.

It was hard to believe all of this natural beauty harbored a family of thieves.

The closer she got to the Annex, the harder her pulse pounded. She would see Zeke in a matter of minutes. Her nerves had been on edge since receiving his text the night before, confirming his brothers were on board and issuing her an invitation.

"No kissing, no touching, no burning take-me looks," she warned herself for the thousandth time. "This is business. Treat him like any other collaborator."

The chant usually worked for about five minutes. After that, images of their night together would creep in, making her hot and achy all over again.

A small parking area appeared and, beyond it, a modern Morton-style office building. The black metal roof and window trim complemented the blue-gray siding. Stone accented the lower third of the building and covered the vestibule. Twin black steel columns dipped in stone at their base flanked the glass entryway. But her favorite feature was the adorable weathervane rising from the highest point on the roof.

Liv pulled into the nearest parking spot. She took a moment to stretch her muscles and don her suit jacket before grabbing her handbag that doubled as a briefcase.

By the time she turned toward the building, a tall woman in her late fifties, early sixties awaited her. Silver streaked her wavy brown, shoulder-length hair and her blue eyes felt like lasers burning straight into Liv's soul. Something about her seemed familiar, as if they had met before, but Liv was certain their paths had never crossed.

The woman stopped a few feet away and stuck out her hand. "I'm Lynette Blackwell."

Zeke's mom. No wonder she seemed familiar.

Liv accepted her proffered hand. "Olivia Westcott."

The older woman's rigid posture, neutral expression, and bone-crushing handshake suggested a military background. Or she'd already taken an intense dislike to Liv.

"Lift your arms, please," Lynette said.

"For what purpose?"

"I need to check your person for any listening devices."

"I'm here to collaborate, not to spy."

Lynette stared at her.

"I'm carrying."

"So am I." The woman's left foot tipped out and she lifted her wide leg pants high enough to reveal a Sig Sauer nine-millimeter cradled in an ankle holster.

Tamping down her annoyance, Liv reminded herself that she was a guest. She set her bag down and lifted her arms, surprised by the woman's efficient technique, despite herself.

Lynette straightened. "My apologies for the measures it took to get you to this point, but privacy is one of the few things we insist upon. Do you have the signed NDA?"

Lowering her arms, Liv leaned into her diplomatic side. "I understand, Mrs. Blackwell." She dug the form out of her bag. "The Bureau is equally keen on privacy."

"Keen on threatening careers, too."

"I had nothing to do with threatening Cameron's job."

"I'm going to be straight with you, Special Agent West-cott, because that's how I roll. If I catch a whiff of dishonesty or the FBI placing my boys in avoidable danger, I'll bring the full force of Blackwell power down on you and yours." Lynette's voice never rose. "Understood?"

Definitely military. "Got it. You have some signed confidentiality agreements for me?"

The older woman pulled several folded papers from her back pocket. "The entire team signed one."

She took the forms and dropped them in her bag at the same time the front door opened and Zeke appeared. Her heart skipped a beat, but Lynette's warning cast a shadow over the nervous excitement of seeing him again.

Zeke's dark eyes took in the scene and asked, "Everything all right?"

Lynette's features softened when she faced her son. "Everything's fine. Just wanted an opportunity to introduce myself to our guest before you boys monopolize her time."

He kept his eyes on Liv, scanning her body as if checking for injuries.

"I'll be in my office if you need me," Lynette said.

"You're not joining us?"

"I'll get the CliffsNotes version from Johona afterward. I have a lot of follow-up paperwork to do for last night's recovery."

Zeke's eyes narrowed. "What do you have in your hand, Mom?"

A muscle near the corner of the older woman's mouth twitched. Liv thought it might have been a smile.

"A nondisclosure agreement."

"A non—when did we institute that process?"

"Today." Lynette turned and reentered the Annex.

Shaking his head, Zeke sent Liv an apologetic smile. "Sorry, she's miffed about Ash."

"I gathered."

"Did she threaten you with dismemberment if you betrayed our trust?"

"I don't recall her mentioning anything about removing my body parts."

He stepped closer, into her personal space. The scent of

his soap—shea butter and citrus—filled her nose, triggering an image of him moving over her, slowly, purposefully.

"Any more trouble?" he asked.

"What?"

"Any more run-ins with angry dudes?"

No kissing, no touching, no burning take-me looks.

She took a step back. "No."

"Would you tell me if you had?"

"Probably not."

"At least you're honest about it." His hand slipped around hers. "Come on. I'll introduce you to the rest of the team."

She didn't move. "Team? I came here to brief you, not a group."

"Like I told Lawson, I'm one spoke in the wheel."

"I didn't come prepared to speak to a group."

"Why do you think I invited you here?"

"To avoid my office."

"True. But you're here to meet the team and to fill in the crater of information we don't know." He tugged on her hand. "Whatever you came prepared to say to me, just say it to four more people. They're not a fastidious lot. Well, most of them aren't. Rohan can be a bit of a stick sometimes."

Liv pulled in a calming breath. Although she was used to dealing with the unexpected, she hated being unprepared for meetings, especially when she was the one in the spotlight.

Zeke returned to her side and lifted her bag. "What the hell is in this thing?"

She snatched her bag away, hefted it on her shoulder, and marched toward the building.

"Putting that much weight on your shoulder isn't good for you."

"Thanks for the tip, Dr. Blackwell. Do you do adjustments, too?"

"I know a woman who used to carry a heavy backpack on one shoulder all the time. Screwed up her shoulder, and now she's in constant pain."

"I'll take your cautionary tale under advisement." She could almost hear his smile creaking into place.

"I don't think your brother liked me too much."

"Don't take it personally. Pierce eyeballs any guy I talk to. Typical protective older brother."

"Do you talk to a lot of guys in your driveway?"

"None of your business." She made to open the door, but he edged past her and put a hand on the door handle, blocking her entrance.

With his body angled in front of her, she had nowhere to look but at his broad chest. Her fingers itched to burrow beneath his shirt and tease his nipple to life. The taste of him, the feel of him against her tongue—

Stop it, Liv!

She would have to add *no sucking* to her mantra.

When she forced her gaze away from so much male temptation, she was ensnared by a pair of rich, brown, all-too-knowing eyes.

"What would you say if I told you I didn't like the idea of you talking to other guys?"

If any other man had said those words to her, she would have ceased any further communication with him. Guys who got that possessive after such a brief acquaintance would be nothing but trouble, notwithstanding the creep factor.

But hearing Zeke's low baritone rumble out the question sent a silent, heart-fluttering thrill through her.

"I would say go get a puppy. You're obviously in need of affection."

"Admit it, Westcott. You want me."

A flush bloomed at the base of her neck. "Are you trying to knock me off balance before meeting your team? Is this some sort of payback for Cameron?"

"Zeke, are you coming in"—a voice blared out from a speaker two feet away—"or are you going to stand out there all day, making calf-eyes at the agent?"

Zeke's sensual smile disappeared. He lifted his hand to the camera and flipped the onlooker the bird.

"We'll resume this conversation later." Before she could protest, he put a hand on the small of her back and nudged her inside.

19

ONCE LIV ENTERED THE VESTIBULE, A MAN IN HIS MID-
twenties opened the interior door, a broad smile on his
handsome face. He wore a pressed—yes, pressed—T-shirt
with Rag and Bone designer jeans and a silver TAG Heuer
wrapped around his left wrist.

A Times Square billboard in the flesh.

"Special Agent Olivia Westcott, this is my brother, Phin.
He's our intelligence gatherer and fabricator."

The younger Blackwell held out a hand. "Nice to meet
you, Special Agent Westcott."

She shook his hand and was surprised to feel calluses on
his palm. "Olivia, please."

Phin's voice dropped an octave. "Olivia."

A firm hand propelled her forward, forcing her away
from Phin and past the large concave natural stone wall
separating the reception area from the rest of the office.
Black metal lettering affixed to the stone read Blackwell
Asset Recovery Services.

Beyond the wall, two rows of spacious offices encircled
an open sitting area with plush chairs and sofas, table,

whiteboard, and a TV screen any Super Bowl party would envy.

"This is the Theater," Zeke said. "Where we plan and brainstorm."

Admiration and jealousy streaked through Liv. The Blackwells' conference room made the one in her office look like a looted tomb.

A short woman with broad hips, silver-gray hair secured at the base of her neck, and kind brown eyes approached her. A beautiful three-strand necklace of red coral beads hung around her neck, a nice complement to her blue blouse, knee-length capris, and colorful Bombas socks inside Birkenstock sandals.

Without uttering a word, the woman held out her hand, palm up. Liv set her palm over the older woman's and, before she knew it, she stood slightly bowed with their hands steepled on top of each other. Strong, slightly curved fingernails carried a thin ribbon of dirt beneath them, indicating the woman liked to spend time in the garden. A gorgeous oval turquoise and silver ring that appeared as vintage as its wearer took up half the space on her middle finger.

Warmth spread from Liv's fingers all the way up her arm and into her chest, stripping away her tension.

"Olivia," Zeke said, "This is Johona Blackwell, my grandmother. Lover of colorful socks and voice of reason."

"It's a pleasure to meet you, Mrs. Blackwell. I understand you served in the Korean War as a nurse."

"It was an honor to serve my country." Johona studied Liv for a long moment. The room grew so still that Liv could hear a clock *tick-tock* in the distance. Then the older woman smiled, and it seemed the entire room exhaled in a single breath.

Releasing Liv's hands, Johona said, "Come meet the rest of my boys." She shuffled close to a dark-haired man, who rose from the sofa to wrap a muscular arm around the woman who barely reached his chest. "This is Cruz."

A strange silence fell over the room as the man turned to Liv. He greeted her with an amiable expression and the most stunning gray-blue eyes she'd ever seen.

She shook his extended hand. "Olivia Westcott."

"AKA mechanic," Cruz said, "or if you prefer the more formal title, Gear Head."

"He's also our pilot," Zeke added, an unusual strain in his voice.

"And slayer of girlfriends," Phin muttered.

Johona shifted to a bespectacled man in a chair on her left and gently pried a tablet from his grip.

He blinked up at his grandmother in confusion, and she smoothed a hand over his wavy, somewhat disheveled hair. "This is Rohan."

"In case it's not obvious," Zeke said, "Technology and surveillance."

"And keeper of weird information," Phin said, claiming a spot opposite his techy brother.

Liv stretched out her hand to Rohan and repeated her name. "I'm Olivia."

The final Blackwell rose, and Liv had to crane her neck to keep her eyes on his face. His eyes were brown, like Zeke's, but where Zeke's were so dark they looked black, amber flecked Rohan's.

Those unusual eyes studied Liv as if she were a frog splayed out on a dissecting tray. Seconds ticked by, her hand warm in his, until a large presence closed in behind her. Zeke cleared his throat.

Humor lit Rohan's features. "This should be fun." He

released her hand and pointed to the chair next to his. "Please make yourself comfortable. This chair will give you the best vantage."

Once everyone was seated, Liv's nerves began to rattle again until her attention landed on Johona's bright yellow with red polka dot socks. The rattle calmed.

"The floor is yours, Olivia." Zeke wedged his body in the corner of a sofa, angling his body in order to have a clear view of her.

She dug into her bag for a folder, giving herself a moment to collect her thoughts. Even after seven years and hundreds of presentations, she still had to mentally prepare herself to be the center of attention for a room full of people. It didn't matter if she was in front of five people or five hundred. She had to talk herself through it.

Thankfully, she had learned to always have a list of talking points, which helped her stay focused and on point. Opening the folder, she read the first bullet, but realized she would have to give the group a little background first.

She cleared her throat. "On behalf of the Bureau, I want to thank you—"

"Save it, Olivia," Phin said, his roguish grin gone. "We're all aware that the FBI is essentially blackmailing us to perform this recovery."

"Zeke also told us," Mrs. Blackwell placed a weathered hand on Phin's knee, "Olivia had nothing to do with Ash's forced leave."

Sweat dampened Liv's palms, and she peered down at her talking points again, but the words wouldn't come into focus. The grandmother's words sent her mind down a dark rabbit hole.

Focus, Liv.

"I'll start with the catalyst that brought us all to this point."

"If you're referring to the informant who's bargaining information for a trinket he wants the FBI to"—Phin mimicked air quotes—"*recover* so they can keep some nasty shi—stuff off the streets, Zeke filled us in on that last night."

Liv's attention cut to Zeke. His betrayal of her confidence left her momentarily speechless.

A muscle jumped in Zeke's jaw as he stared at his younger brother.

"What?" Phin asked. "You told us not to share the information with anyone, and I haven't."

Zeke shook his head, and his unflinching gaze met Liv's. "Tell us about the item we need to recover and what you know about its current location."

"Can I get you something to drink, Olivia?" Rohan asked, as if sensing her churning emotions. "Water? Coffee?"

"If something stronger will get you through this presentation, we have bourbon and wine," Cruz said with a smile, though Liv thought he was only half-kidding.

Bringing alcohol into this volcanic mix wouldn't be a good idea. "Water, please."

Rohan stepped over to the small kitchenette at the back of the room and opened the refrigerator. "Flat or fizzy?"

"Flat."

Liv used the beverage distraction to reorder her thoughts, but her mind kept wandering back to Zeke and his breach of her trust. All she'd wanted to do was make him understand the full impact of a "no" vote when he went back to his team.

If Mitch found out she had shared confidential information with someone not yet part of the case, he might take disciplinary steps that could damage her career.

Rohan returned with her water, and she smiled her thanks. She took a drink, glanced at her bullet list, and plunged in for the third time. "The asset you've been hired to recover is a one-hundred-and-ten-year-old Kämmer and Reinhardt doll."

"A doll," Zeke echoed in a flat voice.

"It's German made and one of a kind. Six years ago, it sold for just under four hundred thousand dollars at auction."

"An informant with a doll fetish," Phin chuckled.

"Does the CI have a daughter?" Cruz asked.

"His youngest is twenty."

"Is he—or his daughter—a collector?" Rohan asked.

"That's what the CI would have us believe."

"But you're not buying it," Zeke said.

"It seems an odd pairing," Liv admitted, sliding her glass onto the oval coffee table, a long, substantial piece of furniture. Absently, she noticed a panel of buttons on the side. "But those involved with drug trafficking tend to have more money than they know what to do with. They get bored and chase blinged-out squirrels and have unusual tastes. But mostly, they want respect. Surrounding yourself with expensive objects can buy a lot of respect in certain circles."

"Where is the extraction location?" Zeke asked.

"In the private museum of a wealthy Asheville businesswoman."

"Guess that rules out getting caught in the middle of a gang war," Phin said.

Zeke leaned forward, elbows on his knees and hands clasped together. A new intensity carved hard lines on his face. "What's the woman's name?"

"Nicola St. Martin."

He didn't so much as blink at the name. Yet his clasped

hands contracted as if his muscles spasmed. Did he know her? Or was something else at play?

"What kind of security are we up against?" Rohan asked.

Liv considered telling them about her family's connection to the St. Martins, but despite Mitch's assertion otherwise, she didn't believe the association would be useful. She'd been to their home a handful of times, though she'd never been invited to see Nicola's famed museum. Didn't even know where it was in her house. But she could make a few educated guesses.

"State-of-the art. She's a serious collector."

Zeke said, "Rohan, we need the layout of the property, museum, and the collector's social calendar. See if she's entertaining in the next few days—"

"She is," Liv interrupted. "Two evenings from now, the St. Martins are hosting their annual masquerade fundraising ball for the Asheville Art Museum, where they display select pieces from their collection for an exclusive viewing."

Zeke looked at Rohan. "Get Phin and me on that invite list."

"You?" Phin asked.

"I'll be part of the recon team."

"There's no team in me. Recon's my job."

"For this one, it'll be ours."

Rohan hesitated a moment, then nodded and headed to his office.

"Phin, once Rohan has the property specs, I need you to work your fabricating magic. "

Still fuming, the youngest Blackwell pushed out of his chair. "I'll start the prep work."

"Cruz, figure out how to get us in there and out."

"Consider it done." He rose and nodded toward Liv. "I look forward to working with you."

"Same here."

Zeke studied Liv for a long second before turning to his grandmother. "Anything you'd like to add, Grams?"

Johona shook her head. "Sounds like you have it under control." She pushed out of her chair and smiled at Liv. "It will be a pleasure to meet your son." With that pronouncement, she strode the short distance to Lynette's office and disappeared inside.

Liv looked at Zeke. "What did she mean?"

He looked at the open office doors, where his brothers lurked. "Come on, I'll walk you out."

Once they reached her vehicle, she deposited her possessions inside before facing Zeke. "Explain your grandmother's comment, please."

He stood a few inches away, one hand hooked over her door. "We only have three days to plan and execute a high stakes recovery."

"I'm aware of our timeline."

"Then you understand it would be best for you to stay here. With your son."

"What? No. I have other cases that need my attention besides this one."

"You can coordinate them from here."

"It's not that easy—"

"Our maintenance manager has a daughter similar in age to Brodie. They can hang out while you work."

"He has school."

"Nowadays, we have the ability to do remote everything."

"We're not staying here."

He leaned in closer. "Afraid you'll be tempted again?"

"Hardly. The mystery is gone." She forced indifference into her features when she scanned his body from head to toe. "I've seen everything you have to offer."

"Ah, but you've only sampled two—or was it three—items from the menu." The back of his finger smoothed down a stray lock of her hair. "You didn't stay long enough for dessert last time."

She shuffled back until her calves hit the door frame. "I'm not bringing my son into this den of thieves."

"Recovery artists."

"You can pretty it up all you want, but we both know you're nothing but thieves for hire." Liv nearly flinched at her own words, but this...man and his gall.

He stiffened. "We're also the ones who are going to save the FBI's ass because you don't have the stomach to do what needs to be done."

"It's called breaking the law, Zeke. Something I'm sworn to protect."

"A little blackmail is okay, though. It's only mildly offensive to your sensibilities."

"What's offensive to my sensibilities is you betraying my trust and deciding where my son will sleep."

Something like regret flashed through his eyes before they hardened into resolve. "I took a page out of your book and gave my team the information they needed to make an informed decision. I'd say I'm sorry, but it would be a lie, because given the same set of circumstances, I'd do the same thing again."

Backed into her own net, she stewed in silence.

"As for Brodie, what boy wouldn't enjoy staying here for a few days?"

Liv scanned the heavily wooded property. A place a

curious child could explore for hours. Unfortunately, her son had pulled the plug on all outdoor activity.

In a low, calmer voice, he said, "Find out why the doll is so important to the CI and report back here tomorrow."

"And if I don't?"

"You can explain to Ash why he has to find himself a new job."

"You wouldn't."

"Oh, I would." He waved toward her bag. "What your files on us evidently didn't uncover was that Ash walked out on the family business three years ago and left me to deal with the aftermath. I owe him nothing."

Liv digested this bit of family intrigue, which explained the undercurrent of tension between the two brothers at the FBI office. Realizing any further discussion would only lead to more harsh, unproductive words, she slid into the driver's seat. She nodded at the hand he still had locked on her door. "Do you mind?"

He splayed his hand and stepped back, allowing her to shut the door.

As she backed out of her parking spot, he said, "Don't forget your kid and suitcase tomorrow."

20

LIV RETURNED TO THE BLACKWELL COMPLEX LATER THE NEXT morning and suffered through the same security measures as the previous day, minus signing another nondisclosure agreement.

Anticipation replaced her irritation when she spotted a runner along the road to the Annex.

Please be Zeke. Don't be Zeke. Please, please be Zeke. DON'T BE ZEKE.

As per usual, her mind roiled in conflict when it came to the BARS team leader. Anger about his high-handedness and his inability to keep a secret still simmered in her veins.

But those thoughts were not the ones causing her heart to break-dance inside her chest as she drew closer to the runner.

He wore dark gray shorts, and his bare torso glistened with sweat. Sinew stretched and contracted across his back with each pump of his arms. Muscled calves carried his six-foot plus body at a fast clip, even though he must be at the end of his run rather than the beginning.

Hearing her approach, the runner turned his head, and

Zeke Blackwell's dark eyes penetrated her windshield, her sunglasses, all the way to that secret part of her that yearned for danger, ached for recklessness.

She glanced at Brodie, who slumped in the passenger seat, his mouth parted as sleepy breaths see-sawed in and out. Halfway to Steele Ridge, he'd fallen asleep while playing his video game. She had saved his tablet before it slipped from his grip and laid it on his backpack in the footwell. But he still wore his noise-canceling headphones.

Slowing to a walk, Zeke shifted to the left side of the road and removed a white earbud. "Morning," he said, around a heavy breath.

The height of her SUV put them at eye level, allowing her to idle alongside him as he continued moving, cooling down. "How was your run?" she asked in a quiet voice.

Damn, he was gorgeous. Back, side, front—every angle tempted the eye to explore and enjoy. She had never been as thankful for a pair of protective sunglasses in her life.

He peered inside, saw her son, and matched her tone. "As long as ever."

"You don't enjoy running?"

"Do I look like a masochist?"

Reaching into the tote bag tucked behind Brodie's seat, she pulled out an unopened bottle of water. "Here."

"You sure?"

"I have another one."

He accepted the bottle. "Probably have a damn case in there." He twisted off the cap and chugged a third of it down. "Thanks." He swiped a hand over his sweaty brow. "Got a towel in that thing?"

"No, but I have a spare T-shirt."

Even though his body stayed in motion, a stillness passed over him. Then he shrugged. "That'll do."

It was Liv's turn to hesitate. She hadn't been kidding about having a spare shirt, but she never thought he'd accept it to wipe the sweat from his face. The action, one she could so clearly see in her mind's eye, seemed far too intimate.

Even so, she found herself digging into her bag once again and retrieving the article of clothing. "Who are you avoiding?"

His big hand reached in and took the folded square of white cotton from her. "What makes you think I'm avoiding anyone?" He blotted his eyes and swiped his face before stuffing the now damp cloth into his shorts pocket.

"The dew point must be in the mid-sixties, it's nearing noon, and you're running outside."

A muscle rippled along his jawline. "It was time to leave my team to their work."

Like with Cameron, she had detected hints of tension between him and his brothers the previous day. Considering his frequent bouts of dictating her movements, she wondered if they suffered under the same treatment.

"They don't like you in their business?"

His thick brows clenched together. "According to them, I have control issues."

"Do you?"

"If staying on top of things to maintain progress is controlling, then I'm guilty as charged." He lifted the bottle to his mouth and drank.

"Staying on top," she mused. "Does that translate to checking on status? Or making pointed suggestions?"

The empty water bottle crackled in his fist. He screwed the cap back on and tossed it in her backseat.

"Got your suitcases?"

"Yes." She had been tempted to leave her son in the care

of Callie and her Aunt Belinda, who was an investigator for the Asheville police department, to make him think twice about commanding her again.

But she couldn't bring herself to separate from her son. Not after her assailant's implied threat. If he knew where Brodie went to school, it wasn't a great leap to assume he knew where they lived.

After she told Callie where she'd be for the next few days, her sister had danced around the kitchen and made suggestive motions with her eyebrows before she finally agreed to camp out at her friend Jessica's house.

"Good girl."

Her teeth clenched. "I don't need to sleep here to do my job."

"Staying here will reduce the distractions."

She braked. "Would you have the same concern if I were a male agent?"

"If he were a single dad, yes."

The matter-of-fact way he answered her took the wind out of her indignation. She released a harsh breath and checked to make sure Brodie was still asleep. A small line of drool eased from his mouth.

She turned back to Zeke. "I'm sorry. Since my husband died, I've had to take time off work for parenting and it's not going over well with some of my colleagues."

He rested a tanned forearm on her open window and leaned forward. "You've witnessed firsthand our security. This is the safest place for him to be, and he'll be close to you."

After their blowup yesterday and a cooling-down period, she had been able to see the benefit of staying on-site during the planning phase. She just didn't like being told what to do with her son.

She also regretted her "den of thieves" comment. Other than some initial surliness from Phin and Lynette, everyone had gone out of their way to be kind to her, despite their feelings on how the Bureau had treated Ash.

"I'm sorry for what I said about your family being thieves. You didn't deserve that."

A charged moment passed before he nodded. "I'll ask Clara to meet us at the Friary."

"Who's Clara?"

"She homeschools her ten-year-old daughter, Sadie. I've already spoken to her, and she agreed to watch over Brodie during the day."

"Thank you." Gripping the steering wheel, she stared down the road. "Brodie's pretty self-sufficient, but if we don't watch him, he—" She broke off, realizing she'd ventured into the too much information arena.

"He, what?" A note of concern entered his voice.

She swallowed, uncomfortable talking about her personal issues with a relative stranger. A stranger that could do such wicked things with his tongue. "He, uh, tends to spend too much time playing video games."

"Doesn't sound too unusual."

"It is for my son. I used to have to drag him into the house. He and his friends would spend hours just throwing a ball around."

"What changed?"

Her throat tightened. "A Charlotte's Knights game and a slicing foul ball into the stands."

"The ball hit his dad?"

Nodding, she bit her lip and looked away.

"Liv, I'm sorry—"

She lifted a hand, cutting off his words of sympathy. One kind gesture from him, and she would spill the whole grisly story. "Are you sure it's a good idea for us to stay? I don't mind driving back and forth."

He studied her features as if re-familiarizing himself with a favorite weapon he hadn't fired in several years. "No, I'm not sure."

Heat gathered low in her stomach, and her breathing grew harder to control. A surprise. Normally, any reminder of Tyler's last days left her cold and hollow.

Something flickered in the dark depths of Zeke's gaze a second before his face cleared. He pushed away from her vehicle. "But there's plenty here to entertain your son." He jerked his chin toward the Annex. "I'll meet you at the parking lot."

"I can give you a—"

He took off down the road.

"—lift." Liv watched him put distance between them.

It was the smart thing to do, the responsible thing to do. The thing she should have done.

One breath. Two. Then three, and Liv blotted her son's drool, released the brake pedal, and followed the one man she feared could release her secret desires from their dark prison.

21

ZEKE PUMPED ALL THE DISGUST AND ANGER AT HIMSELF INTO his leg muscles.

What the hell was wrong with him?

From the moment he'd spotted Liv behind the wheel, his body had come alive with a familiar hum of anticipation.

He'd tried. Tried like hell to keep things professional. Tried to think of her as one of the guys. Someone who had information he needed.

Ask the right questions. Get the answers. Move on.

He'd failed. His damn inconvenient curiosity about her had sparked and ignited and *burned.*

While she spoke about what sounded like a terrible freak accident, one question burned in his mind above all else until he thought for sure she saw smoke billowing from his ears.

Did you love your husband?

No, that wasn't quite right.

Do you still love your husband?

Yeah, there it was. The question that would send him to hell.

"Blackwell, you fuck-wad."

The roll of tires sticking to hot asphalt caught his attention. His hands ground into fists as Liv drove by. He didn't look in her direction. Didn't dare.

One glimpse of her slightly parted lips, and he would cave like a steel door against a block of C4. He followed her vehicle until it turned into the parking lot at the end of the road.

Two minutes.

He had two minutes to get his head screwed on straight and quit panting after Olivia Westcott like a sex-starved sixteen-year-old.

In an attempt to master himself, he forced his thoughts toward the text he'd received from Sardoff two nights ago. The antiquities dealer had received word that a sword matching Lupos's description had recently been sold to a private collector in Asheville. The buyer was none other than Nicola St. Martin, the same collector in possession of the informant's vintage doll.

Who was this St. Martin woman? Did she gain possession of both artifacts through legal means? Or through the black market? All questions he hoped Sardoff could answer for him before their recovery. The more he knew going in, the better.

The cotton shirt in his pocket mocked his attempt to control his thoughts.

Touch me. Bury your nose in me. Draw in my sweet vanilla scent.

He should have said to hell with courtesy and given the soiled T-shirt back to her. The small weight against his thigh made him think of her hand. How her palm had warmed his flesh while she took him into her mouth—

"Fuck!"

Closing his eyes, he ground to a halt and bent over. His fingers dug into the side of his knees while he willed himself to think about spreadsheets and inventory and the gray hair he'd found that morning.

When he had his libido under control again, he straightened and stared down the empty road. The last thing he needed right now was to get involved with a grieving widow whose son had seen a baseball kill his father.

Zeke could barely manage keeping BARS operational at the moment. Phin seemed to be one wrong job away from leaving, Cruz chafed under his leadership style, and Rohan would eventually get tired of mediating the whole mess.

He raked a frustrated hand through his sweat-damp hair, hating the feeling of losing control. The only high point in his life right now was a solid lead on Lupos's location. The rest of it—his business, his career, his family—they were all on a downward spiral, and he had no idea how to stop it all from hitting the bottom.

One thing he did know. He couldn't take on another responsibility. No matter how beautiful or tempting.

22

LIV CHECKED HER PHONE'S CLOCK AGAIN.

Where had Zeke gone?

It shouldn't have taken him this long to run the remaining distance to the parking lot. She'd answered an e-mail and a text and still no hot, sweaty Blackwell.

Did she misunderstand him? Was she supposed to head to the Friary instead? Another more concerning thought surfaced. Did he sprain his ankle? Was he in pain? Forced to limp the final distance?

She started for the road at the exact moment he emerged from the tunnel of trees. A hardness that hadn't been there minutes ago was carved into his features.

"Are you okay?"

Zeke stopped before her. "Arms up."

"Pardon?"

His finger teeter tottered in the air. "Arms up."

"You've got to be kidding me."

"Not in the slightest."

Biting the inside of her cheek, she lifted her arms and stared straight ahead. The moment his large hands touched her, Liv's heart kicked into high gear. Although his effort was no less professional and efficient than Lynette Blackwell's pat down, his hands seemed to leave an imprint, like contrails in the sky.

He knelt before her, and she ached to run her fingers through his hair. She knew from experience how soft and thick it would be. How it smelled. How it felt brushing against her inner thigh.

When his hands paused on her calves, she looked down and found his head bent, the wide expanse of his shoulders frozen.

She lowered her arms, balling her hands to keep from touching the sun-warmed skin that was so, so close. When the already moist air thickened and breathing grew harder, Liv took a small step back and his hand fell away.

He rose, unfolded, really, like the Terminator after his Earth landing. When Zeke's eyes met hers, they weren't flat and mechanical like the Cyberdyne Systems 101. They were molten and wanting.

A keen ache pierced her middle, and she opened her mouth to say. . . something, just as he blinked, and the hardness returned.

"Let's grab your son and suitcases," he said. "I'll show you to your rooms first."

She released a long breath and turned back to her vehicle. Being in close proximity to Zeke Blackwell was going to test her professional conduct—and personal willpower—way freaking beyond their limits.

"He's too big to carry. I'll wake him."

"No need." Zeke used her shirt to wipe the sweat from his chest again before opening the passenger door. Judging by his careful movements, Brodie still hadn't stirred.

Somehow, he hooked an arm through the shoulder strap

of her son's backpack and lifted Brodie out of the seat without bashing either of their heads.

For an eye-tingling moment, Brodie's arms wrapped around Zeke's neck, like they had Tyler's countless times, before they slowly slid down and dangled at his sides.

Conflicting emotions barreled through her. It should be Tyler's arm braced beneath her son's bum and his hand supporting his narrow back as he closed the vehicle door. But seeing Brodie's head balanced on Zeke's shoulder, an untroubled expression on his sweet face, touched her heart in a way she had never thought to experience again.

Zeke glanced at her and came to a full stop.

She swallowed back the tears and rushed to grab her tote and the suitcase she shared with her son.

Without a word, he started down a flagstone path that led away from the offices and wound through a copse of trees. Birdsong chorused around them and a gentle breeze buffed her cheeks. Soon the trees thinned and deposited them before a well-manicured estate that would give the Biltmore a good case of envy.

Not until Zeke turned back to her, a question in his eyes, did she realize that she'd stopped to gawk. "It's amazing."

He looked at the building as if viewing it through her eyes. "This is the Friary. A group of Franciscan monks lived here for a time before the property was converted into a church camp for youths."

Pointing to the center of the building, he said, "This is the original building." His finger touched on either side of the square. "We added two wings. A few of the former staff cabins also survived. We refurbished them into living quarters for staff who care for the property."

"Is there a chapel inside?"

He shook his head. "There's a small one farther along the path. I can take you to see it later, if you like."

"I'd love to."

Zeke continued down the path to the Friary's ten-foot-tall double doors. They opened into a two-story entryway with a rustic chandelier and a beautiful oriental carpet protecting the wood floors.

The entryway spilled into a large rectangular room with enormous fireplaces at each end. Above one mantel, a large elk's head jutted out from the stones. The other was curiously empty but for two ornate hooks positioned horizontal to each other.

Deep-cushioned leather furniture dotted the space as well as high-backed chairs strategically placed around the fireplaces.

The back wall was nothing but glass overlooking a stone veranda housing a firepit, pool, and Jacuzzi. Twin two-person tables sporting a chess and backgammon set were parked in front of the windows, granting the players an inspiring view.

The whole setup had a modern-day medieval vibe that would appeal to any guest.

"This is where the family hangs out in the evenings," Zeke said, avoiding eye contact.

"It's so warm and cozy." She nodded toward the empty hooks. "What are those—"

"Cool!"

Liv jerked around to find her son scrambling out of Zeke's arms and running toward the fireplace with the massive dead head.

Brodie pointed at the mounted trophy. "Mama, look at the moose!"

She strode to his side and placed a hand on his shoulder.

"That's an elk, sweetheart."

His eyes widened. "Can we get one?"

She smiled. "We don't have a fireplace."

"What about above my bed?"

No. If he didn't get nightmares from waking up beneath the thing, she would. "Um, I don't think that's a good idea."

Disappointment replaced his excitement. "But, Mama—"

"Hello, Brodie," Zeke said, cutting off her son's whine.

Brodie took in Zeke's outfit—or lack of—and leaned into Liv.

"You remember, Zeke, right? This is his home."

Her son's eyes flicked to the mount again, then back to Zeke. "Did you shoot him?"

Zeke shook his head. "Once you see one in the wild, you can't imagine viewing them any other way."

"You saw an elk in the wild?"

"When I was about your age, my parents took us to Yellowstone National Park." Zeke paused. "Have you been?"

Brodie looked at Liv.

She placed a hand on his shoulder. "Not yet."

"It's one of the most beautiful and dangerous places in the world. Tens of thousands of elk live there."

"Thousands?" Brodie echoed.

"I only saw a few hundred." He paused as if sifting through memories. "Their call—the way they speak to each other—is like nothing I'd ever heard before. Eerie, but cool." He peered up at the elk head. "The first time I heard their bugle was early one morning near our campsite. The sounds echoed through the ravine. Gave me chills."

"Were you scared?" Brodie shifted out of the protection of Liv's side, his attention fixed on Zeke.

"At first, but my curiosity got the better of me. I crept

through the trees until I reached the bluff's edge, then searched the valley below."

Brodie moved closer to Zeke. "Did you see him?"

"Not at first. A light fog filled the area. I was just about to give up and go back to my warm sleeping bag when a breeze pushed through the ravine until the creek came into view."

Retrieving his phone, he tapped the screen several times, then looked at Brodie. "A bull elk, larger than this one," he nodded toward the fireplace, "lifted its head after getting a drink of water. He seemed to look right at me as he extended his neck and released another ..."

Zeke hit a button on his phone and a high-pitched, keening bugle filled the Great Hall.

Brodie's eyes rounded once again. "An elk makes that sound?"

"Yep."

"Who shot that animal?" Brodie asked, pointing at the mounted elk.

Zeke stopped the audio replay. "No one knows. It came with the Friary."

"His mama believes the trophy adds to the Hall's ambiance," a new, amused female voice said.

Liv turned to find two women and a girl with dark brown ringlets standing at the mouth of the foyer. The fifty-something woman on the left stood at least six feet tall and styled her gray-shot blond hair in two-inch spikes around her head. She wore a bright floral jumpsuit, a studded leather bracelet, and pink On tennis shoes.

The much-shorter and fashionably subdued woman next to her wore her shoulder-length brown hair in a low ponytail. Her slender frame was outfitted in a short-sleeved sage-green top, white pants, and sandals. One arm wrapped around the young girl's shoulders.

Zeke's face split into a broad smile. "Hello, ladies. And Sadie."

The girl's eyes narrowed, and she shoved her hands on her nonexistent hips.

Zeke winked.

The girl grinned and launched herself at the half-naked man. He caught her up in his arms and dug his fingers into her ribs, making her shriek with laughter. "You know you're my favorite lady."

"Stop! Stop! Mama, make him stop!"

The shorter woman smiled. "You got yourself into that hot mess, you can get yourself out."

"You're all sticky. Yuck!"

Chuckling, Zeke stopped tickling her and lowered her to the floor. "Henri, Clara, and"—he squeezed the girl's shoulders—"Sadie, I'd like you to meet my new friends Olivia and Brodie."

Sadie bounced on her toes. "Hi."

"Hi." Brodie gave her a tentative smile.

Zeke waved toward the tall blonde. "Henri takes care of anything and everything to do with the house and gardens."

"Except for Johona's herb garden. That's all hers," Henri said. "If you need anything while you're here, give me a holler."

"Thank you," Liv said.

"Now, if you'll excuse me, I have a crabby toilet in the east wing, then I need to figure out what to feed these giants tonight."

The other woman shook her head as Henri marched away, then came down to round out their small circle. Bending at the waist, she shook Brodie's hand. "Hello, Brodie. I'm Clara. Would you like to hang out with Sadie and me tomorrow while your mama is at work?"

He peered up at Liv, uncertain.

"It's your decision."

"Say yes, Brodie, *please*," Sadie pleaded. "Once we're done with schoolwork, I'll take you fishing."

This excited her son. "Okay."

Zeke angled his and Sadie's body so he could see her face. "Would you mind showing Brodie to his room? I set up the entertainment system. Maybe you could show him the ropes."

"Sure." She reached down and picked up Brodie's backpack. "Wow, what do you have in here?"

Zeke smiled, remembering he had a similar reaction to picking up Liv's bag.

Brodie snatched his pack out of her hands and knifed his arm through a shoulder strap. "Just stuff."

Sadie shrugged and motioned for him to follow. "Come on." They ran up one of two sets of stairs leading off the Great Hall.

Clara sighed. "If only I still had that kind of energy." She touched Liv's arm. "I'll take good care of him. Zeke has my phone number. Call me any time to check in on his status."

"It's so kind of you to take him on."

"Don't pin any angel wings on me. I assure you, I have ulterior motives."

Liv liked this woman already. "Oh?"

"I'm hoping he'll help me tire out my daughter. I'd give a pinky finger for one hour of quiet with my favorite book."

"Are you a Sandra Brown fan?"

"Who isn't?"

"I have her latest in my suitcase. It's amazing—"

Clara held up her hands. "Don't tell me. I'm about five years behind on my reading."

Liv pantomimed locking her lips and throwing away

the key.

"I'll leave you now so you can get settled in. How about I send Sadie to fetch your son at eight-thirty tomorrow morning?"

"He'll be waiting."

Once she disappeared through the front door, a pin-drop silence enveloped them.

Liv cleared her throat. "Thank you for helping Brodie feel comfortable here. He and Sadie seemed to hit it off already."

"I've yet to come across anyone who can resist her." He nodded toward the same staircase the kids ascended. "Your room is this way."

After climbing two flights and traipsing down a short hallway, he nodded to a door on her left. "Brodie's there."

She peered through the half-open door and spotted the two new friends sitting cross-legged on a sofa at the end of the bed. Large AR devices engulfed their heads, and their little hands searched the air around them for something only they could see.

Smiling, she backed away, and Zeke pushed open a door on the opposite side of the hall.

A king-sized bed decorated in cream and gray with navy accents dominated the room. A flat-screen TV sat above a chest of drawers and a desk with a silver lamp stood before a set of double windows.

Zeke reached through an opening and flicked on a light. "Bathroom." Banged a fist on a closed door. "Closet." And pointed toward another open door while setting her suitcase on the bed. "Kitchen."

"Wow." Liv smoothed a hand over the arm of a cushy loveseat at the foot of the massive bed. "This *room* is as big as my first apartment."

"Remember, if there's something you need, find Henri."

"Interesting name."

"Interesting woman."

When he offered nothing more, Liv strode to the windows that overlooked a woodland. The dense canopy made her feel as though she stood in the middle of a tree-house. If she craned her neck to the right, where the ridge slid down into a shallow hollow, she could make out the top of a steeple.

"That's the chapel," he said near her ear.

If she leaned back, would her shoulders touch his broad chest?

Closing her eyes, she imagined the feel of his powerful arms drawing her close until her bottom nestled against the hard ridge of his erection. Feel him pulse against her once, twice—

Her eyes slammed open, and she stepped away from the window and temptation. "This is great. Thank you."

"I hope you'll be comfortable."

"How could I not? Everything I need is right here."

Including you.

A restrained energy seemed to pulse off him as if he wanted to be anywhere but in this room with her. "Settle in while I get cleaned up." At the door, he turned back to give her a cursory glance. "I'll meet you downstairs in ten minutes."

Then he was gone.

Wrapping her arms around her middle to ward off the sudden chill in the room, she wandered back to the window and searched for the chapel's steeple. How many confessions had echoed within its four, stout, hallowed walls?

How many of Zeke's secrets did it harbor?

23

Liv stood in the darkened Theater, staring down at an illuminated three-dimensional model of Nicola St. Martin's Asheville mansion, displayed on the now elevated coffee table. The model was so lifelike that she could almost imagine hearing the clank of crystal and hum of refined chatter.

"This is extraordinary," she said to the room at large.

Across from her, Zeke rested his big hands on the edge of the three-by-five table. His dark eyes shuffled over the diorama as if mentally cataloging every detail.

"You've outdone yourself, little brother," he said.

Although his T-shirt was as wrinkle-free as ever, Phin's rumpled hair, bloodshot eyes, and frequent yawns suggested he'd pulled an all-nighter.

At his brother's praise, the younger Blackwell stood taller and a new energy entered his voice. "Only because Rohan scraped up the mansion's original design and, thanks to the St. Martins' love for entertaining, he was able to pull a bazillion internal photos off the web. The combination filled in the gaps."

"Plus, *Architectural Digest* did a feature article on her home recently," Rohan said.

In an aside to Liv, Phin pointed toward a red line snaking its way through the various levels of the building. "This is Cruz's handiwork. The line shows the path of least resistance."

"Meaning," Cruz said, "that's our way in, and our best chance of not drawing attention."

"Let's back up and start from the top." Zeke lifted his thumb to start a countdown. "The target is Nicola St. Martin, a wealthy collector who likes to show off her latest acquisitions." He held up his forefinger. "We need to send in a recon team to get eyes on the asset and further assess the security situation." Middle finger. "Our recovery team retrieves the asset." He lowered his hand. "Now, what else you got?"

"The private museum doesn't exist on the original floor plan. I've isolated areas of the estate where an extensive art collection could reside." Rohan tapped a screen on his tablet and a blue light outlined a separate building on the estate. "Here." Another tap and the blue light shifted to the south wing of the mansion. "And here." A subfloor beneath the main part of the house lit up.

"That's a lot of options, Ro," Cruz said.

Rohan pushed his glasses higher on his nose. "Agreed, but I can't rule them out either."

"We have to figure out if she likes to parade people through her museum," Zeke placed a blunt finger on the separate building, "keeps it close for family and friends," his finger moved to the south wing, "or hides it in the dark like trophies of war." Everyone's attention shifted to the basement.

"Hoarder or exhibitionist?" Phin added.

"Considering she's only bringing out a few pieces for the donor's viewing," Cruz said, "I'd say she likes to keep her collection closer to the breast."

"Agreed. The standalone would be too easy to breach," Zeke said. "Let's set that one aside for now and concentrate on the other two. What else?"

"As far as I can determine," Rohan said, "only three people have access cards—the St. Martins and their curator."

"After a full body scan, each guest must present an object to the museum curator upon arriving," Phin said.

"What kind of object?" Grams asked, breaking her silence.

"Unknown."

"An identical object?" Zeke asked. "Or are they unique to each guest?"

"Given the level of security," Phin said, "we're assuming unique, but—"

"We don't have time for assumptions," Zeke interrupted. "This event is tomorrow night."

"I'm aware," Phin said through clenched teeth. "The guest list is as protected as the object's identity. Until we have the one, we can't get the other."

"Nothing in cyberspace?" Zeke asked. "No one boasting about attending on social media?"

Rohan shook his head. "Not a peep, other than the one post talking about body scans and the mysterious object. When I went back a few hours later to read it again, in case I missed something, the post was gone."

Liv searched her memory. Hadn't Callie mentioned something about their parents preparing to attend yet another shindig, during their drive to the mechanic's shop this morning?

Could it be the St. Martins' benefit? Would she be able to coax the invitation details from her parents? If so, Mitch had been right about the benefit of her familial connection.

Much of her parents' success could be linked back to the relationships they had fostered over the years. If St. Martin's missing doll got linked back to her parents breaking a confidence, they would suffer a public embarrassment.

And they might never speak to Liv again.

Not that they did a lot of that now. No time in their busy schedules to spare an evening for their daughter or, even worse, their grandson. Hence, the reason Callie preferred Liv's one-and-a-half-bathroom bungalow rather than her suite of rooms in Thornton Manor.

If the St. Martins had invited Regina and Stanley Thornton, there was a one hundred percent chance her best friend and highly successful lobbyist Kayla Krowne had received a coveted invitation as well.

Kayla, unlike Liv's parents, enjoyed a bit of intrigue. She loved nothing more than tweaking the noses of those who were more concerned about their status in society than making sure their community was healthy and safe and thriving.

Could she successfully pry details about the object from both Kayla and her parents?

"Do you have something you'd like to share with us, Olivia?" Zeke asked, picking up on her preoccupation.

Olivia.

Distance.

Something had unsettled him during their conversation on the Annex road. Something he was either still processing or something that had turned him off seduction.

Good.

She hadn't emerged unscathed either. One-night stands

should be one and done. No after-coitus mussy fuss, no disappointment over a refused dinner invitation. No contemplating a lover's deepest secrets.

As much as she craved another physical release with Zeke, she couldn't chance it.

She had loved being married. Loved the companionship. Loved movie night. Loved having another responsible adult she could lean on when parenting got hard.

Zeke was not that guy. She hadn't missed his fleeting *oh, shit* look when he realized she had a son. He might be good with kids, but that didn't mean he wanted to add any to his basket.

"Olivia?" he prodded.

"There's a good chance someone I'm close to has been invited to St. Martin's party."

"Who?"

"Someone who routinely attends high-profile social events, not just in Asheville and Charlotte, but D.C., too."

"Does this friend have a name?"

"Kayla Krowne."

The room fell silent. So silent Liv wondered if she'd spoken the words loudly enough.

"Why didn't I think of Kayla?" Phin murmured.

Liv frowned. "You know her?"

Phin nodded. "I interned at her firm. She's Netflix's Miss Sloane in the flesh."

"Then you know it won't be easy getting her to divulge anything about the object if she decides to abide by the St. Martins' wishes." Liv looked at Zeke. "*If* they invited her."

"Leave Kayla to me," Phin said.

Liv raised an eyebrow.

The younger Blackwell smiled. "Fabricating isn't my only specialty."

Her brow rose higher.

"There's not a woman who can resist little brother's charms," Cruz said.

For a moment, she considered telling them about her parents, but then she'd have to endure the whistles of surprise and shocked expressions. Many in the region knew the Thornton name and had a sense of the family's wealth and influence. She couldn't deny that Thornton money had set her up to be a successful adult—not as successful as her parents would've liked—but it was Liv's hard work that had established her career and earned her the respect of her colleagues.

As always, she strove to keep her personal and professional lives separate. No, she'd keep the parent angle to herself, then share what she learned, if anything.

"The mark doesn't have to be female," Rohan said. "Phin can pull intelligence out of anyone. Not just women."

"That good?" Liv remained skeptical. No one could deny Phin's appeal, but it was dangerous to underestimate Kayla's Bullshit Sensor.

"My second major was in psychology. Humans have basic needs. I excel at uncovering, then exploiting them."

Hopeful smiles erupted around the room.

Phin Blackwell would make a great undercover agent. Should she subject Kayla to that kind of cutthroat manipulation?

Who was she kidding? Kayla was a lobbyist. Queen of Exploitation. If her friend ferreted out Phin's intent, she'd make a meal of his smooth-talking tongue.

As if she'd done it a thousand times before, Liv turned to Zeke for confirmation of his brother's outrageous claims. And maybe a small part of her wanted to experience his hopeful smile. The smile she helped make.

But his mouth didn't tilt upward like his brothers'. Neither did it tilt down. It rode a neutral line.

She shifted her attention to his eyes. Those expressive brown orbs didn't share his mouth's fondness for noncommittal.

No, they bored into her skull, searching. Suspicious.

24

ZEKE SENSED LIV WAS HOLDING SOMETHING BACK, BUT NOW wasn't the time to ask probing questions. She'd presented them with an unexpected gift, and they needed to act fast or this recovery was DOA.

"From what you've both said, Kayla won't be an easy mark."

"No," Phin said, his face one of anticipation. "She'll make me work for the information."

"Is Kayla aware of the family's recovery business?" Liv asked.

"Doubtful," Phin said. "Last she knew, we were in towing and repoing."

"I've known Kayla a long time. She's always had a soft spot for the underdog." Liv smiled. "Think of her as Robin Hood in stilettos."

"What are you getting at?" Zeke asked.

Her lips thinned the slightest bit before she turned to Phin. "I don't mean to tell you how to do your charming, but it might be easier to get what you want from Kayla by giving her as much of the truth as you can."

"Are you authorizing Phin to tell your friend about the drugs?" Zeke asked.

"No." The word came out firm and sharp. "But it sounds like Phin has the skill and relationship to give her the essence of the situation. If she understands the stakes, her heart will overrule society etiquette."

"Why not approach her yourself?" Cruz asked.

"Because despite Zeke's insistence, I can't be part of this operation. I'm strictly behind the scenes. The Bureau cannot be linked to this heist."

"Recovery," Zeke said.

She raised a brow, then turned back to Phin. "Kayla and Nicola St. Martin might dwell in the same circles, but their view of what they do with their wealth is as different as oil and water." An indulgent smile pulled at the corner of her mouth. "My friend enjoys sprinkling pepper on the uplifted noses of her societal friends."

Phin turned to Zeke. "Do I have a green light?"

Zeke didn't like bringing outsiders into their recoveries. It opened up too many variables that were impossible to plan for. One mistake on this would have much greater repercussions than simply failing to retrieve someone's property. It would be on their heads if a shitload of drugs hit the streets. Streets populated with kids like Sadie. And Brodie.

Rohan must have sensed his train of thought, because he said, "If Phin does things his normal way and Miss Krowne proves to be the one target in the world he can't charm, we don't have another viable option. Not in our limited time."

Zeke tapped his thumb against his thigh as his gaze jumped from one expectant face to the next.

"No amount of planning is going to get us the object." Grams's fingers curled around his, halting his telltale sign of his need to control a situation. Her voice lowered so only he could hear. "Intuition and trust will see us through."

Swallowing back his instinctive response, he said to Phin, "Don't fu—screw this up."

Phin rubbed his hands together. "Who else is hungry?"

25

———

Liv followed the group through the Annex, listening to their plans to grill burgers on the back patio. Her stomach growled, liking the plan.

Zeke veered off from the pack and entered an office. Rather than making a quick stop to grab something, he sat down in a chair and swiveled around to fire up his computer.

Not realizing she'd paused, she startled when a presence beside her spoke in a quiet voice. "He takes much upon on himself."

She peered down to find Johona Blackwell staring into Zeke's office with concern pulling at the corners of her eyes. Eyes that had witnessed the horrors of war, the loss of a husband and son, the struggle of a beloved grandson.

"Does he not trust his brothers to share the burden?" Liv asked, matching the older woman's tone.

"Once, he did."

"What happened?"

"He became the team's reluctant leader."

"Reluctant?"

Johona nodded toward the exit. "Walk with me?"

They strolled from the Annex, leaving Zeke to his work. Every step Liv took away from him felt like an abandonment, but she didn't want to miss this opportunity to speak with the Blackwell matriarch alone.

She matched the shorter woman's strides. Neither of them spoke until they were on the path leading to the chapel.

Johona was the first to break the companionable silence. "You like my grandson?"

The question caught Liv off-guard. "Of course. All of your grandsons seem like great guys."

"They are." Pride softened the area around her eyes. "They are the best of men." She clasped her hands before her. "But I believe your affection for Ezekiel goes deeper than admiration. Or have I misread the signs?"

She doubted the older woman misread much. Even so, Liv didn't know how to answer her. She liked Zeke. Enjoyed looking at him. Loved having sex with him. She also admired his strategic mind, his business acumen, and his love for his family.

But he wasn't the guy for her and she wasn't the woman for him. Their personal end games diverged, rather than entwined.

The night they'd spent together in Charlotte was nothing more than a flash point, an exciting, explosive moment in both their lives. A moment extinguished by the reality of those lives.

"Your grandson is an attractive man, but I have a nine-year-old son. I don't think Zeke's in the market for an instant family." She glanced back toward the Annex. "He has enough responsibility, I think."

"Family is not a burden to be borne. It's a privilege. A gift."

"It's also hard work."

"As are most important things in life. Josephine Cochrane did not snap her fingers and the world's first dishwasher appeared. Patricia Bath did not invent a laser to dissolve eye cataracts with her magic wand. Mothers across time did not birth, raise, and send their babies off without shedding a little blood and more than a few tears."

Like a locomotive, scenes from the past blew through her mind. Tyler and Brodie kissing her goodbye, rigged out in their baseball jerseys and caps. Brodie sitting alone in a hospital waiting room, the relief on his blotchy face when she arrived. A trio of six-year-olds, mitts in hand, standing on her front porch, confused by their friend's rejection. A four-by-six frame lying facedown.

Liv couldn't imagine what the next three, five, ten years would bring, but what she did know was that she didn't want her son to navigate the teens without a solid father figure to learn from.

Liv had grown up without the guiding hand of a mother and father. Regina and Stanley Thornton spent their free time engaged in social politics rather than nurturing their three children. If not for her aunt and uncle's intervention, who knew what dark path she might have detoured down.

She could raise her son on her own and do a damn fine job of it. But she didn't want that for Brodie—or for herself. She wanted to find them both someone worthy of filling the void Tyler left behind.

Zeke could be that someone. He had the right tools for the job, but not the heart for it.

Johona interrupted her thoughts. "When my grandson Asher oversaw the family business, Ezekiel was content, even thrived in his role as Asher's right hand. The two brothers were inseparable, had been since they were toddlers."

Liv smiled at the image of two dark-headed boys, hand in hand, causing endless mischief with their curious minds and adorable smiles.

"But Asher's heart never belonged to the business. Always, he wanted to help people, to make a positive impact on society, to be something more, something he would never get at home."

"Why didn't he pursue law enforcement earlier? Why work a job he hated?"

"He was his father's son and would have done anything to please the man."

"Even give up his dream job?"

"Even that. After my son, Ashkii—Duke, died, Asher assumed the mantle of responsibility as his father had wanted. He did so faithfully for eight years."

"That's when he left for the FBI?"

Johona nodded.

"Why did he wait for so long?"

"First, to fulfill his promise to his father. Then to make sure Ezekiel was ready."

"Ready for what? To take Cameron—Ash's place?"

"Ezekiel is a strong, confident man, but he never strove for, nor wanted to lead the business. He, like many, thought Asher would be the one to do so until he retired."

"It must have been a shock when Ash left."

"Devastating. He idolized his brother, even though barely twelve months separated them. Within days of Asher's announcement, Ezekiel found himself in charge of the livelihoods of his entire family. A weight he had never experienced while in his brother's comfortable shadow."

Liv could almost picture the moment. Zeke standing before his brothers, ready to give them directions—and choking. Zeke, with his hands cradling his pounding head while his eyes stared uncomprehendingly at his first P&L statement.

"But I've heard the others mention how Zeke reorganized and rebranded the business, turning it into the multi-million-dollar enterprise it is today."

"Even when his father was alive, Ezekiel had ideas on how to expand the business. But my son"—she paused to watch a small, bright yellow bird bob up and down as it crossed their path—"my beloved son could, at times, be both bullheaded and single-minded."

"And Ash didn't have the desire to try anything new?"

Johona sent her a confirming smile. "Ezekiel will never truly be at peace while there's a possibility of failure or disappointing his family. Because of this, he cannot fully put his faith in his brothers to do their jobs, so he questions and hovers and checks. All of which drives a wedge deeper and deeper between him and his team."

"Which creates possibilities for failure and disappointment."

"It is good you understand the circular trap he has created for himself. It will help you help him overcome his fear."

Johona pushed through the chapel's double doors, and the scent of old wood and dusty corners wafted over Liv.

In one visual sweep, she took in the high ceiling, wooden pews, and simple pulpit. Any other time, she would have gone from corner to corner to rub her fingers over the polished surfaces and to study the hand-painted stations of the cross mounted on the walls. But her mind was too busy formulating a response to Johona's puzzling comment.

"What do you mean 'help him'?" She wasn't a psychologist. How could she possibly accomplish something his family hadn't? "I wouldn't know how."

"You already have."

"How?"

Johona ascended the two shallow steps to the dais and turned to stare down at Liv. "My grandson has allowed no one but family and staff to set foot on this property, let alone sleep in our house."

A warm, satisfied feeling curled in Liv's stomach. "Why do you have so many guest rooms if you don't allow visitors?"

"My daughter-in-law plans for every contingency."

"I don't think Lynette cares much for me."

"She will love who her sons love."

"I'm afraid you have misinterpreted Zeke's drive for efficiency. We have a narrow window with which to recover the asset. My staying here gives us a better opportunity to devise a solid plan."

"No one can recall the last time my grandson joked in a meeting before two days ago."

"Mrs. Blackwell, you're putting—"

"Johona or Grams, please."

Liv's throat tightened at the offer. "Johona, you're putting far too much weight on a few niceties."

The older woman shook her head. "I have known my grandson for thirty-four years. I have witnessed his heartbreaks, his triumphs, and now. . . something that will begin the healing process."

She stepped down from the dais and approached Liv, setting a small hand on her forearm. "You will help him." She continued down the aisle. At the door, she took in the chapel's interior before meeting Liv's eye. "This is a good place for a troubled mind to find a moment of peace. Especially when the moon rides high in the sky."

With that, Zeke's grandma left Liv alone in a chapel.

Surrounded by Zeke's secrets.

26

ZEKE TURNED OFF HIS DESK LAMP, BRACED HIS FOREARMS ON his knees, and closed his eyes as his head dropped forward.

He let the darkness roll over him. Tired. He was so fucking tired.

For once, at the end of the day, he'd like to leave behind the team leader, the decision-maker, the man responsible for his family's well-being, and just be Zeke.

The guy who wanted to shoot the shit with his brothers. The guy who wanted to spend Sunday mornings fishing on Lake Junaluska. The guy who wanted to learn new ways to make Olivia Westcott cry out his name.

"Dream on, Blackwell." He rose and stretched out muscles that had sat knotted for far too many hours.

The other offices were dark, and no one lounged in the Theater. Not surprising. It wasn't unusual for him to lock up for the night.

The Theater was where the magic happened. Where the team ironed out the finer details of a recovery and worked out their problems.

Not with each other. Those stayed locked in silos until a

stray missile blew off a door, releasing a mad explosion of new or ancient wounds. Those moments didn't come often, but based on his brothers' growing frustration, the countdown was underway for the next launch.

On the way out, he tapped in his security code and began the slow process of work detox.

He shoved his hands into his front pockets and drew in a lungful of fresh North Carolina air. Crisp and cool, it was a welcome balm to his heated blood. High above, a full moon ascended, whitewashing every blade, leaf, and shingle.

Liv's guess that the St. Martins had invited her friend Kayla Krowne to the benefit had been spot-on. The object she would present to the curator on arrival was a simple, everyday ballpoint pen with purple ink. Nothing flashy, nothing expensive. Just another means of identity verification.

Zeke could think of a dozen other means of achieving the same goal, but rich people enjoyed their own special blend of high drama and games. He often wondered if they had branched off into their own subspecies. *Homo sapiens opulenta?* It would explain a lot.

Unfortunately, Kayla couldn't tell Phin if the objects were unique to each guest or identical. Until they had that information, their recovery was dead in the water.

According to Sardoff, Lupos was in St. Martins' museum. Dead in the water wasn't an option. Somehow, they had to get both Phin and him on the guest list.

He couldn't get this close to the ancient sword only to be thwarted by a damn purple pen or silver fork or whatever nonsense item the guests were supposed to bring. Once he confirmed Lupos's location, he would make the appropriate modifications to the doll's recovery plan and bring home the sword.

Then finally, he could place it above the now-empty fireplace mantel, where he could see it every day. Draw strength and inspiration from its sometimes violent and troubled past.

He recalled Liv's curious expression as she stared at the empty hooks above the fireplace. If Brodie hadn't diverted her attention to the elk head, Zeke would have been forced to give her the same line he'd given his family for the past year. *I have something special in mind.* But somehow, he didn't think Liv would allow him to get by with such a vague answer.

Thank the Almighty for shrieking children.

Without conscious thought, his steps had taken him to the one place that quieted the conflicting voices in his head. Turning the latch, he stepped inside the chapel and paused, giving his eyes time to adjust to the penetrating darkness.

Once he could make out the former communion table on the dais, he strode between the wooden pews and waited for his mental chaos to quiet. Rather than feeling soothed by the peaceful setting, the small space seemed to amplify the riot in his head. Locating the small box on the table, he removed a match and scratched it along the side.

Light flashed and hissed, pushing back the night. He set the flame to three large candles and stared at the flickering columns as if they held the wisdom he sought in the depths of their singed wicks.

Night after night, he sat in the second pew on the right and replayed the day's events, looking for flaws to fix and holes to patch.

There were always holes.

Many he spotted, some he didn't. The holes made uninterrupted sleep impossible. Waking up in a cold sweat was expected, not unusual.

Tonight, his feet were too heavy to carry him to his favored pew. He stayed rooted before the Lord's table. His hands clenched into fists deep in his pockets. Rebellion roared in his heart.

If Ash were still here, would Zeke be curled around Liv's sated body rather than brooding inside an old chapel?

He gripped the edge of the table and squeezed his eyes shut against the erotic images.

One night.

They had spent one night together, and yet he couldn't get her out of his mind. Out of his blood.

How was that possible? Could this be a classic case of wanting what he couldn't have?

He didn't think so.

From the moment he'd seen her in the bar, she'd captured his interest. Within minutes of sliding into the Jacuzzi, he'd realized he wanted more. More than conversation, more than hot, mind-blowing sex. More than one night.

When he woke to find her gone the next morning, he'd vaulted out of bed, thrown on shorts, and rushed down to the lobby. His dishabille drew several curious eyes from the hotel's fully dressed guests.

He couldn't ask the registration clerk if Liv checked out because she'd never shared her last name. Dumbass that he was, he stayed an extra night, hoping she would appear in the bar again.

She hadn't. He'd known it was a long shot. With her business completed, there was nothing to keep her there.

Not even him.

For days, he'd berated himself for not getting her number or a last name. Then she appeared one day, out of the blue. His lover, his one-night stand. His Jacuzzi mate.

An FBI agent. A widow. A mom.

All day, he'd vacillated between wanting to pin her sweet body against a wall, learning what she liked on her pancakes in the morning, and wishing he'd stayed in a different hotel three weeks ago.

There was no room. No room for a steady girlfriend, no room for a troubled boy, no room for fucking happiness.

An ache started at the center of his chest and climbed into his throat. His breaths came faster, his blood pumped hotter.

A low growl erupted from the dark void, where he pushed every fear, every longing, every sacrifice.

His arm struck out, sending candles and hot wax and match sticks across the dais.

A sharp hiss of breath sounded behind him at the same time the candles snuffed out.

Zeke whipped around to find Liv hovering half in and half out of the chapel, as if she'd been in the process of entering when his emotions had exploded.

Their eyes met across the distance, and Zeke hated her in that moment. Hated that she'd witnessed him at his weakest. Hated himself for hating her.

"Zeke, I'm sorry—"

"Get out."

27

Liv's heart thundered at Zeke's raw, menacing command.

Unable to sleep, she'd padded over to the desk to retrieve her copy of Sandra Brown's latest romantic suspense. She'd heard a lot of great things about the novel and tonight seemed a good time to break the spine.

Once again, Johona's soft assurances echoed in her head. *You can help him.*

Before she could register her actions, her bare feet carried her to the window. The Flower Moon blossomed on a velvety black canvas, washing out the stars and blanketing the landscape in a luminous glow.

The chapel's steeple rose above the shimmering trees, beckoning.

She dropped the book on her bed, grabbed an overshirt from the back of a chair, and stuffed her feet into a pair of slip-ons by the door.

Once she faced the chapel's high doors, indecision gnawed at her. Would he be inside? Should she disturb him? Or leave him to his solitude?

You can help him.

No sooner than her body cleared the door did she realize she'd made a terrible, terrible mistake.

The near-feral man before her kept her frozen in place, even though every instinct urged her to leave him to his demons.

She almost did, until he swiped his arm angrily over his face. Even with the room shrouded in thick layers of gloom, she knew what that motion meant. Any mother of a nine-year-old boy inching his way toward manhood would.

"No." She stepped farther into the chapel and the door swung shut behind her.

He turned his back on her. "I'm not in control, Olivia. You need to go."

Moving closer, she forced a lightness into her voice. "Male tantrums ceased to scare me years ago."

"I'm not a boy," he turned and pinned her with his gaze, "and I'm sure as hell not your son."

Closer. "No, Zeke. You're all man. With all the accompanying burdens and fears and frustrations."

Hands on hips, he lifted his face to a small oval-shaped window high on the far wall, but said nothing.

Closer. "I've mastered the art of listening. What happens in chapel stays in chapel."

His voice dropped several octaves. "And if I don't want to talk?"

The mad ramming in her chest froze and sweat coated her palms. Having sex with Zeke would be a bad idea. Having sex with Zeke in a chapel would be a straight ticket to Hell.

Closer.

Once she put her hands on him again, she wouldn't

want to stop. She recalled how hard it had been to leave his bed last time. That was before she knew much about him.

Closer.

She couldn't afford to get into him any more deeply. If she did, it would hurt like hell when she left. And she would leave. There was no alternative.

"As tempting as you are, Zeke, it's not a good idea."

"I know." He stalked toward her.

"We're working together." His advance didn't slow. "Nothing can interfere with this case."

I won't let you break my heart.

He didn't stop until he was close enough for her to drink in his scent. Heat radiated off his body, and an answering bone-deep ache ignited inside her.

When his warm palm cupped her cheek, she tried again to recite the reasons why this wasn't a good idea. But his touch fritzed her circuit, and logic and reason became a memory that remained just out of reach.

Closing her eyes, she placed her hand on his muscled forearm, marveled at the softness of the hairs beneath her fingers, and turned her head to kiss his palm.

His other hand came up to frame her face, forcing her to meet his hungry, tortured eyes. Something cracked in the center of her chest, and she could no longer draw breath.

What had happened to cause him such pain? Such grief?

She'd been a fool to listen to Johona. Even with all of her training, Liv didn't have the tools to help him. Sure, she could give him—them—a hit of euphoric morphine. But when they both came off their shared high, the rock bottom would be harder, more jagged than ever.

Yet, she didn't—couldn't—pull away. Couldn't stop

staring into his eyes, trying to heal him with the sheer force of her will.

When her gaze traced a languid path to his mouth, she stretched upward on her toes.

He seemed to be waiting for that telltale cue of permission, for he tightened his grip on her face and slanted his mouth over hers. His kiss wasn't gentle, nor was it painful.

The sensual pressure sparked every one of her nerve endings. The feel of him, the taste of him. It was all so thrillingly familiar yet excitingly new.

Angling her head, she drew him deeper into the kiss. But a small, reality-check section of her brain kicked in, reminding her of where they were and the obstacles lodged between them.

She slowed the kiss, bringing it to an end. Before she could pull away, Zeke rested his forehead against hers. The intimacy infused in that gentle contact made her throat clench.

"I've wanted to do that for days," he said in a rough voice. His warm breath buffeted her swollen, damp mouth.

"Me too."

"Come back to the Friary with me," he urged.

The temptation was strong. So strong that words of consent formed on her tongue. But going any further with him could only mean pain in her future.

Unable to stop herself, she pressed her lips to his again, savoring the feel and the taste and the scent of him one last time. When she stepped back, confusion flashed through his dark eyes before understanding settled in.

How had she let things spiral out of control between them? She'd come here on a misguided notion that she could help him understand his value to BARS. Instead, she had compounded the problem by adding one more perceived failure to his list.

He could not know, would never know, how close she'd been to ignoring all her warning bells and losing herself in Zeke Blackwell for a few mind-shattering hours.

"I'll see you tomorrow," she said.

He was silent for a long moment, then the hard lines around his mouth and eyes smoothed out. "Sleep well. We have a long day ahead of us tomorrow."

Regret and unspent passion tangled in her chest as she turned to leave. When she opened the door, Zeke called out to her.

"Once we recover the asset," he said in a low, determined voice, "our professional partnership ends."

Bittersweet warmth filled her chest. "I'll still be the mother of a nine-year-old boy who misses his father, and you'll still be leading a complex, demanding business." She stepped into the night air. "A fact that won't change tomorrow night."

Before she shut the door, she heard his resigned murmur, "No, it won't."

28

Zeke drew in a slow breath, held it, and released the drawstring.

His arrow cut through the thin layer of early morning mist and struck the outer ring of the bull's-eye fifty yards away.

After his disastrous attempt to clear his mind last night, he'd decided to see if he'd have more success at the range than the chapel. The simple repetitive motion of flinging arrows downrange never failed to put him in a meditative state.

Plus, he was far enough away from the house to guarantee no fire-haired beauty would make a surprise visit.

All night, his thoughts teeter-tottered between the scorching kiss he'd shared with Liv and the moment at her vehicle when her expression had clouded upon seeing Brodie in his arms. Had she been afraid he would drop the boy? No, she would have been at his heels, ordering him to do this or that.

A potentially scraped knee wasn't what had made tears glisten in her eyes. Something deeper, something far more injurious to the heart had held her immobile in an emotional chokehold.

He could think of only one reason, one person who could cause such a reaction.

Tyler.

Brodie's dad. Her husband. Taken from them in a tragic, horrific accident. Too soon.

His next arrow sailed wide.

Nocking another one, he anchored the drawstring against his cheekbone, drew in three long, controlled breaths, and on the final exhale, released.

The arrow hit the target.

He fired off several more, each one more precise than the last. As he prepared to send another flying, a faint shuffle behind him snagged his attention.

Biting back a curse, he lowered his bow. "Can't this wait another fifteen minutes?" He turned to deliver a blistering stare to whichever brother dared to intrude. Only it wasn't one of his kin nosing into his sanctuary.

Still wearing his pajamas, Brodie Westcott hovered near a thick tree trunk. He must have heard Zeke pass by his room and followed him.

Zeke wiped the scowl from his face and attempted a welcoming smile. "Morning. You're up early."

Silence.

"Does your mom know you're here?"

A short, negative shake.

"Have you ever shot a bow and arrow before?"

Another shake.

"Interested in trying?"

The boy eyed the compound bow's cams and cables.

"Not this one." He pointed to a ten-by-fifteen secured building where they kept their range supplies. "I have another bow more your size and experience." He refrained from telling him that Sadie used it, knowing how sensitive boys could be about such things.

Brodie nodded.

"Come with me and we'll get you outfitted."

The command seemed to break through the boy's shyness. He smiled and joined Zeke for the short walk to the range building. Zeke shot Liv a text, not wanting her to worry if she woke up early and found her son missing.

By the time they reached their destination, Zeke had shrugged off his irritation at being interrupted and focused on taking advantage of this opportunity to get to know Liv's son.

Other than at the dinner table, he hadn't crossed paths with the boy since Liv's arrival and found himself wondering about this piece of her life.

"Wow," Brodie said upon seeing the array of bows, arrows, and other archery gadgets.

"A few ground rules," he said. "No touching unless I give you permission. These aren't toys. Understood?"

The boy nodded. "Yes, sir."

Zeke lifted a simple, lightweight longbow from a wall peg and held it out to him. "Give this one a try."

Brodie took the bow with hesitant hands, his eyes round with wonder and curiosity. Curling the tips of his fingers around the finger guard, he gave the drawstring an experimental pull, surprised by its tightness.

"Don't worry. You'll get used to it." He took the bow from him and settled it back on the peg. "Let's get you geared up. Safety first when working with weapons. Left-handed or right-handed?"

Brodie held up a hand. "Right."

Zeke strapped a child-sized armguard around the boy's left forearm. "This will protect your arm from string burn."

"String burn?"

"It can take a while to learn how to position your arm so the string doesn't hit it." He grabbed a pair of small safety glasses from a box and hooked them over the boy's nose and ears. "Safety first." The likelihood of an eye injury from an exploding bow was low, but Duke Blackwell had always insisted his boys wear safety glasses while using any weapon. "Now it's time to select your arrows."

Brodie went straight for the wicked-looking metal broad heads.

"Not those." He pointed to a section of shorter arrows with aerodynamic target points. "Those."

"But—"

"No buts. You gotta earn your way to the big dogs."

With a little less enthusiasm, Brodie started pulling out arrows with blue, green, and red fletching, bypassing the whites, yellows, and pinks.

Once he had six in hand, Zeke held out a leather quiver, and Brodie dropped the arrows into the narrow tube. Zeke helped him position the quiver on his back and adjusted the strap before holding out his bow. "You're ready to shoot now."

That perked him up again, and the boy followed him back to the range.

"Sit tight for a second." He strode to the nearest target and moved it to within five yards of the shoot line and returned to Brodie's side. "Ready?"

"Uh-huh."

Zeke grabbed his bow off the rack and notched an arrow, showing Brodie what he was doing each step of the way and waiting for him to follow suit.

"The key to a smooth release is to inhale when you pull back the string and exhale when you let it go."

Brodie looked a bit dubious.

"Watch me."

Zeke put words to action, adjusted his aim so the arrow would land on the outer ring, and released. The arrow *thunked* into the target. "Piece of cake, right?"

Brodie did his best to mimic Zeke's technique, and the arrow whirred drunkenly to the ground four feet away.

"Nice," Zeke said.

The boy gave him an are-you-blind look.

"Archery, like riding a bike, takes practice—and a whole lot of determination."

Zeke notched another arrow, adjusted his aim, and released. The arrow sank three inches closer to the bull's-eye.

"See? Practice." He pulled an arrow from Brodie's stash and handed it to him. "Give it another try."

Brodie got his arrow ready, but Zeke could see he was just going to let it rip in order to get it over with.

"Be patient with yourself. Anchor close to your eye and look straight down the arrow." He demonstrated as he spoke and waited for the boy to comply. "That's good. Now take a deep breath. On exhale, release your arrow."

Brodie did as instructed and his arrow hit the outermost ring of the target.

"Yes!" Brodie pumped his fist in the air.

Zeke clasped a hand around the boy's shoulder. "Well done. Now do that a dozen more times."

"A dozen?"

"Maybe a hundred." He set his bow back in the rack. "Whatever it takes to get good, right?"

Brodie eyed the distance to the target. His back straightened and his grip on his bow firmed.

In that moment, Zeke saw Liv's rock-hard tenacity in every line of her son's features.

"Give it a go."

Brodie loosed two more arrows. Each one hit the target in various places.

When he prepared to let the third one fly, Liv appeared, following Sadie. Her eyes widened at the sight of her son holding a weapon.

Although her motherly instincts no doubt wanted to stop him, her FBI training kicked in and she held her tongue. Instead of startling her son, she fixed a narrowed-eyed stare on Zeke.

Shit.

He must have violated a parental rule or ignored some societal norm about weapons. Zeke's parents had never denied him or his brothers access to guns, knives, or arrows. As long as they were trained to use them, they could. Any time they were caught horsin' around with a weapon, it was the last time they touched it.

Brodie's arrow nipped the edge of the bull's eye. "Holy cow! Did you see, Zeke?"

"Even better," he hooked a thumb over his shoulder. "Your mom and Sadie did, too."

He looked past Zeke and his grin widened.

Liv produced a smile. "Great job, Brodie. Robin Hood has nothing on you."

When the boy's attention shifted to Sadie, a blush heated his ears.

"Do it again," Sadie said, moving closer but staying at a safe distance.

Brodie looked at Zeke, who gave him a nod.

He backed up a few feet, giving the kids some space. A half a second later, Liv materialized at his side, as he knew she would.

In a low, controlled voice, she said, "Thank you for the text."

Zeke nodded, keeping his eyes on the kids, and waited for the ass-chewing.

"Next time you communicate my son's whereabouts, kindly convey more info than—*Brodie at the range*."

"Like what?"

"Oh, I don't know. Maybe he's safe or directions to the damn range or no need to break your neck rushing out of the house."

"You knew he was with me," he said. "I wouldn't let anything happen to your son."

29

LIV HELD BACK THE MYRIAD OF LETHAL RESPONSES THAT CAME to mind. They would be wasted on Zeke. In his mind, he'd communicated all he needed to in order to put her mind at ease.

She glanced up at him, noticing how he never took his eyes off the kids while Brodie emptied his quiver.

Maybe he was right. Maybe knowing Brodie was with him was all the info she needed.

One day, maybe. Not today. Today, she had needed specifics.

"How did you get him to shoot? He hasn't been interested in any outdoor sport since—"

"Since his dad died?"

She nodded, crossing her arms. Even now, she still found it difficult to talk about Tyler's death.

"You mentioned a foul ball before. Brodie was there?"

A piercing pain climbed up her throat, and her vision blurred. "Yes."

Zeke's large, warm hand slid against her lower back and

his big body angled in front of her. "Liv, I'm sorry. I shouldn't have pried."

"Zeke," Sadie called. "Can we get Brodie's arrows?"

He gave the girl a sharp nod and motioned them to proceed downrange.

A year or two older than her son, Sadie seemed at home on the archery field, especially with its safety rules. Impressive for one so young.

"Does she come here with you often?" Liv asked.

"With me, with Cruz, with Phin—anyone. She seems to have a sixth sense about when one of us is here."

"I think you're right. Thankfully, I ran into her during my search for the range."

He gave her a sidelong glance. "I promise to be more specific next time."

"She's the daughter of one of your employees? Besides Clara, I mean."

"My maintenance manager Alejandro Rios. They came with the property."

"What do you mean 'came with'?"

"Employing Alejandro was part of the purchase agreement for the Friary." He looked around the property. "It wasn't a hardship. Alejandro knows every inch of this place. If not for him and his small crew, the Friary and chapel would have fallen into disrepair years ago."

"They live on property?"

"In one of the refurbished camp cabins."

"This is an unusual place for a business such as yours."

"Why's that?"

"Charlotte or Raleigh or Wilmington seems like more profitable places to set up shop."

"Ours is a fairly mobile business. Once we understand the job's scope, we can plan here and execute anywhere."

He cast her a knowing look. "If you don't want to talk about him, just say so. No need to pull the redirect game on me."

Liv's gaze shifted quickly to Brodie. "I have a lot of . . . unresolved anger surrounding my husband's death. I try not to subject people to such unpleasantness. When people ask about the incident, they typically want the gory details, not out-of-control feelings."

"Anger I can deal with, and I could care less about gore." He glanced between her and Brodie. "Maybe you both have some emotions bottled up that you need to pour out."

"Five months of therapy only made my son erect more barriers, and no amount of prodding could entice him outside. Observing his father's death not only put Brodie off of baseball but all outdoor sports."

"Baseball never truly leaves a boy's blood. The game will ebb and flow around school and girls and career and family," Zeke's attention shifted to Brodie, "until one day he hands over his worn, smelly glove to his own son." He looked at her. "Be patient. The game will whisper in his blood again."

"I hope so"—she swallowed back a lump of tears that kept edging into her throat—"Regardless, it's good to see him outside, enjoying himself again."

"He's in a new space with new people. A certain amount of curiosity is natural."

"Whatever it was that coaxed him out of his room, I'm grateful. Thank you for your kindness. I'm sure it's tough to find alone time with so many people about."

"He's a good kid."

Brodie and Sadie ran back to the shoot line.

"Mama, did you see me hit the bull's eye? Well, almost. I clipped the corner."

"I did, sweetheart." She strode over and gave him a quick hug. "Let's return your equipment. Zeke and I need to go to work."

"One more round, Mama. Please. Sadie needs to shoot."

She checked the clock on her phone, then looked at Zeke.

"We have time," he said.

"One more round, then it's time to clean up."

Both kids' faces lit up with grins. "Thank you!"

Sadie encouraged Brodie to shoot three more arrows before they traded places.

As the girl pulled back her first arrow, Brodie exclaimed, "Wait!" He moved the safety glasses from his face to hers and transferred the arm guard from his arm to hers. "Safety first." Sadie smiled her thanks, waited for him to move back, and took aim.

Liv stared at Zeke. "You've made quite an impression on my son in a short amount of time."

"Safety is one of the first lessons my dad taught us. Feeling safe boosts a person's confidence. Safety plus confidence leads to fewer accidents."

Zeke's attraction for Brodie likely had more to do with his easy manner than his lesson on safety, but she'd let it go for now.

A shadow of unease danced around the edge of her conscience. She liked that Brodie felt comfortable around Zeke, but what would happen when the case ended, and they went home?

Was she setting up her son for another devastating heartbreak? She didn't know, but every instinct in her body screamed for her to protect her son from further pain.

Liv's phone chimed with a new text message. She dug it out of her back pocket and checked her screen.

Kayla: *What are you wearing tonight?*

Liv frowned. Did they have something going on? No, everything went into her calendar. If she had something scheduled tonight, she would've received a "one day before" notification yesterday.

Liv: *Uh, why?*

Kayla: *Your mother's dinner?!*

An "Oh, shit" flush washed over her.

Liv: *That's tonight?*

Kayla: *Don't even try to ditch. I'm not facing Nicola alone.*

Liv: *Nicola St. Martin will be there?*

One heartbeat.

Two.

Three.

Kayla: *Are you taking a new medication? Or did Thanos turn the real Liv to ash?*

"Crap."

"Problem?" Zeke asked.

"It's Kayla, asking me what I'm wearing tonight."

He stilled beside her. "You going out?"

"My mother's dinner party. It's not in my calendar and completely slipped my mind."

"That bad?"

"You have no idea." She ripped off another message to Kayla, throwing out the first dress that came to mind, before stuffing her phone back in her pocket. "She said Nicola and Hugh St. Martin will be there, too. Might be an opportunity for me to wheedle some intel out of her about the mysterious object, though I don't see that happening since I don't possess the proper equipment."

Hugh would be a safer bet, but Liv would have to indulge in some liquid courage before going that route. Now she understood why she hadn't been able to reach her mom. Regina had been in party planning mode.

"Sounds like you could use a partner?"

Liv lifted a brow. "You want to attend a dinner party?"

"Hell, no."

His answer made her both relax and stiffen. "Were you thinking Phin, then?"

He mulled over her question. "You think Kayla would take my brother as her plus one?"

"If she doesn't already have one, I don't see why not." Confused, she asked, "If not you or Phin, who did you have in mind for my partner?"

"Me."

"But you said—"

"That I didn't want to go, not that I wouldn't."

"Phin could work on Nicola, while you and I could press her husband for information. Maybe one of us would get lucky."

Liv's heart pounded. "It's a good plan. Phin said he could charm anyone, and Nicola loves a handsome face."

"But?"

"If you go with me, my family will assume there's something going on between us. Their scrutiny could be . . . intense."

"Because you haven't brought a guy home since Brodie's father?"

She nodded. "It would be an *event*."

"I can handle it if you can."

"It won't be a matter of 'handling' the situation. It'll be a series of defensive moves that will leave you dizzy and slightly paralyzed."

"Methinks you're exaggerating."

"Methinks you're not giving this enough consideration."

Zeke was quiet for a moment. "Is there another reason you don't want me to escort you?"

"Like what?"

"I don't know, you tell me." His attention flicked to the kids. "I saw the way you looked at me when I carried Brodie to the house."

He had noticed. She wished she could set his mind at ease, but the truth was she still hadn't worked through the conflicting feelings of seeing her son in another man's arms.

"There's no other reason," she lied. "I'm just trying to protect you from my well-meaning, but aggressive, family."

"Then it's a date."

Although accidentally, she had just presented the team with a potential breakthrough in their recovery effort. But rather than enthusiasm and appreciation, Zeke's tone was flat, unemotional.

As if a light flickered out somewhere deep in his heart.

The practice soon ended, and they stashed away the equipment before leaving the range. As if by written agreement, Zeke and Sadie veered toward the Annex and Liv and Brodie went to the Friary to finish their morning rituals.

The farther Liv moved away from Zeke, the more her unease grew. She wanted Brodie to get to know Zeke. She wanted to know him better, too.

But her cautionary voice took a stab at her floundering resolve.

Would the cost be greater than the reward?

30

Liv sipped her wine as she watched Zeke navigate her mother's numerous and, no doubt, probing questions.

Not once did he exhibit frustration, irritation, or the multitude of other emotions Regina Thornton could bring out in her victims.

On the drive over, she and Zeke had hashed out a back-story on how they met. One that didn't include a steaming Jacuzzi and hot stranger sex, but could withstand a curious mother whose daughter hadn't brought a guy to dinner since Tyler.

Regina wasn't a matchmaking mama. Far from it. She never tried to set up her children with her friends' kids, nor did she pry incessantly into their love lives. But her on-again, off-again parent's insatiable curiosity would discover what made Zeke so special as to warrant a family intro-duction.

Aunt Belinda caught her eye and winked as she moved to join the interrogation. Liv shook her head hard and made a don't-you-dare motion with her finger.

The older woman ignored her. Why she bothered to try

to intimidate a thirty-year law enforcement veteran she didn't know. If she'd been close enough to tackle the old tarheel in order to keep the two Thornton women away from Zeke, she would have.

Although Regina and Belinda were as different as winter and summer, the two found common ground when it came to the Thornton kids' happiness.

"What I wouldn't do to be a fly on your boyfriend's shoulder right now," Kayla Krowne said, absently swirling her wine around her glass.

Liv sent her friend a quelling look. "Enjoying yourself?"

"Immensely." Her generous red lips broadened into a wide smile. "I feel like one of your—What do you call them? Confidential informants?"

Liv's fingers tightened around her wineglass. She hadn't thought to ask Zeke what his brother had shared with Kayla to get her cooperation. Caught up in her own emotional turmoil, she hadn't stopped to consider what she'd say when she and Kayla found themselves alone together. "Informant?" She forced out a chuckle. "How so?"

"Don't play coy with me, *Agent Westcott*. I know you and these Blackwell boys are working a case together. Phin's good, but I wrote the book on the art of artifice."

Liv's mind scrambled for a response that would appease her friend without giving too much away or deepening her involvement. "Why did you agree to bring Phin tonight if you knew he wasn't giving you the full story?"

"To get the full story, of course. I love a good mystery, especially if people like Nicola St. Martin are at the root of it."

Kayla loved nothing more than mingling with strangers and ferreting out their secrets. She had built her lobbying firm on the strength of the connections she had curried over the years. But Liv also knew such demanding work came with a price. One her friend gladly paid, but pay it she did.

Kayla sent her a sidelong look before sipping her wine. "What I don't understand is why you sent Phin to get information from me, rather than ask me yourself."

The note of hurt in her voice made Liv flinch. "Sorry, Kayla. My work on this case is supposed to be behind the scenes. More advisory than anything. Definitely not boots on the ground, but he"—she nodded toward Zeke—"is as tenacious as someone else I know."

Kayla laughed. "You make tenacity sound like a disease."

"Isn't it?" Liv watched Phin work his way toward them. "Besides, your former intern seemed to see you as a challenge." She leaned into her friend and spoke in a conspiratorial whisper. "Anything going on there?"

"With Phin? I'm like six years older than him."

Liv chuckled.

"Wow, that really made me sound ancient, didn't it?"

"Here I thought you were a modern woman."

"Phin's like family. Now, if his older brother were to look my way, I'd be tempted to take an evening off of work and go play."

Liv's heart leapt into her throat. "They're all older. Which one would inspire the mighty Kayla Krowne to ignore politics for an entire evening?"

"Since you don't have a claim on Zeke..."

An image of Kayla's curvy body snuggled in Zeke's arms caused the blood in her veins to sizzle. "Bossy isn't your type."

"Not out of bed, no." Kayla slanted a glance at her. "In bed, I do love a man who—"

"He has a lot going on right now."

"Including you?" Kayla sent her a knowing smile and

held up a hand when Liv started to protest. "Good thing I was talking about the eldest-of-them-all brother."

"Cameron? Have you two met?"

"Briefly." Kayla grinned as if reliving the memory. "He seemed to take an instant dislike of me."

"Hello, ladies," Phin said, arriving at Kayla's side and giving them both a megawatt smile. "Sorry, Liv. Do you mind if I borrow Kayla?"

"Not at all," she said with great meaning.

Kayla laughed, hooking her arm around her escort's. "I believe I've worn out my welcome, Phin. Do you have a new victim for me?"

"As a matter of fact, I do."

"Lead away." Kayla's gaze caught Liv's. "Tenacity is just another word for passion." The power duo sauntered away.

Liv barely had time to digest the lobbyist's cryptic remark before she heard her sister's voice calling to her.

Turning, she took in Callie's shimmering black, knee-length bodycon dress with a deep V-neck and matching black stilettos. Her little sister looked stunning. Not surprising though. Caledonia Thornton, like Kayla Krowne, would look terrific in a potato sack cinched up at the neck.

What surprised Liv was the handsome, brown-haired man at her side. Liv smiled a greeting and bussed her sister's cheek.

Callie linked her arm with Liv's and leaned into her, as she'd done a thousand times before—right before she stirred up trouble. "Liv, this is Mason."

Liv moved to shake his hand, but Callie's next words stopped her cold.

"Your date."

"Pardon."

"Your date." Callie gave her a conspirator's smile. "I told

you I'd take care of you."

Panic whirled in her stomach, and her gaze instinctively sought Zeke. He still held court with her mother and aunt. As if her mortification wafted across the spacious room and found refuge in his nose, Zeke's head lifted, following the scent, until his dark gaze locked on her, then Mason.

A large, powerful hand wrapped around Liv's, wrenching her attention back to Callie's latest devilry.

"Nice to meet you, Liv," Mason said.

A month ago, Mason's smiling green eyes, roguish mouth, and broad shoulders would have kindled a warm, anticipatory flutter low in her stomach. Tonight, his presence made her guts cramp.

Extracting her hand, she smiled. "I believe there's been a misunderstanding. I already have a date."

"You do not." Callie searched the room for likely suspects.

"I can find male companionship on my own, dear sister."

"Where is he?"

"Mother is currently extracting his ancestry and personal history, decade by decade."

Callie craned her neck. "Oh, my." Then her eyes widened. "That's *him*. Why didn't you tell me?"

"Funny, but I believe that's my line."

In a huff, Callie moved to Mason's side and linked her arm with his. "Looks like you're stuck with me tonight, handsome."

Mason studied Liv for a heartbeat longer before covering Callie's hand with his. "I could think of worse fates."

Something over Liv's shoulder caught her sister's attention before she announced, "Let's find the Swedish meatballs." She yanked her escort in the opposite direction.

"Olivia, darling," a velvety, cultured voice crooned. "It's

been an age."

Nicola St. Martin materialized at her side. The wealthy socialite's midnight hair was pulled back into an elegant chignon, complimenting the boat neckline of her caped sheath dress. The blush color was a stunning contrast to her sun-kissed complexion.

A casual observer might peg her for early forties. But a closer inspection would detect the unnatural firmness around the woman's eyes, mouth, and forehead.

Money was a great preservative.

After the obligatory cheek bussing, Nicola gave Liv's navy-blue chiffon dress with its tulip hem an approving glance. Liv might have turned her back on her mother's lifestyle, but that didn't mean she lacked an eye for fashion. She simply preferred comfort ninety percent of the time.

"Gorgeous, as always," Nicola said. "I understand you have not come alone tonight. Do you want to point him out? Or shall I guess?"

Liv nodded toward the trio on the other side of the room. "He's currently undergoing Thornton interrogation."

Nicola followed Liv's gaze, and smiled. "Your mother has been waiting years to sink her teeth into another marital prospect. Callie is too young, and Pierce has yet to present an eligible young woman." She angled her head in the way predators do when sizing up their prey. "He's quite extraordinary, my dear. If only I were twenty years younger."

Liv didn't miss the fact that she didn't include "unmarried" in her list of qualifications.

It was widely known that the St. Martins enjoyed an open marriage. According to those in the know, Hugh spent his winters at their Miami home and Nicola preferred the Vail scene.

She tried not to judge people's choices, especially if

those choices hurt no one. But she simply couldn't wrap her mind around sharing someone she loved with another woman—women.

Watching woman after woman, young and old, approach Zeke tonight had proven one thing to her. Her starving heart had already attached itself to the dark-eyed devil. The splintering that she had hoped to head off would begin the moment she said goodbye.

Something of her thoughts must have registered on her face, for Zeke extricated himself from his interrogators and made a beeline toward her.

"Interesting," Nicola said.

Liv tore her gaze away from Zeke. "Pardon?"

"Your escort is more than a convenient plus-one. Regina suspected as much."

"My mother spoke to you about Zeke and me?"

"Of course. We have been friends since high school. There are few topics off-limits."

It shouldn't bother her that this woman knew her mother better than she. But it did.

Many times, over the years, she had wished for a closer relationship with Regina Thornton. One where they gossiped together, shopped together, went on long walks together.

No such relationship existed between the two of them. Liv didn't even know her mother's favorite color or food or book.

Parties and travel and meetings occupied her mother's time, and Liv didn't see her busy schedule changing any time soon.

When Zeke joined them, he snaked an arm around Liv's waist and drew their bodies together like two Kit Kat bars. If the lack of personal space didn't tip everyone off that they had slept together, his lingering kiss to her temple set aside anyone's doubts.

"Did I miss anything?" he asked in a low, sexy voice.

Despite knowing the warmth in his voice was for their audience, she still had to draw in a calming breath before answering.

"Zeke, let me introduce you to Mrs. St. Martin, my mother's dear friend."

"Nicola, please." She held out her hand. "Mrs. St. Martin makes me feel so old." Her mouth curled into a suggestive smile. "And I do not want to feel old in your presence."

"Impossible," Zeke said.

In true James Bond fashion, he kissed the back of her outstretched hand, never taking his eyes off the older woman's. Nicola's chest seemed to expand twice its size, though Zeke's attention never wavered from her face.

A moment later, he straightened, releasing her hand slowly, almost reluctantly.

A woman would have to be stone cold inside not to be affected by such sensual masculinity. Nicola, with all her sophistication, didn't prove to be an exception.

"Hmm," the older woman all but purred. "I can see why Olivia is protective of you." Her hazel eyes took on a speculative look, then cleared as if she had come to a decision.

In the distance, a deep voice called the guests into dinner.

Nicola gestured to her husband, then snaked her arm through Zeke's. She looked at Liv. "You don't mind swapping partners for dinner, do you, dear? Hugh will be happy to escort you."

The socialite didn't wait for an answer. She swept forward, displaying Zeke as if he were a newly acquired Van Gogh.

31

Zeke needed a drink. A real drink. Not this fruity red stuff mellowing in a stiletto-style glass, but a stout tumbler full of amber liquid that burned a path all the way to a man's gut.

Five would do the trick. Enough to give him a good buzz, but not enough to take away his capacity for logical thought or ability to enunciate his words. He would need both in order to achieve tonight's mission.

Rather than succumbing to Phin's obvious charms, Nicola St. Martin had taken a fancy to Zeke. It didn't seem to matter that he was here with Liv. If anything, the fact appeared to incite the socialite's competitive instincts.

Nicola was a master at verbal swordplay. She'd spent the last thirty years sharpening her weapon on some of the brightest minds in North Carolina. According to Liv, the socialite had influenced the outcome of many local elections with her wit and financial generosity.

Six. Maybe he could eke out a sixth bourbon and still deliver an Oscar-winning performance.

When Nicola leaned toward him for the dozenth time,

her full breast brushing his arm, he wondered if she'd marked him as her next acquisition. Zeke swallowed, feeling an invisible snare tighten around his nuts.

"Do you like art?" Nicola asked.

His pulse ratcheted up at this first sign that their plan was working. He looked across the table at Liv, who appeared to be engrossed in cutting her salad into tiny, even squares, rather than following the unfolding drama.

At least she'd been spared the other St. Martin's attentions. Hugh, another space invader, had set his predatory sights on Kayla, who seemed extraordinarily amused by the situation.

Another breast brush against his arm brought his attention back to his dinner partner. Producing a slow smile, he said, "I do."

Play the part, Blackwell. Play the damn part.

He forced his eyes to roam over her features. Still a beautiful woman in her mid-fifties, Nicola St. Martin must have been a stunner in her unblemished youth. Not as beautiful as Liv, but she would have turned many a masculine head. "The older, the better."

She chuckled, low and melodic. "I'm hosting a fundraiser tomorrow night for the Asheville Art Museum at my home. Donors will be treated to a viewing of a few pieces from my private collection."

"Private collection?" he teased. "Like a cabinet of curiosities?"

Another soft laugh, followed by an admonishing squeeze of his forearm. Her hand didn't move away.

In a louder voice, she said, "My collection is much too big for a cabinet."

"Turned my entire basement into a museum for her *trea-*

sures," Hugh interjected, sitting opposite his wife and between Liv and Kayla.

Nicola stiffened beside him, but her lighthearted expression never wavered.

"It must be difficult to keep such a large collection secure," he said.

She turned a provocative smile on him. "Nothing is difficult to achieve with the right amount of money."

Any thought of coaxing intelligence from her about the museum's security system vaporized. She was too savvy and too protective.

But was she also possessive? If she was, his Plan B would sink in the water as well.

"Having a museum of artifacts in one's home is so intriguing," Zeke said. "I can't imagine anything more stimulating than strolling down aisles of history whenever the whim struck me."

Nicola's fingers slid from his arm to his thigh for a moment. "If only my husband shared your enthusiasm."

"Any time you would like an appreciative observer, I'm only a phone call away."

When she didn't take the bait, he nodded toward her other dinner partner. "My brother Phin is also an appreciator of the arts and will ooh and ahh at all the right moments."

"I'm a brilliant ooh-er," Phin said immediately, as if he'd been waiting for an opportunity to get into the game.

Nicola lifted her wineglass to her lips, directing her next comment to Zeke. "You are becoming more interesting by the minute, Mr. Blackwell."

Every cell in Zeke's body screamed for him to bring up the fundraiser again, to secure his invitation, and to end this painful charade. But Liv had cautioned them that Nicola loved the chase as much as the capture.

So he would sit here and endure her exploratory fondling and suggestive glances until he got what they came for. The only way he could survive the evening, though, was by imagining that it was Liv next to him instead.

"As are you, Nicola," he said.

"I always hold back a few tickets for my fundraisers." She studied him from the corner of her eye. "For last-minute special guests."

Zeke raised a brow. "Is that an invitation?"

"It depends." Her expression transformed from playful to shrewd. "The price per ticket is far above the average person's means."

He swallowed back a surge of bile and hit the fastball as hard as he could. Lowering his voice to an intimate whisper, he said, "Have I given you reason to believe that I am in any way average?"

Heat pulsed in her eyes as they tracked their way down his body, pausing on his lap before meeting his gaze. "My assistant will be in touch."

With that, she turned to Phin and began a lively discussion about the weather.

The triumph Zeke had expected to feel upon securing entrée to the St. Martins' fundraiser never came. Instead, he felt as if someone had dumped a truckload of foul-smelling sludge on his chest.

A sound to his left shifted his attention from his cooling plate of food to Regina Thornton. The woman wore a murderous expression, and it was directed at him.

When he looked at Liv in confusion, he found her chair empty.

32

ZEKE CAUGHT UP WITH LIV IN WHAT MANY WOULD CALL A library, but the statues, artwork, and other foreign bric-a-brac occupying every surface suggested the room was much more than a place to kick up one's heels and read.

The faint scent of incense hung in the air, reminding him of the earthy aromas that always clung to Grams's hair and clothes.

Liv stood before a pair of tall windows overlooking a distant mountain-scape. The setting sun painted the three tallest peaks in liquid gold while the valley below rested in shadow.

"Every time my parents would return home from one of their trips," Liv said, not turning around as he entered, "they would add a memento to this room."

She turned away from the window and moved toward a cream throw that draped one corner of the pinstriped sofa. Her fingers slid over the material as if wiping away dust to reveal one childhood memory at a time.

"They would gather the three of us together and unveil their newest acquisition with a flourish." She continued moving around the room, touching each surface she passed. "Unlike Nicola St. Martin," she glanced at him, "my parents brought home items that held personal meaning to them. They weren't necessarily old or of any particular value."

"True treasures, then."

"After the unveiling, my father would spin a tale of how they came into possession of the piece. The tale always included bits about the country, its history, and its people and their customs."

"Sounds like you've been training for your position since childhood."

"I never thought about that." Her expression grew even more thoughtful, as if reevaluating those early years. "I suppose you're right."

Zeke moved farther into the room, not sure what to make of her mood. He wasn't sure what he'd expected when he left the dinner table to track her down, but it wasn't measured contemplation.

"Once Callie and Pierce hit their tweens," she continued, "they dreaded, no, make that resented, attending my parents' recap of their trips. But not me. I gobbled up those precious moments with my family, even though I wished they would've taken us all with them." She paused her circuit to meet his eye. "It wasn't until I brought my future husband home to meet my parents that I realized my parents had collected no memories of my childhood. None."

Zeke felt an answering pang in his chest. A bookshelf in the Friary's Great Room was dedicated to family photo albums. The albums started out thin, but as the family grew, so did the thickness of the albums.

Knowing how tough it was for his mother to be away from her boys while serving in the military, Grams had documented every missed birthday, scraped knee, touch-down, and slippery fish for his mom.

Once Lynette Blackwell retired from service, the albums got thinner again, eventually giving over to cloud storage.

"Your parents probably have a pile of photos hidden away in shoe boxes somewhere," he said.

"The only photos that track my youth are the obligatory school pictures. Many of which I would prefer to burn than keep." She crossed her arms over her middle, one hand absently rubbed her bare arm as if chilled by the retelling. "Don't get me wrong. My parents are good people—just preoccupied by their own pursuits."

Preoccupied was one word for their treatment. Others might call it neglect.

Although he enjoyed learning more about her, no matter how heart-wrenching, he didn't understand why she chose this moment to share this bit of her life with him.

His tête-à-tête with Nicola St. Martin had obviously bothered her, but he couldn't see a connection between the two events. "Why are you telling me this?"

"For years, I sought whatever small morsel of time my parents would give me. I craved it from one adventure to the next, not realizing what I really wanted, what I searched for in their cool smiles, stiff hugs, and feigned interest, was their love."

She stood before him. Close enough for him to see the vulnerability in her eyes. Far enough away for him to recognize the Do Not Cross Line etched between them.

"What is it you're searching for?" she asked.

Sinew gripped bone. "What do you mean?"

"Your performance back there. It was more personal than professional."

"I did what I needed to do to accomplish the mission, which was to get intelligence from the St. Martins."

"Bravo. She practically drooled an invitation to her fundraiser into your lap."

"You're jealous."

"Irritatingly so." She crossed her arms. "You still haven't answered my question."

"There's nothing to answer. I did my job."

"Does Nicola have the sword?" she asked in a low voice.

33

Liv watched Zeke's body jerk, as if his heart rocked to a sudden, jarring halt.

"Sword?" he asked, his voice razor-sharp.

"A longsword with wolf heads on the pommel and *Family First* inscribed on the guard. Been in your family since the sixteenth century." She held his gaze. "Sound familiar?"

"How did you learn about it?"

"From you."

His eyes flared for a moment before they returned to suspicious slits. "Not possible."

"Five weeks ago, I spent the night in your hotel room."

His stare could have set forests ablaze. "You went through my files?"

"You left a folder splayed open. I rarely sleep through the night. Even after such," her attention dipped down to his mouth, remembering how attentive it could be, "rigorous activity. There's not much else to do at three a.m. than read."

She didn't think it was possible, but his eyes narrowed more. "If you were looking for something to do, you should have woken me." His voice lowered. "I would have been happy to give you something to do with those hands besides thumbing through my personal papers."

An image of his hard, naked body against the white sheets surfaced, and her hands tingled with the need to run them over every hard plane and smooth crevice.

Something of her thoughts must have shone on her face, for his expression turned molten. Or was that fury?

She reached for levity. "Noted. The next time I'm in a hotel room with a stranger and can't sleep, I'll shake him awake instead of reading his luggage tag."

Rather than breaking the tension, her comment made the atmosphere around them stretch tighter.

He stepped closer. "No."

"No, what?" she asked carefully, though her voice remained firm.

"No more fucking strangers in hotels."

Even while his possessive tone stirred something primitive and wanton deep inside, it contrarily tripped her independence wire.

"Until I have a ring on this finger," she flipped him a ring finger, "I'll fuck whoever I want to fuck."

His eyes blinked twice in rapid succession, and Liv reviewed her angry words.

Shit.

"That's not a hint or a suggestion or whatever else is scrambling your mind," she rushed to clarify. "But my body is mine to give to whom I want until I'm committed to another."

He reached out to cup her cheek. Warmth spread along the side of her face, compelling her to lean into his touch. Her eyes fluttered closed.

"Then commit to me," he said in a guttural voice.

Her eyes snapped open in time to see his head descend toward hers.

When his mouth molded with hers, she could no longer remember the myriad of reasons it was a bad idea to sink deeper into Zeke's kiss.

Why she shouldn't bury her fingers in his soft, thick hair. Why she shouldn't press her body into his.

Logic and reason and motherly instincts faded into the background as his hands blazed a path up the long curve of her back. His mouth seared her cheek, her neck, and the sensitive hollow at the base of her throat.

A moan escaped. She needed to be closer. Her leg followed the telepathic command and hooked itself around his hip.

His mouth sought hers again, ravaged it while his hands clasped her bottom and lifted.

Even though her brain had stopped functioning minutes ago, her legs seemed to have developed their own consciousness. They wrapped around him the moment her feet left the floor. Anchored him to her in an intimate embrace.

Their tongues tangled in long, drugging kisses. She wanted to feel the hot press of his skin against hers, the thickness of his cock stretching her, soothing her with long, slow glides, and fast, pounding possession.

A throat cleared.

Like she would a mosquito, she mentally batted the irritating noise away and reached for Zeke's zipper.

The throat cleared more loudly, breaking through the erotic haze. As one, she and Zeke stilled and rolled their heads toward the open doorway.

Kayla and Phin stood arm-in-arm, both grinning. But where Phin averted his gaze, her devilish friend did not.

"Parents this way come," Phin said. "You might want to . . . disengage."

Heat scorched her face and she tried to do just that. When Zeke didn't oblige her frantic pushes against his chest, she chanced a look at his face. What she saw there made her heart stutter to a halt. But her mind didn't have time to fully process it before he kissed the corner of her mouth and eased her back to the floor.

Zeke looked at his brother. "Buy us a minute."

Phin's smile grew louder. "It'll cost you."

A growl erupted from Zeke's throat.

Giving Kayla a conspiratorial wink, Phin asked, "Shall we save the evening?"

She pushed him into the hallway and sent Liv a we'll-talk-later smile.

After they departed, Zeke tucked a stray hair behind her ear, and she straightened his tie and re-buttoned his jacket. An awkward silence filled the air space once they finished putting each other back together.

"Promise me," he said, "that you won't do that with another."

"I don't think you understand what you're asking."

"I damn well do."

Liv stopped her lips from twitching. As sexy as he was in his earnestness, she had to make sure his lower half hadn't siphoned off every drop of blood going to his brain.

"You don't get just this body. You get the total package—career, kid, and," she motioned toward the door, "Thorntons."

"And you."

"Yes, and—" She waved at the growing volume of voices down the hallway.

With thumb and forefinger on her chin, he nudged her attention back to him. "You."

She frowned.

His finger traced a path from her chin to her left breast, to the area covering her madly beating organ. He rested the pad of his finger there. "You."

"Zeke, I—"

"There you two are." Regina Thornton marched into the room, followed by Liv's sister and brother. Her keen eyes traveled over Liv as if reassuring herself that her daughter hadn't suffered harm at Zeke's hand. "I see you're showing Zeke the place where we spent so many happy moments as a family."

Liv said nothing, still off-kilter from Zeke's revelations and now her mother's lioness behavior. A person could only take so many shocks to the system in a five-minute time period.

"You and Mr. Thornton have enjoyed a full life," Zeke said to fill the silence.

Regina glanced around the room before her gaze fell on Callie, Pierce, and finally Liv. "In some ways, yes."

Was that regret forming deep lines on her mother's forehead? Liv looked at her sister and noted that she wore the same confused expression.

Zeke said something else, but the words flowed over her as if she were sinking below water. She might have drowned there if it hadn't been for the large, warm hand at her lower back, keeping her afloat.

34

The following afternoon, Liv's mind still reeled with the previous evening's events. She couldn't stop it from replaying Zeke's intimate conversation with Nicola or his reaction to her mention of the sword or the fact that they'd almost made love in a house full of guests within hearing range.

But none of that compared to his *commit to me* comment. She'd been so shocked, then aroused, then embarrassed, that she never got a chance to find out if he threw the words out on a whim or if he meant them.

She sighed and continued picking up her son's dirty laundry off the floor. Even if Zeke meant what he said, how would he fit her and Brodie into his busy life?

Her phone vibrated in her back pocket, and she shuffled soiled underwear and socks to her opposite hand in order to fish her phone out. At the sight of the women's center's director's name, her pulse leaped.

"Hi, Gina. Everything okay?"

"I'm sorry to bother you, Liv, but I thought you'd like to know that Claudia Rogers is here."

Liv closed her eyes a moment. "How bad is she?"

"He broke her nose, and she now has a missing front tooth."

"I can be there in forty minutes."

"Actually, rather than making the trip, I had hoped you could help her get an emergency DVPO."

A domestic violence protective order was a court order that required the abuser to stay away from the victim. They weren't foolproof, but they allowed the police to make an arrest on the spot if the abuser violated the order.

"Consider it done, but I'd like to come see her."

"She won't be here. I've already helped her make arrangements to stay with her cousin in Raleigh."

"Claudia has agreed to go?"

"Yes. I don't know how long she'll stay, but we can at least put some distance between them."

"I'll let you know when I have the protection order."

"Thanks, Liv."

After disconnecting, she called her Aunt Belinda and relayed the information. Her aunt didn't question Liv on the legitimacy of the claim, having assisted her with other battered women from the center in the past.

Liv found herself standing in the hallway between her and Brodie's room, staring at nothing.

"What are you doing?"

She looked toward Zeke's voice and watched him stride toward her, a fierce expression on his handsome face. Drawing in a deep breath, she pushed Claudia's situation to the side and stood her ground.

Last night, on their drive back to the Friary, she had studiously avoided the commitment topic and tried to question him again about his research on the longsword, but he'd stubbornly refused to quench her curiosity. Irritating man.

"Where can I find a kitchen garbage bag?" she asked, delaying the inevitable.

That pulled him up short. "How should I know? Did you ask Henri?"

"Not yet." She sent him a chiding look. "You really should know where the garbage bags are located."

"Quit trying to redirect me." He scowled at the bundle of clothing in her arms. "Why do you need one?"

She continued into her bedroom. "For our dirty clothes."

"Just give them to Henri. She'll wash them for you."

"I'm not asking a member of your staff to wash my dirty underwear."

"But it's her job."

"She's paid to take care of you and your family, not my son and me."

"But—" His gaze took in the open suitcase on the bed. "What's going on, Liv?"

"Tomorrow morning, Brodie and I are going home."

"You can't."

She stuffed Brodie's dirty clothes in the front zippered pocket of her suitcase. "I absolutely can. After tonight, there's no more reason to stay."

"No reason? Didn't I give you one last night?"

A cold lump settled in the center of her chest. If only she could believe he wanted to explore a life with her and Brodie.

The team had spent all day working through scenario after scenario until everyone knew their part. And all day, she'd waited for a sign from Zeke that he didn't regret his passionate plea for commitment.

But the only signpost she located was *Keep Your Distance*.

She couldn't even be upset with him. How many times had memories of their one night together led her down the dangerous path of envisioning there could be more between them?

Too many.

She cleared her throat. "Things got a little heated—"

"Dammit, Liv. That wasn't my dick talking last night."

"You don't know that."

"*I know.*" The words came out guttural and raw.

"Mama!" Brodie ran in, pulling something from a wicker basket that bounced against his hip. He proudly displayed a bluegill the size of his hand. "Look at what I caught."

Liv forced a smile. Felt it wobble. "You did great, sweetheart."

"Look how big it is, Zeke!"

Zeke tore his attention from her and made a show of inspecting the fish. "Perfect frying size."

Brodie stared at his catch. "You want to cook it?"

"Of course, silly," Sadie said, breathless, as if she'd run all the way from the pond. They probably both had. "It's dead. Not cooking it would be wasteful." She scrunched up her nose in thought. "We could throw it in the field and leave it to the varmints, but bluegill taste so good."

Sadie's smile faded when she realized Brodie was no longer listening. Liv looked at her son and found him staring at her bed. Or rather, what was on her bed.

"Mama, why are you packing?"

Liv swallowed, reached for a reassuring smile. Sure she failed. "For our trip home tomorrow."

"We're leaving?" Brodie stepped closer to Zeke and leaned into his side.

"Yes, sweetheart. You knew we would only be here for a few days."

"But Miss Clara was going to take us to the creek so we can search for mussels and macro—macro. . . " He glanced at Sadie for help.

The girl stepped forward and slipped her hand into his. "Macroinvertebrates."

"We get to wear waders and turn over rocks and, and—please, Mama."

Locked in unity, the trio stared at her as if their lives hung in the balance on her next words. She understood the feeling. Two paths spread before her. One led to a world of color and hope and happiness. The other to an existence in shades of gray, heartbreak, and loneliness.

For many, the choice would be clear. Yet Liv worried the life she wanted would converge with the life she feared in the near distance, when Zeke finally understood the magnitude of his choice.

Setting aside her packing, she bent down and kissed her son's forehead. "Why don't you and Sadie go downstairs and ask Miss Henri for help with your fish, while I speak to Zeke."

"Does that mean we can stay?"

"Let me think on it."

Brodie nodded, misery weighing down his narrow shoulders. He placed his catch back in his basket.

Zeke squeezed his shoulder. "I'll see you later, sport."

Her son hesitated a moment, then wrapped his arms around Zeke's waist.

Zeke stood immobile for a stunned second before he returned the gesture. Brodie broke off and ran down the stairs. Sadie followed.

Zeke stared after her son for a long second before turning back to her.

"The threat is still out there," he said.

"I'm aware."

"He's safe here."

"I know how to protect my son, Zeke."

"The man who assaulted you knew where you worked and where your son went to school. He likely knows where you live, too."

"He won't catch me unawares again."

"Liv." He took a step forward.

She held up a hand, stopping him. "I appreciate what you're trying to do, Zeke. But we're not your problem." She took in their surroundings. "You have enough on your plate."

The skin on his face tautened. "You're not a damn problem. I—care about you. And Brodie."

She swallowed hard. "I've enjoyed our time together, but I can't take this"—she waved her hand between them— "whatever this is between us, any further."

He closed the space between them and traced the side of her face with the back of his finger. "What if I don't agree?"

Unable to stop herself, she lifted a hand to his chest, absorbed his warmth, his strength.

He leaned down and kissed her. Drugged her with his taste, his heat, his temptation. She would never get enough of this, of him. It was then she felt the first crack in her heart.

Easing out of the kiss, she brushed her thumb over his damp lower lip before meeting his eyes.

"I could fall in love with you, Zeke. No matter what you think, you're not ready for that kind of commitment. I have to stop this now while I can walk away with my heart intact." She edged around him. "I'll see you this evening."

"Liv—"

She managed a smile. "Can't wait to see your costume."

Turning away, she kept her strides unhurried, even though every cell in her body begged her to run.

But the special agent in her, the Thornton in her, would not allow her emotions to take control. An abundance of emotion destroyed friendships, careers, families.

Love.

35

Zeke paced the expanse between the foyer and Great Hall, alternating between checking his tie in the small oval mirror by the entrance door and glancing up the wide staircase for Liv.

I could fall in love with you.

For the first time in his life, he wondered what it would be like to be loved by such a strong, beautiful, and caring woman. The thought didn't overwhelm him, didn't make the veins in his temple throb or the muscles in his chest constrict.

The prospect of waking up next to Liv every day brought a sense of peace to his mind. He didn't want to run from it. On the contrary, he yearned for it.

He wanted to be the one to take Brodie fly-fishing, teach him how to knot his first bowtie, and reintroduce him to baseball. No one could ever replace the boy's father, but Zeke wanted to help fill the gap.

An image of Liv, Brodie, and him attending a Charlotte Knights game surfaced. He would get seats deep into the outfield to avoid any possibility of unexpected balls zinging their way.

He'd buy them a huge tub of buttered popcorn, hot dogs smothered in ketchup, and a giant soda pop that would have the kid sugared up for the next week.

If he got lucky, Brodie would smile, which would make Liv smile, which would make him—

"Why are you grinning at yourself in the mirror?" Cruz asked around a mouthful of food. He stood with one hand on his hip and another wrapped around an enormous hamburger. "You clean up well, but you might be taking self-appreciation a little too far."

Zeke turned away from his reflection. "Shouldn't you be camped out at the St. Martins' place?"

"I'm on my way. Not all of us get to dine on lobster rolls and sip champagne for dinner."

Zeke peered up the stairs for the hundredth time. Where was she?

A low, burger-muffled whistle echoed in the foyer. "Someone's got date night jitters."

"This is hardly a date, and she's"—he checked his Rolex —"three minutes late."

Cruz frowned. "Where's your costume? Aren't you going as Zorro or a Musketeer or something?"

"In the car." He would wait until the last possible minute before donning his black cape and mask. The costume, including his stainless-steel watch, black Armani suit, Gucci necktie, and Ferragamo boots were all selected by Phin, of course. Zeke couldn't tell a Rolex from a Rolodex.

Why his brother bought designer everything for a costume party, Zeke had no idea. He was just thankful to be spared the shopping trip. The only accoutrement he cared about was the voice-activated ear insert Rohan had handed the entire team an hour ago.

Although Phin still eyed him with suspicion, he'd finally accepted Zeke's presence within his territory. Sort of. Once this recovery was over, Zeke would happily cede the spotlight back to his little brother's loving arms.

But not tonight. Tonight, he'd traipse beneath the chandeliers, dine on gourmet cuisine, and smile during inane conversations. Whatever it took to get into Nicola's museum and search for his ancestral sword and the antique doll.

"Want me to go up and check on Liv?" Cruz asked in a low, suggestive voice, knocking Zeke out of his thoughts.

"Stay away from her." Where Phin's words charmed women into his bed, Cruz had only to look at the opposite sex before they dove beneath his covers.

It was annoying. The incident with Tina still stung after fourteen years. He'd met the raven-haired Nebraskan through a forced group project in his Business Analytics class at UNC. They enjoyed each other's company, but were content to hang out with their own friends, too. They helped each other study for exams and the sex had been good. Real good.

Until Zeke invited Tina home for a long weekend. Her shift in affection had started at the dinner table that first night, when Cruz had given her his focused attention while she shared a story about rescuing a duck tangled up in discarded fishing line.

His brother had done nothing more than look at Zeke's date. But by the end of the weekend, Tina had slipped her number into Cruz's hand and tried to kiss him. Zeke had watched the whole disastrous scene unfold.

Tina brushing past Cruz, his brother's confused expression at the piece of paper she'd pressed in his hand, Tina lifting on tiptoes, grasping Cruz's face, and planting a kiss on his mouth, Cruz stumbling backward, angrily swiping his mouth against his shoulder, his brother telling her to stay the fuck away.

She hadn't been the first girl to become smitten with Cruz's smoky good looks. Every one of them—Ash, Phin, Rohan, Zeke—had lost a lover to him. Outside of the initial pissed-off rejection phase, none of them held their loss against Cruz. It was difficult to be mad at someone born with eyes women find irresistible, even though he could be a supreme asshat, sometimes. Like now.

So far, Liv had treated Cruz no differently from the rest of his brothers. No longing looks, extreme blushing, or accidental body brushes.

Zeke had been watching, especially during their first meeting at the Annex. But that didn't mean her attention wouldn't shift if Cruz actively set out to seduce her.

Not that his brother would, despite his antagonizing suggestion, but the mere thought of Cruz kissing Liv set off a torrent of fury.

"Stay the fuck away from her."

A broad smile swept across Cruz's face, making him even more handsome. He ripped off another bite of his sandwich and garbled out, "You got it bad, bro."

Zeke rolled his fingers into fists and stared at the empty staircase. He didn't bother denying it. Cruz knew him too well.

"She's obviously into you, too, so what's with the pained expression?"

"It's complicated."

"Aren't they all?"

Zeke slid a glance at his brother, who seemed to not have a care in the world as he systematically snarfed down his dinner. Whereas, Zeke's nerves were stacked so tightly on top of one another that he found it hard to breathe.

They had so much riding on the success of this operation. If it failed, Zeke would be responsible, and he didn't know how he'd live with himself if he were the cause of ruining Ash's career and unleashing a torrent of lethal drugs onto the streets of his hometown.

And losing his chance to recover Lupos.

Yet he couldn't seem to keep his professional distance from Liv. A guilty flush crawled up his neck as he recalled how good she'd felt in his arms last night and how much he wanted moments like that with her for the rest of his life.

How he'd said as much and how she couldn't get away from him fast enough.

"I've got a lot on my damn plate right now," Zeke growled, "in case you hadn't noticed."

Cruz's smile disappeared, and tension sharpened his shoulders. "Whose fault is that?" He wiped his mouth with the back of his hand. "I've asked you more than once to let me take on some of your responsibilities and Neuman is ready—"

"Neuman's not ready. He hasn't even gone on an active recovery yet."

"There's no reason he couldn't have joined us on the Warner recovery. It was low risk, but challenging enough to test his mettle. After the botched dry run, he practiced for hours until he perfected his technique—and carried enough backup equipment to make Big Foot groan."

"He never said anything—"

"You never asked." The same eyes that melted many women's hearts were now savage and unrelenting. "You never ask. You do and do and do like you're Super-fucking-man, then get overwhelmed and pissed off when mistakes are made."

Every word Cruz uttered stoked a rising inferno inside him. Who was he to criticize how Zeke led this team? He—like the rest of his brothers—had reaped the rewards of BARS's success, then went about the rest of their lives without a thought for the future because they knew big brother had it covered.

A disturbance at the top of the stairs cut off Zeke's retort. Barefoot and wearing a turquoise fringed flapper dress, shot with geometric patterns of gold, that did nothing to hide the luscious curves of her body, Liv skidded to a halt at the top of the stairs.

"I'm sorry." She held the banister while squeezing her foot into a break-your-neck pale gold stiletto. "My blasted hair wouldn't cooperate."

In a low voice, Cruz said, "Trust your team, Zeke. We'll all be a lot happier." Then he lifted his attention to the beauty at the top of the stairs and smiled. "Your hair looks great, Liv. Despite my brother's annoyance, we're still on schedule. Good luck tonight. We've got your back every step of the way." Cruz's luminescent eyes cooled when they returned to Zeke. "Yours, too, shithead." He stuffed the last bit of his burger into his mouth and left.

Zeke stared after his brother for a long, uncomfortable moment, playing his words over and over in his mind.

Trust your team.

We'll all be a lot happier.

Got your back.

"Is everything okay?" Liv asked into the silence.

All thoughts of Cruz evaporated at the sight of Liv gliding down the staircase. In one hand, she held a delicate half-mask and beaded clutch that matched her shoes, while her other hand skimmed along the railing, reminding him of how they felt when they traced a line down the hollow of his back.

She paused on the last stair, placing them eye-to-eye. As if he'd done it a thousand times before, he leaned forward and gave her a soft, thorough kiss. Seconds later, he pulled away, and they were both breathing hard.

"Everything's fine," he whispered against her lips.

"You're not wearing a costume?"

"I'll put it on once we get there." He caressed her cheek with his thumb. "You look stunning."

Her hand smoothed down his lapel, flattened over his heart, and pushed until he took a step back. "We can't do this."

"Sorry, turquoise is my new favorite color."

She gave his tamed hair, smooth jaw, tailored black suit, and silver-gray tie an admiring look. "Black is mine."

He would never harass his little brother about his fashion sense again.

As she brushed past him, his nose followed the delicate scent of vanilla through the foyer and out of the front door.

It was going to be a long, *hard* night.

36

THE ST. MARTINS' ASHEVILLE MANSION WAS EVEN MORE impressive than Liv remembered. She had attended a similar benefit here five years ago on the arm of another man who, unlike Zeke, loved high society parties.

Tyler Westcott could work a crowd like a seasoned politician, but without the bile-inducing flattery and meaningless conversation. Tyler knew how to listen and ask questions that set the receiver at ease.

Much like the youngest Blackwell.

On the opposite side of the room, Phin and Kayla held court with several outrageously costumed guests. Whether by design or accident, the two crowd-pleasing powerhouses were the epitome of yin and yang. Black and white. Modern and ancient.

Rather than don a full-on costume, Phin had decided instead to keep it simple with a Dolce and Gabbana black suit and a Columbina, a Venetian eye mask. But it wasn't a plain black mask like Zeke's. Phin's had just enough flare to set his apart from all the others.

A series of jet-black crystals curved over one eye,

swooped down to the bridge of the nose before arcing over the other eye. Decorative black trim surrounded the perimeter of the mask and raised scrolls and little wisps gave the mask an elegant old-world feel.

Kayla, on the other hand, was dressed in an eye-blinding white chiffon Grecian gown with silver and diamond clasps holding the front and back sections together at the shoulders and a matching accessory around her slim waist. With her blond hair piled high on her head, she looked like she should be lounging on Mt. Olympus rather than standing in the St. Martins' ballroom.

Her white paper-mache Columbina was as exquisite as its wearer. Two majestic swan wings arched upward on one side of the mask and more diamonds lined the upper and lower edges of the eyeholes.

Kayla and Phin were an eye-catching couple, both beautiful and sleek and cunning. Like two mountain lions marching through a den of mice.

The Yin and Yang broke away from the knights, queens, fairies, and werewolves and strolled toward their host, Hugh St. Martin. The vascular surgeon didn't have the same collector's heart as his wife, but he enjoyed giving private tours of his wife's museum, especially if the group included a young, beautiful woman.

St. Martin had already shown an interest in Kayla's company at the Thornton dinner party. Her friend would not have to work too hard to coax him into a tour.

As fun as it was to watch Kayla and Phin work their magic, Liv's attention never strayed far from the tall, broad-shouldered man, making his way toward her through the animated crowd.

Where Phin charmed, Zeke observed. Listened. He

nodded at the right moments and moved on when conversations got too personal, leaving an air of mystery in his wake.

He was James Bond in the flesh. Not the polished Pierce Brosnan version, but the flawed and brooding Daniel Craig.

Dangerous Daniel Craig.

Before handing the St. Martins' valet his keys, Zeke had buckled a sword to his waist, whipped a long cape around his shoulders, and tied on a half mask. Within seconds, Mr. GQ had turned into Zorro. She'd been charmed by his costume, until she got a good look at his sword.

The weapon dangling from his hips was not a rapier, but a longsword. One that bore a striking resemblance to the one she'd spotted in his research folder all those weeks ago. Had he found the family heirloom? Or was this a replica?

Why bring either of them to the fundraiser? A suspicion began to form in her mind until Zeke caught her staring. The small, private smile he sent her, while pretending absorption in the pair of women who'd intercepted him, kicked all thoughts of ancient weaponry to the background.

No matter how hard she tried to barricade her heart against further assault, he continued to smash her barriers with little more than a sexy grin, a warm glance, or a reassuring hand on her son's shoulder.

She forced herself to shake off his effect and refocus on reconnaissance. Between the four of them, they had prowled the entire mansion in short, coordinated bursts, checking security details, exits, cameras, and anything else that would help them finalize their recovery plan that they would execute in the wee hours of the morning.

If they located the CI's doll.

"Olivia," a cultured feminine voice called. "I've finally caught up with you."

Liv air-kissed her hostess's cheek. "Fabulous party, Nicola. Thank you for inviting us."

She took in the older woman's jeweled crown, ruby and diamond choker, and shimmering red ballgown. "Or should I say, Your Majesty, though I've never seen Queen Elizabeth looking so gorgeous or so . . . modern."

"Elizabeth?" Nicola shuddered and waved a hand over her costume. "Behold Queen Máxima of the Netherlands, not some four-hundred-year-old doddering Englishwoman."

"Of course, I can see the Dutch now."

Nicola tapped her fan, none too gently, against Liv's hand. "Where is your handsome escort?"

Four women surrounded Zeke's caped figure now. She was surprised the gathering hadn't sent her jealous flag flying.

Maybe it was the occasional amused smile Zeke would tilt in her direction that made the sight more amusing than concerning. Or maybe she didn't feel deeply enough for him to cause such a visceral reaction.

Liv thought back to the Thornton dinner party, to Nicola's hand on Zeke, to her generous breasts nearly dripping into his lap, and decided she definitely had the capacity for jealousy.

She nodded in Zeke's direction, amusement lacing her words. "Fighting his way through the adoring horde."

"Shall we go save him?"

"Two more women vying for his attention might blow his big head through the roof."

Nicola chuckled.

"Here comes Zorro now."

"Good evening, Nicola." As he did at the dinner party,

Zeke kept his eyes on the socialite as he kissed the back of her hand.

"Black suits you."

Zeke moved to Liv's side and slid an arm around her waist. "So I've been told."

A rotund man with a head full of thick, wavy hair and a large camera strapped around his neck paused before them to snap a picture.

"How about a group shot?" The photographer waved a hand. "Mrs. St. Martin, please join the other two."

"Fabulous idea, Glenn." Rather than move to either Liv's or Zeke's side, the socialite wedged her svelte body between them.

Glenn counted off, "Three, two, one. Smile." He took a series of pictures, adjusting his lens and orientation in between each snap of the shutter. "Thank you."

As the photographer ambled away, Nicola snatched a flute of champagne from a passing server and began walking away. Over her shoulder, she said, "Come along, you two. I have something *old* to show you."

The museum?

Liv looked at Zeke, who gave her a triumphant smile before twining his fingers with hers and following the socialite through the ballroom.

When they neared Phin and Kayla's location, Zeke nodded. It wasn't much in the way of communication, but Phin seemed to understand that their plan just got hijacked. Again.

By a horny hostess, of all things. Liv kept her expectant expression in place while her mind raced through scenario after scenario like a hummingbird flitting from one flower to the next.

On one hand, Nicola might provide additional intel that

her less art-interested husband wouldn't know. However, they had targeted Hugh St. Martin because he would be easier to manipulate and distract.

Although Nicola obviously enjoyed a bit of flirting, she would watch them like an eagle as they strode amongst her treasures.

Which meant Liv would have to do her least favorite thing in the world.

Wing it.

Many, many moons ago, she had loved winging it. Enjoyed the thrill of the unknown, the adventure of balancing life on a razor's edge. That now-dormant part of her was one of the reasons she'd been drawn to the Bureau.

However, the birth of her son had blunted her wild gene and the death of her husband had killed it all together.

"My queen," Hugh St. Martin called in a kingly voice, with Phin and Kayla on his heels. "Where are you off to with these scoundrels?"

Unlike his wife, who preferred modern royalty, Hugh was rigged out in full, gaudy Henry VIII regalia, with his slash-sleeved doublet and striped hose. A bejeweled crown sat atop his head at a jaunty angle.

Liv had no idea how he kept the heavy thing from sliding off.

Nicola halted near a roped-off tiered glass table at the base of where two curved staircases ended. Pin lights from high above shone down on twelve black-velvet-draped figures, all unique in shape and size.

The art pieces for the fundraiser. Could she be inches away from the Kämmer and Reinhardt doll?

With the exhibit pieces already in place, the lack of security surprised Liv, until she spotted an eagle-eyed man in a suit on the other side of the table and the cameras attached to the long balcony running between the twin staircases and directly above the display table.

"To the museum," Nicola said in a low voice for their ears alone.

"Might my delightful subjects join you below?" Hugh gestured to Kayla and Phin. "They've shown a keen interest in the artwork adorning the ballroom's walls."

"Have they?"

"I'll never hear the end of it if my big brother sees your famed private collection and I don't." Phin pressed a hand against his chest. "Take pity, dear Nicola. My appreciation for your treasures will far exceed Zorro's."

"The tour will be brief. I must return here"—she waved a hand at the display table—"for the unveiling in twenty minutes."

Phin wrapped an arm around Kayla's shoulders. "We'll take brief."

A strained smile stretched across Nicola's lips as she studied the yin and yang pair for a long moment. They were clearly not in her plans, whatever those were. "Come along."

Kayla shot Liv a triumphant smirk, but something about the entire exchange pricked her sixth sense. Zeke squeezed her hand as if sharing her concern.

Their growing party followed the couple through the mansion until their tour guides paused before a mirrored wall near one of two studies in the house.

Nicola's fingers sank into a hidden pocket, drawing something from her silken skirts. She waved the gold proximity card over the smooth surface of the wall until a green button was illuminated.

She pressed the button and it turned red.

A hidden elevator.

A chime went off, and Hugh fished his phone out of his

voluminous short trousers. "Apologies." Reading the display, his jaw slackened a moment before he produced a weak smile. "I'm afraid I won't be able to join you for the tour."

Liv's heart sank, and her hold on Zeke's hand tightened.

The mirrored door slid open, revealing a small elevator. Nicola stepped inside and motioned for Zeke and Liv to follow, filling the small space. "Is everything all right?"

"A small business situation I must address." Hugh handed an identical gold card to Phin. "You'll need this to call up the elevator."

Nicola stiffened. "Hugh, can your business not wait five minutes?"

"Afraid not, my queen." He bowed and left.

Nicola stared at her husband's retreating back as if she'd like to send him to the guillotine.

"Is there a problem?" Zeke asked.

The socialite blinked. "Forgive me. There are only three access cards for this elevator, and my husband just handed one to someone I met only a few days ago."

"Miss Krowne will ensure I do not run off with your card," Phin said with a grin.

Nicola forced a smile. "I meant no disrespect, Mr. Blackwell. But my museum is precious to me."

Phin's face sobered. "If my having this distresses you," he stepped forward and held out the card, "I will be happy to take a rain check. Or the stairs."

Liv's heart bucked and thrashed inside her stomach.

More winging it.

37

ZEKE'S EYES NARROWED ON HIS BROTHER. WHAT THE HELL WAS he doing?

Having the museum's access card in hand was an unexpected turn in their favor. Even now, Rohan would be working his way to the nearest window, having heard their conversation through his earpiece.

A quick scan, a little Rohan magic, and they'd have their own gold card within the hour.

At Phin's suggestion, tension eased from Nicola's royal frame. "Thank you, Mr. Blackwell, but the only way in and out of the museum is via this elevator." She released the button holding the door open. "We will see you both in a few minutes."

The door closed, and silence settled over the trio before the elevator began its slow descent.

"One ingress and egress," Zeke said. "Ever worry about getting stuck down there?"

Nicola's shoulder pressed against his. "No. I have too many backup systems in place. It would take an apocalypse to stop this elevator from running."

"How do you get the larger pieces below?"

"We manage."

She said nothing more, which led him to believe that the museum had a hidden service elevator as well.

"Do you have a curator for your museum?" Liv asked.

Nicola nodded. "Dr. Bentley. You might have noticed a sandy blond-haired man hovering near the display table."

"I thought he was a security guard."

"He might as well be."

The elevator door binged open, and a hundred lights flickered to life across the room, illuminating hundreds of artifacts that stretched over centuries and continents.

Zeke's blood pumped hotter, faster. If Sardoff's intel was good, Lupos was in this room.

After years of searching every corner of the black-market world, his family legacy was right here. In his own backyard.

Maybe.

Liv released his hand and strode to the nearest table. A six-inch, centuries old, ceremonial mask stood on a metal pedestal. The piece appeared to be made of wood, though in certain places he could see a sheen of gold.

Behind the piece rose an illuminated concave glass with the artifact's provenance etched onto the surface.

"No wonder you're so protective of this space," Liv said, moving on to the next priceless display. "Every piece is unique. The history you have contained within these four walls is incredible."

Nicola beamed like a proud mother. She took in all the pieces on the large round table. "I inherited these from my father. They're very special to me and the impetus to what has become a lifelong obsession."

"I can see why. Is everything in your collection one-of-a-kind?"

"With a few exceptions, yes."

Their conversation faded into the background as Zeke turned toward the far wall, where an array of clubs, spears, firearms, knives, and swords were displayed.

Leaving Liv to search for the doll, he shoved his hands into his pockets and made slow, steady progress toward the ancient weapons. It took every bit of self-control he possessed—and then some—not to sprint across the room.

His pulse shot up several digits with every step. As a collector of antique weaponry, he couldn't help but feel awed by the history splayed out on Nicola's wall.

He stared at implements that were handcrafted to hunt, kill, and protect various cultures around the world, through war, famine, peace, and prosperity.

Eight longswords. He searched the pommel of each one, looking for the unique four-headed wolf.

Nothing.

Searched each guard for the *familia primum* inscription.

Nothing.

He went through the process twice more. Same result.

Lupos wasn't here.

An avalanche of disappointment blinded him to his surroundings. For days, he'd envisioned drawing the heirloom down from its place of honor and tracing the fine etchings in the polished blade, then smuggling it home.

The whole exchange would have taken less than a minute. A minute toward setting his life back in order.

But Sardoff's intel had been bad. Despite Zeke's own insistence that he not get his hopes up, he had. Badly.

The moment his damn eyes started to burn, a small

hand curled over his shoulder and a slim body pressed into his side.

"It's not here?" she whispered, as if she struggled to contain her own disappointment.

"No." He didn't even bother trying to play it cool. His emotions were too raw, too close to the surface.

The hand on his shoulder squeezed. "We'll find it."

"We?"

She nodded and sent him a conspiratorial grin. "I'm not without resources."

Words of appreciation lodged in his tight throat. He found her hand and wove their fingers together, and squeezed.

No one but Rohan knew of his quest to find the sword. Although his brother had promised to keep his ear to the ground for any digital whispers, Rohan hadn't actively sought the blade. None of his brothers had ever felt the sword's loss like Zeke.

Hell, he hadn't exactly been looking for it until the team started falling apart. At that point, finding it had become imperative, for reasons he didn't fully understand.

Sardoff had a lot of explaining to do.

The elevator door opened, and Phin and Kayla spilled into the room. Phin gave him a short nod before striding toward Nicola.

"Did you find the asset?" he asked Liv in a low voice.

"Sort of. I found where it's displayed. The case is empty."

"Empty?"

She nodded. "I think it might be one of the twelve items on display upstairs."

"Dammit." Now they wouldn't have an exact location for the doll when they returned later to extract the asset. More than likely, the pieces upstairs would be returned to the museum at the close of the fundraiser, but there were no guarantees.

"Delivered safe and sound," Phin said to Nicola.

The socialite accepted the gold card and pocketed it. "Thank you." She sailed up to Zeke's other side. "Leave it to a man to sniff out my weaponry collection."

"An impressive display." He slid his arm around Liv's waist, wanting her to know that she was the woman—the only woman—on his mind.

"Extraordinary, aren't they?"

He nodded. "I have a small collection, but nothing like this."

"Careful, Zeke. Collecting antiquities is like collecting money. You can never have enough."

"From the lack of space on this wall," Liv said. "It looks like you won't be adding any more pieces to this genre."

Nicola's mouth stretched into a Cheshire cat smile. "I have three more acquisitions waiting in the wings. Once my designer finishes etching their origins onto their glass placards, I'll start a new panel." She pointed to a curtained off area to their right.

"Are the new pieces here in the museum?" Zeke asked.

"Of course. I would not trust them anywhere else."

"May I see them?"

"They're not ready for viewing yet. Dr. Bentley still needs to have them restored."

"We don't mind a bit of dust." Phin sidled up next to Nicola. Placed his fingertips on her waist as he leaned across her to look at Zeke. "Do we, bro?"

"Not at all."

Zeke watched Nicola stare at Phin's mouth, inches from hers. She inhaled a slow breath before snapping the fan open at her wrist and setting it into motion.

"Follow me," Nicola said in a husky voice.

Another conquest.

Phin winked at Kayla, who rolled her eyes.

Liv smiled.

Zeke trailed after the group, heading toward what would no doubt be another heart-wrenching letdown. But he wasn't strong enough not to hope.

38

Zeke tapped his thumb against his leg, silently urging their hostess to hurry the hell up as Nicola fanned herself over to a closed door, waved her magic card near the proximity reader, and waited for the telltale sound of the electric strike unlocking.

She opened the door, flicked on the light switch, and led them into a large room that appeared to act as part storage, part workshop, and part office.

All the high-tech, elegant simplicity displayed in the other room had not carried over into this one. The utilitarian, no-nonsense space seemed to mock their outlandish costumes. Half-open wooden crates dotted the floors and other flat surfaces. A large magnifying glass anchored to a wide table that held various instruments and containers hovered over an oil painting the size of a cereal box. Metal cabinets and an L-shaped desk with stacks of paper and two enormous monitors lined one wall.

Take away the electronic devices and it would be a scene straight out of an *Indiana Jones* movie.

Nicola strode to one of the wide metal cabinets and pulled open the center drawer. Nestled inside were several more weapons. Each one had a manilla envelope attached to it via a jute string.

Although Zeke could have spent hours learning about each artifact, the one he sought wasn't here. His chest constricted until he found it difficult to breathe. He turned away, wanting nothing more than to get out of this underground tomb.

They had what they came for. No sense in drawing out this charade any longer.

In his single-minded focus on leaving, he didn't notice Liv bending over one of the wooden crates strewn about. As he stormed by, she grasped his cape, jarring him to a halt. The protest died on his lips when she smiled at him and held out her hand.

Without thinking, he curled his fingers around hers and allowed her to pull him closer to the crate.

"Look," she whispered.

A wild pounding vibrated through his entire body. He wanted to. Sweet Mother, how he wanted to, but he couldn't withstand another devastating blow.

He shook his head. "It's not here." She peered over her shoulder to ensure Nicola wasn't within earshot before she said, "Once I've committed a piece to memory, I don't forget it. Your research was quite detailed." She squeezed his hand. "This is it." When he made no move to see for himself, she said, "Trust me."

He did, he realized. With his life.

But his hopes had been battered too hard and too frequently for him to muster a confirming smile. He crouched down and waited for her to brush back the rest of the packing material before peering inside.

When he did, every drop of blood in his head vanished, as his gaze roamed over Lupos for the first time. He swayed, dizzy with relief and happiness. His knees crashed to the concrete floor, and Liv's hold on his hand tightened.

It was here. It was really fucking here.

An almost childish giddiness filled his chest. He looked at Liv, unable to temper his wide grin. He couldn't think of anyone he'd rather share this moment with than her.

Not his brothers.

Not his mom.

And not Grams.

The only person he wanted with him was her. Liv.

If the depth of his feelings for her hadn't been abundantly clear in her parents' library last night, they were now. The fact should scare the shit out of him. Send him running into the next county.

Feelings like his led to engagement rings and weddings and children—and a lifetime of happiness.

Tears rimmed her eyes before she leaned over and kissed the corner of his mouth. When she straightened, her eyes were clear. Intent.

She glanced between him and Lupos.

Do what you have to do, her eyes commanded.

Zeke stilled. Somehow, she had figured out his plan to swap out Lupos with the reproduction at his waist. She didn't try to talk him into waiting until they returned to recover the doll later tonight. Somehow, she knew he wouldn't be able to part from the heirloom once he found it. And Special Agent Olivia Westcott was giving him the green light.

Yeah, his feelings ran fucking glacier deep for this woman. But there was nothing cold about them.

She brushed the back of his hand with hers, then joined

the others. For the next few minutes, she kept Nicola busy, going through drawer after drawer.

While he did what he had to do.

39

FOR THE LAST TIME, ZEKE BENT OVER NICOLA ST. MARTIN'S hand. "Thank you for sharing your museum with us. It's an evening I will always cherish." Not for the reasons she would assume, but he would not correct her assumption.

Her hand slid slowly from his. "It's a rare treat to tour the collection with such like-minded enthusiasts. Most people endure my yammerings about antiquities because they want something from me or wish to get into my good graces." She took in the four of them. "Thank you for allowing me to be me for a while."

Guilt snaked across his mind, but he didn't allow it to burrow deep. He appreciated Nicola St. Martin's charitable endeavors, but he'd spotted at least six pieces of question-able origins below, not including Lupos. The socialite had the funds to get what she wanted, when she wanted it. Something told him if she had to break a few laws along the way, the act wouldn't cause a single sleepless night.

In the distance, a crowd had formed around the display table where tonight's main event would take place. Excited chatter pulsed and grew in volume.

"Now," Nicola said, "if you'll excuse me. I believe it's time for me to say a few words before the unveiling."

"Mrs. St. Martin, where have you been?" asked a harried man in a business suit and scuffed dress shoes.

"Showing the museum to my guests. What is the matter, Dr. Bentley?"

"I've been trying to call you for the past fifteen minutes."

"You know cell reception is nonexistent down there."

The curator's ears turned bright red at the admonishment. "My apologies. It's just that . . ." His voice trailed off as if he feared his employer's reaction.

"Spit it out, Dr. Bentley. My guests are waiting."

"The Kämmer and Reinhardt doll."

"What about it?"

"It's missing."

Zeke caught Phin's eye, and his brother peeled away from the group to see what intel he could uncover.

The doll was gone.

If it was gone-gone, their entire mission had just gone nuclear.

All of his elation at discovering Lupos dried up like the Sahara. If they couldn't recover the doll, the CI wouldn't cooperate and a half billion dollars' worth of fentanyl, heroin, and methamphetamines would explode into the streets of Steele Ridge and other small towns like it across Western North Carolina.

Zeke's stomach soured.

Had his obsession with a family heirloom just cratered his brother's career? Had his distraction opened the gates to an insidious poison that would rip apart lives, one by one?

"If you'll excuse me," Nicola said, already storming away. Her curator in tow.

"Well, this ought to be interesting," Kayla said with amusement before gliding off.

"Who would be bold enough to steal one of the exhibit pieces in the middle of the party?" Liv asked.

"Why the doll?" Zeke didn't like coincidences. His elbow pressed against the sword strapped to his side. What he wouldn't give for a Glock at the moment.

"You think someone here knew we wanted it?"

"I don't know. But something feels off."

"Zeke, is that you?"

He turned toward the familiar voice, wishing he hadn't eschewed the costume's Cordovan hat to help shield his identity, and found one of his long-estranged cousins. Slick, high-powered sports agent and current city manager of Steele Ridge, Griffin Steele, eyed him with a mixture of surprise and suspicion.

Great. Just what he needed.

40

Liv's attention sliced between Zeke and the tall, golden-haired man decked out in a tuxedo and a black mask. The two seemed to be deciding whether they should duck a punch or go in for a man-hug.

"Grif." Zeke shook the other man's hand. "Should have known you'd be here."

"Can't say the same. Ballrooms aren't your normal habitat."

"What would you know about my habitat?"

"I know you like to prance around in the damn woods."

A provocative smile dented Zeke's cheeks. "Don't have the faintest idea what you're talking about."

"The Steeles aren't taking the fall for a Blackwell prank."

"Don't see why they should."

"Glad you agree. Now, go confess to the Kingstons, so they'll stop planning their retribution against us."

"Confess, what?"

"Dammit, Zeke. Whatever those assholes are planning, it won't be good."

"Gotta admit, I'm intrigued now."

A low growl erupted from Grif's throat, and he took a threatening step forward.

Liv moved to stand between them, when a pretty strawberry-blond woman, wearing grimy denim overalls, goggles, and a welding helmet tipped back on her head, appeared at Grif's side with two drinks.

"Are you boys at it already?" The woman offered the tumbler of amber liquid to Grif, who never took his eyes off Zeke, and kept the wineglass for herself. She smiled and stuck her hand out toward Liv. "I'm Carlie Beth Steele. This Instigator of Trouble next to me is my husband, Grif."

Grinning, she took the woman's hand. "Olivia Westcott."

Zeke kissed Carlie Beth's cheek. "I'd hug you, but I'm afraid of getting clonked by that thing on your head." In an aside to Liv, he said, "Carlie Beth is a badass blacksmith."

"And an artist," Grif added, earning him a grateful smile from his spouse.

"Do you have a shop in town?" Liv had to raise her voice to be heard over the growing crowd. "Or do you have pieces on consignment at a gallery?"

"Consignment right now, but I hope to sell enough soon to justify opening my own shop."

"I love handcrafted artwork, as does my friend Kayla. Maybe we could swing by sometime to see your collection and get a tour of your forge."

"I'd be happy to. You're welcome anytime."

"Pardon my lack of manners," Grif said, shaking Liv's hand. "My cousin has a way of bringing out the worst in me."

"Cousin?"

Zeke drew her to his side. "Mom and his dad are siblings."

"Are there a lot of you?" she asked Grif.

"Four boys and two girls."

"What about the Kingstons?"

"Three and two," Grif said. "My mom and their mom are sisters."

Liv looked at Zeke. "Y'all live in Steele Ridge?"

"Unfortunately, yes."

Carlie Beth laughed. "That's not even all the cousins."

Liv couldn't imagine having that much family close by. Most of hers were scattered across the country, so she rarely got to see them in person.

"What do you do for a living, Olivia?" Carlie Beth asked.

It was the one question Liv dreaded answering at parties. People's reactions ranged from impressed to wary to downright hostile. "I'm a special agent with the FBI."

"Do you work with Cameron?"

"Ash," Zeke grumbled.

Liv ignored him. "Yes, we've worked on a few cases together. He's a terrific agent."

"Are the other G-men in your office as handsome as the ones on TV?"

Grif sent his wife a blistering look, which she ignored.

Liv chuckled. "Some are. Some aren't. Probably the same odds as any office."

Carlie Beth's hopeful expression fell. Grif smirked.

"I could give you a tour, so you can decide for yourself."

"You're on, girl."

The decibel level had risen to such a degree that conversation was almost impossible and a thicket of guests blocked Liv's view of the exhibit table.

"A lady at the bar said one of the showpieces—a doll—disappeared," Carlie Beth said, noticing her distraction.

When neither she nor Zeke remarked on the incident,

Grif pinned his cousin with a glacial stare. "What do you know about the missing doll?"

"Only what Nicola's curator told us."

"Which was?"

"That it was missing."

"Dammit, Zeke. Do you always have to be an ass?"

"Only when the right elements are present."

Carlie Beth slipped her arm through her husband's. "That's enough family reunion for now." She scowled at Zeke, then smiled at Liv. "Don't forget your promise to visit."

"I won't. It was really nice meeting you both."

Grif nodded at Liv and allowed his wife to usher him away.

As soon as the couple was out of earshot, Liv stepped out of Zeke's embrace. She wasn't sure why she'd stayed next to him through the volatile exchange with his cousin. But she'd sensed in him a need for an ally, a need for connection.

Then again, maybe it wasn't his need at all, but hers.

"What was all that about?" she asked.

"All what?"

She waved her hand toward the departing couple. "That. Why so much tension between you and Grif?"

"Every year, the Kingstons host a holiday festival at their farm. This past Christmas, the boys and I spiced it up a bit." He grinned. "Evidently, we were the only ones who enjoyed ourselves."

She shook her head, holding back her own smile. "Something else was going on. Something that's been roiling for years."

He shrugged. "In the early days, we kept to ourselves. Mom was gone, Dad was busy, and Grams did her best keeping us from killing each other."

"Let me guess—hell-raisers as young men."

He fingered the wispy black feather jutting out of her flapper headband. "Entirely possible."

"What about as adults?"

"I suppose we'd settled into our public persona of reclusive badasses."

She studied his unrepentant, no, proud expression. "You enjoy your renegade status."

He grinned. "Why destroy a good thing?"

A male voice rose above the pulsing cacophony. Beyond the mass of humanity, Liv followed a single-file line of bobbing heads moving toward the exhibit table.

"Phin," Zeke said, "you got anything."

Phin's voice came through her ear insert. *"Nothing concrete yet."*

"Dammit." Zeke clamped her hand in his and tunneled through the guests like a lawnmower through tall grass.

When they reached the edge, Queen Nicola stood halfway up one of the curved staircases, holding a microphone and smiling at her subjects. Hugh stood at the base of the stairs, white-knuckling the newel post and smiling up at his wife. Dr. Bentley prowled below in the shadows, a green cast to his countenance. Photographer Glenn dipped and swayed around the balcony above like a one-eyed cyclops focusing in on his prey.

Each of the bobbing heads—eleven gorgeous, masked men dressed in unrelieved black, except for their white satin gloves—now stood around the table, beside items draped in black velvet and drenched in LED illumination.

Liv counted the men again, and her heart sank into her stomach. She leaned toward Zeke. "Earlier, there were twelve items on the table."

Zeke did his own count, holding out hope that the rumors and Dr. Bentley were mistaken about the doll. They weren't. *"Shit."*

The Kämmer and Reinhardt doll was gone, gone.

41

Twenty long minutes later, Zeke, Liv, Phin, Kayla, and several other guests began filtering out of the St. Martin mansion.

The big unveiling took less than five minutes, and Nicola did an admirable job of pretending nothing was amiss.

Fear for Ash gathered in Zeke's chest. Would Ash lose his job? Or get buried in some FBI basement and be forced to sift through seventy years of UFO sightings? Would the CI stand back and allow the drug shipment to go through? When would the first child die from an overdose?

Question after question tore at his mind. But the one he focused on now was who had stolen the Kämmer and Reinhardt doll, and why?

As they neared their hosts, who stood at the door, thanking their guests as they exited, Zeke activated his ear insert.

"Rohan, you got an update?"

"I hacked into the St. Martin surveillance system in less than a minute. For all their money, their security is for shit."

"What can you tell me?"

"Someone tampered with the feed. Put it on a continuous loop, allowing someone to walk right up to the table and take the doll."

"Good job. Keep digging. See if anything else pops."

"Ten-four."

Having heard his conversation with Rohan through her own earpiece, Liv mused aloud, "Who could have smuggled out a two-foot doll undetected?"

A growing suspicion formed in Zeke's mind, but he let it percolate there for the time being. Right now, he had a more pressing concern.

Getting out of this mansion.

Finally, they reached the head of the exit line. Zeke shook hands with Hugh and Nicola. "I hope you track down your missing artifact."

"I have no doubt we will." Nicola projected a calm confidence that seemed out of place for one who treated her acquisitions as if they were household pets. "Good luck with your," she considered him a moment, "endeavors."

Liv slipped a hand into his. "Goodnight Nicola, Hugh." She nodded at the curator, who stood on the opposite side of the socialite, holding a tablet. "Dr. Bentley."

Their quartet streamed into the cool night air. Rather than feeling a sense of relief, Zeke's shoulders bunched tighter and tighter. He couldn't shake off the dread that made every step to freedom a slog.

When they reached the end of the walkway, two Goliaths in suits blocked their path. One held a device in his hand similar to the curator's. The display flashed red.

The security guard with the tablet said, "The two of you need to follow us."

He peered over his shoulder and found two more guards behind them. Liv gripped his hand tighter.

Phin registered what was happening. Confusion flickered across his brother's face.

Maybe he could gut it out. "Is there a problem?"

"This will only take a moment, sir."

Zeke looked at the guard's tablet, at the flashing red light. "You're looking for the missing display piece, aren't you? A doll, if rumor can be believed." He released Liv's hand, opened his cape, and rotated in a circle. "No doll here." With a roguish smile, he nodded at Liv's flapper dress. "No doll there."

Tablet Guard didn't share his amusement. He indicated a cobblestone path leading to the opposite side of the house. "This way, sir. Ma'am."

The desire to run arrowed through his body, but Zeke knew the attempt would be futile and ridiculous, since he wasn't exactly a stranger. Plus, he would never leave Liv to clean up his mess, but there was a segment of his renegade mind that wanted the confrontation with Nicola. Wanted her to explain how she'd come into possession of an antique sword that had been stolen a century ago.

"I'll go with you, but there's no reason to involve Mrs. Westcott."

Liv grabbed his hand. "I go where you go."

He shook his head. No way would he allow her to get tangled up into this anymore, no matter how much her words made him want to haul her into his arms and kiss her senseless. "This isn't your battle."

"I'm not leaving you."

Jeez Almighty, she was a stubborn woman. The last place an FBI agent should be at the moment was with him.

"Liv," he disengaged his hand from hers. "Go home to Brodie. He needs you." He hardened his voice, even while his heart splintered at his next words. "I don't."

.

A stricken look crossed her face, and she took a sharp step back. Kayla was at her side in a second, shooting him a glare.

"We have orders to bring Mrs. Westcott, too," Tablet Guard said.

"Fuck your orders. She has nothing to do with this."

The guard stepped away for a moment. When he came back, he said, "Come with us, sir."

Zeke followed the guard with Lupos slapping lightly against his thigh. He didn't look back at Liv, because she would have seen in his eyes all the things he wished he had said, instead of delivering hurtful words designed to protect her.

LIV WATCHED ZEKE AS HE FOLLOWED THE TWO ENORMOUS guards down the walkway. According to Phin's model, the path led to a private entrance to Nicola's study.

After she recovered from the initial shock of his harsh words, her blood boiled. He had only said what he did to make her get as far away from him as possible. Did he really think she would abandon him when he needed someone the most?

"Phin?" Kayla said, nodding at Zeke's departing back.

"Yeah, yeah, I'm going." He looked at Liv. "Do you know what this is about?"

The youngest Blackwell's initial confusion had given over to a much more volatile emotion—betrayal, hurt, anger, something that made his body vibrate with violence. By the look of him, he didn't even know what he was fighting to contain.

Liv hesitated a moment, then nodded. "It's ...very important to him."

In her earpiece, Cruz said, "Super-Fucking-Man."

Phin's jaw turned to steel, then he stomped after his brother, muttering beneath his breath. "I'm going to rip off his fucking red cape and stuff it up his—"

"What's going on?" Kayla asked, her earlier amusement gone.

Liv was torn. She didn't want to betray Zeke's secret, yet the situation had exploded out of control. Then she considered how Zeke's insistence on locating the sword on his own had dropped them into their current circumstances and decided to not make the same mistake.

She glanced down the walkway. What if Nicola's goons had noticed Zeke's or Phin's earpieces and were listening in?

As if reading her mind, Rohan said, "Liv, you can speak freely. I've switched you, me, and Cruz to a private channel."

She closed her eyes and took a deep breath. "Nearly a century ago, someone stole a Blackwell family artifact. A longsword."

Cruz's voice filled her ear. "Lupos."

"Yes, Lupos," she repeated for Kayla. "He found the heirloom in Nicola's museum and attempted to smuggle it out."

Silence surrounded her, then Rohan said, "Nicola must have placed a security chip on the sword. The moment he walked out of the house, the chip's radio frequency must have triggered a silent alarm."

That would explain the flashing red light on the guard's tablet, and Nicola's smug conviction that she would locate the doll. Only it wasn't the doll that alerted her security system, but the Blackwell sword.

"He's going to need provenance," Kayla said. "Something that will top whatever phony paperwork Nicola has in her possession."

"There's an antique dealer in Charlotte who might be

able to help us out," Rohan said. "Zeke has a standing order with him to have first right of refusal on any antique weapons he comes across. He might know someone who can authenticate Blackwell ownership."

Liv recalled Zeke's research file, and a plan started to formulate in her mind. A risky one. One that Zeke might not be able to forgive her for. Better that, than him going to prison.

"Okay, this is what we're going to do."

42

As Zeke followed the two guards through a side entrance into what appeared to be someone's office, he wondered what the hell his team was cooking up.

One moment they were chattering in his ear and, the next—dead silence.

Like the public areas of the mansion, the office—or was it a study?—looked as if it had been staged for an *AD* photo shoot.

Even though it had to be seventy degrees outside, a gas fireplace cast flickering yellow-gold shadows against the hardwood floor at the far end of the room. A sideboard containing an array of hand-cut crystal decanters filled with amber liquid sat below a large oil painting of stampeding horses. A stonework wall with black metal shelving housed modern and antique books as well as illuminated frames bearing smiling mugs of miniature St. Martins. A large, severely clean desk sat facing away from a bank of windows and short-legged, squat-backed chairs and a matching sofa dotted the space.

His well-mannered, but firm, escorts *encouraged* him to

sit on the trendy, but uncomfortable, creamy sofa. He tore off his mask, shrugged off his cape, and unfastened his scabbard before taking a seat. He rested Lupos against his right knee. Within easy reach.

Phin stormed in after the last guard, avoiding the Goliath's big paw.

Zeke sat forward. "What the hell are you doing here?"

"The better question," Phin said in a savage voice, " is what are *you* doing here?"

Zeke looked at the guards, then sat back. "Go home, Phin. I can handle this on my own."

"Like you're so good at handling things on your own."

Crushing his teeth together, he kept his mouth shut. Now wasn't the time to work through his family's grievances with him.

Phin held his stare. "I'm not leaving your side until I find out what the hell is going on."

Shaking his head, Zeke draped his arm over the back of the sofa and focused on the door. Waited for the performance to begin.

Minutes later, his patience was rewarded when Nicola, Hugh, and Dr. Bentley sailed into the room.

Hugh continued on to the sideboard and poured himself a drink, Bentley moved to stand in front of the marble fireplace, and Nicola glided toward Zeke. She stared at him in that disappointed way mothers do when they catch their son placing maggots in his sister's underwear drawer.

Despite his body's desire to squirm under her regard, he kept his gaze steady and unflinching.

She held out her hand. "I believe you have something that belongs to me."

Zeke crossed his ankle over his knee and rubbed his thumb over a small scuff on his boot. "I assure you, I don't."

"The sword, Mr. Blackwell. Give it to me."

He rested his free hand on the sword's hilt. Something he had worried would never happen in his lifetime. He smoothed his thumb over each of the four wolf heads on the pommel. "How did you come into possession of this piece?"

Nicola's hand slowly lowered to her side, and anger burrowed into her forehead. "The same way I acquire all my treasures. I bought it."

"From whom?"

"I don't discuss my business dealings with anyone."

Hugh lifted a glass in their direction. "Not even me."

"Then we have a problem."

"You have a problem." She signaled to one of her guards.

In a blink, Phin moved to stand beside him. Zeke wouldn't have been able to articulate the depth of his appreciation at that precise moment if he tried.

Nicola held up a staying hand to her guard.

Zeke couldn't help but note how calm he felt. A few weeks ago, he would've been yelling or punching or blowing up shit to get himself out of this. A few weeks ago, he didn't love Liv.

Now, all he wanted was to watch Nicola burn in a cauldron of her own bullshit.

"Normally, I enjoy a good verbal dance," Phin said, "but could we get to the damn point now?"

"The point is," Zeke said, "this sword belongs to our family, and I'm not leaving here without it."

"A costume sword?" Phin looked at him as if he'd lost his mind.

Understanding lit Nicola's eyes. "Seems your brother likes to keep secrets, even from you." She flicked a manicured finger at the weapon. "What Zeke's holding hostage is a sixteenth-century longsword."

Phin frowned. "But—"

Zeke followed the play of emotions on his brother's face and knew the exact moment the misshapen pieces clicked into place.

"You switched them. While we were in the museum. You switched the one in your scabbard with one in Nicola's collection."

Which must have been equipped with a tracking device or hidden chip. So much for Rohan's assessment of their security. Zeke made a mental note to take that up with his normally infallible brother.

If an unpacked artifact already had a security chip, then every item in Nicola's collection had to be similarly equipped. Which meant the only way someone could remove the doll from the house was by extracting the radio frequency tag.

In order to do that, the thief had to first know of device's existence. Either someone close to the St. Martins took the doll—or the doll was still in the house. If the latter was the case, that scenario gave rise to a whole new set of headache-inducing questions he and his team would need to sort through.

He considered inspecting the sword but didn't think the guards would appreciate him unsheathing a weapon in their presence.

Instead, he gave his brother a level look. Answer enough.

"I have a bill of sale for the longsword," Nicola said, though he heard the first crack in her unwavering confidence.

"If I were you," Zeke said, "I'd focus on discovering who among your intimate circle took the doll, rather than clinging to someone else's family's heirloom."

Hugh's drink paused halfway to his mouth. "What are you saying? Someone on our staff or a family friend stole from us?"

"Staff, friend...family."

Hugh's eyes widened and his attention shot to his wife.

Nicola waved her hand in irritation. "The Kämmer and Reinhardt is none of your concern. I'm here to retrieve my property."

"A twenty-first-century receipt won't hold up against the original," he said, "nor a one-hundred-year-old newspaper clipping about the theft that included a picture of my great-great-grandfather standing beneath the sword."

Phin's eyes clashed with his. "This is the stolen sword?"

He nodded. "Lupos."

"Lupos," Nicola repeated slowly as if it was the first time she was hearing the sword's name.

"You've been searching for it all this time?" Phin asked.

"Off and on, but seriously in the past year."

A mixture of hurt and anger clouded Phin's features before they molded into resolution. He turned to Nicola. "We're taking the sword with us."

"I paid a lot of money for that piece. I won't let you just walk away with it."

When the guards fanned out around them, Zeke rose and refastened the scabbard around his waist. "Your Rent-a-Guards are no match for my brother and I."

"Or us," Liv said, entering through the door that led to the outside. Kayla on her heels.

"Liv," Zeke growled, shouldering his way past the guards to her side. *"What are you doing here?"*

She smiled up at him. "Trust me?"

His gaze settled on the curve of her lips. Swallowed hard. "You know I do."

"Then stand aside, Blackwell." Her hand brushed over his abs as she strode away to face off with Nicola.

Kayla winked at him and followed her friend.

Zeke moved to Phin's side, needing masculine support for whatever the two friends and, no doubt, Rohan and Cruz had cooked up.

"In order to avoid bloodshed," Liv said. "I suggest that we allow Kayla to take the sword into her safekeeping."

"Absolutely not," Nicola said.

"No way," Zeke said at the same time.

Liv continued, "Tomorrow, the two of you can produce the documentation necessary to prove ownership."

"The sword will be quite secure, I assure you." Kayla crossed her arms in that way goddesses do to impart their impatience. A silver leaf arm cuff glinted in the light, mocking their resistance.

"You're hardly impartial," Nicola said.

"Are you questioning my integrity?" The look Kayla leveled on the older woman made the socialite seal her ruby-painted lips. "I know a gentleman who can review your paperwork and verify the artifact's provenance."

"Who?" Zeke asked.

"Lan Sardoff. He's an antiquities dealer out of Charlotte. Extremely reputable and a local expert on ancient weaponry."

"You can thank me later, bro," Rohan said in his ear.

Cruz made a grunting noise.

A calculating gleam entered Nicola's eyes. "I'm familiar with Mr. Sardoff."

"So am I," Zeke said, keeping his expression neutral.

"Then you both agree?" Liv asked.

Even without Sardoff's involvement, their plan was a good one. He had no doubt his ownership would be verified.

But the thought of letting Lupos out of his hands felt like a shard of ice scraping its way through his veins, inch by inch.

Hugh stepped forward, a fresh drink in hand. "Sounds like a perfectly reasonable solution to our little problem."

Nicola looked at her husband as if he'd grown a second nose. "Little problem?"

"It's settled then." Liv stepped toward Zeke. "Kayla will take good care of it. Her collection is not so large as Nicola's, but it's significant and well-protected."

Zeke forced his hands to unwind before unfastening the scabbard from his waist and handing it to her.

The smile she sent him warmed a path straight to his heart. He disliked disappointing people, especially his family. But with Liv, disappointing her would be like Thor's hammer flying into his gut.

When Kayla accepted the sword from Liv, Nicola's shoulders snapped into perfect alignment. "I will see you tomorrow and will expect a full apology for your abuse of my hospitality." Her green eyes bore into Liv. "Your parents would be so ashamed."

The consummate professional, Liv's expression didn't change, but Zeke knew the socialite's words hit their mark.

Everyone watched Nicola's exit, even her husband, and Zeke had a feeling they had all made a serious enemy, no matter the outcome of tomorrow's verification process.

43

After escorting Kayla home, Liv and Zeke had stayed long enough for him to inspect the lobbyist's home security and the safe where she'd keep Lupos until the authentication meeting. When he still seemed reluctant to leave, Phin, Rohan, and Cruz offered to stay overnight.

Amused rather than offended, Kayla kicked off her shoes, grabbed four beers from the refrigerator, and challenged the brothers to a game of pool.

The ride with Zeke back to the Friary had been a silent one. Volatile in a way she didn't understand, but had witnessed once before. On a rooftop.

That night in Charlotte, he'd been exorcising demons. So had she.

For her, the fourth anniversary of her husband's death.

For him, his brother's desertion at his birthday dinner—and a deeper scar she was only now figuring out.

Together, they had expelled their demons in a hot splash of water and cool sheets.

But tonight, the farther they drove away from the sword, the more distant Zeke grew.

Did his failed attempt to smuggle the sword out of the St. Martins' museum replay in his mind? Was he upset with her for offering a compromise? Or did something else drag him deeper into silence?

Once they reached the Great Hall, he made a direct line to the sideboard full of liquor and she climbed the stairs. The moment she reached the second floor, she wrenched off her beaded six-inch torture chambers and groaned when her feet leveled out on the plush carpet.

She inched open Brodie's door and, using the glow of moonlight through his window, padded across his room. He lay on his side, turned away from her. When she bent forward to kiss him goodnight, something propped against the spare pillow caught her eye.

Every muscle in her torso clenched tighter and tighter until all the air was forced from her lungs. Tears gathered, blurring her vision. She couldn't blink—wouldn't blink—for fear of the small glove and grass-stained baseball vanishing like a mirage on a heat-soaked Nevada highway.

Tilting her head, she read the faded markings on the palm of the glove. Four awkwardly written letters just below the *Rawlings* logo.

ZEKE.

Until one day he hands over his worn, smelly glove to his own son.

The tears spilled over, plip-plopping on the bedcover, as she recalled Zeke's prediction that the game would whisper to Brodie again. She swiped a hand over her damp cheeks and placed a trembling kiss against her son's soft cheek.

He roused at the spidery touch. A sleepy whine rumbling from his throat until his hand raked across the bed, seeking the comfort of an old friend, the smooth texture of worn leather.

The tension released, and his body sagged into the mattress, his breathing deepening as visions of home runs and double plays pulled him back to sleep.

Liv straightened and backed away, closing the door on a soft click. In the hallway, she stood with one hand on the door handle and her forehead pressed against the smooth wood panel while she fought to get her own breathing and emotions under control.

Did Brodie toss a ball around with Zeke? Sadie? One of the other Blackwells? Or did he quietly sit with the glove and ball, considering?

In truth, she didn't care which. Seeing him in such close proximity with a tool of a sport he once loved so much was enough.

Pushing away from his door, she glanced between her bedroom and the stairs leading down to the Great Hall. Down to Zeke.

She wanted to thank him for what he had done for her son, wanted to thank him for the priceless gift. She wanted. . . *so many things.*

Would he welcome her company? Or be counting down the seconds until she returned upstairs?

The latter possibility made her hesitate. But only for a moment. Leaving her shoes in the hallway, she eased down the stairs until Zeke came into view.

Drink in hand, he stared up at the empty space above the fireplace's mantel. The space where Lupos might be right now if not for her.

As she watched, he drained his glass and, in a violent move, launched it into the stone cavern. Crystal shattered and flames shot upward.

Frustration and fear blasted through the room and rammed up the staircase, pushing her upward and away.

She retreated, her heart aching for the part she'd played in causing his pain.

In her suite, she shimmied out of her clothes, caught her long hair up into a topknot, and allowed the hot shower spray to rinse away the heaviness of the evening. She stayed there for several minutes. Hours, maybe. Long enough for her throat to loosen and her breaths to even out.

After drying off, she traipsed across the bedroom naked to the still-packed suitcase lying open at the foot of the bed. She tugged out clean undergarments, pajama bottoms and a *Don't Moose with the Boss* graphic T-shirt and slipped them on.

Like a nicotine-addicted smoker, her fingers automatically went to the bag containing her late-night snack. Wrenching open the plastic, she unraveled a string of strawberry flavored licorice and bit down on the waxy treat as she strode to the window.

No halo of light pierced through the darkness above the tree line. Instead of finding solace in the chapel, Zeke sought a blue devil oblivion. If only she could have found another way to settle the matter of the sword's ownership. One that wouldn't have ended in imprisonment or bloodshed but would have allowed Zeke to finally bring the heirloom home.

She released the licorice to let it dangle from her mouth as she continued nibbling away at the end. Even though it had been a long day, she wasn't sleepy and, for once, reading didn't appeal.

Maybe she'd finish packing. Nails scraped across her heart, stealing her breath. Maybe not.

Sighing, she turned away from the window and found a large masculine frame silhouetted in her open door.

· · ·

LIV SUCKED IN A SHARP BREATH AND A BIT OF LICORICE SHOT to the back of her throat, forcing an involuntary cough. The now gooey candy rocketed out of her mouth and landed between them.

A wave of heat climbed up her throat.

Thank goodness she hadn't turned on her bedroom light, preferring the gloom after spending hours in dazzling brightness. The knowledge didn't stop the flush from stinging her ears.

Zeke didn't so much as twitch.

Had he knocked? Called her name? If he had, she'd been too lost in thought to hear.

Squinting through the dim moonlight, she noted his once crisp Bond elegance looked as if a drunken hurricane had attacked it. His coat, shoes, and socks were gone and his tie hung loosely around his neck. The unfastened top buttons of his shirt revealed a V of tanned, golden flesh.

Two squat glasses dangled from his strong fingertips. This was not an innocent pause at her door to say goodnight before he ambled on to his own rooms. He intended to linger.

Liv breathed in through her mouth, afraid to engage any more of her senses. One was already burning at the sight of him. She blinked hard to hold back the inferno.

"May I?" he asked in a surprisingly normal voice. No sign of anger, no hint of frustration. How many more acts of violence against the fireplace had it taken to smooth out his edges?

Liv hesitated a moment before nodding.

He stalked inside, shutting the door with the heel of his foot and shooting down her notion about the healing qualities of breaking things. Emotions still churned inside him, and she was now alone with him in a room that suddenly seemed too small.

He held out a glass of sloshing liquid. "You look like you could use one, too."

Taking his offering, she cradled the tumbler between her hands but didn't drink. Not only did she not care for the taste of hard liquor, the stuff had the uncanny ability to knock her on her ass.

Not Zeke. He downed half of his in one gulp.

Another wave of guilt swept over her. "I'm sorry about the longsword. I know how much it meant to you."

He began a slow circuit around her room, stopping every so often to inspect the few personal belongings she hadn't yet packed. "You couldn't possibly."

"Pardon?"

"It's more than an heirloom." He paused near a framed picture of Brodie taking off on his electric blue bike after she'd removed his training wheels. He traced a thumb over the frame and murmured, "It's a talisman, a symbol." A momentary pause, then, "My family's lifeline."

"I don't understand."

"Neither do I, really. Though I can't help but believe—"

He cut himself off, as if embarrassed to go on. His finger fell from the frame.

"Believe what?"

Finishing his drink, he set the empty glass on the desk and faced away from her. The moon shone on his features as he gazed out the window, highlighting a fragility she'd never witnessed there before.

He closed his eyes a moment before he spoke in a tear-roughened voice. "That a three-foot hunk of metal could help me keep my family together."

Liv's mind chased several images—Zeke dining alone,

Grams laying a gentling hand on his arm, Cruz whispering harsh words in his brother's ear, Phin's look of betrayal.

Carefully, she asked, "What's wrong?"

A small, sad smile kicked at the corner of his mouth. "A complicated answer, though I suppose I can sum it up by saying with every decision I make, every question I ask, every job I accept, I shred my brothers' reasons for staying. One day, soon, I will do something that will snap their tie to this place—to me—in two."

Liv frowned. "That can't be true. I've seen y'all together. You're as close as any family can be."

"But did you look beneath the surface? At the rot and decay and their—their disappointment?"

"Disappointment and frustration and annoyance are natural emotions in every family." She moved closer. "You'll work through it."

"The tension has been worsening over the past year. They're reaching their breaking points."

"You believe the longsword's presence will fix this, how?"

He stiffened, yet still kept his back to her. "The sword itself won't fix what's broken, but . . ." His voice faded.

Silence stretched.

"But?"

He shook his head, either unwilling or unable to form the words.

Her conversation with Johona surfaced, and a sudden realization cleaved through her confusion. Somewhere along the way, he'd lost confidence in his ability to lead BARS. It could have been one disastrous incident or a hundred insignificant ones.

Confidence could go two ways. It could soak up the world around it and grow stronger. Or it could turn inward and feed on itself until nothing but crumbs remained.

She'd seen the way his brothers all but leaned forward when he spoke in meetings. They respected him and would follow him anywhere. All they needed were his respect and his belief in them in return.

Sometimes a thing had to fail before a truth showed itself.

"Lan Sardoff will pronounce you as the rightful owner, then we can bring Lupos home."

When he finally angled his head around to look at her, his gaze held something even more powerful than hope. "We?"

She stared at him, feeling exposed and uncertain. No matter how hard she tried, she couldn't stop her growing attraction to this man. Sleeping in his home and seeing how good he was with her son had not helped her cause.

Neither did being alone with him in her bedroom, behind a closed door, in the middle of the night. Although raw, unchecked danger pulsed off him, there was something vulnerable in his unkempt state that made her want to enfold him in her arms and whisper everything would be okay into his ear.

"Of course. I got you into this." She tapped her glass against the air between them. "I won't abandon you now."

She tipped back her drink, remembering too late what nastiness lurked inside. Gulping down the whiskey, she willed herself not to cough or, worse, throw up.

Fire ignited in her throat, streamed down her esophagus, and fanned through her stomach. She attempted a breath, but the fire vaporized what little she had in her lungs.

She tried again.

Nothing.

A large hand whacked her between the shoulder blades and air wheezed past her lips.

"You okay?" His face filled her tear-blurred vision.

She nodded. "Wrong hole."

He gave her a knowing look and disappeared. The faucet in the bathroom turned on, and the whiskey faded to the background.

Had she picked up her dirty underwear off the floor?

She whipped around and squinted into the bathroom. Zeke hadn't bothered to turn on a light, so it was murky by the shower. Enough for him to miss her black panties?

Zeke reappeared, holding out a small glass of water. "Try this."

Once again, she accepted his offering, but this time she didn't hesitate to take a drink. The cool liquid soothed the bourbon's fiery path. "Thanks," she said.

He finished the rest of her drink before sliding the empty glass onto her nightstand. His fingers balanced on the rim of the expensive crystal.

"Would it be so bad?" he asked.

She searched her mind for the thread of their conversation.

We.

Us.

She waited for the inevitable fear to surface. But it didn't.

"No," she whispered into the silence.

Slowly, he turned to face her. Hunger gripped his features, and Liv felt an answering desire deep in her bones.

Every part of her longed for him, wanted him with a passion that frightened the hell out of her.

He closed the distance between them. Feathered the backs of his fingers along the side of her face. "I want to be so deep inside you." Along the arch of her brow. "Tell me you want me there, too."

With his words alone, she recalled the long, slow pressure of him gliding into her, widening her, pleasuring her until both their cries rent the air.

She swallowed, reached out, and grabbed what she wanted. The consequences—well, she would face those later.

"Yes." Her fingers toyed with a button on his shirt. "But not here. My son—"

Before she could finish the thought, he grasped her hand and rushed her down the hall to his bedroom. A quick survey of her surroundings revealed the layout was similar to her own suite, yet his tastes ran to darker colors and sturdier furniture.

Drawing her to a halt next to his bed, he placed her hands on his broad chest. "Continue." A heartbeat. "Please."

Unable to deny him—or herself—the pleasure any longer, she grazed her fingertips over the hard ridges of his stomach through his shirt. She reveled in the way the muscles bunched and twitched beneath her touch. But the tentative contact wasn't enough.

Smoothing her palms around his waist, she tipped back her head and fell into the dark depth of his gaze. "Kiss me, Zeke."

His mouth dove in for hers as if he'd been waiting for the green flag. The moment their lips touched, the last of Liv's caution blinked out.

She melted against him, and her hands burrowed beneath the edge of his shirt. The overwhelming need to reacquaint herself with every square inch of his body sent her fingers exploring.

The impulse to close her eyes and see him with her

hands made her eyelids heavy. He was so warm and smooth . . . and large. So large, everywhere.

The pulsing length of him pressed against her lower stomach, compelling her to cup his ass and pull him closer.

The exquisite friction made them both groan.

Zeke reared back to remove his shirt. He didn't bother unfastening the remaining buttons. Ripping it apart was far more expeditious.

Flying buttons bounced off the wall, the bedside table, and even the ceiling. His garment landed in a soft *thwat* by the window.

The ache at her center pooled into her legs, making them restless with the desire to wrap around his hips. Her heated inner muscles clenched and unclenched, seeking the part of him that would release the explosive pressure building inside her.

She reached up and touched the black onyx hanging from a braided leather rope around his neck. "Does this stone carry meaning for you?"

"The woman I bought it from said—" He broke off and his eyes looked everywhere but at her.

With two fingers on his chin, she gently drew his gaze back to hers. "Said what?"

He swallowed hard, yet he couldn't seem to form the words.

"Nothing you say to me could change how I feel about you, or," she smiled, "stop what's about to happen." She rubbed the stone between her fingers. "Please tell me."

Releasing a long, shuddering breath, he said, "The stone is supposed to help me with decision-making and self-confidence. Ridiculous, I know."

"It's not. I believe in the healing power of gemstones."

"You do?"

She nodded. "I have an uncut rose quartz sitting on my bedside table."

"Why?"

Unable to stop herself, she leaned forward and pressed a kiss where his heart thundered beneath his warm skin. "I put it there four years ago to dull the pain of my grief." Another kiss. This one, a few inches to the left. "I leave it there to—" She skimmed her fingertips over each side of his ribcage, enjoying how her touch made his flesh quiver.

He cupped her face and recaptured her attention. "To what?"

Now it was her turn to break eye contact, but he was having none of it. He bent down to eye level and forced her to look at him. "Don't leave me alone in the Bare Your Heart Club."

She chuckled, but quickly sobered. "Open my heart to love again."

His hands briefly tightened around her face before he rested his forehead against hers. "How's that going for you?" he whispered.

"Showing promise."

He kissed her, tangling his tongue with hers and making her go mad with need. She could no longer recall why it was imperative that she leave tomorrow. What harm would there be to stay a few more days?

She broke away long enough to lick and kiss her way down his neck to his chest. "You are so breathtakingly gorgeous," she whispered against his heated flesh.

His head dropped back as his hand cradled the back of her head, encouraging her toward his taut nipple. In the warmth of her mouth, it hardened even more as she laved the bud, over and over.

Wanting more, she smoothed her hands over the hills

and channels of his stomach to the long length of him. She molded her palm over his thickness and squeezed.

Zeke hissed out a breath above her. It thrilled her to know she could have such an intense effect on him.

He bent and kissed her again. This time with a wild urgency that made her heart explode and the area between her legs tingle.

Working on opening his trousers while drinking in every drop of his drugging kisses made her hands clumsy, but she finally managed to unbutton, unzip, and push his pants and underwear down to his bare ankles.

Their mouths broke away long enough to allow him to kick free of his clothes.

He stood before her, naked.

Pulsing with desire.

Magnificent.

44

THE AMOUNT OF SELF-CONTROL ZEKE HAD LEFT COULD FILL A rain drop. He forced himself to stand still and allow Liv to look her fill.

Admiration flared in her eyes and her lips parted, making the long hours he spent in the gym worthwhile. But when she reached out again to set those wicked fingers on his bare flesh, his control snapped.

"Liv." He tried for a normal tone, but her name emerged on a low, feral growl.

Her hand halted, and she lifted desire-filled eyes up to his. She blinked hard, once, twice, before concern knit her brows.

"Playtime is over." He forced the words between his teeth. "For this round."

Concern gave way to a slow, nefarious smile. "Don't you want me to undress?"

"Hell, yeah."

For days, he'd imagined her naked in his bed, naked in his shower, naked on his desk, naked. . . everywhere. If he put his hands on her now, he would be too rough, too primitive in his need for her.

Grasping the edge of her T-shirt, she drew the thin cotton material, inch by fucking slow inch, up her torso and over her head. The baby blue scrap dropped between them. A line in the sand.

With her head tilted slightly to the right, she gave him a sidelong glance, all but daring him to cross the cotton divide.

"You're toying with danger, Agent Westcott."

Her thumbs hooked into the waistband of her pajama bottoms, though she made no move to remove them.

At his sides, his fingers curled to keep him from yanking her into his arms.

"Danger," her voice husky, "is exactly what I'm looking for tonight."

His mind splintered. There was before, when he heard Gram's voice gnawing at him to treat women with respect, to be a gentleman. And after, when the silent animal in him uncoiled and urged him to give her what she wanted. What he wanted.

"Take them off."

She didn't flinch away from the fire in his voice, as he'd expected. Instead, excitement flared in her eyes.

"These?" she taunted, her thumbs gliding along the rim of her waistband.

"If you want them to remain in one piece, remove them now, or I'll be happy to rip them off."

Interest whirled across her features, yet the practical side must have decided to protect her sleepwear. She pushed them down, along with her panties. First one hip, then the next, her eyes never leaving his. Over and over until her PJs drooped around her ankles.

By the time her foot flicked them to the side, Zeke realized he'd misread her. Practical had nothing to do with her choice.

Strategy drove her every action. She understood either intellectually or instinctually the best way to drive him out of his ever-loving mind, to slam a mental door on his family, the business, and the sword, to live in this moment—with her—was to capture his undivided, lust-induced attention.

Mission accomplished, agent.

He crossed the cotton divide.

Releasing her hair from its topknot, he speared his fingers through her silky locks and clamped his hand around the base of her head. He bent forward until his lips grazed her ear. "The rest, Liv."

Her breath shuddered against his chest as she reached behind her to unfasten her bra. It slid down her arms before joining the shipwreck of clothing on the floor.

Curling his other hand around her hip, he added pressure until her body was flush against his. Every nerve ending tingled and writhed beneath his skin. Sandwiched between them, his erection pulsed and stretched, seeking her internal warmth.

Her homecoming.

Wrapping her arms around him, she smoothed her cheek against his pec like a kitten rubbing its soft head against its human's palm. Her nails raked and soothed, raked and soothed along his spine.

A wild need to be deep inside her drove through his veins, and his hips thrust forward. The exquisite friction of their pressed bodies compelled him to do it again. And again.

"Zeke," she gasped, "I need—I want . . ."

His hands cupped her sweet ass, lifting her until her hot,

wet center clamped over him, sending him to new levels of torturous pleasure-pain.

"Liv," he whispered against her neck. The word a plea and a demand.

"Put us both out of our misery," she breathed against his lips before sliding her tongue into his mouth.

The slick heat of her inside his mouth ignited a fire in his veins that only she could stoke. Every cell in his body reached for her. Demanded that he take what she offered.

Striding to his high bed, he laid her against the soft cover, his mouth never leaving hers. Their kiss grew wilder, stronger, hotter. It explored and plundered, retreated and advanced.

Breaking off, he pressed a fiery trail of possession down her throat, over one ruched peak, along her firm stomach to the length of her toned thigh. The musky scent of her desire filled his nose, and he almost came right then.

He wanted to taste her, tongue her until his name ripped from her throat.

But he had wanted her for too long. His time was up.

"Do not fucking move an inch," he growled against her inner thigh.

At Zeke's guttural command, Liv couldn't lift a brow, let alone her head, to see why she no longer felt his scorching heat.

While her body writhed against the bedcover, she heard the tinkling of a belt buckle, the slap of something heavy hitting the floor, then the blessed rip of packaging.

Soon, his big body loomed over her again. The arm balanced near her shoulder trembled slightly as he bent to kiss her again, while his knuckle grazed her opening, checking her readiness.

"Now, Zeke," she all but begged.

Their eyes met, and he slowly licked her essence from his index finger, then bent low to run his tongue along hers. The taste of him mixed with her had her hips lifting off the bed, seeking, begging for release from his sensual torture.

Reaching down, he positioned himself at her entrance. Rather than plunge inside, as she wanted him to, needed him to, he reached up to remove a lock of hair stuck to the corner of her mouth.

Something elemental, something that had survived lifetimes and spanned universes, shifted between them.

Connected.

Multiplied.

Spread like a virus at soul level. She grasped his head with both hands and savaged his lips with hers, letting him know that what happened next between them meant something more to her than a simple expulsion of desire.

It meant *more*.

Her lust-fogged mind couldn't work out exactly what *more* was, at the moment, but she needed to warn him, needed him to know.

He pushed into her.

Every inch sizzled and pulsed and pierced the fragile layer of control she kept wrapped around her, day and night.

From the first moment his dark eyes had latched on to hers, as he'd lowered himself into the rooftop Jacuzzi, she'd sensed she could let go with him.

Halt the endless, exhausting cycle of *what-ifs*, put to rest the *what-comes-next* decisions, and simply be a woman desirous of a mind-blowing orgasm.

"You feel so fucking good, baby," he whispered, watching his slow withdrawal.

When the tip of him hovered at her entrance, his eyes sought hers.

He pushed into her with more force, and Liv dug her heels into the bed, meeting him halfway. They kept this rhythm, once, twice, but on the third stroke, he braced both hands on the bed and drove into her, over and over and blessedly over.

Grasping his arms, she did her best to meet his bruising, soul-searing pace. Much too soon, electricity flickered to life, low in her stomach. It grew and grew until it shot into her core and lightninged into her extremities.

Her back arched, and Zeke tensed above her, releasing a pleasure-packed, *"Fuuuck."*

Moments later, their chests heaved against each other, and Zeke's breaths fanned across her damp skin.

Lifting his head, he kissed her tenderly, so tenderly that tears gathered in the corners of her eyes. He pushed himself into a standing position, raked his gaze down her satiated naked body before padding to the bathroom.

She should feel ridiculous, lying there with her legs dangling over the side of the bed, but the emotion that rose to the surface was joy.

Pure joy. Happiness that she hadn't felt in a long time.

For the first time since Tyler's death, she looked forward to the future. Somehow it no longer stretched out before her like the endless, barren wild-scape of a Mojave winter.

The miles of undulating sand of before now blossomed with red, orange, white, and purple spring flowers. A vibrant landscape of possibilities and hope.

She prayed a late-night frost wouldn't descend and kill it all.

45

THE FAINT SCENT OF COFFEE PULLED ZEKE FROM AN incredible dream, hard and aching.

Not an unusual state for him since Liv had been under the same roof. But after last night's lovemaking, he once again dreamed about her in 3D, full-color, and with a room full of subwoofers.

Lying on his stomach, he pressed his lower body into the mattress and moaned out Liv's name as he reached for her.

"What do you think?" a masculine voice said. "Should we wait for the finale or call for an intermission?"

Zeke bolted up on his elbows, blinking moisture back in his scratchy eyes.

At his desk, Phin reclined in his leather chair with an ankle propped on one knee, lifting a mug with the words "Coffee. . . because murder is messy" etched on the side.

"What the fuck—?" Zeke looked at the other side of the bed to make sure Liv was covered.

Only her side was empty.

The sheets cold.

"Looking for someone?" Cruz asked, leaning against the closed bedroom door, a knowing smirk on his face.

Rohan stood at the window, drenched in a ray of morning sun, his expression pensive.

A knot of apprehension formed in Zeke's gut, killing his hard-on.

"What's going on?" He had his suspicions, but he couldn't seem to chisel the muck off his brain.

"A question I've been asking myself after hearing about your little run-in with our target last night," Cruz said. "Why didn't you tell us about the sword?"

Zeke threw his feet over the side of the bed and strode bare-assed into his closet. After throwing on a pair of track pants and a T-shirt, he headed to the kitchenette tucked into one corner of his suite and dropped a biodegradable K-cup in the Keurig machine. No one said another word until a stream of piping hot coffee filled his cup.

"Zeke," Cruz prompted.

Even though he knew he shouldn't, he sipped his coffee and was predictably rewarded with a scalded tongue. He focused on the pain while formulating his thoughts. In the end, he only stalled the inevitable.

"I didn't tell you because you didn't care about it."

Phin stared at the opposite wall, taking in the small display of weapons, old and new. "Why do you?"

"Because it's our family legacy."

Phin shook his head. "It's more than that. You went to a damn masquerade ball. Willingly. You've been unusually invested in this case from the start."

"That's bullshit, and you know it," Zeke said. "I do whatever I need to do to get the job done."

"Oh, yeah? Where exactly does stealing a sword and

jeopardizing our sanctioned mission fall into that equation?"

He set his cup down with a sharp clunk. "Are you questioning my commitment?"

"I'm questioning your motives and your actions."

Stepping forward, he rolled his hands into nose breakers. "My actions have kept this company alive."

"I'm not talking about the past three years, for fuck's sake. I'm calling you out about last night, you damn dipshit."

Rohan put a restraining hand on Zeke's arm. "Perhaps we should postpone this discussion until after breakfast."

Phin honed in on Rohan. "Don't you have anything to say about our brother working a clandestine case without informing us?"

"No."

"Why the hell not?"

"Because I've been helping him."

Cruz and Phin stared at Rohan as if he'd just announced he found a third testicle.

Releasing a breath, Zeke took advantage of their distraction to calm his bubbling emotions.

Logically, he understood that his current ill-temper had more to do with finding Liv gone than any nonsense Phin flung at him about the sword.

Why had she left his bed again?

When had she left?

From the cold sheets, she'd been gone well before the guys barged in.

In a way, he was glad. He didn't like the idea of his brothers seeing Liv naked and disheveled. She was hard to resist clothed and put together. Rumpled and bare beneath a thin sheet would send any red-blooded man's mind down a path of fantasy.

"Dammit, Rohan," Cruz said at the same time Phin demanded, "What do you mean you've been helping him?"

Rohan resumed his place by the window. This time, he leaned a shoulder against the frame. "Searching the dark web for any mention of a sword meeting Lupos's description."

"Did you also know in advance about the hat trick he performed at the St. Martins'?" Phin asked.

"No," Zeke said. "I didn't even know what I was going to do last night."

Not entirely true. He'd worn the Zorro costume, with its cape and sword, knowing if he found Lupos he would attempt to walk out of there with it.

Phin snorted. "Your choice of costume was a happy coincidence, then?"

"I'm that good, bro."

"Enough of the bullshit, Zeke," Cruz said in a tired voice. "How'd you know the sword would be there?"

He took a drink of coffee, relishing the liquid's burn down his throat.

"I got a tip from an associate."

"An associate?" Cruz echoed.

"Sardoff?" Phin guessed, incredulous. "You told him about your quest, but not us?"

"What's it going to take to get you off my back about this?" Zeke's body itched to pace. His suite wasn't small, but when four Blackwell men breathed the same air, most spaces tended to shrink.

Besides, he refused to give these nosey-ass jamokes the upper hand. He would present the appearance of calm, even if it killed him.

"An apology?" Zeke pressed. "I'm sorry. I should have told you about my hunt for a stolen heirloom you couldn't give two shits about. I'm sorry for taking advantage of a prime opportunity to get our family's property back." He took in each of his brothers. "We good now?"

With Flash-like speed, Phin pushed out of his chair and stormed across the room. "You can be a real asshole, Zeke."

Cruz opened the door, and their little brother disappeared down the hallway.

Shaking his head, Cruz said, "Shitty apology accepted."

Zeke bit down on the inside of his cheek as his second-in-command left. A heavy silence descended on the room, and he glanced up to find Rohan studying him.

"Go ahead, say it."

"Told you, bro." Rohan paused, as if considering humankind's presence in the world. "Felt as good as I thought it would."

Zeke dropped into his favorite chair, a camel-colored recliner that doubled as a bed when the muscles in his lower back decided to throw a torture party.

He planted his elbows on his thighs and clamped his hands around his head. "Who's surprised I screwed up something else?"

In a quiet voice, Rohan asked, "How did it feel to hold it?"

Unable to speak around his tight throat, he nodded.

"Was it everything you expected?"

Lifting his head, he said, "It was...more than I expected. So much more."

"Do you feel different after having had it in your possession?"

Sighing, he sank into the cushions and leaned his head back. "Do you mean do I feel smarter, stronger, more capable of leading this motley crew?"

"That's what you thought, right? That holding the

symbol of our ancestors' power would imbue you with their wisdom, respect, and strength?"

"Too fantastical?"

"Too easy."

"What am I going to do, Rohan? I can't—none of us can —continue on as we are."

"It's simple."

Zeke raised a brow.

"Trust your team."

"*I do.*"

"No, you don't. Not fully."

"Eighty-eight percent of our business comes from word of mouth. If we fail to recover an asset, it not only affects getting more clients, but the livelihoods of every member of this family."

"We won't fail, because we're a team," Rohan said. "We'll make mistakes, yes. No matter how talented someone is— even you—mistakes are inevitable. But BARS is made up of highly motivated, highly competitive men and women. No one will stop until the asset is in the rightful owner's hands."

"I understand what you're saying—what everyone is saying—but the reality isn't so fucking black-and-white."

Rohan removed his glasses and hooked them in the collar of his button-down shirt, as if he didn't want any barriers between them. His brother could see fine without them, but wearing them made the world more crisp. Revealed nuances he couldn't pick up with the naked eye. Or so he said.

"You know how Mom refuses to throw away the scratched album the five of us bought for her when we were kids?" Rohan asked.

Snoopy's Red Baron. They had pooled together their minuscule resources and given it to her as a Christmas present. She'd been so happy that tears had slid down her cheeks. A rarity. He could count on two fingers the number of times he'd seen his mom cry over the years.

Zeke nodded. "There are so many scratches that it's impossible to listen to without sitting beside the record player."

"Why do you suppose she keeps nursing it along?"

"Sentimental reasons, I suppose."

"Most likely." Rohan regarded him with eyes too ancient for his twenty-nine years. "Or was it an inability to let go? The record is obviously more frustration than pleasure now. Why not get a new album, one that doesn't hiccup every ten seconds, and store the old one away?"

Times like this solidified his fear that the right Blackwell wasn't leading BARS. It seemed any one of his brothers could do a damn sight better job than him.

But he wasn't a quitter and, despite recent history, he could adapt. It only took banging his stubborn head—like his mom's—against the Rock of Reason two, five, a hundred times before he got it.

"Message received, bro." He pushed out of his chair, a new energy firing through his veins.

"Now get out of here. I need to shower and speak to Liv before we huddle up this morning. Something about the doll's disappearance is bugging me, and I need to talk it out with everyone."

When Rohan said nothing, Zeke grew still. "What haven't you told me?"

Rohan's eyes flicked to the bed, then returned to him. "She's gone."

46

HEART POUNDING, LIV FAST-WALKED UP THE SIDEWALK leading to her open front door, a testament to the number of law enforcement officials coming in and out of her home in the past two hours.

Minutes before dawn, she'd untangled herself from Zeke's warm body to pad down the hall to her own bathroom. She used her phone to light the way, and it was a good thing. No sooner than she finished her business, she received a call from her alarm service, letting her know they had dispatched the police to check on a tripped alarm.

Instinct told her this wasn't a false one. A quick look at her weather app confirmed there had been no thunderstorms in the area last night, no power outages, nothing that would easily explain why the alarm went off.

Thank goodness Callie was still staying with friends. Although she didn't need one more thing on her plate, she could deal with replacing a few stolen electronics.

By the time she rinsed off Zeke's scent and shrugged on fresh clothes, the expected phone call came in.

Home invasion.

What the reporting officer told her chilled her bones.

After writing Zeke a note, she crossed the hallway to rouse Brodie from his warm bed. While he used the restroom and dressed, she finished packing their belongings.

The whole sequence had taken less than ten minutes, but every second that ticked by felt like a year of her life falling away.

She didn't want to leave, had even contemplated staying a few more days. But this morning's phone call had changed everything.

While she'd waited in the hallway for Brodie to emerge from his room, she stared at Zeke's bedroom door. She ached to slip inside and kiss him goodbye, but she couldn't, for so many reasons. Mostly because she didn't trust herself enough not to climb back into bed beside him and let him kiss away her fears.

AFTER DROPPING BRODIE OFF AT HER PARENTS' HOUSE, SHE'D driven across town in record time. Even though the R/O had given her the skinny on the damage, Liv still couldn't believe her eyes when she found the family room and kitchen still intact.

No hint of the intruder's passage through these rooms. No forewarning of the utter destruction she found within the ten-by-ten space, first door to the left.

Brodie's bedroom.

Standing in the doorframe of her son's room, she tried to mentally process the chaos inside.

Smashed toys covered every inch of the floor like shattered crystal and only ragged strips remained of the super hero posters dotting the walls. Mattress padding bulged from dozens of twelve-inch slashes across the surface and the new computer and gaming devices on the desk now looked like roadkill. Every stitch of clothing in the closet lay in a shredded heap on the floor.

Liv's breath seemed stuck inside her chest. Every shallow inhalation hurt with the effort to fill her lungs. But what froze the blood in her veins and caused her heart to flame out were the words carved deep into the drywall above Brodie's bed.

A Loss 4 A Loss.

This was no random burglary.

Whoever destroyed her son's room and belongings had done so with calculation and malice.

But why? What loss was the intruder referring to? And why did her son pay the cost?

Two evidence technicians worked the room, taking pictures and dusting for prints. It was doubtful they'd find anything, given how methodical the intruder was in their messaging. But no crime was perfect, and Liv prayed the techs got lucky.

"How are you doing?" a low feminine voice asked.

Liv looked up to find Detective Marissa Schuler of the Asheville Police Department at her elbow. She'd had the pleasure of coordinating with the detective two years ago on a case involving the theft of a rare Japanese print. It had taken them five days to track down and recover the asset.

Schuler was solid, and Liv was glad to have her working this B&E.

"Detective," Liv said, "I'd like to say it's good to see you again." Her gaze raked over her son's destroyed possessions. "But I can't quite pull off sincerity right now."

"Don't even try. If this was my son's room, I'd either be babbling in an inconsolable heap on the floor or booking passage to some remote, faraway island with a state-of-the-art security system."

"A faraway island has some appeal at the moment." Anything to nuke the threat to her son.

But the longer Liv stared at the violence, the more pissed off and determined she grew. Tracking down the coward who'd decided to terrorize her through violating her son's bedroom would be an absolute pleasure.

"Somehow I don't think the asshole who did this would be so lucky as to have you retreat."

A ghost of a smile fanned over Liv's lips. "No, they wouldn't."

"Our preliminary assessment is that he entered there." Using her fifty-cent conference pen, Schuler pointed to the window next to Brodie's desk. "The window frame is busted on the outside, and the burglar left the pry bar behind."

Sweat broke out on Liv's palms at the thought of what could have happened if Brodie had been here at the time of the break-in. She had Zeke to thank for not having to face that nightmare.

"We didn't find any surveillance cameras pointed at this side of the house," Detective Schuler said. The suffocating band around Liv's chest tightened. She had cameras on the front and back doors, but not the bedroom windows. "That's correct." She tried her damnedest to keep the recrimination from her voice. There would be plenty of time later to beat up herself. "Just the entrances."

"I'd recommend pulling the recordings. You never know. We might get lucky."

"I'll get copies from my alarm service." Liv took in the room again. "I was told this was the only part of the house affected."

"As far as we can tell, but it would be best if you did a

walkthrough. You would know better than us if anything's missing or been tampered with."

With near robotic movements, Liv pivoted to do as Schuler suggested. The detective laid a hand on her forearm. "We'll get whoever did this, I swear it."

Liv didn't doubt the detective. As a mother of two, Schuler would want to ensure this didn't happen to another little boy. But in that moment, all Liv could think about was how she was going to break the news to Brodie.

Until she noticed that the framed photo—the one Brodie had kept facedown on his desk since the day of his father's funeral—was missing.

47

HOLDING A LARGE BLACK TRASH BAG, LIV ONCE AGAIN STOOD on the threshold of her son's bedroom. Now that she had the house to herself and an okay from the police, she wanted to see what, if anything, was still salvageable, then pitch the rest.

The heaviness in her heart kept her immobile. A tear crowded into the corner of one eye before it flung itself over the edge.

She was no closer to knowing how she would explain this travesty to Brodie. He'd lost so much already. First his dad, then his favorite sport, and now the safety of his room.

Given the nature of her job, she had stood in the center of many crime scenes before. None had made her feel like an army of ants were stampeding beneath her skin.

The front doorknob rattled.

Dropping the bag, she drew her firearm before easing down the hallway to the family room. She peered around the corner, but her entryway contained no sidelights for her to identify who might be on the other side.

A Reacher-sized fist slammed against the fiberglass door, making her jump. "Liv!"

The pent-up breath she'd been holding hissed between her teeth, and she splayed her free hand wide to release the tension.

Another savage pound. "Liv, open up!" Zeke's silhouette appeared before the large picture window facing the street. He cupped his hands around his face and peered inside.

Even though he shouldn't be able to see her through the sheer curtain, his eyes seemed to latch onto hers as he stabbed a finger toward the door.

A contrary mixture of joy at seeing him and irritation at his high-handedness held her in place.

His eyes narrowed and his jaw firmed, yet he still said the magic word in a low rumble. "Please."

Any other time, she would have smiled at his disgruntled tone. Not today. Smiling would tax the short supply of energy she still had in the tank.

She stalked forward, flipped the dead bolt, and shielded her handgun behind her thigh before swinging the door wide. "What are you doing here?"

He thundered past her. "That's my line."

Frowning, she closed the door. "Didn't you find my note?"

He rattled a wrinkled piece of paper in the air between them. "This doesn't qualify as a note." He recited from memory. "Something's come up at home. Good luck this morning."

Eyes wide, she checked her watch. With her mind still half-buried in the destruction down the hall, she'd forgotten about his appointment with the authenticator.

"Why aren't you at Kayla's?"

He stilled, noticing the weapon she tried to hide. Then

he took in her ripped, decades-old jeans, faded T-shirt, and sloppy bun at the back of her head.

Slowly, he scanned his surroundings, his head cocked slightly to the side like a wolf trying to pinpoint the exact location of a juicy rabbit moving through tall grasses.

"Where's Brodie?"

"I dropped him off at my parents' house."

"I didn't take your parents for the babysitting kind."

"Callie is on her way there."

"What's going on, Liv? Something doesn't feel right."

"Don't worry about it. You need to get to Kayla's." Reholstering her gun, she retrieved her phone from her back pocket and tapped through until she brought up her contacts.

"What are you doing?"

"Calling Kayla. I'll ask her to push back the meeting long enough for you to get there."

He ripped the phone out of her hand.

"What the hell, Zeke?"

"I'll deal with that later." He tossed her phone onto the couch. "What happened?"

"What if there is no later? What if Nicola takes the sword? She could bury it so deep in one of her many estates that we'll never find it."

His dark gaze remained steady on hers as he said, "So be it."

She stared at him, uncomprehending. "You've been searching for your family's heirloom for years. All you have to do is show up, flash a document, and take it home."

When he said nothing, she threw up her hands. "I don't understand you. Why would you jeopardize something so important to you?"

"A wise woman once told me, 'A sword does not make the man, the man makes the sword.'"

"Johona?"

He nodded and strode to the window, crossing his arms. "In my misguided mind, I had convinced myself that once I set the sword in its place of honor in the Great Hall, that everything wrong with BARS would magically right itself. That we would all unite, rally around an artifact that had survived wars and all manner of hardships." His voice lowered. "I thought. . . I thought it would somehow reveal the secrets to being a good leader." He shook his head. "Horseshit, of course, but I needed to believe in something. Something that could fix what I had broken."

She moved to his side. "And now?"

A self-deprecating smile appeared, and he tilted a side-long look her way as he knocked a knuckle against the side of his head. "A battering ram of logic by enough people I care about and trust. Including you." The back of his finger whispered along the edge of her jaw. "Especially you."

The warmth of his touch heated the cold pit in her stomach. "I'm happy for you, Zeke. Awareness is the first step to healing." She placed a hand on his lower back. "But you need to go claim Lupos."

He shook his head. "I'm where I need to be."

His caress shifted to include her bottom lip. She wanted to lean into it, allow him to brush away the dread creeping over her flesh. But her mind kept returning to Brodie's room, to the message carved into his wall.

As if sensing her thoughts, he dropped his arms and turned away from the window. "Enough about the sword. What forced you to leave my bed and"—paper rumpled in his fist—"write this useless note?"

"I left it intentionally vague so you wouldn't do something stupid." She narrowed her eyes at him. "Like follow me."

"Well, your little slight of pen trick didn't work." His voice grew hard. "Tell me."

A rush of defeated air puffed between her lips. "Someone broke into my house."

His eyes turned to molten onyx as he scanned the room again. "What did they take?"

"Only one thing that I've discovered so far. They seemed more focused on leaving me a message." She headed toward the bedroom. "Follow me."

48

ZEKE FOLLOWED LIV THROUGH THE HOUSE, WILLING THE MASS of caterpillars in his gut to disappear. They had fallen there, bulbous bodies writhing and tiny feet scrapping, after Rohan's early morning announcement.

During the endless drive, he'd convinced himself that the "something's come up at home" was nothing but an excuse to flee what she perceived was a terrible mistake.

Not him, though. Having Liv in his bed again was like taking the first bite of Grams's pecan pie. Delicious and warm and like Dorothy's Kansas.

Home.

Pausing outside Brodie's bedroom, Liv glanced at him as if to say "brace yourself" before motioning him in ahead of her.

One look inside, and the caterpillars drop-kicked him in the solar plexus. "What the fuck?" The place looked like a gang of Tasmanian Devils had played ping-pong inside. Then he noticed the jagged carving above the bed.

A loss 4 a loss.

"What the hell does that mean?"

"I don't know." She stooped to pick up a large garbage bag. "I've plowed through memory after memory, trying to find a connection. But nothing's popping."

"Do you think they were looking for something? Or was this some sort of payback?"

"Your guess is as good as mine. I've run through my recent cases and can't tie in any of them to this." She stooped down and picked up a decapitated Wonder Woman from the pile of disfigured action heroes. "This was personal. Deeply personal."

Zeke gently pried the toy from her fingers and dropped it into the garbage bag. "What about the guy stalking the social media influencer?"

"Jeremy Jackson."

"Is he still bothering Ivy?"

"I checked in with her a few days ago, but she hasn't returned my phone call."

"If he was that into her, he wouldn't like being cut off."

"Jackson's a coward. I can't see him risking a B and E. He likes to play in the shadows."

"Just because he avoided a face-to-face confrontation with you doesn't mean he's not capable of violence."

She rubbed her right temple. "You're right." If anyone should understand the vagaries of human behavior, it should be her.

"What about your volunteer work? Callie mentioned once that you help women in need. Any recent issues there?"

"Everyone I've assisted through the women's center has been nothing but grateful."

"What about a pissed-off spouse, significant other, brother, father, son—someone negatively impacted by your good works?"

"Nobody who would have cause to react like this—" Her words cut off abruptly while she stared at the boarded-up window.

"You've thought of something."

"One of the women, Claudia Rogers, is married to a man who likes his habitat—clothes, home, meals—a certain way. In the past year, when his wife's efforts fell short of his expectations, he let her know. The abuse started with a few isolated outbursts, then came the gaslighting, rough handling, and finally the beatings."

Men who used their strength to intimidate those weaker than them ranked right up there with pedophiles and serial killers in his book.

"Yesterday, the center's director called me. Claudia returned with a bloodied nose and a busted-out front tooth."

"Fucking bastard."

She nodded. "The director made arrangements for Claudia to go to her cousin in Raleigh, while I worked with my aunt to get an order of protection."

"What changed?"

"Claudia believes he'll go back to normal—whatever that means—once he's done with some high-profile project at work."

"What about kids?"

"One adult son. I'm not sure what kind of hold the father has on him. Claudia seemed reluctant to get him involved."

"He's a grown-ass man."

She shrugged, bending to pick up a shattered frame. The torn picture inside was of her and a younger Brodie in swimwear going down a water-gurgling slide. "Mothers are wired to protect their cubs, no matter their age."

"What does the husband do for a living?" He moved toward the wall of superhero posters.

"Owns a shop that specializes in performance of turbocharged vehicles. Don't ask me to explain."

"It means they make sports cars look cooler and go a helluva lot faster." He ripped down what was left of the posters and removed the thumb tacks. "Think she'll go back to him?"

"The odds aren't in her favor. On average, survivors leave and return to their abusers six times before getting out for good."

"Damn."

"Every situation is unique, but survivors generally have multiple, complicated reasons for staying—or returning." She rubbed her forehead with the back of her hand.

"I take it the husband knows you've been assisting his wife?"

Her expression turned sheepish.

"Spill it."

"Before this," she waved her hand around the room, "I would have said no."

"But now?"

"She must have told him or maybe he saw me or—I don't know."

"Saw you, when?"

She winced. "When Claudia left the shelter the first time, I followed her home."

"You did what?"

"It was stupid, I know." She released an exhausted sigh. "But I wanted to see."

"See what?"

She shrugged. "That she was safe. The bastard's face.

Birdshit on the window. Hell if I know. There was no logic to my actions. I just wanted to see."

"And?"

"They hugged, then went inside." A line of concentration creased her forehead. "Her son Alan was there, too, though that fact didn't make me feel any better about the situation."

"Why not?"

Another shrug. "The only thing that would have felt right was Claudia staying at the center." Sadness entered eyes. "Seems I was right. Hooray."

He avoided bringing up the O'Fallon case. Reminding her about the former politician who had decided to establish a legacy for his five kids by selling priceless artifacts on the dark web—or wherever one sold stolen antiquities these days—might put her over the edge.

He slid a hand around the back of her neck and drew her close. "You did what you could."

"Did I? I'm not convinced. The poor woman suffered a broken nose and lost a tooth and had to leave her home."

"She's safe now, thanks to you." He brushed a thumb over her cheek. "We have to do the same for you and Brodie."

She placed a hand on his uplifted arm. "You have enough to worry about back in Steele Ridge." Her gaze slid down to the remnants of her son's toys. "My aunt will help me figure out who's behind this."

Desperately wanting to remove the look of devastation from her face, Zeke hooked a finger under her chin until her beautiful eyes met his. "There's nothing in Steele Ridge more important to me than keeping you and Brodie safe."

As the meaning of his words sank in, her eyes flared wide and the garbage bag sagged to the floor.

"But your family, BARS, the sword—"

"Are number two, number three, and number four."

She rolled her lips between her teeth as if to keep them from trembling. "Zeke, I don't know what to say. If you're alluding to what I think you are, my position and your business—"

"Let me be clear," he interrupted. "I love you, Special Agent Olivia Westcott, and Brodie's carved on my heart, too. The rest, we will figure out." He smiled. "Because that's what we both do best—figure shit out."

For a long moment, her features remained in a stasis of cautious hope and complicated reality.

Then a muscle twitched at the corner of her mouth and her gaze made a languid journey from his eyes to his mouth.

His body went rock hard and his mind turned laser-sharp. The desire to protect and possess waged a mini damn war, both on equal footing, until she reared up on her toes and whispered against his lips.

"Figuring shit out is number two."

His free hand snaked around her waist. "Number one?"

"Making each other scream."

49

"WHAT DO YOU MEAN, YOU LOST THE DOLL?" ASH ASKED.

In the distance, Liv sat at a picnic table, earbud in place, while she FaceTimed with someone. Zeke kept his attention fixed on her as he and Ash made a circuit around the park's asphalt trail.

After a hard and fast round on her bed, where they screamed their release in unison, Zeke had pulled Liv into the shower for a slow and thorough lovemaking.

Once they fed their sated bodies, he finished cleaning up the mess in Brodie's room, while Liv made a few phone calls. She checked in on Claudia Rogers, tried Ivy again, scheduled tradesmen to fix Brodie's window and walls, and sent Pierce to relieve Callie so her sister could go on a shopping expedition.

Returning Brodie's room to what it was before the break-in would be impossible, but Liv was determined to get it close.

Sometimes it was good to be a trust fund baby. Money made shit happen fast.

"Are you thinking?" Ash asked after a protracted silence. "Or avoiding?"

"If I was avoiding, I would've called instead of standing beside you and enduring your scowl of disappointment."

Liv lifted her eyes from her phone to look their way. Even from here, he could see the worry on her features. She'd wanted to help him explain to his brother how they failed him, but Zeke had refused. This was his shitshow to set right.

But he wasn't about to let her out of his sight, so this was their compromise.

"Nicola St. Martin offered to show us her private museum. Which was our primary purpose for attending the event."

"Yeah, I got it. You needed to confirm the artifact's location and know how to get in and out of there for when you swiped the doll later."

"Recovered."

"If that verb helps you sleep at night, great."

Zeke stopped. "The FBI, *your agency,* hired BARS for a recovery. Are you telling me the CI isn't the doll's owner?"

Ash's jaw clenched. "What does it matter? You lost it."

"I didn't fucking lose anything. Someone stole it while I was doing my job." His attention drifted back to Liv.

"When did you start doing recon work?"

Since getting a bead on a priceless fucking heirloom with mystical leadership voodoo.

"I had a personal interest in seeing the St. Martins' museum."

Ash studied him for a long moment. "What are you not telling me?"

Zeke resumed walking. This was a mistake. He should have called Ash, told him the case went south, apologized for fucking up his career, then gone on a twelve-hour bender.

Ash caught his arm. "Slow down."

He shrugged him off, keeping his eye on his destination. Liv.

"Zeke," Ash planted himself in his path, an arm stretched out between them. "Talk to me. What happened at the St. Martins' party?"

"I just told you."

"Tell me the part you don't want to tell me."

He'd already looked the fool enough today. Telling his big brother that he thought having their family sword at the Friary, where he could see it, touch it, absorb its mystical, nonexistent power, was a humiliation he would not endure.

When he made to sidestep Ash's bulk, his brother said, "You found Lupos."

Zeke froze. His eyes squeezed shut briefly before he glared at Ash. "Who—?" His accusatory gaze shot to Liv, who looked up at the precise moment as if she felt his confusion. His hurt.

Had she called Ash? Had she felt compelled to notify her colleague of the aborted mission without him?

Seeing the direction of his thoughts, Ash said, "I didn't hear about the sword from Olivia."

"Who?" Then it came to him. "Phin."

"He called me, demanding to know if I was aware of your unauthorized side project."

"I don't need permission from the FBI to retrieve our family's property."

"His words, bro. Not mine."

Zeke pushed out a frustrated breath. "He could give two shits about the sword, yet he's pissy about not knowing I was searching for it."

"Phin feels things more deeply than the rest of us. Always has."

"He needs to suck it up. I'll be damned if I'm going to run every personal project I'm working on by my kid brother in order for him to feel involved in my life."

"He wants the family united again."

"So do I." Zeke gave his brother a level look. Thanks to Ash's defection, their family dynamic would never be what it once was. "But that's not gonna happen."

Ash looked away, and Zeke took a perverse pleasure in his brother's discomfort. But Ash never dwelled there long.

"Are you sure you didn't tell any of us about your Indiana Jones expedition because you were afraid of failure?"

Something snapped in the deep recesses of his mind like the restraints holding down a thrashing patient.

One second, he was facing his brother and, the next, his shoulder was plowing into the bastard's solar plexus. The force swept Ash off his feet long enough for Zeke to pin him against the nearest tree.

Air whooshed out of Ash's lungs, and his brother stood frozen for a full second before he growled, "You're going to regret that, little brother."

His fist cut into Zeke's jaw. Pain shattered his skull, but his hold on his brother didn't break.

In the distance, Liv yelled his name. He ignored her. Blood lust and years of resentment had taken control, and he wanted nothing more than to vent his rage on the selfish prick who'd lit the flame.

"The only thing I regret is that I didn't do it years ago."

"Still blaming me for your inability to not be a control freak?"

"Picking up your slack while still doing my job isn't being a control freak. It's doing what needs doing."

"What needs doing is for you to delegate."

"To whom? Everyone's plate is full."

"You're going to tell me that Rohan, Cruz, and Phin, who all spend their evenings and a good portion of their weekends in pursuit of reading ancient tomes, working on muscle cars, and visiting nightclubs, can't pull another hour each day to reduce the load on your shoulders?" He shoved Zeke away. "Bullshit, little brother. *Bullshit.*"

A truth he couldn't deny, and one he'd come to realize in the past year, yet he still convinced himself to give them space to do their jobs.

In many ways, he had. In other ways, he hadn't.

His mind never rested. It constantly jumped from point to point. Always analyzing, always ticking off items on a never-ending to-do list. Always asking for a status update from his brothers.

"When was the last time you took time for yourself?"

A vision surfaced of Liv lounging in a hot tub across from him, a small smile playing across her lips. His birthday. He'd indulged every one of his senses that evening. For hours.

The thought of her turned his eyes into heat-seeking missiles as he sought her out. His heart stuttered inside his chest.

She wasn't at the picnic table. He searched the nearby area, his panic growing.

Nothing.

He noticed her bag was still on the picnic table.

"*Liv!*"

. . .

ZEKE TOOK OFF, HAULING ASS AT A PACE THAT WOULD'VE MADE Usain Bolt proud. Distantly, he heard Ash's shoes beating the pavement behind him.

When he neared the table, he found her in a dazed heap on the other side. She tried to push herself upright, but appeared to be favoring her left shoulder.

Red bloomed on her pale yellow top like a Nickelodeon paint splatter.

He landed hard on his knees at her side. "Liv." His throat was tight. "I've got you, sweetheart." Over his shoulder, he yelled, "Call 911."

"Already on it," Ash said in a calm voice.

Red rivulets trickled down her face from a wound on the left side of her forehead. A black-and-blue knot was already forming beneath the thin layer of skin.

Holding her in his arms, he eased down the neckline of her top for the source of the blood on her shoulder and found a half-inch stab wound in the meaty part where the neck and collarbone met.

"Sonofabitch." He glanced around in search of something to stuff into the blood-pumping wound. Finding nothing, he started pulling at the neck and shoulders of his shirt.

"Here." Ash ripped off his pristine white dress shirt, balled it up, and handed to him.

The wail of sirens reached him as he stuffed the material against her wound. She winced and emitted a low groan.

"I'm sorry, Liv, but I need to get the bleeding under control. The ambulance is almost here." He kissed her forehead while pressing down harder.

"Do you see anything?" he asked his brother in a low voice.

"Nothing out of the ordinary. The curious are starting to approach, though."

"Same voice as before," Liv whispered, her eyelids fluttered open. She blinked several times, as if batting away a thick fog.

"You're looking for a guy, Ash. He might try to blend in with the onlookers."

"Got it." His voice held no trace of annoyance, only unremitting calm, even though Zeke was telling him something he'd probably learned in FBI 101.

When Liv's eyelids fluttered closed, he tapped his fingers against her cheek. "Stay with me, Liv."

Her eyes widened, then drifted closed again. "No, Liv. Stay awake."

When her lids continued to fall, he elevated his voice and smacked her cheek harder. "Agent Westcott, you will not fall asleep." His throat ached with a crush of emotion. "Not until I hear the words."

Out of the corner of his eye, he saw Ash wave down the ambulance.

"What words?" she asked, her voice so freaking weak.

He said nothing, feeling like a damn fool suddenly.

"What. Words?"

"I love you."

"I did—"

"Hell if you did."

Her eyes shot open.

"I'd remember something like that."

"But—"

"I need the words. Not just actions. The words, Liv."

A large hand clamped around his shoulder. "The paramedics are here, Z. They need to look at her now."

Zeke brushed her lips with hers. "Rain check."

She gave him a faint smile. "Deal."

Loosening his hold on her, he allowed the paramedics to lift her onto a gurney.

Something white on the ground caught his eye. He reached over and picked it up.

An earbud.

Ash held out his hand to help him up. Zeke stared at the device in confusion. His worry for Liv fracturing his critical thinking chip.

"I got you, Z," Ash said as he hauled him to his feet.

Z.

It had been years since he'd heard the nickname.

As the paramedics carted Liv away, she blurted out, *"Brodie,"* and reached for her phone on the table.

The sudden movement jostled her concussed head too much, and she heaved the contents of her stomach onto her shoulder and the gurney.

"Stay still, Mrs. Westcott," the paramedic near her head said, forcing her to lie back down.

Liv ignored the woman and sent a last desperate glance at Zeke before she disappeared into the back of the ambulance. *"Brodie!"*

Zeke rolled the earbud between his fingers as he stepped toward the table. Dread crowded into his chest as he picked up Liv's phone. A FaceTime call was still active.

Brodie's red, tear-streaked face and his uncle's concerned one filled the display in a jittery Blair Witch-style videography.

Zeke shoved Liv's small white device into place.

The boy's scream-wail pierced his eardrum.

"Mama!"

50

LIV EASED HERSELF UP INTO A SITTING POSITION. WHEN HER stomach stayed anchored in place, she sent out a mental thank-you to the genius who invented anti-nausea meds.

Careful not to jostle her left arm, she slid her legs out from beneath the warming blanket and sat on the edge of the bed.

Even with pain meds, she nursed a dull ache behind her eyes. The attack had been swift and violent. One moment she'd been talking to her son and brother and, in the next, fire exploded in her shoulder while her forehead kissed the rough picnic table. Not once, not twice, but three damn times.

A wave of nausea that had nothing to do with her mild concussion worked its way up her throat. Although she hadn't been able to see Brodie's face, she'd heard his screams of terror in her ear before she lost consciousness.

Had he seen the entire attack? Or had the first hit thrown the phone from her hand?

She hoped God wasn't so cruel as to force a boy to first

watch his father die by a baseball, then observe his mother getting stabbed and beaten.

Please, please, please, no.

Two fat drops landed in quick succession on the tiled floor. She blinked, and two more fell.

She'd failed her son in the worst way possible. The fragile security net she'd started weaving from the moment he was born now had a massive hole in its center.

At the moment, she couldn't be sure the two assaults were linked to the break-in. Was she dealing with one assailant or two? Could both Sam Rogers and Jeremy Jackson be exacting separate revenge schemes? Or had only one come unhinged? Maybe it wasn't either of them. What if someone from the O'Fallon brood was none too happy about her locking their inheritance away in a warehouse?

"Mama?"

At the sound of her son's hesitant voice, Liv slid off the ER bed and swallowed back the burn of tears.

He ran forward, then hesitated when he noticed her bandages and IV.

She held out an arm. "It's okay, sweetheart."

"Watch her shoulder," Regina Thornton warned in a gentle voice, following behind her grandson.

Brodie rushed forward and wrapped his thin arms around Liv's waist. His narrow body shook as his silent tears joined hers on the floor.

"I'm fine," she whispered, kissing the top of his head. "Just a few scratches."

She looked up at her mom, shocked to find the other woman's eyes red-rimmed and her face blotchy. "Thank you for bringing him."

"I, uh," Regina swallowed, "I had to see for myself that you were all right."

Having her mother near somehow soothed the ache in her heart. It didn't make sense. Regina Thornton had rarely been around for the pivotal moments in Liv's life. They didn't have a close mother-daughter relationship.

Not because Regina was a cruel or unfeeling person, because she wasn't. When present, she hugged and gushed and complimented like the best of mothers. What kept them from sharing pajama nights and wine nights and movie nights was Regina's busy social calendar.

"Your father, aunt, and brother are in the waiting room. They're limiting the number of visitors you can have at a time."

"Daddy's here?" If her mother's visit shocked her, her father's nearly made her heart go into A-fib. Everything Regina did was to help further her husband's ambitions. Stanley Thornton preferred to leave the messy bits of life to others.

Regina's smile wobbled as she nodded. "He's anxious to see you."

An almost giddy sensation flared in her chest, and she returned her mother's smile with a guarded one of her own.

Brodie looked up at her. "Mama, who was that man?"

Her son's question wiped her joy away like an eraser against a whiteboard. She didn't have to ask what man he spoke of. With a bone-deep grief, she knew her little boy had witnessed the entire horrible act.

The helplessness and fear he must have felt.

Pain splintered her heart.

"I don't know, sweetheart." Her thumbs smoothed over his damp cheeks. "But I'm going to make sure he never hurts anyone ever again."

"How?"

Blow him to smithereens. Tear his head off. Hang him by his nuts—

"The *how* is not for you to worry about, young man," Regina said in her most hoity-toity voice. "All you need to know is that your brave, smart mama will *always* win the battle against evil people."

His grandmother's outlandish prediction seemed to be what Brodie needed. The fear clutching his sweet face faded, though his next question revealed his need for things to return to normal. "Can we go home?"

She lifted her head to speak to her mother. "Anything from Callie?"

"Not yet. I left her a message to call me."

A new misery wrapped around Liv's chest. She couldn't expose him to another bombshell today. Until her sister sent word that his room was ready, she had to keep him away from the house.

Looking into Brodie's hopeful eyes, her mind blanked on how to tell her distraught son he couldn't go home.

"Mom, would you mind if we imposed on your hospitality awhile longer?"

"Absolutely. You're both welcome anytime."

"I have a better idea," a newcomer said.

Zeke filled the doorway, and Liv had to force herself not to move, not to run blubbering into his arms. The same gale of emotion whirling inside her was evident in his beautiful brown eyes. Fear, fury, helplessness, joy, and. .
.

"Let me be clear. I love you, Special Agent Olivia Westcott."

The echo of his declaration was like a warm waterfall washing over her. She wanted to stand beneath it for hours, days, years. All of their years.

A small bundle of energy bounced up and down before

him. No doubt the weight of Zeke's hands on the girl's shoulders was the only thing keeping her in place.

Sadie Rios, with a smile as big as the sun, waved at Brodie.

"How about you and Sadie take a trip to the water park?" Zeke suggested, then looked at Liv. "If it's okay with your mom."

"They have eleven slides and a game room," Sadie added, excitedly.

Interest sparked in Brodie's eyes, though he didn't move from her side. "Can we go, Mama?"

"Your mother isn't going anywhere," Regina said. "She needs to rest."

Liv didn't want to disappoint her son, but she couldn't fathom letting him out of her sight at the moment. Regina was right, though. The last thing she should do right now was go to a noisy, manic water park.

Zeke said, "My mom and your aunt have agreed to escort them."

An army vet and an active police detective. A mother couldn't ask for better guards. She recalled the torn picture of her and Brodie screaming their way down a water slide. The joy on his face.

"We even brought you a pair of swim trunks and a beach towel," Sadie said. "Hope you don't mind Marvel. The store didn't have any DC towels."

"I like Marvel," Brodie said, his arms slipping free of Liv's waist.

No matter how much it pained her to be parted from him, Liv couldn't deny her son an afternoon of escape. She bent to kiss his head, lingering there for a few seconds to drink in his familiar scent, praying she wasn't making a horrible mistake.

Decision made, she lifted her head and met Brodie's hopeful gaze. "Do you promise to listen to Mrs. Blackwell and Aunt Belinda?"

"Yes, Mama."

"No hiding from the adults."

"I won't, Mama." He took a step closer to Sadie, sharing a quick triumphant smile with the girl.

"Text me when you get there and when you leave."

He nodded. "I can go then?"

She smiled. "Go have fun, sweetheart."

Sadie broke free of Zeke's hold to high-five Brodie.

"Mercy," a shocked, commanding voice said over Zeke's shoulder. "I don't know how y'all sardined your way in here, but now it's time for you to skedaddle."

"Brodie, kiss your mama," Regina said.

He did as commanded, and Liv hugged him until he wriggled against her hold.

Regina stepped forward and pressed a palm to Liv's cheek. "Don't ever give us a scare like that again, you hear?"

"I'll do my best."

Regina kissed her forehead. "I'll send your father and brother to you," she glanced at Zeke, "in ten minutes."

Liv squeezed her hand. "Thank you."

Regina gathered herself before ushering the kids out the door. She paused near Zeke to pat his arm before marching out and taking the ER nurse with her.

Liv placed a hand on the edge of the bed to steady herself.

Suddenly, Zeke was at her side. "Here, let's get you back into bed."

"No, I'm fine."

"You have a mild concussion and a stab wound. You're

not fine." An anger she understood all too well laced his harsh words.

She stroked a finger along his stubbled jaw. "What happened to me was not your fault."

"You were under my protection. It bloody well was my fault."

"I'm a trained FBI agent. My body. My responsibility." It could be argued that she hadn't done a bang-up job of protecting herself in the past week. But she wasn't into splitting hairs. "I need to speak with Pierce. He might have glimpsed my attacker."

"Ash and I already spoke to him. He's meeting with a forensic artist in an hour."

"Kimber Wu?"

"Sounds right."

"Good. She's the best."

"Will she really be able to get a decent sketch from a 'glimpse'?"

"She's done it before. If anyone can do the impossible, it's Kimber."

Spotting her phone and purse on a chair beside the bed, she went to retrieve them and noticed five missed phone calls.

Recognizing the number to her parents' restaurant, she frowned.

"What's the matter?"

"I'm not sure."

She checked voice mail and found three messages. Tapping the Play button, she listened.

"Hi, Liv. This is Hailey Wright. Can you call me when you get a chance?"

"Hailey's the server who waited on us at my parents' restaurant."

"I remember. You scared off her sister Ivy's stalker." He raised a brow. "But I didn't know your parents owned Plate It."

"That's because I didn't want you to know at the time."

"Why?"

"Some people change once they hear I'm a Thornton. It's like a light switch, once they associate me with their money. One moment I'm interesting and, the next, I'm *very* interesting."

The second message came in twelve minutes later. This one, she put on speaker.

"Liv, I'm sorry to bother you, but this is about my sister, Ivy," her voice lowered to a whisper, "and that issue you helped her out with. Call me, *please*."

The skin on Liv's chest prickled as she detected the first rumbling of fear in the server's voice.

She hit the Play button on the last message.

Hailey's cries filled the air. *"Ivy is missing."*

51

Liv called Hailey back, counting the seconds while waiting for her to pick up. The server's last voice mail message had come in thirty-seven minutes ago.

"Hello," Hailey answered on the first ring. "Liv?"

"Yes, it's me. I'm sorry for the delay. What's happened?"

"Ivy was supposed to pick me up at the end of my shift, but she never showed." She spoke fast, her voice filled with anxiety. "She's never late."

"When did your shift end?"

"One o'clock."

Fifty-seven minutes ago.

"You tried her cell, I assume."

"Nonstop. At first, it was ringing. Now it's going straight to voice mail. I think it might be off. Why would she turn off her phone?"

She and Zeke shared a glance. "Have you contacted the police?"

"Yeah, I just finished speaking with an officer. Liv, he looked like he was right out of the academy."

A person can go missing for a million different reasons.

Some folks simply waved bye-bye to their old lives, not giving a second's thought to the chaos they left behind. But Ivy didn't seem like the kind of person to ghost her life or her sister. She was enjoying it far too much.

"Let me make a few phone calls to my colleagues at the police department," Liv said. "Can you get into Ivy's house?"

"Yeah, I know where she keeps the spare key."

"Good. Go there and wait. There's a chance she could show up."

"Okay, you'll keep me updated?"

"Absolutely."

When Liv disconnected, Zeke said, "What do you think? Truly missing? Or pissed off at her sister, for some reason?"

Liv hadn't considered that possibility. She knew how wicked sisters could be to each other when upset, but Hailey and Ivy shared a close relationship, like she did with Callie.

"My gut tells me something's wrong. I can't imagine Ivy scaring her sister like this."

"What's the plan?"

Blinking up at him, she noticed for the first time the way he was talking through the problem with her rather than trying to take control. She thought of his well-loved glove standing vigil while her son slept and of the way he'd set aside his yearslong quest to pick up the remnants of Brodie's beloved toys.

She thought of the three ginormous words he'd uttered without hesitation hours earlier. Of the knot of uncertainty wedged beneath her sternum that was now slowly, happily, unraveling.

She cradled his strong, stubbled jaw in her palm. "Weird timing, I know."

He leaned into her touch and brushed a kiss against her palm. "What's weird timing?"

"I think I'm in love with you."

He stilled like a hare following the slow glide of an over-head hawk. His eyes didn't blink, his breath didn't stir.

Then his chest rose high, and a large, warm hand clamped about her waist. Suddenly, no space existed between them. He nuzzled her nose, and his lips whispered over her brow, her temple, her ear. "I missed waking up next to you."

Breathing became more difficult as she imagined what it would have been like if she hadn't scampered off to her suite, if the alarm service hadn't called, if an asshole hadn't trashed her son's room. "Me too."

"Seeing you on the ground," he said in a choked voice, "the blood." He reared back. His eyes burned into hers. "Can you forgive me?"

"I told you, there's nothing to forgive."

"If I hadn't been fighting with Ash, I would have noticed the bastard and could have—"

She pressed a finger against his lips. "There's only one person at fault for what happened to me, and that's not you."

"I'm going to track him down and make him pay with a thousand lifetimes of pain."

The ferocity of his vow and the promise in his eyes made her heart topple over into his hands. She loved this big, beautiful man. Probably had, from the moment she saw him sitting alone, staring at his glowing birthday cake.

Her finger traced a path over his full bottom lip, and he drew the tip into his mouth.

A place deep in her core quaked with need. In a voice barely above a whisper, she said, "A relationship with me comes with an insta-family, with all its lumpy richness.

Then there's my job and yours. They'll likely have a head-on collision at some point."

She tried to smile, tried to show him that despite the numerous challenges, she still chose him. Chose to do everything she could to make this exciting, terrifying thing work between them.

But the smile never bloomed and persuasive words clogged in her throat like matted, wet hair in a drainpipe.

He raised a hand and smoothed it along her arm until it enfolded her hand still cradling his face. He lifted it a fraction of an inch, kissing each fingertip, one by one.

Liv's phone rang and she reluctantly lifted it to her ear. "Olivia Westcott."

"Special Agent Westcott," a low baritone voice crooned.

Something in the man's tone dried the smile on her face. She checked her phone's display and realized the caller wasn't someone from her contacts. "Who is this?"

"How's your head and shoulder? Do they burn with pain?"

Liv's eyes flared, and she quickly hit the Speaker button. In the caller's background, a door slammed.

"I hope so," he continued in a hard voice. Footsteps crunched against gravel. "I hope you feel the bone-deep agony of someone stabbing you in the back. As I did."

"Jeremy Jackson?" Liv ventured.

He ignored her, bent on spewing his vile message. "You shouldn't have stuck your nose in men's business, Oliv—" The signal broke off. "—going to like what comes next."

"What are you talking about? Who is this?"

A long silence, then a muffled woman's voice. *"Fifteen dollars."*

More voices. Dozens. Some talking, some yelling, some laughing.

"I promis—" Another signal break. "—a loss for a loss, Olivia. It's time I kept it."

A child screeched. Then another. And another.

Water splashed.

"But unlike you, I won't steal away those you lov—" Dead air for two breath-stealing seconds. "—last look."

Her phone chimed, indicating a new text.

"Goodbye, Olivia—" Liv's eyes burned as she stared at the call's seconds ticking by on her screen. *Thirty-three, thirty-four, thirty-five.* "—rot in a puddle of your own misery."

The line went dead, and Liv tapped over to her text messages, knowing before she opened it what nightmare awaited her, but unable to stop herself from sinking deeper into the darkness.

"Zeke..." she said in a voice that sounded nothing like her own.

His warm hand grasped the back of her neck as he leaned in.

The message held a single image. No words. She tapped the jpeg and stretched two fingers across the image to blow it up.

There, at the end of a long orange slide, Brodie climbed a ladder out of the water. A smile as big as a moon on his sweet, unsuspecting face.

52

ZEKE'S BIG TRUCK THUNDERED DOWN THE HIGHWAY WHILE LIV
dialed her aunt's cell phone number yet again. "Still no
answer." She switched to Zeke's phone, tapped the first line
on his Recents list, and tried to calm the quaking in her
chest while she waited for Lynette to answer.

The phone on the other end rang and rang and rang
until his mom's voice mail kicked in.

"Shit." She disconnected, having already left two
messages. "Shit, shit, *shit*. Why aren't they answering?" She
switched back to her phone and started the process all over
again.

Zeke laid his hand on her thigh. "There's a lot of activity
and noise at those places. Maybe they can't hear their
phones." Engaging his turn signal, he swerved into a left-
hand turn lane.

"Neither one of them thought to put their phones on
vibrate or turn up the damn volume?" She shook her head,
unable to shake the feeling something else was at play.

Guilt engulfed her. She should never have let Brodie out
of her sight. She should have borne his disappointment.

Better that than never hugging him again. Never cleaning up his dirty dishes or corralling him toward the door in the morning.

"I can't lose him, Zeke."

"We won't let that happen. The police are on their way."

The overhead traffic light blinked from yellow to red. Already committed to the turn, Zeke accelerated. Out of the corner of her eye, Liv caught a flash of blue barreling toward them.

"Watch it!" The warning erupted from her mouth at the same time the car blew through the intersection, horn blaring, wheels swerving to the right.

"*Fuck!*" Zeke's truck came to a sudden, deafening halt. They sat in the middle of the intersection for three heart-racing seconds before he eased off the brake and finished his turn. "Sorry," he said. "You okay?"

She released a breath through her mouth, nodded, and resumed her futile effort to contact Brodie's guardians.

Despite the near collision, they made it to the water park in record time, pulling into the lot seconds behind Detective Marissa Schuler. Liv had never been so glad to see another human being.

"Thank you for coming," Liv said.

"Luckily, I was in the area. Uniforms are on their way."

"I'm not waiting."

"Glad to hear." The detective nodded toward the large, imposing building. "Let's go find the bastard."

Liv and Marissa flashed their badges at the guy in the ticket booth before pushing their way inside, Zeke tight on her six.

The moment they cleared the double doors, a blast of humid air and the screaming laughter of hundreds of kids assailed her senses. Liv winced at the impact on her already pounding head.

Natural light shone through the see-through roof, bathing all the water worshippers in sunlight. Bright, cheerful blues, greens, yellows, oranges, and reds covered the surface of every slide, tube, chair, table, and wave machine.

How could a place that brought so many people joy allow a hideous person like Jeremy Jackson through its doors?

Although everything pointed to Jackson, she couldn't help but wonder why he didn't acknowledge her guess at his identity. Had he been hyper-focused on releasing all the dammed-up vitriol he'd been harboring since their last encounter? Or had her phone cut out, and he never heard her say his name?

Marissa split off to speak quietly, but adamantly, to a woman wearing the park's purple and black uniform. Liv did a quick scan of the enormous space, then she slowed it down. Although her instinct was to look for Brodie, she knew isolating her son from all the other wet-haired, bare-chested boys would be like singling out one bee in a massive hive.

Concentrating on the adults, she alternated searching for Belinda's athletic build, Lynette's curly brown hair, and any males who seemed off or didn't belong.

"Anything?" Zeke asked, scanning.

"Not yet."

They moved farther into the chaos. So many people. As hard as she tried to focus on the adults, she couldn't stop herself from searching every face.

Kids and adults alike lined up for their turn down winding slides. Little ones wearing floaters on their arms alternated between stomping their feet in ankle deep water and butterflying in and out of liquid geysers.

A mother should be able to pick out her child no matter what, shouldn't she?

If a zebra could locate her young in a herd of thousands by her offspring's call alone, shouldn't Liv be able to identify her own son in this mass of wet humanity?

When the pressure on her chest became too much, she did the one thing every parent dreaded doing. The one thing that signaled to the rest of the world that you're a terrible mother. That you've lost your child.

"Brodie!" she yelled, startling a teenaged girl next to her.

Taking her cue, Zeke did the same, adding his deep baritone to her calls.

They moved through the indoor water park, calling Brodie and Sadie's names, eliciting a range of spectator responses from concerned to irritated to where's-my-own-child to indifference.

Liv's pulse quickened when she spotted two familiar figures standing on the far side of the room. They watched something in the pool before them, faint smiles on their faces.

No terror, no confusion, no distraction.

Releasing a long, shuddering breath, she got Zeke's attention and pointed to the spot where her aunt and his mother watched over their charges.

The moment she reached the water's edge, she peered down to find Sadie's father, Alejandro, rising from beneath the water, a gun in his hand. Brodie and Sadie shrieked, tried to run away, but the pressure from the water made their movements sluggish. Alejandro squeezed the trigger and a line of water bolted from the weapon and hit Brodie in the back of the head. Her son's body jerked, and he melted beneath the water.

With wide eyes and an even wider smile, Sadie yelled, "No, Papa! No!" as she dove away from her father.

"You can't hide from me, my pretty," Alejandro said in his best Wicked Witch of the West voice.

Liv grappled for the nearest Adirondack as her legs buckled. She covered her mouth and nose with her hands, dragging in deep, ragged breaths. Zeke cocked a hip on the chair's wide arm and placed a hand on her shoulder, massaging away the tension.

The firm warmth of his hand almost made the tears crowding behind her eyes surface, but somehow she kept herself in check. Somehow, she held back the puke.

"What are you two doing here?" Aunt Belinda asked, her gaze snapping to scan the surrounding area.

"Where's your phone?" Liv asked.

"Right here." She raised her hand where she'd held it at her side.

"Battery dead?"

"Shouldn't be. I charged it before I left the house." Her aunt glanced down at the display and frowned. "Ninety-two percent."

Zeke checked his own phone. "The reception is for shit here."

"What's going on?" Lynette asked, joining them.

"They've been trying to call us, but there's no signal," Aunt Belinda said.

"But we sent you a message as soon as we arrived," Lynette said.

"Were you inside or outside?" Zeke asked.

Her aunt frowned. "As we were coming in."

Liv met Zeke's eyes. "He kept cutting out."

Zeke nodded. "It got harder to hear him after he cleared the ticket booth."

"He who?" Belinda asked.

Liv peered over her shoulder, and Brodie waved right before making a dive for Alejandro's water gun.

"The man who stabbed me. He was here." Something had niggled at the back of Liv's mind ever since the disturbing phone call. It hunkered in the shadows, though she could see its glowing eyes mocking her. No matter how hard she tried, she couldn't coax the thought forward into the light.

Hoping distance would eventually jog it free, she released a tension-filled breath and shook the abundance of adrenaline from her trembling hands. Lifting her phone, she showed the two women the picture Jackson had sent her less than thirty minutes ago.

Lynette went as still as a heron searching the water's edge for its next meal. "We haven't taken our eyes off the kids."

"Which is why they're still here and safe," Liv said. "Thank you."

"Considering our less than stealthy entrance," Zeke said, "he's long gone."

"I'll call the kids out," Lynette said.

Liv shook her head. "Please, let them play for a while longer. This is probably the safest place for them right now."

The older woman didn't look convinced, but she didn't try to persuade her either.

"What now?" Belinda asked, though Liv suspected her aunt had already gone through a battery of scenarios.

Liv stared at her son playing with his new friend as if the world hadn't almost crumbled down around him. She was glad. Glad this one piece of his youth had been preserved.

A loss for a loss.

Why didn't Jackson at least try to take Brodie? Why go through so much trouble and not even make the attempt?

"It doesn't make sense," Liv said. "He was here, yet all he did was take a picture."

"Maybe after observing his target's bodyguards, he realized his plan wouldn't work," Zeke said. "If he somehow nabbed him under that kind of pressure, he'd still have to carry a kicking and screaming kid through a building full of parents without getting tackled. Bad odds, even for a sociopath, psychopath—whatever he is."

In today's world, murderers blew through schools, malls, churches as if they were invincible. If he'd wanted Brodie, he would have waited for that one moment of inattention that happens with even the most attentive parents, and made his move.

With shocking clarity, Liv said, "He never intended to take Brodie."

Sadie, finally noticing the new arrivals, gave them an exuberant wave.

"His texts would suggest otherwise," Zeke said, lifting a hand to the little girl.

The exchange was so normal, despite the fact that somewhere out there, an unstable man was playing *Wheel of Fortune* with her life.

"A loss for a loss. That was his promise," Liv said. "After he trashed Brodie's room, I assumed he intended to make me pay by hurting my son. He knew my mind would go there, encouraged it by sending me that picture."

Liv's phone chimed, and dread darkened the edges of her vision until she saw only her phone. She tapped through to her text messages. An image filled her screen.

The concrete beneath her chair crumbled away, and she *fell, fell, fell.*

Zeke leaned close, and he growled low and hard. "Sono-famotherfuckingbitch."

On her screen, she stared into the terrified eyes of her sister.

A loss for a loss.

Callie.

53

ZEKE SAT ACROSS FROM LIV AND ASH AT THE LARGE, OVAL conference table. The same table where the FBI had first approached him about recovering a doll for a confidential informant with ties to a drug dealer.

The meeting felt like a lifetime ago, but in reality, little more than a week had passed. A week that had altered his life forever.

In the last twenty-four hours, he had held Lupos, figured out how to save his family, lost Liv, found Liv, loved Liv, declared himself to Liv, lost Brodie, found Brodie, and lost Callie.

Yet, despite the horrifying reason for their presence at the FBI's office, Zeke found himself happier than he could ever remember. He'd told Liv that he loved her, and she hadn't run the other way.

She hadn't exactly said the words back, but he could see the emotion brimming in her eyes. Once Callie was safe and her kidnapper was behind bars, or six feet under, Zeke would remove every obstacle her brilliant mind threw between them.

For now, he set aside their future and focused on the present.

On Liv.

He had sat across from her in order to monitor the slightest variation in her condition. With every passing minute, she seemed to shrink in on herself.

The mother who had stormed into the water park, ready to take down the world to protect her son, was slipping away. The woman across from him was fragmenting, tormenting herself with a million *what-if*s and *if-only*s. She kept glancing at her phone, at Callie's picture. No doubt blaming herself and feeling an overwhelming helplessness.

The distance between them also took away the temptation for him to offer her comfort. Something she wouldn't appreciate in front of her coworkers.

Always, she had to be in control. Show nothing that could be construed as weakness. Juggle all that life threw at her without help.

Somewhere along the way, she'd gotten it in her head— or someone put it there—that she had to be all, do all. Alone.

Horseshit.

No one was built to do everything by themselves without incredible sacrifices. Something that had only recently penetrated his thick skull.

When her chin trembled, he knew she'd reached her breaking point. She'd held it together during the entire time she thought her son was in jeopardy and while navigating the park's lack of indoor security.

But here, where her body was no longer in motion, her mind was venturing into cavernous dark holes of fear and dread and self-recrimination.

Fuck it.

Rising, he circled the table and sat beside her. Rather than draw her to him and coax her head onto his shoulder, as he wanted to, he reached out and covered her hand with his.

Cold. It was so cold.

She jerked beneath his touch, and he was certain she would pull away. Then her eyes closed, and she drew in a long, deep breath before placing her free hand on top of his.

A sharp ache split down Zeke's throat, and his hold tightened.

He looked at Ash, who was hunched over his laptop, grumbling beneath his breath. True to her word, Liv had ensured his brother's forced leave was revoked the day Zeke accepted the FBI's job offer.

Despite the current circumstances, he was glad to see Ash in his element. He belonged here, just as Zeke belonged at the helm of BARS.

His realization didn't mean he wanted to be chummy with the asshat just yet, but he was finally understanding why Ash chose a career he could be passionate about rather than a job that paid the bills.

"Still no video from the water park?" Zeke asked his brother.

Ash shook his head and tapped a key on his laptop, no doubt refreshing his e-mail for the thousandth time. "I don't know what the hell is taking them so long."

RSA Mitch Lawson entered the conference room, phone to his ear. "They found Ivy Wright," he announced to the room, though his eyes were on Liv.

Liv's head jerked up. "Where?"

Lawson held up a finger while he listened to whoever was on the phone. A few seconds later, he said, "The details are still coming in, but evidently Jeremy Jackson climbed into Miss Wright's vehicle as she was preparing to leave to pick up her sister."

Liv's grip on his hand became crushing.

"He ordered her to drive to a nearby park," Lawson continued, "where he spent the next two hours crying out his sob story in order to make Miss Wright understand why she shouldn't ignore her fans. Or some stupid shit like that." Phone still at his ear, Lawson seemed to be speaking and listening at the same time. "Anyway, Miss Wright is shaken up, but safe and with her family. Jackson is in custody."

"Reason five million and one why not to be on social media," Ash said, shaking his head.

Liv dropped Zeke's hand and stood. "What about Callie?"

Lawson's harsh expression softened, though he said nothing. He gave her the few seconds it would take to make the connection that everyone else in the room, whose sister wasn't missing, already had.

If Jackson had been with Ivy for the past two hours, he couldn't have kidnapped Callie.

As understanding dawned, Liv's shoulders drooped and her body sagged back into her chair.

Lawson's face hardened again. "We'll find her." Then the RSA left as abruptly as he'd entered.

"Got any coffee or tea in this fancy office?" Zeke asked his brother with a slight nod toward the door.

Without a word, his brother pushed his chair back and rose. "I'll make a fresh pot and check on the team's progress."

Once they were alone, Zeke turned to her fully and did his best to massage warmth back into her hands. "We'll find her," he reiterated.

She swallowed several times before words emerged. "I can't stop thinking about the terrified look on Callie's face."

Nor could he. Silver tape had covered her mouth and encircled her head, black mascara ringed her eyes, snot dripped from her nose, and strands of brown hair hung in frazzled disarray around her red-blotched face.

What drew his attention more than all of that was her eyes. They held something more than terror.

Something like—

"About what her kidnapper might be doing to her right now," Liv continued, interrupting his thoughts. "While I'm sitting here doing nothing."

"You've done everything you can for the moment. But I think you should tell Lawson about O'Fallon and Rogers. They might be a long shot, but they're leads the agency can follow up on, and we can take them off the table if they prove fruitless."

She nodded, but her mind was firmly in sister country, not special agent. "Even if we get to her in time, if he—" She squeezed her eyes shut. "She might not recover from this. If only I had—"

"No." He shook her hands until her eyes opened. Tears crowded in their corners. "This is not on you. You couldn't have foreseen this. None of us could."

"Something I did caused this, Zeke. Made my family a target."

"Maybe, maybe not." He gentled his voice. "But turning your back on someone in need—that's not you. Your calling, your gift, is to help those in need, to right injustices. That's who you are, that's who you'll always be."

One of the many reasons why I love you.

"But at what cost to my family?"

He cradled the side of her face. "We will get through

this, Liv. No matter what happens. We will get through this together."

She burrowed her face into the crook of his shoulder and inhaled, as if his scent bolstered her strength. Rocking her gently, he rubbed his palm in large circles over her back.

In the quiet moment that followed, Zeke thought again about the kidnapper's picture of Callie, about the young woman's eyes, and that something else besides terror lurked along their edges.

His heart *thunked* against his chest once, twice, three times before the answer finally surfaced.

Fury.

54

CALLIE THORNTON CAME AWAKE SLOWLY, CAREFULLY. BEFORE opening her eyes, she listened to the world around her. Listened for the creepy guy who'd abducted her.

Shame washed over her.

How could she have fallen for the puppy ploy? *The freaking puppy ploy!*

She had seen how many movies and shows where the kidnapper had used a cute, wiggly dog to entice a woman?

Countless. Yet one too few, as it turned out.

Granted, her puppy hadn't been wiggly at all, but sad and forlorn.

With the sun blazing down, she'd paused near her trunk, arms full of replacement bedding and toys for Brodie, when she heard the whining. She stowed her purchases in her trunk before going in search of the distressed animal.

Following the whimpers, she peered down the length of her vehicle and spotted a yellow lab puppy pacing at the end of its leash near a blue car in front of hers. The back passenger side window was down about halfway, and the puppy's leash appeared to be caught on something in the backseat.

Had the puppy jumped out? Callie moved along the driver's side of her car, peering into the front windshield of the blue car for a sleeping teenager—anyone who might be inside and oblivious that their new pup had flown the coop.

No one was inside.

At the sight of her, the puppy surged toward her, only to be caught up short by its leash. The puppy yelped, and she rushed to its side.

When she kneeled on one knee, the hot asphalt burned her bare skin and a slow trickle of sweat slipped down the back of her neck.

How long had the pup been tangled up in its own leash? What heartless person had left their dog inside their car on such an unusually stifling day for May?

A yellow bone tag dangled from the pup's collar. Hopefully, the owner's phone number was engraved on the tag, and she could call and give them a piece of her mind, er, notify them their dog was loose.

Intent on her task, she didn't immediately register the sound of a sliding door. Before she could react, a brawny hand covered her mouth with a damp cloth and pulled her into the van. The pup scrambling out of her arms.

The last thing she heard was the ominous sound of the door slamming shut, throwing her into complete darkness.

Callie's throat ached at the thought of the pup's fate, at Liv's disappointment.

How many times had her big sister warned her about vans in parking lots? About guys and puppies?

During her years in college, she'd heeded Liv's dire warnings, even though she knew the chances of her coming across any of scenarios Liv painstakingly laid out for her were minimal.

In the past few months, while staying with Liv, she'd become more complacent. Less watchful. It had always been so when with her big sister. Liv made her feel safe, protected. But not in a smothering, gooey way.

The sweet puppy was all but hanging out the window by its collar! Who wouldn't be moved by such cruelty?

Being moved by the sight and throwing caution to the wind are two different things, Cal. She could almost hear Liv's admonishing voice.

Stupid, stupid, idiot.

Having not heard anything for several minutes, Callie blinked her eyes open while engaging her other senses. She was lying on her back in a relatively soft, yet starting to get ripe, bed in what looked like a bedroom.

The musty, damp air combined with the sound of a nearby HVAC system kicking on and the deep window wells confirmed what her eyes had already determined.

She was in someone's basement.

The realization dismayed her, but not as much as the handcuffs binding her wrists to the headboard or the immovable duct tape strapped across her mouth.

She glanced down her body and almost cried with relief. Still clothed in her V-neck top and denim shorts, though her flip-flops were long gone.

Knowing it was futile, she still jerked hard on the restraints. The cuffs bit into her wrists and clanged against the metal-framed bed. Her breaths turned shallow as the full weight of her situation pressed upon her chest.

How long had she been unconscious? Was he here? If not, how much longer did she have before he came back and—

She broke off the horrible thought before it could form a debilitating image in her mind. The last thing she needed was that shit floating around her head. Every part of her needed to be focused on escape.

What would Liv do?

She snorted. Liv wouldn't have allowed herself to be in this situation.

Think, Callie. Think!

Posters of beautiful women draped over muscle cars hung on each side of a large-screen TV and a set of true crime books lined a small bookshelf beneath an engraved cross that read, "God Loves You."

Clumps of dirty clothes dotted the floor like heaps of cow poop in a pasture. To her right stood an oak dresser with a rectangular mirror above it. If she leaned forward a bit, she could see her entire reflection. She avoided looking at that bound girl's eyes, not wanting to observe the desolation building in the back of her mind taking root.

Even though the bedroom was sparsely furnished, it appeared to be in great condition. No gouges, no stained carpet, no wet spots on the ceiling. Which likely meant the furniture would be of good quality. Aka unbreakable.

Only one way to find out.

Being careful not to make too much noise, she gave her body an experimental jiggle. The bed didn't make a sound.

She tried again with a little more force. One tiny *creak-creak.*

Lifting her head, she sent a desperate glance around the room, looking for inspiration. That's when she noticed the framed picture and keys sitting on the dresser. The silver keys looked small enough to fit inside her handcuffs.

A flurry of excitement built inside her before realization snuffed it out. Freedom was eight feet away, but it might as well have been on the other side of the continent for all the good it did her.

Instead of the keys, she focused on the picture. There was something familiar about it.

She leaned sideways, as far forward as her restraints would allow. Her breath caught as the image became clearer.

Brodie stood between his dad and first baseman Jimar Baker. A huge hero-worshipping smile split her nephew's face. It was the last picture father and son would ever take together. A happy moment captured mere hours before a baseball changed the boy's life forever.

White-hot fury blazed through Callie's body, and she struggled in earnest. No way would her creepy kidnapper keep that photo. It belonged to Brodie. One day, when the wound wasn't so raw, her nephew would cherish that four-by-six like nothing else he owned.

It took a moment for her to realize that the bed was rocking with her movements.

The tight duct tape couldn't stop her smile from flourishing.

Old bed.

She could work with that.

55

"I NEED TO SPEAK WITH MY TEAM," ZEKE SAID TO LIV. "Shouldn't take but ten to fifteen minutes. You okay here?"

She nodded. "Go do what you have to do. I'll track down Mitch and tell him about Rogers and O'Fallon."

He leaned forward and kissed her temple, then made his way to a smaller conference room down the hallway. He sat down at the laptop that Ash had set up for him, typed in the visitor password, clicked a few more buttons, then stared up at the FBI logo emblazoned on the large, wall-mounted screen while waiting for the clock to strike the top of the hour.

His gut churned like a combine disk cutting through the soil's crust for the first time in spring. After clearing the water park, he'd sent a text to Cruz, asking him to gather everyone together for a videoconference. He checked his phone's clock. Two more minutes.

Sweat gathered at his temple, and he swiped it away.

Using the mouse, he double-clicked the browser icon and, with a few keystrokes, he opened his web-based e-mail, clicked on the link Cruz sent him, and waited for everything to connect.

Seconds later, the Theater appeared and everyone, except Lynette, who he knew wouldn't leave Brodie's side until she delivered him back to Liv, was seated and waiting.

After a quick audio check, he got right to it. "Thanks for dropping everything to meet with me." A cocktail of dread and failure mixed with an unassailable determination filled his chest. His gaze landed briefly on each person present, and he cleared his throat. "I need your help."

Phin's propped-up foot fell from his knee, Rohan began plucking away at the laptop in front of him, doing God-knew-what, and Cruz sat forward, bracing his forearms on the table.

Grams smiled.

"Mom gave us the bare bones," Cruz said. "What do you need us to do?"

Months—years—of pressure lifted from his shoulders, and Zeke released his first full breath in hours, even though it felt like a thousand stinging bees crawled up his throat and clung to the backs of his eyes. He loved this lot of pains in the ass.

Clearing his throat one last time, he filled his team in on Liv's attack, the taunting call and pictures, Callie's kidnapping, and their thoughts on possible suspects. "The police and FBI are doing what they can to find this guy, but they have to do it all by the book." Images of Brodie's room, Callie's taped face, and Liv's quivering chin blasted through his mind. "I want this guy. Whatever it takes."

Everyone nodded their agreement.

"Whatever you need," Rohan said, "it's yours."

"After this," he swallowed against the sharp ache in his throat. "Whoever wants out can go with my blessing."

Rohan stopped typing. The silence couldn't have been thicker if someone had dropped a smoke grenade between them.

"But I hope you'll choose to stay. When this is done, I'll finish training Neuman and delegate some of my other responsibilities so I can focus on the business side." As he said the words, his voice grew stronger, more confident he was doing the right thing, for them—and for him. "From this point forward, Cruz will take the lead on operations, and I'll try my damnedest to stay out of everyone's way." A smile pulled at one side of his mouth. "I can't guarantee that I won't slip or piss you off at some point, but you have my word that I'll try and that I'll listen."

Everyone either grinned or nodded their head again. Everyone but Phin.

"You got something you want to ask, little brother?"

"What about our shadow op recoveries? Will we still take those on?"

In other words, would they still be required to stretch, and sometimes break, the law.

"Yes."

Phin's hand fisted on the table.

"This is what we do, Phin. We return property to its rightful owner. We right injustices when the legal system falls short." He leaned toward the screen. "But every person on this team can decide for themselves which recoveries they'll take part in."

Phin's body relaxed. "I can work with that."

The heavy stones Zeke had been carrying on his shoulders crumbled to the floor, and he released a breath.

"What's the plan?" Cruz asked into the silence.

"I don't have one."

Eyebrows rose, and his brothers shared a glance.

Grams continued smiling. Her unshakable faith in him sparkled in her dark eyes.

"Do what you do," Zeke said. "Just keep me updated, and I'll do the same."

Rohan tore into his computer again.

The tension that had been slowly building for months—years—dissipated. Now Zeke had to make sure he never stoked it into existence again.

"We won't let—" Phin began, but seemed to struggle to get the words out. "We won't let you down, bro."

Zeke's own throat tried to shut down. "I know it. I have all along. It's just that I—" His gaze lost its focus, unable to look any of them in the eye. "I was afraid of . . . "

His words were all balled up in his throat, clawing to get out, like a terrified crowd trying to cram themselves through a narrow doorway.

"Ezekiel." Grams's voice cut through the thickening darkness.

He blinked and focused on her brown, wrinkled face, on the serenity she brought to every conflict.

Her beloved voice pierced the digital distance. "Family first."

Zeke's hand curled into a hammer.

"Through blood," Phin said.

"Through hate," Rohan added.

"Through fear," Cruz said.

Steel sharpened his back.

"Through joy," Ash said quietly from the doorway. "Don't forget the joy."

Had he knocked? Zeke couldn't recall. He'd been so focused on the screen before him that his surroundings had blurred. Ash had never participated in their rallying cry before. Zeke wasn't even aware he knew about it.

Having his big brother witness this moment was cataclysmic. Unfortunately, he couldn't decide if he should be celebrating the moment or scraping it from history.

Either way, he and Ash had a reckoning coming. But not today. Not now.

Now was about unity.

Zeke nodded, joining the chorus. "No exceptions."

The audio fell silent for a moment. Love, determination, and a unified desire wove around each of them.

"Let me know when you have something." Zeke didn't doubt that they would, and soon.

"Count on it," Cruz said.

Having this long-overdue conversation behind him should have relieved some of his tension. In a way it did, though almost immediately his shoulder muscles bunched and tightened until he thought the sinew would snap.

Sensing the conversation wasn't over, Rohan lifted his attention from his laptop and asked, "What's the matter?"

Tiny needles pricked the nerves running down his spine. What he had to discuss with them would either strengthen their newly formed bond or it would rip off the bandage and leave them all broken and bloody.

Family first.

He took a leap of faith. "One more thing . . ."

56

After Zeke left her alone in the conference room, Liv had sought out Mitch and told him about the possible motives that might incite the O'Fallon clan and Sam Rogers to strike out against her through her family.

The small action felt good. Since leaving the water park, she'd been utterly useless. Nothing but a mute ghost occupying a place at the table.

The only sensible decision she'd made in all that time was allowing Brodie to return to the Friary with Lynette and Alejandro. She hated letting him go, but he would be safer and happier with the Blackwells and Sadie.

Inhaling the sweet, earthy scent of the chamomile tea she'd made for herself on the way back to the conference room did little to dispel her roiling stomach. She was sick of herself, sick of doing nothing but waiting on other people to find her sister.

To hell with that.

She tapped a key to wake up Cameron's laptop and saw that the park's surveillance recordings had finally arrived. Following the link provided by the park's director, she opened the file for the entrance door and fast forwarded to a few minutes before the kidnapper called her.

She might have been useless over the past hour, but that didn't mean her mind had stopped analyzing every minute of her conversation with the caller. His voice wasn't one she recognized, though that didn't mean much.

He could have disguised it with a phone app or voice modifier or maybe he simply modulated his accent—all were good possibilities. But none of those things would alter the inherent arrogance in his tone.

If Jackson had still been a suspect, she would've ruled him out on that fact alone. The guy outside Ivy's house had turned into a mouse when challenged by an authority figure. Whereas the caller broke into her house, attacked her in the park, and kidnapped her sister. Not the actions of a mouse.

Hitting play, her attention shifted between the time stamp and the people flowing into the water park's building. The black-and-white image was grainy, but clear enough to make out a lone white male wearing swim trunks, T-shirt, flip-flops, and a bulky beach towel slung over his right shoulder at the time of the kidnapper's call. The guy was even talking on the phone.

But Liv didn't recognize him. She watched the playback for several more minutes, but didn't see any other lone males enter the building. Frustrated, she tapped the fast forward button through the next hour and a half, until she saw her and Zeke's figures exiting.

Not one lone male had left prior to her and Zeke.

Had he left through another exit? No, she recalled the park's director telling them the other exit doors were hooked up to an alarm.

She hit rewind.

Maybe they were wrong. Maybe the kidnapper had still been in the building when they left. Liv shook her head even before she completed the thought. The picture he'd sent of Callie had been taken in a vehicle, a cargo van of some sort. It's true he could have taken the picture before going into the building, but Liv's gut rebelled at the suggestion.

She allowed the video to play, fast forwarding through inactivity and zooming in on all the men. Her earlier bout of crying combined with the unblinking, hard stares she was throwing at the screen made focusing for long periods of time difficult. She rubbed her eyes, trying to force clarity and moisture into her abused orbs.

Blinking in rapid succession, she squinted at the screen again. Her heart took a polar dive into her stomach. She leaned closer, zoomed in.

There, at the edge of what appeared to be a large family calling it a day, a man trailed after them. Not too close, to creep them out, but close enough for the casual observer to mistake him as one of the group's members.

When he peered over his shoulder, giving her a clear view of his face, Liv sat in stunned disbelief.

Then slowly her disbelief turned to terror.

57

CALLIE PAUSED TO CATCH HER BREATH. THE METAL SPINDLES on the bed frame wouldn't budge. No matter how hard she yanked, they remained stubbornly seated. She had even managed to contort her body so that she could kick the hell out of them.

Nothing.

She was no closer to escaping now than when she started. A scream of frustration tore from her lungs. She didn't worry about her kidnapper hearing her. If he were upstairs, he would have come down to investigate the sounds emanating from the basement long ago.

Scooting up, she rested her back against the headboard to take the pressure off her wrists and shoulders. If only she had a similar remedy to decrease the pain in her filling bladder.

The bastard had better show himself soon, or she'd be forced to wet herself on his bed.

Part of her mind dreaded the moment he would return and the other part prayed he'd come back soon. She couldn't escape this place without shedding the handcuffs and she couldn't shed the handcuffs without her kidnapper's help.

The distant sound of a door slamming made her heart stop in its tracks. Her instincts warned her to be quiet, which was ridiculous. It wasn't as though he'd forgotten she was down here.

But what if it wasn't her kidnapper? What if it was a family friend or neighbor stopping by?

Once again, she tried to think about what her sister would do in this situation. Liv would develop a plan and execute it.

Problem was, she sucked at planning.

As she did with most things, she plunged forward and damned the consequences. Only this time, Liv wouldn't be at her back to clean up the chaos. This time, Callie was on her own.

She filled her lungs and yelled through the tape, "Ith thomeone dare? Hel eee!"

The footfalls above her stopped, and a long silence followed. She could almost picture the person cocking their head left and right, trying to locate the source of the sound.

"Leez, hel ee!"

Boards creaked as hard sole shoes retraced their steps.

Callie's pulse galloped toward the edge of the cliff. Every muscle bunched and knotted, anticipating the crunch of bones and twisting of flesh as she cartwheeled into an abyss of unknowns.

The door to the basement opened, and the newcomer paused as if expecting an attack or the waft of something foul-smelling.

Callie's icy fingers curled around her handcuffs. The short chains sank deep into her palms.

She welcomed the pain, needed it to keep her mind focused on her goal, rather than her rising fear.

Fear paralyzes the body and mind.

Liv's cautionary words echoed in her ear as clear as the day she'd uttered them years ago.

Stay calm. Use that brilliant mind of yours to outwit your opponent. Use whatever is within reach to get the upper hand.

The urge to pee grew stronger. She forced her thoughts away from her body's needs to once again scan for potential weapons.

Once free, her options were limitless, given this was someone's actual living quarters. But right now, she had nothing but her mind.

Sweet baby Jesus, she was in trouble. This was a mistake. A terrible mistake.

A heavy footfall landed on the top step, then the next, and the next, until a rhythmic descent brought the newcomer's work boots into view. His short legs came next, wrapped in dark blue pants.

The beginnings of a beer belly hung over a belted waistband and tufts of gray hair peeked above his collared shirt. Bushy brows angled into a tight vee over his dark eyes and thick black hair, sprinkled with silver, covered his pate.

Was this him? Her kidnapper? Or her savior?

Her body trembled and tears spilled over her cheeks. "Get ee out of ere." Callie knew her words were indecipherable, but she had to try to make him understand the urgency. She shook her restraints. "Leez."

The man halted at the bottom of the stairs and stared at her. His expression didn't reflect surprise, nor interest.

It was blank. Completely, utterly blank.

The hairs along her spine vibrated in apprehension.

He strode closer, and she noticed he was clean shaven,

even though it had to be late afternoon. Maybe early evening, considering the gathering shadows. He wore a crisp white, short-sleeved shirt and blue uniform pants. Well, sort of crisp.

Crease lines marked the shirt and pants in different places, as if whoever had attempted to iron out the wrinkles didn't know what they were doing. The scent of oil and grease hovered in a cloud around him, yet not a speck of either marred his clothes.

Everything about this guy, and his room, screamed mechanic. The scent triggered a distant memory, one she couldn't quite place. Something Liv had told her, or was it Jessica?

Then she recalled the recent problem she'd had with her car. Did this guy work at the same shop where she'd recently taken her vehicle to get it fixed?

Had he been stalking her? Did he trash Brodie's room?

His gaze roamed down her body with a boldness that sucked what little breath remained in her lungs right out. When his dark eyes returned to hers, she could read his intent as clearly as if he had sent her a text.

This man was not her savior.

Reaching out, he placed the pad of his index finger on her bare thigh. In a faraway cavern in her mind, she noted his hands and nails were devoid of grease or grime, as his finger smoothed a line down to her knee, then retraced its path. Up, up, up. . .

58

"RIGHT THERE," LIV SAID, POINTING A SHAKING FINGER AT THE grainy image of Alan Rogers. "It's Claudia's son."

Zeke braced his hands on the table and leaned in, squinting. "I've seen him before."

"What?" she asked, pacing behind him. "When?"

"At the conference hotel in Charlotte. I thought of him as Intense Dude for the way he was"—he glanced at her over his shoulder—"staring at you."

"Alan was in the restaurant?"

He nodded. "I couldn't decide if he was suffering from unrequited love or simply struck stupid by the beautiful redhead at the bar." He scowled at the screen again. "Then my brother arrived and I lost sight of him."

"That would have been about three weeks ago." Liv thumbed through her memories, searching for a connection. The process took longer than she would've liked, but she gave her tired, battered brain some grace. "I didn't set eyes on Alan until after the conference. The time I saw him outside his parents' house after following Claudia home."

"You're sure you never met him before that?"

"Positive."

"Maybe his appearance at the water park is a coincidence."

"Then why is there no video of him entering the building?" Before texting Zeke to get back to the conference room ASAP, she had replayed the video twice more, specifically looking for Alan.

"You mentioned another lone male who arrived at the same time the kidnapper was on the phone with you. Let me see him."

Liv rewound the video, then hit play once he appeared on the screen.

Zeke tapped a finger against the screen. "Does the towel draped across his shoulder appear bulky to you?"

She remembered thinking the same thing when she first saw him. "He's wearing a wig."

"With an extra change of clothes beneath the towel."

Their eyes met. Held.

"It would explain why you weren't able to locate his arrival."

Liv shot out of the conference room, Zeke close behind. She stopped by her cubicle to grab her purse, then went in search of Mitch.

His office was empty.

"Are you looking for the boss?" Peppy Patsy asked as she streaked by.

"Have you seen him?

"I saw him leave about fifteen minutes ago."

"What about Cameron?"

"No clue."

She looked at Zeke. "We're on our own."

A predatory smile creased his face.

. . .

Liv ran-walked out of the FBI building, digging into her purse for her car key. Her fingers tripped over hand sanitizer, lip balm, sunglasses, travel-size Excedrin bottle, and something that stabbed the pad of her pinkie.

"Dammit!" She checked the wound to make sure it wasn't bleeding before doing a free dive back into her bag.

"I'll drive." Zeke jangled his keys and pushed ahead of her.

"No." She checked another pocket and felt the familiar shape of her key fob. "Last time, you nearly got us killed. My vehicle has lights and sirens."

"That wasn't my fault."

She hit the unlock button and slipped into the driver's seat. "Why is it that guys never accept fault?"

He opened the passenger door. "That's a pretty broad statement."

She sent him a reproachful look. "Yet, oh-so-true." A rush of movement caught her attention. "Behind you!"

But her warning came too late. The assailant struck Zeke, and his wide eyes met hers briefly. In them, she saw fear. Fear for her before they rolled back, and he was thrust into the passenger seat.

Alan Rogers stood outside the open door, wearing a T-shirt and swim trunks and pointing a gun at Zeke's slumped figure. "A loss for a loss, Olivia."

Liv's death grip on the steering wheel kept her grounded in the present, when all her mind wanted to do was spin out of control. Peering into the rearview mirror, she met Alan Rogers's cold stare before glancing at Zeke's unconscious body, now wedged between the passenger door and seat, at the shallow rise and fall of his chest.

Still breathing.

Breathing meant he was alive. Alive meant there was a chance for her to get him out of this.

But the blood. There was so much of it sliding from an unseen wound at the back of his head. It curled around his neck and disappeared beneath his shirt.

Alan had a thing for sneak attacks and traumatic head wounds.

She kept reminding herself that head wounds bled like drama queens acted. Over the top.

"Keep your eyes on the road, Olivia. We wouldn't want to get into an accident. Your lover isn't buckled in. One hard brake, and he could go flying through the windshield. You wouldn't want to break Brodie's heart a second time, would you?"

Beneath her fear for Zeke's safety roiled a fury that made her hands shake. "Why are you doing this?"

She peered at the repulsive reflection in her rearview mirror again. Alan sat in the center of the backseat, buckled in as if he were on a road trip and enjoying the sights. The handgun trained on the back of Zeke's head shattering the illusion.

"A loss for a—"

"Yeah, yeah, I fucking get it. A loss for a loss."

Anger wiped the self-satisfied look off his face. He kicked the back of her seat. "Don't forget who's holding the gun."

"Tell me. Who did your mom leave? You or your dad?"

"She left because you stuffed a bunch of modern feminist bullshit into her head."

"Shit like, 'You shouldn't fear living in your own home?' or 'Your adult son and husband can wash their own underwear'?"

"She was content, knew her place, until you came along, flashing your business card, promising her things."

So that was how he found out about her and tracked her down. He must have suspected something was going on, searched his mother's purse, and found Liv's business card.

Stupid mistake, Westcott. She made a mental note to get a burner phone and generic cards just for her volunteer work.

Alan's scowl turned into a terrible smile. "Claudia doesn't matter anymore. I'm done with that. . . that *woman*." He said the word as if he wanted to use a different epithet, but years of conditioning wouldn't allow such blasphemy. "I have a replacement lined up. One much easier on the eyes. One I'll enjoy breaking in."

Callie.

Bile congealed in the back of her throat, neither coming up nor going down. Stuck in the center of her chest, burning, eating away at the walls of her esophagus.

If she still had possession of her service weapon, she would have drawn it and blown the bastard's head off. But her weapon now rested in the hand of her enemy.

"Where are we going?" she asked.

"Home." He smiled. "I need to demonstrate to my mother's replacement what will happen if she tries to leave me."

He was going to kill her and Zeke in front of Callie. The steering wheel grew slick beneath her palms.

Think, Westcott. Don't let this pansy-ass loser get into your head. Think!

"You didn't keep your promise, Alan."

"What do you mean?"

"You promised me a loss for a loss. By my calculation, that's one for one. Not two for one." She nodded toward

Zeke, who remained utterly still, though his chest seemed to expand on deeper breaths. "Why did you attack him?"

He shrugged. "My father lost his wife. Seemed only right that you should lose your lover."

"He's not—"

"He is! Don't effing lie to me." He tapped the barrel of the gun against his temple. "I have eyes. I see. *I know.* First, at the hotel, then at your house, then at the park, before that other guy showed up, then at the water park. The two of you can't keep your hands off each other."

The mind focused on the strangest things when under extreme pressure. Liv didn't give thought to the eeriness of him watching her and Zeke making out and it didn't surprise her that he, in his new disguise, had watched them storm into the water park, into the chaos he'd created.

No, what her mind fixated on was his use of the word "effing." Had he grown up in a 1950s-style household where it was frowned upon to curse in front of one's parents, even as an adult? Or had the family's religious beliefs forbidden such lingo?

Evidently, he'd dropped out of Sunday school before they got to the *honor thy mother* bit. And let's not forget *do unto others as you would have them do unto you.*

"What was that for?" he asked.

"What are you talking about?"

"You snorted."

"I was contemplating how some men have selective religion like they have selective hearing. It's annoying."

She knew the moment she had pushed him too far. Felt it, actually, in the form of a teeth-rattling impact of the pistol grip glancing off the side of her head.

Not because he reined in his anger at the last second, but because Zeke's arm slashed out to block the blow. It still hurt like hell, and she lost control of the steering wheel for a second.

The jostling vehicle threw Alan off balance enough for Zeke to whip around and cram his fist into the other guy's nose. Blood spurted.

"You broke my effing nose!"

He fired the gun. The world shattered around them.

59

Zeke flinched as the gun ignited inches from his ear, blowing out the front passenger window and sending blades of ice through his already pounding skull.

Which fucking pissed him off.

No doubt seeing murder in Zeke's eyes, the guy reared back in his seat like a younger brother who'd finally had enough and fought back, but didn't anticipate the aftermath of his rebellion.

Gutless little shit.

Zeke ripped the weapon out of his now slack hand and gave him a taste of what it felt like to be cold-cocked. Still belted, the guy hung in a half-seated position with his head flung to one side. Lights out.

"Are you hit?" Liv asked, stealing glances at him, while bringing the vehicle under control.

Zeke swallowed back a bout of nausea. Every movement took an abundance of concentration to keep the contents of his stomach where they belonged. Moving and speaking at the same time required more fortitude than he possessed.

After checking the unconscious man for more weapons, he sagged back into the front passenger seat on a groan.

"Zeke, are you all right? Are you hit?" she all but screamed.

It was then he felt the sting-throb in his shoulder. He glanced down to find his shirt torn and blood soaking the material. "Well, damn."

"What?" She chanced another look around him and saw the blood. "You *are* hit." She stuck her hand behind his seat and fished out a pair of multicolored leggings from a duffel. "Here, apply pressure."

He wadded up the proffered spandex and pressed it to the wound, gritting his teeth against the pain.

Liv turned right at the next intersection.

"Where are we going?" he asked.

"I'm taking you to the hospital."

"The hell you are."

"Besides being shot, you took a hard blow. No telling how much damage was done."

"Not enough. Get back on route."

The vehicle continued on its current path.

"Dammit, Liv." Every word tore through his brain. "We need to get to Callie."

"I will, once I drop you off at the ER."

"You're wasting time. I'm not getting out of this vehicle until we're outside jerk-off's house."

Her hands gripped the steering wheel. "I can't lose you both."

"No chance of that. You're stuck with me. For life."

"This is no time for joking, Zeke."

"Do you see a smile anywhere on this ruggedly handsome face?"

The corner of her mouth twitched once before she folded her lips between her teeth.

"Turn around, Liv."

Although not happy about it, she made a U-ey at the first opportunity.

He held up a pistol. "Yours?"

"Yes." She bit out the word, holding out her hand. He understood. Losing a service weapon had to be an agent's worst nightmare.

He handed over the gun, and she slid it into her underarm shoulder holster.

"What are we up against?" he asked.

"I haven't been inside the house, so I don't know the layout. It's a ranch, probably built in the seventies. Based on the size, I'd say two or three bedrooms."

"Basement?"

"Unknown, but he," she jerked her head to the backseat, "gives off the creepy lives-belowstairs-vibe." She stared at the road ahead for a long moment. "I keep replaying my conversations with Claudia, trying to remember if she gave any indication of being afraid of her son. My focus had been on her husband. It never occurred to me she could have feared her entire family."

"Why would you, Liv, unless she told you?"

"I'm trained to pick up nuances the average person wouldn't, trained to dig around in the dirt until I uncover the root."

"You might not have discovered everything wrong in the Rogers's household, but you figured out enough to get Claudia out of there. You couldn't have predicted the son would unhinge and threaten your family."

They drove in silence for the rest of the ride. A few

houses from their destination, Liv slammed on the brakes and let out a sharp curse.

"What's wrong?"

"Mr. Rogers's truck is in the driveway." She edged to the side of the road, pulled up her phone contacts, and tapped a name.

"Who are you calling?"

Before she could answer, the line connected on the other side. "Detective Schuler."

"Marissa, it's Olivia Westcott. Sorry to be abrupt, but can you tell me if anyone has contacted the police from 1421 Englewood Drive?"

"Is this about your sister?"

"Yes, I've apprehended Alan Rogers, Sam Rogers's son. He's the one behind the attacks and he all but admitted that he has Callie. I need to determine if his father is also involved. His vehicle is in the driveway."

"Give me a second. I'll get some uniforms headed your way."

Zeke took the opportunity to send a quick update to Ash and his team. Within seconds, Ash responded. *ETA 10 minutes.*

Their eyes remained fixed on the navy-blue single-story home and silver F-150 while they waited for the detective to return.

Zeke dropped the bloody leggings and curled his hand over Liv's. Her fingers were like icicles, yet her palm was damp. He tried to infuse reassurance into his grip, but he suspected the only thing that would accomplish that feat was for Liv to see that her sister was safe and unharmed.

"He knows," she predicted.

Zeke squeezed her hand in agreement. The moment he saw the dad's truck in the driveway and zero red-and-blue lights bouncing off the aluminum siding, a sickness had gripped his stomach. In this case, the apple had not only fallen directly beneath the tree, it had rooted and grown into something far more insidious than its parent.

Or had it?

60

THE OLD MAN'S FINGERS GROPED HER LEG, HEADING FOR THE area on her body where no one had yet touched. This weirdo wouldn't be her first. Couldn't be.

In that moment, she wished she'd worn something besides her denim cutoffs. But the look in his eyes told her no amount of clothing would have been barrier enough. Bound as she was, the advantage was all his.

The helplessness that washed over her paralyzed every muscle in her body. Even her brain was frozen and unable to formulate a plan. With growing horror, she watched his finger move closer and closer. Thoughts scattered through her mind like shrapnel, too fast and scattered for her to latch onto.

An echo pushed against her paralysis. It grew louder and louder until the reverberation turned into a memory. The memory transformed into Liv's voice.

"If ever you find yourself under the control of another, you fight, Caledonia." Liv tapped a finger against Callie's forehead. "Use this and do whatever it takes to survive. Whatever. It. Takes. *Promise me."*

Callie rolled her eyes. "I promise, G-lady."

Without a doubt, Callie knew Liv was on her way. She had to keep this sick bastard at bay until her sister reached her.

Hurry, Liv.

When Sam's nasty finger closed in, Callie clamped her thighs together and twisted her body away.

His hand fell to his side, and eyes that held no empathy met hers. "Lucky for you, I don't have to go back to work. The night is ours to play."

When he reached for her again, she kicked out. Her bare foot slammed into his surprisingly hard stomach. The impact had no ill-effect on him. He didn't grunt, let out a *whoof* of air, stagger back a step, yell curses, or hit back.

He did something far worse. Something that felt like a thousand wolf spiders gang-rushing her body.

He smiled.

Ice crystals cracked across her chest and her mind went blank.

You fight, Calendonia.

But that's what he wanted. He wanted her to resist, wanted her to scream and cry and pray for release. He vibrated with the need to deny her, to repress her, to tame her.

Callie's throat grew tight with tears. Tears she refused to shed even while the terrible paralysis still held the strategic part of her mind captive.

Thick, calloused hands grabbed her ankles and yanked her down until she was lying flat on her back. Even knowing she was playing into his fantasy, she twisted and screamed and bucked.

What other option did she have? Allow him to rut on top of her until help came? If help came?

Bile pushed into her throat.

No. She refused to allow that part of her fear to take hold. Liv would come.

Do whatever it takes.

His fingers worked on the fastenings of her shorts. Ignoring the feral desire to watch his progress, she instead took in his well-groomed hair, smooth jaw, poorly pressed clothes, and grease-free fingernails.

An idea sparked. One that made every muscle in her body rebel.

But no better options came to mind, and she was running out of time. She had to wrest control of the situation before it was too late.

She calmed her see-sawing breaths and forced her body not to resist him as he yanked her shorts off, folded them, and laid them onto the edge of the bed. When his attention returned to her, he frowned at her unmoving body and dry eyes.

Survive.

Every strand of willpower went into keeping her body motionless and filling her gaze with unmistakable challenge.

Uncertainty shivered across his features, and he shifted away.

Callie's heart pumped so hard in her chest that she was certain the bed shook beneath her.

From one blink to the next, his uncertainty disappeared and calculation returned. He pressed a hand into the bed beside her head, leaned in, and said, "You think to manipulate me, little girl?" His hand clamped her mound, startling her. "I'm the one who will manipulate you."

Even terror-drenched, her mind worked out the double

entendre. The bile entered her mouth but had nowhere to go.

Whatever. It. Takes.

Fighting against twenty-plus years of conditioned behavior, she kept her promise to her sister. She set free the inner muscles forcing her bladder to behave.

The warm rush of liquid against her panties was both a relief and a humiliation. When the sensation registered against her attacker's palm and his face contorted in disgust, another emotion surfaced.

Victory.

Instead of trumpets and fireworks heralding her achievement, she heard the sweet sound of Sam's curses and deranged screams barreling up the basement steps.

Close enough.

61

WHILE WAITING FOR DETECTIVE SCHULER TO GET BACK TO her on whether a 911 call had been placed from the Rogers's house, Liv and Zeke worked in quiet unison to secure Alan in her vehicle. Despite what happened after the water park, sitting idly by and doing nothing wasn't in her DNA.

Liv's phone vibrated. "What do you have, Marissa?" she said by way of greeting, while peering around the back of her SUV at the blue ranch across the street, two doors down.

"No callouts, emergency or otherwise, for 1421 Englewood Drive."

"Okay, thanks for checking."

"Olivia, don't go in there. Wait for my uniforms."

Her sister was inside with a man who liked to beat and subjugate women. Callie could hold her own with him, at least, for a while, but Liv couldn't stand the thought of her little sister's catalog of terror growing while she stood outside waiting for backup.

"Will do." She disconnected, then jerked her head toward the house. "Give me thirty seconds to get in place."

Zeke pulled her in for a swift, hard kiss. "Be careful."

She squeezed his hand. "You too." Then she took off.

Half a minute later, Liv stood pressed against the house, near the door, watching Zeke stride up the walkway, a forced smile on his face. A towel from her workout bag hung over his right shoulder, doing a pretty good job of covering his blood-soaked shirt.

Hastily hatched, their plan was simple. Get Sam to open the screen door.

Once he opened the door, Liv would cram the muzzle of her weapon into the man's throat long enough for Zeke to knock him down. It should be her facing the threat head-on, but they couldn't take the chance that Sam might recognize her.

The whole thing was damn risky. Sam might sniff out a setup and never answer the door. He might shoot first, ask questions later.

Or he might not even know his son was holding a woman captive in his basement. How many people walked by their basement doors without a glance, especially if their adult child had claimed the space?

But every instinct in Liv's body rebelled against the latter. Alan might not have let his dad in on the kidnapping scheme, but he was comfortable enough to bring Callie here. A telling decision.

And Callie was trapped in this house. She could all but feel her sister's fear.

Zeke reached for the doorbell.

62

A split second before Zeke depressed the doorbell, a man's muffled yell had him snapping his hand back and reaching for the knife sheath looped on his belt. A quick look at Liv confirmed she'd caught the disturbance.

She motioned for him to move to the side of the door.

"No way," he whispered in a harsh voice. Every instinct he possessed shouted for him to stand between her and danger. He didn't want to give way. Not an inch.

"Stand back," she said, matching his decibel level, "so I can do my job."

The yelling continued, sweeping through the house like a toddler with a shitty diaper on fire.

Zeke wished he had a pistol. He'd intended to have Liv stop by his truck so he could grab the handgun he kept stashed inside, but then that fucker had ambushed him. It was the second time Rogers had bypassed the FBI's parking security. When this was all done, he and Mitch were going to have words.

"Zeke, stand back," Liv ordered again.

Trust was a bitch. In order to get it, one had to give it in equal measure. Hadn't he said as much to his brothers on their teleconference?

A line of sweat trickled down his back as he took one step, then two, away from the door. He held his breath as Liv knocked and shouted, "FBI."

She waited three seconds before testing the knob. The door popped open.

They both stared at the two-inch gap for a heartbeat before Liv lifted her gun and called, "Mr. Rogers, this is the FBI. We're coming in."

"Disgusting creature!" the guy wailed from the back of the house. "Vile, unclean whore!"

Zeke met Liv's eyes once more, hoping she read in his gaze everything he wanted to say but couldn't. The severity of her features softened for a nanosecond before she slipped inside.

Zeke followed in her wake. He might not be trained in how to deal with kidnappers, but he sure as hell knew how to cover his partner's back.

63

T<small>HE FIRST THING</small> L<small>IV NOTICED WHEN SHE ENTERED THE FAMILY</small> room was how normal it was. Accent throw pillows sat in the corners of the sofa, a big-screen TV perched on a cherry wood stand, framed pictures of Alan's ascent to adulthood adorned the wall, and, somewhere beyond her line of sight, a fish tank gurgled and hummed.

At a glance, everything appeared clean and tidy. Then she noticed the open magazine on the sofa, the empty glass on the table beside the recliner, the layer of dust on the TV stand, and the faint scent of burned toast lingering in the air.

With Claudia gone, the men had to fend for themselves. Neither one had probably performed a domestic chore in decades, if ever. Poor babies.

They did a quick circuit of the first floor before following the sound of running water and muttered curses to a half bathroom off the kitchen. With her back to the wall, she leaned toward the edge to peer around the doorframe.

The man's head was down, furiously washing his hands.

Soapy water splattered over the rim of the white pedestal sink.

As if sensing he was no longer alone, his furious mutterings halted, and he shut off the water.

Liv met Zeke's eyes across the opening. He nodded his readiness.

"Who's there?" Sam Rogers asked in a low, controlled voice that carried none of the hysteria of a few seconds ago. "Alan?"

"FBI," Liv said. "Come out with your hands above your head, Mr. Rogers."

"What is this about?"

"Callie Thornton."

"Name doesn't ring a bell."

Liv drew in a breath, forcing every fear and abhorrent image her mind had conjured on the drive over into a dark corner. Although she hadn't spotted a weapon, she wasn't going to take any chances with Zeke standing three feet away.

"Come out of the bathroom, Mr. Rogers, and show us where you're holding Callie."

"Do you have a search warrant—"

"Where is Callie?" Liv shouted, her calm dissolving like a pad of butter in a hot skillet.

"There's no one here by that name."

"That's not what your son told us," Zeke said, breaking his silence. "Right before I broke his face."

Something shattered inside the bathroom. "And you are?"

"Not the FBI."

"Where's my son?"

"Bleeding all over Agent Westcott's back seat."

A muffled crash from deep within the house reached

their ears.

Callie.

Liv vibrated with the push and pull of wanting—needing—to be in two places at the same time. Was someone down there with Callie? They hadn't known about Sam. What if someone else was helping Alan?

"I got this," Zeke said, reading the struggle on her face.

"I can't leave you here alone."

"Yes, you can. Backup will be here any moment."

"Lif, I down here!"

Liv peered over Zeke's shoulder, at the open door on the far side of the kitchen.

"Go," Zeke said.

She nodded. "Don't let him out of there until you have backup."

Moving away from the wall, he positioned himself for a better angle on the doorway. "He's not going anywhere."

The rectangular layout of the house meant there was only one way out of this hallway. In order to get to the other side of the kitchen, she would have to expose herself to the open bathroom door, where a slightly unhinged bear of a man stood seething.

Claudia had once sworn her husband didn't own any weapons. She had also left out the fact that her son was a Mini Me version of his dad.

Channeling her inner Flash, she nodded at Zeke and rushed past the opening. Next thing she knew, something solid slammed into her shoulder, knocking her off-balance and into Zeke.

Her already concussed head ricocheted off the wall, and she went lights-out for a brief second.

"Liv!"

She blinked and her world upended as Zeke rolled their

tangled bodies just in time to take the brunt of Sam's attack. The older man swung a free-standing toilet paper holder at Zeke. It wasn't one of those flimsy aluminum contraptions that you picked up at Walmart. No, this one, with its inner construction of steel pipes, reeked of Etsy.

The solid hunk of metal came down on Zeke's injured shoulder, making him lose his grip on his knife. The weapon dropped to the carpet with a thud. Sam took another swing at Zeke, catching him in the ribs.

An ominous crack rent the air, and Zeke grunted as he slammed to the floor.

Still dazed and on her back, Liv lifted her gun. *"Stop, or I'll shoot!"*

Her warning bounced off the guy like a rubber ball. All his focus was on Zeke, who was struggling to his knees.

"Hurt my boy, did you?" Sam snarled, lifting his ridiculous, yet effective, weapon in the air.

Maybe he already knew what she hadn't yet realized. If she pulled the trigger, she was as likely to hit Zeke as him. Or maybe the guy was drunk on adrenaline and rage.

Shaking the black spots from her vision, she took a knee and steadied her aim. When Sam reared back for another swipe at Zeke, she pulled the trigger. The older man froze as chunks of plaster rained down on him.

The momentary distraction was all Zeke needed. He ripped the stand out of Sam's hand and landed a solid to his jaw. The older man staggered back from the blow, then regained his senses and charged again.

Having climbed to her feet, Liv jammed the RIP end of her gun into the back of Sam's head. He froze, and she pushed him, face first, into the wall.

"Spread your legs and put your hands behind your back," she ordered.

Zeke picked up his knife and sheathed it before pulling a zip tie he'd taken from her supply box out of his back pocket.

"All I was doing was protecting my home from a threat," Sam said.

"Does that protection include holding a young woman hostage in your basement?" Liv asked, pressing his face harder into the wall while Zeke secured his hands.

"That's my son's room. I respect his privacy and don't go down there."

"Yeah, right. Callie had you sniveling like a baby when we arrived."

His palms rubbed together as if he were trying to wipe them free of something. "Disgusting whore."

She grabbed a handful of hair and yanked his head back. "Call my sister a name like that again, and I'll *end* you right here, right now."

Sam pressed his lips together.

Grasping the other man's arm, Zeke jerked his head toward the basement. "Go get her."

Liv looked at Zeke's injured arm. Seeing her line of sight, his jaw clenched. "I got this." True to form, he forced Sam down until the older man breathed carpet fibers.

She squeezed Zeke's hand and shot toward the basement. The moment she hit the family room, Ash entered the house, gun drawn.

"One suspect is hogtied in my vehicle." She pointed down the hall. "Your brother has the other one subdued, but he needs medical attention. Uniforms should be here any second."

Ash nodded, and she continued toward the open door.

Toward Callie.

64

CALLIE STRAINED TO MAKE OUT WHAT WAS GOING ON upstairs. Her heart pumped so furiously that she could almost taste the blood in her mouth. Maybe that had more to do with her efforts to remove the tape from her mouth than any biological osmosis miracle.

Although the metal bed was unbreakable, it had a flaw. She couldn't exploit it to free her wrists, but she had used the flaw—also known as headboard decoration—to get under one corner of the tape.

With slow, methodical movements, she ripped away the adhesive, centimeter by centimeter. Until she heard her sister's voice.

She abandoned slow and methodical to frantically drag her face over the pointy bit, cutting her cheek on the metal and her teeth until she'd freed part of her mouth.

A small part.

Everything became a blur of movement after that. Swinging her body around, she'd kicked out, sending a bedside lamp to the floor along with everything else on the small square table.

When she could reach no more, she'd filled her lungs with air and engaged every one of her inner muscles to push out four little words.

Liv, I'm down here!

Because her mouth was still essentially closed, the words emerged in a drunken gargle. She'd kept the tears at bay until then. But the fear and frustration and humiliation all congealed together and twin tears trailed from the outer edges of her eyes and into her hair.

Rustling above pulled her out of the cauldron of emotions, boiling away her hope. Getting her mouth free was something she could do, something that might aid in her rescue.

She attacked the tape again and, by the time her sister called down, half her mouth was exposed.

"Callie?"

"I'm here!"

"Are you alone?"

"Yes, it's clear."

Just me and the pinup girls.

Her sister eased down the stairs, handgun at the ready, eyes searching, confirming for herself that no one held Callie at gunpoint or lurked in the shadows. Once she was satisfied, she holstered her weapon and looked at Callie.

At her bared legs and soiled underwear.

The overwhelming relief Callie felt at seeing her sister was quickly banished by humiliation. She clenched her legs tighter together, though she refused to look away, for fear of her sister disappearing.

It was an irrational worry. Liv would never leave her. She would always come for her, no matter how busy or bananas her own life was.

And she would never, ever judge her for doing whatever it took to protect herself.

"Liv," Callie choked out.

65

Liv's mind was on an acid trip.

Images plucked from the past couple of weeks whirled behind her eyelids, preventing her from reaching a deep sleep and transfixing her in a state of semiconsciousness.

What finally pulled her from her weird state was the feeling of being watched. She opened her eyes and reared up on a forearm.

"Easy," Zeke whispered, moving away from the curtained window, "it's just me."

She blinked several times to lube her dry, sticky eyes. Next to her, Callie slept on, her arm flung over Brodie, whose body was contorted in a way only nine-year-olds could pull off.

Zeke moved around the spacious bedroom to her side. It had been strange to sleep under her parents' roof again. To her surprise, Regina Thornton hadn't changed a stitch in Callie's room.

Muted plum-and-white graced the satin bedding and softened the curtains framing the windows, a white-legged glass desk dominated one wall, and black-framed sketches of structures yet to be built, each one more beautiful as Callie's technique improved, created a mosaic on the opposite wall.

It was a beautiful room, a tribute to Callie's impeccable taste and accomplishments. Maybe her mother's reason for preserving the room wasn't so surprising after all.

"How are you feeling?" Zeke asked in a low voice.

Careful not to wake her bedmates, she rolled over and sat up, assessing her body as she moved. "Good. I think."

After the paramedics had treated Callie and Zeke, Liv pulled a pair of short leggings from her duffel bag for Callie to wear before they were shuffled off to the police station to give their statements. On the way, Liv contacted her parents and filled them in. Predictably, they were shocked and concerned. Even more predictably, her father had speed-dialed the family attorney.

Less predictable was her parents' camp-out in the station's waiting room. When she and Callie emerged hours later, neither parent had looked their normal immaculate selves. Stanley's close-cropped hair stood out in odd places and his facial skin drooped in ways it hadn't the day before. Regina's red-rimmed eyes and trembling lips were devoid of makeup and her Gucci jacket was inside out.

Pierce had been there too, looking his normal, unflustered self. No telltale signs of misery, concern, or anger. Demonstrative emotion had never been his way. A skill he'd adopted from their parents, then perfected to a diamond-cut precision.

But last night, Regina and Stanley Thornton had set aside their societal obligations and simply been parents. One look at the utter exhaustion on their baby girl's face had them running toward Callie and enfolding her in a tight cocoon of safety and familiarity.

Before Liv knew what was happening, Stanley had coaxed her and Pierce into their group hug. Shocked to her bones, Liv stood there, unmoving, until her mom's hand snaked out and rubbed small circles on her back.

She couldn't recall the last time her mother had laid a genuine, comforting hand on her. The remembrance made emotion ball up in Liv's throat.

In true Thornton style, Regina had taken a deep breath, lifted her chin, and declared everyone would return to their house. Liv hadn't wanted to. She'd wanted to hug her son and smother him in kisses, then curl against Zeke's big, warm body and let him love away the day's events.

When she opened her mouth to decline, Callie had clutched her hand with the same tenacity with which she clung to her father's waist. Liv had never been able to deny her sister anything.

So the Blackwells—all of them—had brought Brodie home to her. The three of them had slept in the same bed because Liv couldn't stand the thought of another separation. Not even for sleep.

Liv looked from Zeke's shoulder to his ribs. "You?"

"A scratch, a bruise. Nothing to worry about."

It was far from nothing. Alan's bullet had left a furrow in his arm the size of her index finger and the toilet paper holder had indeed cracked a rib. He'd been injured because of choices she'd made. They all had—Brodie, Callie, Zeke. Who knew how far Alan would have gone in his vengeful obsession.

The irony of it all was that the threat hadn't come from her job as a special agent. It had stemmed from her desire to protect those who couldn't protect themselves. But she'd failed on every level, putting her family and the man she loved in jeopardy.

Zeke grasped her hand and tugged her up. His thumb brushed over her cheek, and he kissed the corner of her mouth. "You're wrong."

Vision blurry, she spoke to his chest. "About what?"

"About whatever dark self-recriminations are churning in this," his lips pressed against her forehead, "amazing mind."

She wrapped her arms around his waist and buried her face in his chest. "I could have lost any one of you. I w-wouldn't have survived it. I wouldn't."

"Yes, you would have. Had the worst happened. But it didn't. Thanks to you, we located Callie, and you made sure the guy never had an opportunity to harm Brodie."

"If I had stayed out of Claudia's business, they never would have been in danger. *You* wouldn't have been hurt."

"Look at me, Liv."

If she did, he would see her every vulnerability, every fear, every aching desire to be the best mom, best sister, best agent, best wif—

"Please," he said, rearing his head back to see her.

It took the last dregs of her courage to lift her eyes to his.

"If you had not helped Claudia, she would likely be dead or severely injured. Protecting people, that's who you are. That's who they"—he nodded at the two sleeping forms on the bed —"love." His voice lowered even more. "Who I love."

She closed her eyes and gritted her teeth, swallowing back the clump of emotion pushing into her throat. Her chin wobbled, and she was afraid to breathe for fear of releasing an ugly, sobby noise. Her fingers dug into the material of his shirt, and she held on until the tumult of her emotions passed.

They didn't.

All of her effort couldn't hold back the ugly sob.

Zeke's arms went around her, holding her until her body stopped trembling. Despite her initial outburst, she released all her tension, all her anxiety, in silent tears against his chest.

"Come," Zeke said, "let's get you cleaned up. I have something to show you."

Liv turned back to her son and sister, reluctant to leave them. Other than adjusting to new everything in his room, he would come out of this unscathed. Not so for Callie. Her baby sister was strong and resilient, but for a few hours she hadn't known if she would live or die. And if she lived, what horrible acts she would face.

Callie had assured her that neither man had sexually assaulted her, but she refused to tell Liv what she'd done to set off Sam Rogers. From the wet patch beneath her sister, the scent of urine, and the man's furious handwashing, it didn't take a physicist to figure out what went down.

Good for her. She hoped the bastard scrubbed his hands to the bone for the rest of his life.

"I'm worried for her," Liv said.

"Detective Schuler gave her a number to call if she needed to talk about what happened. She'll call when she's ready."

No doubt Regina would have a legion of specialists lined up as well.

She turned back to Zeke, grasped his neck, and pulled him down for a kiss. It was neither chaste nor passionate. But it consumed, it reassured. It promised.

Callie's sleepy voice interrupted them. "Would you two get a hotel room already? All that sucking noise is disturbing our perfectly good sleep-in."

Liv smiled, leaned over her grumpy sister, and pressed a

smacking kiss on her cheek. The contact elicited a frustrated groan from Callie right before she swept the covers over her head.

Sliding her fingers between Zeke's, she followed him from the room, relinquishing mind, body, soul, and heart into his keeping.

66

LIV STOOD ON HER FRONT PORCH, WONDERING IF ZEKE'S notion of a surprise was the same as hers. "Bringing me home is my surprise?"

"Wait for it."

She stared at his broad back as he unlocked the front door. Even though she'd showered and changed into a new set of clothes that Zeke had retrieved for her, she still felt . . . off. Unsettled.

Over the years, she had been involved in any number of cases. Some big, some small. Some so routine she could've dealt with it blindfolded, some so disturbing the images still visited her in the dark of night.

But having violence hit so close to home felt almost surreal, as if it had happened to another person. Yet it had a realness to it that made her insides quiver and hands sweat.

The door clicked open, and Zeke glanced back. Smiling, he threaded his fingers with hers. And just like that, her world recalibrated and she was back on course.

Would his smile always mend her wounded thoughts? Would his touch always set her pulse on fire?

As they stepped over the threshold, the answer seemed to be there. Right there for her to embrace. But thoughts of her son held her back.

How would Brodie feel about sharing her with someone else? A man, not his father?

Until this past year, when Callie had moved in, it had just been the two of them. Together, they had survived the loss of a beloved father and husband, survived the first day of school, and the first falling-out with his best friend.

What would it be like to bring another person into their lives? Their home. Someone who might have a different way of doing things. Someone who might not enjoy Avengers binge night.

Endless questions kept swirling around her mind until they stopped in front of Brodie's bedroom door.

"I hope you don't mind, but my brothers and I—we did some things."

Her gaze flickered between him and the door. "What sort of things?"

His hand closed around the handle. "Might be best if you see for yourself."

Bracing herself, she nodded as Zeke eased the door open. Liv stepped inside. And stared.

The room looked . . . right. Like it had never been trashed. The window, his bed, the computer—they all appeared untouched. She rushed over to the closet. Clothes —familiar clothes hung on hangers. Underwear and pajamas lay stacked in dresser drawers. Toys lined his shelves and desk.

The picture. The one Callie had retrieved from her basement prison, the one of Brodie, Tyler, and Jimar, sat upright next to her son's computer.

"How on earth—how did you do all of this?"

"The tradesman you hired had already fixed the window by the time we arrived, and I found the replacement clothes and bedding in Callie's trunk when we retrieved her vehicle from the mall parking lot."

"The toys and computer?"

"Phin and Cruz. They like to fix broken things."

She scanned the smooth, freshly painted wall above Brodie's bed. "The message?"

"Rohan." He smiled. "When he's not lost in cyberspace, he's actually quite handy in the physical world." When she continued to stare, he said in a rush, "Your aunt helped us put things back in place. If we got it wrong, let me know and I'll—"

"You didn't get it wrong. You got it perfect."

He released a heavy breath, as if he hadn't been sure of her reaction.

"When?" she asked.

"Last night while you were sleeping. It seemed a shame not to put all that brawn and mental power to work. Ash helped me with the posters."

"Y'all must be exhausted."

"It's a good exhaustion. I can't recall the last time I've seen my brothers so energized and joking with each other. It was like old times."

She threaded her fingers through his and kissed the back of his hand. Happiness for him bubbled inside her chest.

"I dreaded coming home," she admitted. "It's part of the reason I didn't put up much resistance to staying at my parents' place last night. I had no idea how I would put his room back to rights." Her eyes lifted to his. "Thank you."

He placed a soft kiss on her lips.

"I don't know how," she said in a broken whisper, "don't

even want to think about how differently yesterday would've turned out had you not been there with me."

"I'll always be with you. If you'll have me."

Her hands skimmed up his chest and smoothed them over his shoulders, careful not to press anywhere it might hurt. "Are you truly ready to be a dad?"

"Brodie already has a dad. But I'm more than ready to be the man who will protect him and help you guide him through all the tricky parts of life."

Outside of his father, Liv couldn't think of anyone else she would trust with such an important role. "It could get really complicated, at times."

"I'm not afraid of complicated, Liv." He brushed the backs of his knuckles along the edge of her jaw. "What scares the hell out of me is not having you and Brodie in my life."

A spark of hope ignited in her chest, then the antithetical nature of their careers doused the budding flame with arctic water.

"What about our jobs?" Had he thought this thing through? How could she, an FBI agent, turn a blind eye to breaking, entering, and stealing?

Amusement lit his eyes. "You mean cops and robbers?"

A surprised laugh escaped. "Yes, exactly."

"What do you think about coming over to the dark side?"

She blinked. "Are you offering me a job?"

"As it happens, I'm making a few operational changes to BARS. I've handed over the management of the recoveries to Cruz and will finish Neuman's training. I suppose the company could use another recovery artist." He studied her for a moment. "But what we most need is an expert to authenticate provenance *before* we take on a recovery."

Liv's mind was utterly and completely blank. He wanted her to ditch her career with the Bureau.

Was he freaking mad? Did he understand what he was asking her to give up? She'd busted her butt for years, gone up against ginormous egos, and fought the disdain of her fellow agents who wanted to shove art crime to the bottom of the barrel.

Cracking the O'Fallon case had finally put North Carolina's art crime problem on Shanice's radar. Charlotte's SAC was talking about creating a special unit—right here in Asheville.

Who better to lead that team than Liv? Everything she'd been working toward was finally coming together.

And yet she continued to listen. Began running through the pros and cons. Considered how it would affect her son—

"The team leader can be a bit of a prick sometimes," Zeke continued, interrupting her spiral into Confusionville, "but his girlfriend has figured out how to smooth out his edges." He brushed his thumbs over her cheeks. "Can't beat the five-minute commute."

She placed her hands on his forearms. "Zeke, I don't know if I could fully get behind BARS's mission."

"Which part?"

"The robber part."

He grinned. "You and Phin. So black-and-white." His thumb smoothed along the rim of her lower lip. "Did Callie steal the photo from the Rogers's basement? Or did she recover Brodie's treasured picture of his dad?"

Liv froze as her mind sifted through his words. Never in a million years would she label Callie's actions stealing. In fact, Liv would have done a lot worse than merely lifting the picture frame off Alan's dresser in order to return it to her son.

Even breaking and entering.

The prospect of an impending disaster lifted from her mind, giving it a weightlessness that she hadn't felt since leaving Zeke's hotel room. Now, his single-minded determination to do whatever it took—even tight-roping the law—to recover stolen assets made sense. How satisfying it must be, reuniting people and their treasures.

Hope thundered in her chest. "Brodie—his friends, his school."

A new intensity entered Zeke's voice. "There's an excellent school down the road. Full of kids waiting to be someone's friend. Or, if you like, he could homeschool with Sadie. Either way wouldn't prevent us from setting up visits with Brodie's friends."

Could she do it? Could she pull Brodie from everything he knew? Could she give up her dream job at the FBI?

If her parents had taught her nothing else, it was how resilient kids could be. Despite missing his father and his refusal to play sports, Brodie led an otherwise normal nine-year-old's life. He already had one friend—Sadie—in Steele Ridge. He could make others, couldn't he?

What did the FBI offer her that BARS couldn't? She respected the agency and its mission, but she hated the office politics and the layers of red tape she had to plow through.

BARS was nimble. They didn't have to play by the same rules as a governmental agency. The parts she loved about her job—recovering art and cultural property—she could do at BARS, without the frustration. Not to mention the other, more insidious reasons to consider Zeke's offer.

She would no longer suffer that unique layer of stress reserved only for single parents. The one that thickened every time she was late, every time she called in sick, every time she left early.

Then there was the issue of Mitch's inappropriate feelings for her. Feelings she didn't share and which would likely combust once her relationship with Zeke became common knowledge.

A low hum of excitement vibrated in her stomach. "What if we don't work well together? What if we turn into *Mr. and Mrs. Smith*?"

"I promise I won't try to shoot you or throw you across the room when we have a disagreement."

Although a laugh bubbled in the back of her throat, she said, "I'm serious, Zeke. Some couples should not work together."

His lips brushed against hers. "Sweet, Liv. Did you not notice our flawless teamwork over the past week?"

She raised a brow. "Flawless?"

"Close enough." He sobered. "There will be bumps— just ask my brothers—but we'll figure things out."

"Speaking of your brothers, I can't imagine they'd welcome an outsider, especially a law enforcement officer, into the fold."

"They would and they do."

She couldn't keep the surprise from her voice. "You've discussed this with them already?"

"Why do you think they were so lighthearted last night?" His thumbs traced twin lines over her cheeks. "It's one reason I asked to use the conference room at your office. I wanted their blessing, and they gave it. Without hesitation."

From one breath to the next, Liv's world tilted in a direction she'd never thought possible. She loved this man, and the offer he proposed for the future was a temptation she couldn't refuse.

"I accept your offer," she said, somewhat breathless. "But my services don't come cheap."

The smile he sent her washed away any lingering doubts, and he sealed the deal with a ferocious, mind-melting kiss.

What felt like hours later, he lifted his head. "You and Brodie will move into the Friary?"

"Yes."

"Soon?"

"Yes," she whispered.

When his mouth covered hers again in a slow, thorough possession, she poured her acceptance, her dreams, her future into one hopeful word.

Yes, yes, yes. . .

67

Two weeks later

Night whispered beyond the thick fog pulsing closer to the Friary, snuffing out buildings and trees and patio furniture until nothing but a wall of gray existed.

Many would find the meteorological phenomenon eerie or even claustrophobic. Zeke found comfort in the isolation, like a warm fire on a chilly night.

It was home.

He'd only been gone for two weeks, yet he'd missed this place, missed his family, including his pain-in-the-ass brothers. Even missed the demanding, frenetic pace of BARS.

Standing before the Great Hall's floor-to-ceiling windows, he peered at a reflection of the room behind him, while pouring a finger of bourbon into four crystal tumblers. Only a few hours ago, everyone who possessed a piece of his heart had filled the space. Everyone but Ash, who had unexpectedly been called back to Charlotte by his SAC.

Although Ash had come through for him with Brodie's room, the two of them still had unfinished business. But he would deal with his big brother later. Much later.

Zeke's eyes unfocused as the phantom scene appeared in the window, and he felt his mouth stretch into a smile. His brothers lounged on the overstuffed furniture arranged around the unlit fireplace and Liv occupied a cushion on the raised hearth. Happy tears glistened in her eyes.

Everyone's attention centered on the nine, er, ten-year-old nestled between Grams and Lynette. Brodie's hands moved like lightning as he shared the exciting details of his afternoon with his captivated audience.

For the first time since his dad's freak accident, Brodie had attended a baseball game.

A few days after Callie's rescue, Zeke had come home to grab some clothes and informed his brothers that he was going MIA for a while. Rather than grumbling about him leaving them hanging, they had all enfolded him in rough hugs and told him it was about damn time.

While Brodie finished the school year and Liv exited the FBI, he'd stayed busy packing the items Liv wanted to take to the Friary and stretching his handyman skills on what seemed like an endless honey-do punch list to make the house ready for Callie and her friend Jessica to rent.

For the first week, he'd watched for signs that Liv regretted her decision to say goodbye to the FBI. But the only time her forehead creased with concern was when she broke the news to Brodie.

If it hadn't been for the boy's previous visit and his friendship with Sadie, Brodie's reaction might have been a lot different. But when Liv had told him they would be moving to the Friary, he jumped off the couch, ran to his bedroom, and started packing.

From that point forward, they had all worked toward a common goal—flipping the proverbial page to the next chapter of their lives.

Today not only marked the pivotal "flip" in their lives but also Brodie's tenth birthday. When the boy had first unwrapped Zeke's gift that morning and stared at the tickets in silence, he thought he'd screwed up big time.

But after a few minutes, Brodie's smile appeared, then widened when he learned Sadie would join them. The boy had even dressed for the occasion, wearing a new pinstripe Charlotte Knights jersey and black cap, bearing the team's logo.

Zeke blinked away the image and stretched his neck left, then right, before carrying the drinks over to his brothers and wedging himself in the corner of one of the leather couches.

"I never got around to thanking you guys for what you did." He held up his glass. "I owe y'all one."

"'Bout damn time," Phin said, belting back his drink. "I was dying over here."

"That's not what he's talking about," Cruz said.

Phin looked at Zeke as if he'd botched something. "It's not?" He looked at the fireplace, then squeezed his eyes shut. "Fuck. Sorry, guys."

Zeke frowned, glancing from one brother to the next.

"Tell him," Rohan said.

"How can you be so oblivious?" Phin said to Zeke.

"Oblivious to what?" Zeke's frustration cut through his the-world-is-a-beautiful-place mood.

Cruz shook his head and buried his nose in his glass of whiskey.

"Tell. Him," Rohan repeated.

"Why me?" Phin gave Zeke another you're-unbelievable look.

"Because you did most of the damn legwork."

"Oh, for fuck's sake," Zeke said. "Just spill it, already."

"That," Phin pointed to the fireplace. "We've been waiting all night for you to take your eyes off Liv long enough to notice *that.*"

Zeke followed Phin's finger to the empty mounting brackets above the mantel. Only the brackets were no longer empty. They now cradled a sword. *The* sword.

Lupos.

He set down his drink, sloshing its contents onto a side table, and bolted from his seat. In three long strides, he stood inches below the object of his obsession.

"How?" he croaked out around a throat that had gone dry, despite bourbon lubrication.

The protracted silence behind him forced him to face his circle of brothers. "You went to the provenance authentication meeting for me?"

"Yeah." Phin jumped up and headed for the sideboard for a refill.

"Why didn't you tell me when I stopped by to pick up my things?" He now recalled a slight reticence among them before they hugged him and pushed him out of the house.

"Timing wasn't right." Cruz stretched an arm along the back of the couch. "You had a few things on your mind."

Zeke stared at Phin's back. "How much of a fight did Nicola put up?"

When Phin said nothing, Rohan interjected, "She threatened to get a second opinion."

"And?" Zeke wished they'd just tell him what the hell happened, but he had a feeling Phin was dealing with something that had nothing to do with the sword, and the other two knew or, at least, suspected what it was and were navigating tricky Phin waters.

"Thanks to your tip about Nicola's photographer, Phin persuaded him," Cruz rubbed his thumb and forefingers together in the age-old sign for money, "to make a second set of *all* of the pictures he took the night of the benefit. One of them clearly showed Hugh St. Martin removing the doll from the display table."

"Hugh stole his own artifact?" Zeke stared in disbelief. "Why?"

"The St. Martins had a con of their own going." Rohan's eyes sizzled and his voice held a barely contained rage. "I found several phone calls between Hugh and the person who I believed was the FBI's confidential informant. After digging a bit deeper, I confirmed my suspicion."

Now that Zeke thought about it, Hugh had been acting squirrelly the night of the benefit. His last-minute disappearing act, his nerves at the unveiling, his shock at Zeke's suggestion they should search for the thief closer to home. Then there was Nicola's inexplicable calmness at learning that one of her "treasures" had gone missing.

"Who's the CI?" Zeke asked.

"Your old friend Joe Lederman."

"Lederman?"

The greedy bastard who'd stolen Lan Sardoff's vintage comic book years ago. The comic Lederman had caught him recovering. The same man, who had promised retribution as he watched Zeke's ass clear the windowsill.

His heart felt like it hovered on the edge of an abyss, and he was certain that the next revelation would send it tumbling into endless darkness.

Phin rejoined the group, handing Zeke a fresh glass of

whiskey. This one, three fingers deep. "You're going to need this."

Zeke nodded his thanks and took a bracing sip. "Let me have it. All of it. Don't sugarcoat anything."

Cruz jumped in. "Ash's job was never in jeopardy."

"What?" Zeke demanded.

"You said no sugar."

Zeke rolled in a breath, then gave himself a mental warning to not interrupt again. He sent his brother a sharp nod to continue.

"Ash learned that someone went to the FBI and informed them about one of your pre-BARS shadow operations. The one where you recovered the baroque violin for the finance guy in Arden."

"I remember it." After initiating a search warrant, the police had found nothing at the thief's house. Soon after, the case turned cold. So Zeke had heated it back up.

"Ash explained the situation to Lawson and thought he'd settled the matter. Until a few weeks ago, when Lawson and his boss approached him at a conference."

Zeke recalled Mitch Lawson's poor attempt at his office to diminish the significance of their initial meeting at the hotel and Shanice Williams's intent regard of him before pulling Ash away from their dinner. At the time, he'd thought her interest was one of empathy. Now he saw it for what it was.

Calculation.

"Let me guess," Zeke said, as some of the puzzle pieces fell into place. "The FBI would look the other way on my 'illegal' activities if Ash could convince me to recover their CI's antique doll in order for them to get the information on the drug shipment."

Rohan nodded. "But Ash knew how you felt about the

FBI and sensed you were going to turn them down, so he devised a different story to get you to take the job."

One that made it seem as though Ash's career was on the line if he didn't cooperate.

Family first.

Thanks to Phin—hell, maybe all of them—his bastard brother knew he was struggling to hold BARS together, so he probably hadn't wanted to add to the strain Zeke was already under. In other words, Ash had lied to protect him and to keep the drugs off the streets.

Sonofabitch.

"Lederman worked a double-cross with the St. Martins," Cruz said. "He promised Nicola a three-thousand-year-old Mayan artifact she's coveted for years if she made the doll disappear."

"Jeez Almighty." Zeke scraped a hand down his face. "He must have been the one who contacted the FBI about my violin recovery. When that didn't produce the results he'd intended, he went to Plan B, the St. Martins scheme."

Cruz nodded. "He devised the plan to make sure that you would fail, assuming the FBI would be furious about their blown case and would resume their investigation into your shady business practices."

Zeke shook his head. "All of this because of a damn comic book."

Rohan raised a brow. "Not just any comic book. You cost him over a quarter of a million dollars."

"Besides fucking with me, what else did Lederman get out of this elaborate scheme?"

"When he didn't get his so-called property back," Rohan said, "Lederman cut off communication with the UCA."

Zeke took a large drink. "The fucker never intended to

share the drug shipment information with the undercover agent."

"Which allowed him to stay on the good side of a homicidal drug lord."

"Lederman played the perfect tune, and the FBI hummed along." Zeke squeezed his eyes shut. "Now that shit's going to hit the streets of Steele Ridge."

"*If* they can get through Maggie and her deputies," Cruz said. "Not a bet I'd be willing to gamble on."

Over the years, many people had underestimated Steele Ridge's sheriff, much to their later regret.

"The FBI briefed Maggie, and several other authorities in the region, on the situation," Rohan said. "She'll be ready."

Fury welled in Zeke's chest. "Rohan."

"Yeah?"

"Find Lederman."

His brother nodded. "With pleasure."

Zeke looked at Phin. "What happened after you showed Nicola the photo of Hugh taking the doll?"

"Tried to deny it, of course, until we presented the phone log and some very damaging texts Rohan uncovered."

"We?"

"Kayla and I." Phin smiled. "She enjoyed Nicola's downfall more than a little."

Zeke opened his mouth to ask his brother if he had shared the details of the FBI's case with the lobbyist, then closed it. Everything was so tangled right now, he couldn't muster a single gives-a-shit.

"She backed off the sword?"

Phin nodded.

"So Lederman fades into the shadows, and I suppose the

St. Martins go free since there's no law against stealing from yourself."

"Liv saw several pieces in Nicola's museum that were on the FBI's Most Wanted list," Rohan said. "Thanks to Liv and Ash, Nicola's black-market dealings are over."

Why hadn't Liv told him any of this? For two weeks, they had been each other's shadow. At least, at night. Evidently, during the day, she was putting together an airtight case while he pulled hair from a clogged sink and packed up toys.

Reading his mind, Rohan said, "She wanted to tell you, but we made her promise not to say anything."

"Why the hell not?"

"For one," Rohan nodded toward the sword, "we wanted this moment with you."

His brother's quiet words ripped the wind out of his self-righteous sail. They hadn't just pushed a piece of paper into Nicola's face and walked out with the sword. They had annihilated the threat to him.

"And two," Cruz said, picking up the baton, "you needed, no, deserved, two weeks where the hardest thing you had to worry about was how to make love to your lady without the boy hearing you. You deserved to be happy." He swirled a hand in the air. "All of this could wait."

All of this they did without him. Without his hovering, without his two cents. Without his constant management of, well, everything.

They loved BARS as much as he did. Failure was bound to happen, but it wouldn't be due to less than one hundred percent effort.

Zeke's throat tightened. His gaze touched on each brother—Cruz, legs stretched out before him, his back buried deep in the cushions, Rohan, tapping out something on his phone before clicking it off and sending him a rogue's grin, and, Phin, one hip propped on the edge of Rohan's chair, staring pensively into his drink.

He loved these guys and mentally reaffirmed his promise to give them the space they needed to do their jobs and to always have their backs.

"Thank you," he said. "I don't know what else to say, but thank you."

"It's more than enough, bro," Cruz said.

"You going to speak to Ash?" Phin asked.

Zeke nodded. "I owe him my thanks, too."

"That's not what I'm talking about."

He gave his kid brother a half smile. "I know."

"Someone's looking for her bed warmer," Rohan said, indicating the staircase.

Liv's sudden appearance explained the reason for his brother's nefarious smile and dancing fingers.

She looked beautiful with her hair down and clad in a simple T-shirt and pajama bottoms. The hesitant look on her face, as if she feared he would be upset with her for keeping her activities secret, had him draining the last of his whiskey and bidding his brothers good night.

There was still a lot there to unpack, but all he wanted in that moment was to hold her. Kiss her until her knees grew weak, then carry her upstairs and show her in a thousand different ways how much he loved her.

He paused on the step below. "Hey."

She gave him a small smile. "Hey."

"You've been busy."

"I'm sorry—"

"Don't be. The only thing that matters is that you're here, with me." He lifted something from his pocket and pressed it into her hand. "Always, I hope."

She stared down at the royal blue box with unblinking eyes. "Zeke?"

"Open it."

With excruciating slowness, she lifted the lid and gasped. "Zeke, it's beautiful."

"This isn't how I'd planned it, but the moment felt right. Only—" he glanced down, "I don't think it would be wise for me to get down on one knee on these stairs."

"Ask me," she whispered, a lone tear sliding down her cheek.

He removed the engagement ring, a white gold, emerald cut halo design with diamond accents, from its satin cushion and allowed it to hover over the end of her ring finger. "Will you"—he swallowed back the onset of his own tears—"have me, Olivia Thornton Westcott?"

"Yes." Her chin trembled. "Always."

He slid the ring onto her finger, and a roar of masculine voices shook the Great Hall.

Smiling, she cradled his face between her hands and whispered, "Always." She kissed the corners of his eyes. "Always." Her lips whispered over his cheek to his ear. "I think it's time for number one."

A slow smile pulled at his mouth, as he thought of all the ways he'd make her scream again.

And again.

And again.

SMOKE SCREEN

ADRIENNE GIORDANO

Enjoy an excerpt from Adrienne Giordano's *SMOKE SCREEN*, Book Two in Steele Ridge: The Blackwells series:

"So, you're a repo guy."

Phin stood smack in the middle of Kayla Krowne's living room—the one inside her massive twelve-thousand square foot home—peering out over her small private beach and the still waters of Lake Norman.

He'd expected more boat traffic. Particularly with the streaks of purple and orange lighting up a summer sky. Who wouldn't want to be floating around watching that spectacular sunset?

He supposed Tuesday nights in June weren't big boating nights. He didn't mind so much.

The entire scene gave him a sense of peace. And quiet.

At least on the lake.

Inside Kayla's house?

Les Blakely, the senate majority leader from Charlotte, put his finger on Phin's hot button and pressed that fucker hard enough to break it.

Phin dragged his gaze from the lake, looking down at Blakely, who—eh-hem—happened to be a good six inches shorter.

"Asset recovery," Phin said.

The senator shrugged a boney shoulder and... snorted.

Seriously?

Phin cocked his head and hit the guy with the flashing, toothy smile his brothers said caused men to shit themselves and women to lose their clothes. Either way, Phin had perfected it, learned to use it in a variety of ways.

A tool in his arsenal.

At times, like now, it kept him from pounding men like Les Blakely into the ground. And that was something because Phin still burned — a damned month later — about Blakely vaporizing a domestic violence bill that Kayla had lobbied hard for. Shelters around the country needed that funding and Blakely managed to bury the bill for probably another year.

Fucker.

"Asset recovery," Blakely said. "Is that what we're calling it these days?"

Phin focused on keeping his face neutral. No hard stare, no clenched jaw or pressed lips. He stood there, shoulders back, doing his Mr. Smooth thing, while a hot knife carved up his intestines.

Fucker, fucker, fucker.

"Gentlemen." A hand clamped on Phin's forearm, dragging him from the near-homicidal rage brewing inside him.

He glanced down at the hand squeezing his arm, then at its owner.

Kayla — thank you, sweet baby Jesus — stood beside him. He'd known her for years now and, as usual, her timing couldn't be better.

A woman – an exceptionally noticeable one – with a mane of dark curly hair and deep blue eyes accompanied her. And who might this lovely creature be?

Maybe she was what Phin needed to relieve his now-pissy mood. Female company. Never a bad thing. Especially if it led to Phin's hands rifling through those wild curls.

"Kayla," Blakely drawled. "Lovely party."

"It is," Kayla agreed. "Senator, could I pull you from my good friend Phin? I have an important matter to discuss that requires a bit of privacy."

Ha. Privacy his ass. Clearly, Kayla had overheard the exchange and wanted to keep Phin from getting blood on her marble floors.

As one of the country's premier lobbyists, Kayla had power. Not the kind Blakely had. Hers was subtle. Back room influence where she'd wheel and deal senators and congress members on behalf of her clients.

A world Phin had left behind three years ago.

"Of course," Blakely said.

The weasel nodded. "Blackwell, good to see you."

Not in this lifetime.

"Kayla," Phin said, "maybe you can talk him into reviving that domestic violence bill."

Kayla drilled him with a look that should have blown him clear through the floor-to-ceiling windows.

Tomorrow, she'd call him and ream him. Today? He'd gotten his jab in. After all, she couldn't expect Phin to stand there and listen while the man insulted his family.

"Later," she told Phin. "Now, I want to bend his ear about the appointment of our next Secretary of State."

Oh, boy. Kayla ushered the senator away, leaving Phin thinking he'd like to be a fly on the wall for *that* conversation.

"Hello."

The brunette.

He banished thoughts of Blakely-the-weasel and flashed *the* smile again, offering his hand. "I'm Phin Blackwell."

She accepted his hand, gave it a perfunctory shake. "I know."

Interesting. This chick with her soulful blue eyes didn't seem the panty dropping type. But, dang, that mane of curly hair combined with the black dress that managed to hug her body while revealing absolutely nothing made for a fascinating sexy-librarian package.

He made quick work of the handshake, making sure not to squeeze too hard or linger too long. He didn't need those slime ball tactics. His mother had taught him better.

Inside though? His brain filled with visions of lowering that little side zipper on her dress and peeling it off.

With his teeth.

He let the fantasy play out while his body hummed. Things might be looking up after the Blakely incident. "And you are?"

"Madison — Maddy — Carmichael."

Phin ran through his mental contact list. Carmichael. If he knew Kayla at all, chances were she'd brought this woman to him for a reason. A reason that probably included a job.

And wasn't that why Blackwell Asset Recovery Services — aka BARS — paid ten grand a plate to send him to these political shindigs?

"A pleasure, Maddy Carmichael," Phin said. "Why do I feel like Kayla engineered this meeting?"

"Because she did. I need your help."

Interesting indeed.

A woman about his mom's age — Congressman Jenkins' wife — squeezed behind Phin, eyeing him with the hunger of a Bengal tiger.

The things he put up with for his job.

Ignoring the tiger, he focused on Maddy. "Always happy to oblige a woman in distress."

At that, she rolled her eyes. Definitely not the panty dropping type.

"Easy, Charlie Charm."

Charlie Charm?

Phin laughed. An honest to God ripple that flew right up his throat. How he loved a woman capable of verbal swordplay. "Is that why my friends call me CC for short?"

This time, Maddy laughed. "Good one. But this is serious."

"Whatever *this* is."

She leaned in. His cue to dip his head in anticipation of whatever apparently naughty secret she'd like to share. He had a few of his own, if she'd be willing to play.

"I'm the acquisitions manager at the Thompson Center," she said, her breath warm on his neck.

And oooh-eeee. Phin concentrated on staying in character. Mr. Smooth. Mr. I-see-this-all-the-time-and-am-not-completely-fucking-stunned.

"As in President Thompson?" he asked.

"Exactly."

After two terms that ended three years ago, former United States President Gerald Thompson shook things up in Washington by foregoing a traditional presidential library. Instead, he'd opted to spend the twenty months before leaving office fundraising for a presidential *center*. One housing memorabilia, clothing he and his wife had worn, exhibits, a theatre. A gym to get kids off the street.

Thompson's vision? To revive the Charlotte area he'd grown up in, but now suffered from the killer combo of economic decline and rising crime.

Phin cocked his head. His curiosity exciting him for reasons that suddenly had nothing to do with Maddy's hair. "What can I help you with?"

Please let it be what I think it is.

"I'll assume you've heard about the robbery at the Center?"

"Priceless jewels designed by a former president's father? You bet I have."

She leaned in again and he dipped his head, letting her get right next to his ear. "Can we talk in private?"

They sure could.

Find out what happens next and order SMOKE SCREEN

ACKNOWLEDGMENTS

The first spark for the Blackwell clan came to us in March 2018, while plotting the final books in The Kingstons series. Each time thereafter, when Adrienne, Kelsey, and I would get together, we would flesh out the concept of these mysterious, black sheep cousins.

A lot has happened in the world and in our lives since the first spark, and there was even a moment in early 2020 when I worried The Blackwells series wouldn't be written. But thanks to our avid Steele Ridge fans, who kept asking about the Blackwell boys, we pushed through a few personal and professional crises and got busy writing. I hope you love their stories as much as we enjoyed writing them!

My thanks and love to Adrienne Giordano for reasons too numerous to list here, but mostly for being the *bestest friend in the world*.

Enormous gratitude to the professionals at the Federal Bureau of Investigation who patiently answered my many questions, especially Supervisory Special Agent Ray Hall and Program Manager of the Art Crime Program and Supervisory Special Agent for the Art Crime Team Randolph Deaton IV.

Thanks to Sarah and Dan Walker for getting me up to speed on the latest gaming craze and ensuring I didn't sound like "an old one."

Huge thanks to editor Kristen Weber for helping me dig

deeper, copy editor Martha Trachtenberg for your wicked, keen eye, and Stuart Bache for *Flash Point's* amazing cover.

Mega appreciation to our powerhouse behind-the-scenes team—Sandy Modesitt, Leiha Mann, and Heather Machel. Y'all rock!

As always, I couldn't continue going on these literary adventures without the generous support of readers, booksellers, librarians, reviewers, and bloggers. Thank you, thank you!

ABOUT TRACEY DEVLYN

 Tracey Devlyn is a *USA Today* best-selling author of historical and contemporary suspense, which often contains elements of mystery, romance, and environmental crime. Despite the thrilling, emotional ride she crafts for her readers, Tracey enjoys an annoyingly normal lifestyle with her husband and rescue dogs at her home in the mountains of North Carolina.

For access to exclusive content, new release notifications, special promotions, and behind-the-scenes peeks, join Tracey's VIP Reader List at https://TraceyDevlyn.com/ Contact.